LEGEND OF THE SORPHA

SAPHO
ECONOMIDES

Astral Plane

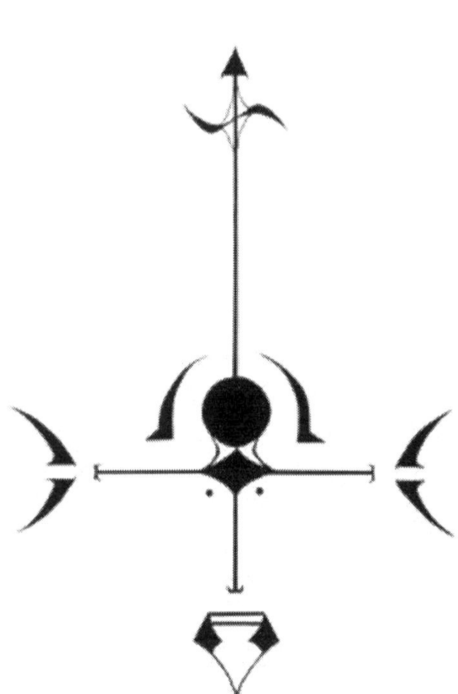

Astral Plane Publishing

First published in Great Britain in 2018 by Astral Plane
Astral Plane Publishing, Nottingham, United Kingdom.

Graphic editing by Deborah Leonardi, 2018.

ISBN 978-1-9996244-0-8

ISBN 978 1 9996244 1 5

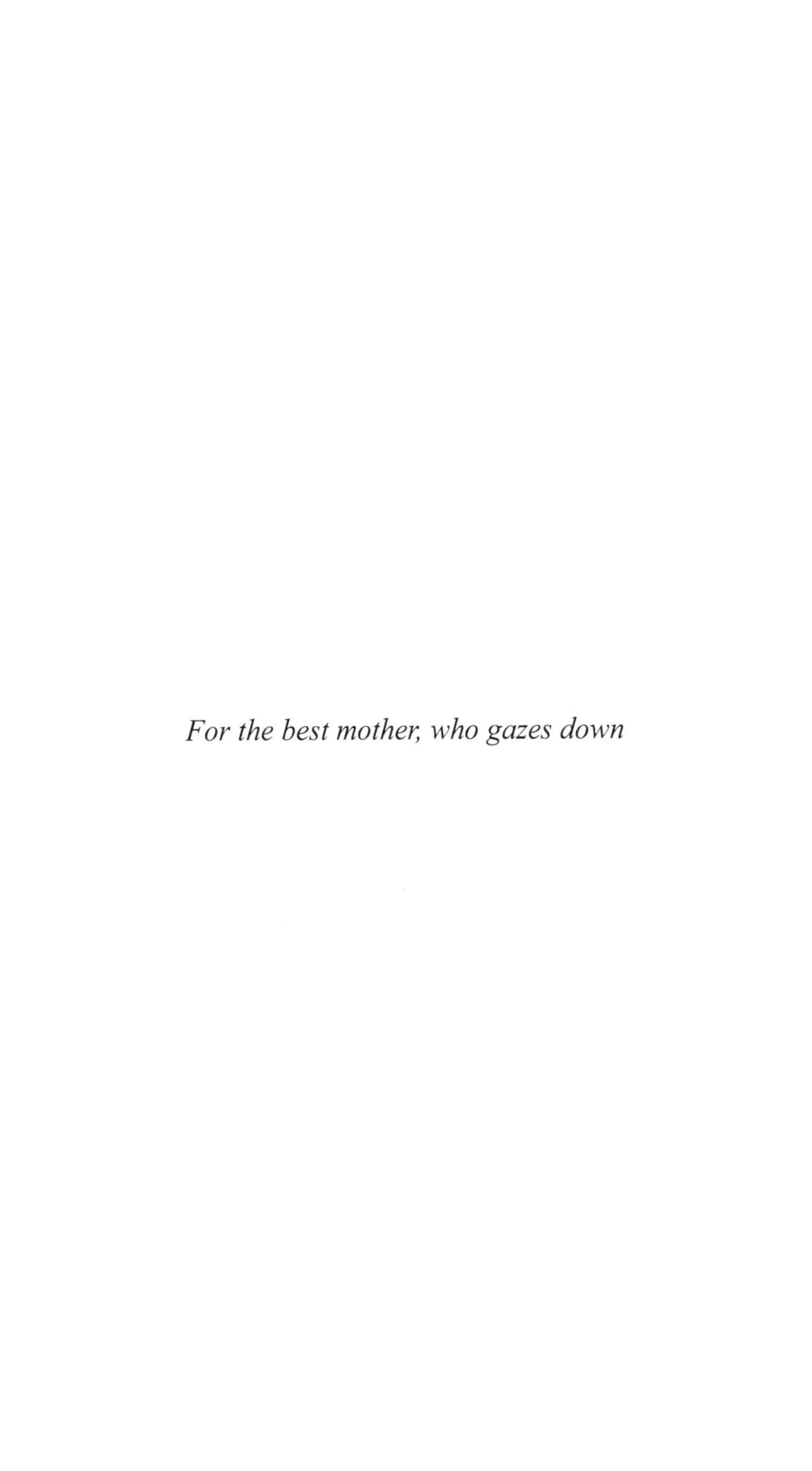

For the best mother, who gazes down

Pronunciations

A

Adrenache	A-*dren*-a-kee
Afax	Ay-fax
Ahone	A-hon-*nee*
Akeon	A-*kay*-on
Aphlicohn	Af-li-*kon*
Ataleka	A-*tal*-lekka

B

Belarahn	Bel-a-*ron*
Betharanei	Beth-ara-*nee*

C

Cercha	Ser-sha
Chandre	Can-dra
Chriah	Kree-a

D

Droha	Dro-a

Dynetii	Din-*ay*-tee

E

Ebenaea	Eben-*nay*-a
Ebrat	Eb-ret
Elenia	Elenn-ya
Eraiik	Eh-*ry*-ek

F

Fadre	Fay-der
Fitaeba	Fit-*tay*-ba

H

Halemedra	Hall*em*-med-dra
Halemer	Hal-em-*mare*

I

Ilysehr	Il-iss-er
Inyenaphe	Inn-*yen*-a-fee
Isbre	Iz-bree

K

Kolhr	Kol-er
Korsthr	Kor-ster

L

Lampaea	Lam-*pay*-a
Leao	Lay-o
Leohreten	Lee-*orra-ten*

M

Maliste	*Mal*-iss-ter

N

Nago	Nay-go
Nephele	Neh-*fel*-ee

O

Orpegh	Or-pay

P

Phaos	Fay-os
Plineah	Plin-ee-a

R

Raneao	Ra-*nay*-o
Rukurehn	Ruk-a-*ren*
Rydha	Ree-da

S

Skepreo	*Skep*-ree-o

V

Varehna	Va-renna

X

Xenor	Ksen-or (X sound is pronounced as in ‘ks,’ no *Z* sound present).

A Word on Esilence

Esilence is the world that has stood against an infinity of ages or more, the world that has nurtured children who would one day destroy it, much as earth is to us. A mother of unrequited love.

A person once described Esilence as a man who stood in the sea, with only his crown to show. But he is not alone; he stands shoulder to shoulder with tens of thousands of others, yet these others all remain submerged. They are unseen to the man, and for his sanity, unknown. But he feels them nearby, he rubs shoulders with them when they move, and he feels the water rush against his skin when they breathe. But will he venture to open his eyes and see them, or reach out a hand and touch them? To make known what stands in the dark surrounding him – it is inevitable.

'The boy asked me, so very profoundly, of Esilence. If Esilence were to take a bride, he said – a love to conquer all loves. I told him not to bother me with the riddles of fools, Esilence sits as the head of a pin, lost somewhere amidst the rest of the bridal gown.'
Anon.

A Brief History of Esilence: Enphiah, Pyra and Orpegh

Valistehn Period (Val.) - The ‘Unknown Period’ before Enphiah, Pyra or Orpegh were founded by men. The lands were uninhabited and referred to as the 'Wild Lands' during this time. Various village tales state that this was the period in which Blackcraft was created and lay dormant in the earth until it was accessed by Belarahn, large early horla-like creatures that stamped the earth. Whilst some in the present day believe that these creatures attempted to keep the Blackcraft underground, others believe that they are the cause of its creation. The Belarahn became extinct due to the Dirim hunting them, although many believe that two or three survived and that present-day horla are the descendants.

Menistehn Period (Men.) - The period of the founding of the three lands, including the Nyvean war and the settlers arriving across the sea from the north. Often known as The Age of Silence as cooperation was scarce and disputes erupted between the three leaders, Rukurehn, Nago and Sethra, leading to the outbreak of war. These men were known as the Luminors; Rukurehn claimed the west, Nago the midlands and Sethra the east. During this time Pyra was left forgotten as Enphiah's size, diversity and resources were deemed too valuable not to fight for. When Chrie, Sethra’s highest-ranking captain, mutinied against him, he looked to Pyra in the south, however there were tribes of people already found in Stura known as the Artons, and they were banished to the Isle of Ira when they refused to give up their land. The daughter of the Arton's leader, Illeno, was rumoured to have blessed her homeland before leaving, so that its plants and crops would thrive for any but those who banished them. As it was, crops failed for all those who served under the power of Chrie, and they were forced to move to the east of Pyra, later becoming the Chriahks. Years on, Stura became occupied by people from the Mid and West Enphiahn regions, once they had won the war. The Menistehn Period lasted around 200 years.

Existehn Period (Exis.) - The period after the war in which the 'recovery of death' occurred, and the six divided lands were established under their corresponding leaderships: Orpegh, West Enphiah, Mid Enphiah, East Enphiah, Stura and Chriah. Many cities, ports and villages were also established. Overseas trade began. Western and Mid Enphiah were kept informed of the actions of the east regularly. Many successors and descendants of the leaders from the West and Mid Enphiahn regions were murdered under mysterious circumstances in Exis.97. It was believed that the killers were Setrans, tired of being 'spied on,' though they were never identified. Any surviving potential successors were taken to Orpegh for safety, but authority became weak, negligent or avoided due to fear or a lack or right to the position. Exis. lasted 426 years.

Stalespic Period (Stal.) - also referred to as The Age of Independence, as the people became responsible for their own well-being and were able to develop their own systems owing to an absence of rule from the Luminors, such as the transport of mercantile goods and trade between the regions. Surprisingly, the lands worked well and efficiently from their own, private functions rather than under a greater power. This enabled the families and working people a 'voice' and prevented anyone who wanted to restore single power authority from doing so, though the shadows of people from the former powers still lurked within Lor and Penthor. In Stal.649, the Chriahks threatened the Sturans with violence and held some of them captive in dungeons for torture, accusing them of stealing Stura and cursing its earth with Blackcraft. The tortured Sturans learnt of the Chriahks' secret, yet few survived to tell of it. Stura received help from Beltro and Ferin and fought Chriah until they yielded and agreed to end their brutality. Rumour broke out amongst the Sturans that Chriah held a precious secret. The rumours were too vague and the stories too varied for the Sturans to know exactly what it was, however they allowed the Chriahks to believe they knew it and threatened to take the information to Enphiah unless the attacks ceased. Stal. lasted around 700 years.

Bleth Period (Blet.) - Early in the Bleth Period people from nearly every land were complaining about the Chriahks; worse, Setra became equally unpredictable and allied with Chriah. The people of Enphiah felt vulnerable and did not want to live in fear. In response to this, men from all lands volunteered to form a potential reserve force against Chriah and Setra, although they were not required to take action unless necessary, for the greatest priority was to avoid another war. These men laid down their names in the Halls of Lor and Penthor upon a 'Paper of Loyalty' known as the Ranis in Blet. 63. Lor and Penthor therefore became the 'central forces' and were responsible for the constant maintenance of peace in Enphiah. The Chriahks knew Enphiah was far too great and powerful, and permanently retreated. Any male descendants of the men who laid down their names to serve were instantly assigned the same duty on the Ranis once they reached sixteen, although the majority in the present day are not aware of this duty they serve. The Bleth Period lasted 610 years.

Bartrixehn Period (Bar.) – The period of Feletra and her great plight; Feletra was born in the year Bar.52. The Bartrixehn Period to date has enjoyed peace between all nations, villagefolk and townsfolk in particular have taken for granted the luxuries of a quiet life, until Bar.45-68, when rumours began to break out of an unrest in the east. Some would foretell of the 'evil reborn' that would spill out of Setra and Chriah once more, reunited and bringing with them a force to be reckoned with. Orpegh, dubbed 'The Banded Land', was deemed neutral in the Nyvean War, and now the country begins to watch her neighbours fearfully from afar; secretly they begin to prepare for the innocents that may seek refuge.

Down in dark'd Chriah,
Slept deceit and mystery
Dead be the thought
Hers the black history

Chapter 1
Delirium

A shift in time, a shift in fate, a shift in soul. She used to hear these words as a child, as a baby, as a glitter of a glimpse in her mother's eye. Then they stopped. As adolescence crept through, she ceased to repeat these words ever again; her brothers could stop teasing her, her parents relinquished the concept of abnormality. She would be dull. And happy. Nevertheless, they were the words she would always remember, and never utter again for years after they ceased to be first heard.

Estra once told her daughter many stories that would puzzle her in such a way to believe that some of these stories might be true. She heard them all outside with her six other siblings, where it was warm and three suns smiled down on them like radiant entities. Pytheria, of light and heat, the largest ruler of the sky burning brilliant gold and silver. Desporsa, the only sun with mood, bringing volatile gales when fiery red and serenity to the land when a placid blue. The third and smallest was the Black Dwarf, the enigma of unknown purpose, merely an unmoving dark circle, owning a constant position above them, never to set nor rise.

Estra's words had her children paralysed with intrigue; whilst their father would work the fields to the back of the house, she would sit in her usual chair, with her usual needle and thread, and her usual sombre expression, regaling each tale as accurately as the last. Her eldest daughter always wondered how she managed to sew so quickly and keep a watchful eye on the young ones at the same time. But now she shared some of that watching with her mother, for the girl had soon reached sixteen, and now she leant against the corner of the house listening to those stories being carefully absorbed by her eight-year old sister, Briapora and what should have been her six-year old brother, Leao.

Leao had taken sick and was confined to the inside of the house where he said the light would not hurt his eyes. Estra had tended to him for fifteen days, the illness had been sudden and without cause, she feared he was too weak, for he was showing no signs of recovery. Every day he coughed, every day there was pain inside him, he said, everywhere. The herra, a person professed in medicine, had already visited three times, though he confessed he had never treated an ailment like Leao's before, and options were running short. Leao was unaffected in his spirits, he had always been the happiest child of the seven, joyous with all those he met, a conversation starter and an imagination like no other. His eldest sister prayed every day for his recovery, for it was becoming too serious to ignore.

She missed seeing him outside with Bri, listening to their mother's stories. Sometimes she would snatch a moment during her brother and sister's awe at the end, and attempt a clever remark, 'And what is the moral to that one?'

She was only ever greeted by the same answer, 'No moral, much like many other stories. Away with you, Feletra.'

She left as instructed, both her parents had taken pride in raising obedient but strong children. Ignorance was unheard of and punished forthwith. They had not been entirely successful, however; two of the children, now eighteen and twenty, had always been the most destructive for their parents' tempers. Lampaea and Skepreo had grown up as partners in crime, their misbehaviour was their sport and everyone was given reason to be wary when the two were missing together for more than half a day, for their schemes and pranks were ungovernable. Her brothers were now separated, Lampaea having left home to travel across Enphiah once he had turned sixteen. Skepreo felt the loss, and Feletra knew she would feel the same when finally separated from Ataleka, her closest brother, only a year younger than herself. Bri and Leao appeared to be repeating the same pattern; it was only Flior, the eldest, who had grown up without a closely bonded sibling. Before he had also left home, he had been a pillar for Estra and Padryl, the brother who watched and protected all of his siblings and was still a valuable confidant to every one of them when they could not confide every detail to their parents.

Ataleka appeared at the house during a break from working the fields and called Feletra over, wearing a smirk of delight.

'Did you see Bri this morning?' he said gleefully, 'I climbed up the aghaia tree and told her I was stuck, she cried no end to Mother, thinking I'd never get down. She's always so gullible.'

'She *is* eight, Ataleka,' his sister responded reasonably, though nonetheless amused, 'and I'm sure Mother was less than pleased.'

Ataleka rolled his eyes. 'She sent me off to the fields early. Missed breakfast, and now I'm starving.'

'Not as bad as Lampaea then, missing two days of food

once. And that was just for saying he had walked to the Sorpha.'

'Do you think he really did that?'

'Of course not. He just needed something to compete with when Skepreo said he had jumped off the roof.'

Ataleka then had a pondering look about him. She didn't like it, he was thinking of something exciting to do and she wanted to be a part of it, but the older she became, the more parental shame pinned her down. Juvenile playtime was just that, juvenile. And yet here she was, still stuck firmly in her youth. Her mother had noticed it before and greatly disapproved, even more so it seemed that she was to be a woman, *'Women are more grounded than men, they grow up faster.'* It was not so easy to succumb to with five brothers.

'I will see the Sorpha,' said Ataleka, speaking his thoughts aloud as predicted, 'and I will be the first of our family to do it.'

Feletra sighed in exasperation. 'Ataleka, don't tempt fate –'

'Everyone is so scared of it, I will prove that you don't need to be, and I will bring some of the water home.'

The Sorpha was a vast and beautiful river, stretching across six lands in the Western and Mid Enphiahn regions, its waters were the clearest and purest ever known, giving a great sense of pride to the lands it ran through. But there came a price for its purity; rich in vitality, the waters of the Sorpha were terribly heavy in weight. Whilst this was a burden in itself, the price did not end there. There was an old Enphiahn myth attached to the river, one which warned that to receive the waters of the Sorpha too often or even to live too close was to lead a sinful life, and their greed would be reflected in illness. A curse, many called it, that brought a medley of symptoms: vomiting, unexplained bleeding, a gradual loss of the senses and dark visions. The worst, however, was extended life. Many had been said to have taken their own lives before preparing to suffer years of the unbearable disease.

Although it had been dubbed a myth by some, the majority of Enphiahns did in fact spare strong belief for the notion. Naturally, Estra had been sure to teach all her children the stories of those unfortunate souls who had fallen ill to the Sorpha's curse.

'Of course it's true,' she would say dryly. 'Does Pytheria rise and set every day without question? Well, then. It is as true as that.'

Feletra was fully aware, however, that both her parents feared the river, and that fear had been instilled in them from their own parents. Lampaea's punishment would have, after all, been greatly inappropriate were this not the case. And still, her intrigue for the Sorpha had only festered and bloomed over the years; she had basked in her brother's gloating upon his return, whether he had truly seen it or not, for the details were enchanting, fascinating and foreboding all at once. When she was a young child, she would imagine herself as the river itself, flowing freely through the six lands and commanding them with her presence. The thought was liberating, and she had always remembered it.

She stepped into the shade of the house with Ataleka, the coolness swept under her skin and into the marrow of her bones in an instant, it sent a shiver down her spine. The house was altogether small for nine people to share, seven of which now remained; there were but four main rooms and a lavatory. Two were bedrooms, one that was large enough to house all seven siblings, and another for their parents. There was a kitchen and scullery area, known as the basin room, and a wide, little-used room to the front of the house. This area was more of an open space, scattered with chairs, a meagre table and toys for Bri and Leao, for the most part this was their play area during the evenings. The entire house and all furniture had been handmade by their father, Padryl; wood and stone he had mastered to perfection, Flior and Lampaea had been taught these same skills, and Skepreo was also fast becoming fully competent with the technique. They acquired few things with money, for they had little to give. Some home-grown produce they sold on or traded to a merchant who rode by every five days or so, the transaction was often limited but no one ever went hungry.

Ataleka led the way into the basin room, spied a fresh loaf of bread on the table in the middle, and handed it to Feletra who had fetched butter. She plunged a knife down into the loaf, slicing off two clean cuts, the crumbs sprayed everywhere. The flattened bread took some moments to rise again, but she noticed it would never look the same again.

'Not the crust end for me,' said Ataleka, ever the most particular one of the family. At the age of six, for no reason, he had insisted that his bed be turned facing diagonally from the corner.

'How could I forget?' came the audacious reply, and she passed him the second buttered slice, accepting the crust end herself.

Ataleka was chewing his bread thoughtfully. 'I've been thinking again about the Sorpha.'

He was met with an aggravated sigh. 'Don't start.'

'No, listen, just listen. What do you think about giving that water – to *Leao?'*

She ceased to chew the bread for a moment and stared at him intently. *Completely absurd,* she thought, but failed to eliminate the idea altogether. Leao's illness was not improving, they didn't know if he ever would. And the Sorpha...those waters were known to be pure for a reason; taken without greed, the water brought prosperity to the drinker, good health, and limitless energy. Mother's stories of the thriving fortunate had nonetheless been far fewer than the impoverished unfortunate.

From Ataleka's impatient expression, she realised she had been cogitating too long.

'No,' she said finally.

'What? He needs it, sis! We could help Leao in a day when the herra could take years! I still can't believe Mother and Father haven't considered this already –'

'Because they know it is too risky, Ataleka! It's a cursed river – what if it went wrong?'

'It won't. We will collect it carefully, not wasting a drop. And it's for our brother, making it completely selfless. The laws of the Soprha say we can do that, don't they?'

Feletra couldn't help but pause again to digest his argument. It was good. She wouldn't admit it, but it was good, and she agreed. But she had to play the responsible part, the sensible sister, didn't she? Her thoughts were suddenly interrupted when Leao's coughing from the bedroom broke the silence, it was harsh and hollow like an angry dog marking its territory and making it known. Estra marched inside swiftly.

'Bring a fresh jug of water to me with honey,' she

ordered without turning around.

Feletra wasted no time in running to the barrel outside with a tall metal jug, filling it to the brim, she added honey quickly and mixed, dashing back in to the bedroom where Leao rested. He was whiter than ocean's foam, his once bright eyes dulled and lolling around and his spirit dampened to the point of being pushed into a deep grave, alive just but scrabbling with bloodied fingernails into the earth, desperate to reach the surface but always too weak to escape the formidable pit.

Estra guided a cup of the water to Leao's lips, he struggled to drink without coughing, and then fell back onto his pillow. They had never seen him this bad.

'We should call back the herra,' said Feletra.

'The herra can do nothing,' Estra replied frankly, walking out of earshot of Leao and closing the bedroom door behind them, 'spend time with your brother, won't you?'

And her mother traipsed back outside, leaving Feletra somewhat stunned. Spend time with him? Then her mother was preparing for the worst, but surely she would not lose her little brother, surely he would fight this, whatever it was...it was incomprehensible, she had never dealt with a death before.

As she returned to the basin room, she found Ataleka waiting patiently. He raised his eyebrows at her as if in challenge to his suggestion now that the evidence was pressing.

Feletra half rolled her eyes, 'Don't say it.'

'The answer is obvious, Fel,' Ataleka shrugged. He paused and stared at her for an answer, but she remained silent. Her head began to throb and she no longer wished for conversation and hearing outlandish ideas.

Ataleka shook his head at her in vexation. 'I'm going back to the fields.'

Feletra was torn. She knew exactly what she wanted to do, she wanted to risk everything, go with Ataleka and fetch that water from the Sorpha. Mother would be so overjoyed (inside perhaps, Estra withheld most emotion outwardly) to see Leao well again, venturing outside in the sun, playing with Bri, laughing gaily...but there was still a risk. There was no illness like the curse, what if they took too much water? How much even was too much? What if they spent too long gathering it? Did they have to collect it quick-sharp if they must at all? She had no answers, and the fear of the unknown restrained her.

Aimlessly, she prepared a bowl of warm water with oils from the aghaia tree, this tree had become something of a landmark of the family home. The house was situated on the barren Elpuran plains, and the land was instead scattered with serris, short trees that appeared distorted and mangled with branches set at odd angles like broken bones. In various areas, the soils of Elpura were plentiful and rich, and Padryl was among the few to have taken advantage of this, building a home next to a fortunate patch of land where the soils ran promising. The aghaia tree and its survival remained a mystery however, for it was native to Naxor Forest in Lira and occupied a dry plot of earth here, good enough only for serri trees. Estra had stocked years' worth of jars of the oil, she swore by its soothing and sleeping properties.

Feletra re-entered the bedroom quietly, Leao's violent coughing had subsided but still he shook with it, he would not be able to sleep easily. Feletra dipped a cloth into the water and dabbed at his forehead, his cheeks and under his nose, she could hear him inhaling the scent.

'Feletra?' he stuttered.

'You should try and sleep, Leao. The aghaia oil will help,' Feletra went to sit on the bed next to him, she laid a hand on his head. He felt cold, colder than yesterday.

'It's hurting.'

'I know, I know. I wish I could take it off you.'

'No, it's hurting more.'

Feletra hesitated. More? Should she call her mother back?

'Where, Leao?' she asked softly, 'Your head?'

'No!' Leao's voice suddenly raised with agitation and took Feletra aback, 'It's hurting more over there! Over *there*!'

Unexpectedly, he pointed impatiently to the corner of the room, directly next to his bed. Feletra followed his direction but failed to make sense of it. She exercised patience carefully, children were like that sometimes, they could refer to something that did in fact cohere in some shape or form but an adult would only grasp it later.

'What are you pointing to, Leao? There is nothing there.'

But Leao fervently continued pointing, his head was buried in his pillow and the pain he felt reduced him to suppressed sounds of anguish rather than words. There was only the basin room on the other side of that wall, was something happening there? Perhaps he had heard something. Feletra swiftly marched back there in search of the answer, but there was no one. She even followed the same direction and looked outside, nothing but the empty plains.

When she returned to the bedroom, Leao was curled up,

his arms over his knees beneath the blanket, his breathing was calmer, and the coughing seemed to have benefited from the aghaia oil a little. Feletra knelt down next to him, though his eyes were closed and the sleep finally appeared to be taking him.

'Does it still hurt?' Feletra whispered, 'Over there?'

Leao nodded without opening his eyes, then he pointed one last time to the corner to confirm, and fell into slumber. Feletra opened her mouth to ask more, then thought better of it and returned to the basin room as silently as she could. What answers did she really need? Leao was delirious, the sickness was making him ramble, she almost felt foolish for believing she could interpret what he was saying. This was new though, she was sure Mother would have mentioned such strange behaviour if he had done it before, perhaps it was a sign of his debilitation. Whatever it was, it unnerved her terribly.

The land darkened quickly in Elpura following the sunset, and once Pytheria had been put to sleep later that evening Feletra found herself busy setting the table for dinner whilst her mother cooked the food with Bri's help. When she saw her father stride in with Skepreo and Ataleka, she dropped the knife and fork she was laying with a clatter and raced on over to him, he saw it coming and groaned idly.

'Father...'

'Not again, Feletra.'

Every night for the past fortnight Feletra attempted to twist her father's arm into teaching her the art of combat, she was far more interested in competing with her brothers in a sport that would push her every limit than learning how to sew or when to take a roast bird out of the oven before it burnt. Granted, she could sew, she could cook, she was even adept with medicine, all of these domestic tasks she could achieve...to a degree. Feletra knew she was not and never would be the best, she felt distinctly average in most of her abilities and was not encouraged by her mother finding some insignificant fault in each of these, such as the end thread of Bri's pillow coming loose four days after Feletra had made it from scratch. Estra had been aware that Bri had been playing a particularly energetic game with it teasing Byte the cat, but a good seamstress would have made the pillow too well to unravel, she had claimed. But where was the challenge? The thrill? The expectation that she could fall and lose at any moment? If she fell and dropped the dinner, she might indeed lose her family's respect for one starving evening, but only because they only expected one job of her. She could do that, she could carry a plate of potatoes to the table. Anyone could. But it was the fact that *anyone* could that was suffocating her.

'Just the important parts at least,' Feletra implored, 'you taught Flior, Lampaea and Skepreo has just finished his training as well. Even Ataleka is starting now! Why not me?'

'It just doesn't feel right, Feletra,' Padryl sighed, 'I am not the only one who thinks it. In the case of war, do you think they would choose you, or your brothers?' He took a seat at the head of the table earlier than everyone else as he always did, began to remove his heavy work boots and shot her a stern look.

'They might choose me if I ever had a chance to prove myself,' Feletra said somewhere between a mutter and a retort, and her father raised an eyebrow, hearing every word. Padryl portrayed a strong patriarchal figure, from day one he had established to each of his seven children that he was the alpha, and demanded respect for both himself and Estra. And yet somehow his youth was locked in his face; his vision was impeccable, professed from two horizon-coloured eyes, the colour of the sea before the sun leaves the world, not dark, not light, but perfectly golden, the uniform of baked bread. In there his old mischief twinkled and he saw it in his children, it took little for them to coax it out, and they could make the same nooks that stretched to his temples change from lines of the most quelling look to pure creases of laugher and back again. Lampaea, Skepreo and even Leao had his look. Feletra wished she had it too sometimes, it was a lamentable thing to know she had inherited her mother's face of appearing miserable even when she wasn't.

'I meant the fact that only the boys are conscripted,' said Padryl. Although there was ample reason in his tone, Feletra could detect none in the content. 'Besides, your mother teaches you plenty of useful skills.'

Estra overheard. 'She tires of what she learns with me,' she commented, 'I'll not force her to be a housewoman if it's not what she wants. Perhaps you should teach her a thing or two.'

Feletra turned back to her father with high expectation after the unexpected support of her mother (perhaps she was sick of her daughter's distinct lack of enthusiasm as a student), though Padryl stared accusingly at the back of Estra's head, somewhat surprised at her suggestion.

'She will not be as strong as the boys,' he said through gritted teeth, cupping his hands on the table, at which point Estra spun around and calmly approached them to finish laying the table from Feletra.

‘Seven children, Padryl,’ she said, lining up a fork meticulously, ‘seven. Do you think I gave our girls no strength?’ she shot him a silencing look and wandered back into the basin room to find Bri.

Feletra couldn’t help but smirk.

Padryl gave one of those brief laughs that showed his momentary amusement whilst maintaining his strict expression. Feletra’s parents were ayres, the term used to describe two people who had chosen to live together and had created a long-term relationship, usually beginning a family. Individually, the man was referred to as the aaron, while the woman was still called the ayre. It was very natural to have an ayre, and more common than having an estehss, the term used to describe a person who has undertaken a special ceremony with their lover as a form of marriage, viewed as unbreakable and lasting an eternity.

‘She has a point then, no?’ he admitted. Feletra could see it was painful to do so, her father was as competitive as her brothers and disliked losing.

‘So...?’ Feletra couldn’t yet tell if she could stop wheedling or not.

‘I will teach you some manoeuvres –’ Feletra beamed at him, ‘– *some* manoeuvres. And you can learn after Ataleka.’

And then Feletra’s smile faltered. ‘After?’ she repeated, ‘I am older than Ataleka, that makes no sense –’

‘It makes sense because he has already begun,’ Padryl reasoned.

‘Why not pit Feletra and Ataleka against each other?’ Skepreo interjected as he and Ataleka followed the smell of food and took their seats at the table. ‘They will both learn twice as fast that way.’

‘Now you are being ridiculous,’ Padryl leant back into his chair on two of the legs and rubbed his golden eyes.

‘Why? Listen...’ while Skepreo reeled off a list of advantages to training the two simultaneously to his father, Feletra glanced at Ataleka as if asking for his opinion privately and he returned it positively with a nod.

‘We’re in,’ said Feletra abruptly, and she and Ataleka awaited Padryl’s response intently like mirror images of each other. He placed his hands on the back of his head tiredly and looked from one to the other.

‘Alright, fine,’ he said in defeat, and Skepreo appeared particularly proud of his successful proposal, ‘but if I spot any sign that this is too much for you to handle,’ he pointed at Feletra earnestly, ‘we stop at that moment. No more.’

Feletra gave a half-hearted nod to keep him quiet and close the deal. She hoped he wouldn’t withdraw on the agreement by tomorrow and blame his succumbing on evening tiredness, though he was an unlikely character to do so. The thought that she would learn a skill, or several skills, that were once prohibited from her was a gripping notion. She had not merely pursued the lessons to show her family that she could do just as good what her brothers could, it was not even about them. It was about the fulfilment. Everything her mother had taught her would indeed prove to have its use, but it was all average. She was still searching for a skill she could be good at, excellent at even, and hopefully then it might define her.

‘Alright, Briapora,’ Estra could be heard in the basin room, ‘set aside a small plate for Leao. I will take it in to him in a moment.’

Feletra was reminded of Leao’s outburst earlier. She thought it was the illness causing the derangement and told no one, but couldn't shake off the feeling that something was wrong. Hastily, before the food was brought out, she rose from her seat to help her mother fill the bowls and stepped in close to her side.

Ataleka was watching from afar.

'Mother?' said Feletra in a hushed voice.

'Take the bread in, will you?' Estra was handing Feletra a basket, then saw the look of concern in her eyes, 'Feletra, what is it?'

'It's Leao, he was acting strange earlier.'

'Strange, how?' Estra continued to bustle around with plates, bowls and utensils.

'Well, he...' Feletra felt unsure how she would react to the update, but she had to tell her, 'he was pointing to his corner and saying that was where it hurt. He said it hurt more there.'

'Where?'

'The corner,' Feletra sighed, 'I didn't understand what he was trying to tell me. It makes no sense. Is it delirium?'

Estra paused, it seemed she too was at a loss and had no feasible answer.

'I do not know anymore, Feletra. All I do know, is that Leao is running out of time.'

Chapter 2
The Sorpha

Incredibly, everyone could sleep with ease, and not for the first night. Leao had been sick for so long that his family had learnt to live with the coughing every night, the coarse breathing in between the hours of the silent night.

It had been five days since Feletra had witnessed Leao's delirium when he pointed to the bedroom corner, seemingly at nothing. Delirium. She could barely bring herself to call it this, it just didn't feel right, it didn't feel true. There was something real about his reaction that day, something she couldn't ignorc. Fclctra was the only one now unable to sleep at night; she sat up in her bed and looked over at Leao. He writhed and sweat more than usual.

The bedroom was shared by all seven siblings, although two beds now lay empty. On the far side of the room, Ataleka began to stir, Feletra knew he had sensed her awakening. He looked over his shoulder instantly in her direction, as if responding to a summoning, the blankets strained over his neck and back.

Feletra turned her head to him slowly, and placed a finger to her lips. She gestured outside, and he nodded. Together, they crept out of the bedroom, silent as mice, and stood outside the front door in the cool night air. Ataleka looked at her expectantly.

'I think we should go,' said Feletra without a flinch.

Ataleka's face contorted with surprise, 'The Soprha?'

'Yes. I can't keep seeing Leao like this, he is getting

worse and nothing we do is working.'

Ataleka paused for thought at that moment, 'Do you really think it will help him?'

Feletra couldn't decide whether to find his sudden deliberation an irritation or indeed whether to take another moment herself and consider the plausibility. Many generations had passed since any evidential properties of the Sorpha had come to light, and none had dared investigate a single drop of the river. She took the former, it had been five days already of consideration. Enough time had passed.

'It has to. Put something on, if we leave now no one will stop us,' she said determinedly.

'Now? Fel, we need the whole night to get there unseen, more time. Tomorrow –'

'Time is what we do not have,' Feletra interjected urgently, struggling to contain her voice to a whisper, 'it's what Leao does not have. We go *now.*'

Without waiting for any further objection, she made to sneak back inside, but Ataleka had one more point to remind her of.

'Feletra, you do realise...the curse?' he said reluctantly.

She paused a little. Yes, she had realised. 'He would be an innocent receiver, Leao would not be cursed.'

'And us?'

Yes, she had realised that too. 'Family is all we have, Ataleka. If we do, if we don't, it doesn't matter.' Out of the ambiguity for everything she was about to do, that one thing was certain. If it were for Leao's benefit, then the curse was truly, and utterly, inconsequential.

x

A woman stopped halfway up a foreboding and cold staircase in a narrow tower. A man named Akeon looked down on her from the top, his expression defined by severity in the inert lines that bent into his skin. He had a distinct lack of sympathy in his eyes, and in the central divide of his collarbone lay a small, sharp-looking branding in black. The woman paused upon it with recognition.

'You knew I was coming?' she said, and continued to the top of the stairs.

'Are you surprised?' Akeon replied, casually allowing her entry to the room. He inadvertently fell into a red leather chair, his favourite.

'I suppose not anymore. You have your ways and means, and they are the reason I am here.'

Akeon appeared suddenly interested and proceeded to sit up. 'You have everything, what could you possibly need me for?'

'Not quite everything, but you know that. I need to change something. I need you to use...' she glanced plainly towards a wide, spiralling staircase at the opposite end of the room and then up to the ceiling, '...them.'

Akeon left a pause between them, he had listened carefully without astonishment. 'And your white knight downstairs, will he be joining you?'

The woman did not look at him, she toyed gently with a pendant that hung from her neck, fingers curling, tucking, coiling around the edges that had warmed from her skin, her wrist folded inwards on its side, resting there on her breast.

'I would imagine so,' she replied with a reassurance

somewhat more to herself, 'he is unlikely to take no for an answer. However, you and I know we are not friends, Akeon. Name your price.'

Akeon smiled a little and began pouring himself a glass of wine from a decanter. 'I would ask only one thing, but I do not think you want this that much.'

There was firelight that bounced back dangerously from the woman's eyes, 'I want this more than anything, what do you think I've been doing all these years? There is no one else I can turn to, except you. Am I not humbled enough for you by just being here? Name the price.'

'Very well. You will bear a child –' the woman laughed mockingly, '– and when it is born, in no matter what state of being you find yourself in, and no matter what realm, you will give it to me and renounce any connection you had. That is my price.'

'Dorsyn already foresaw that I would never bear children. This bargain is empty.'

'Dorsyn does not have what I have. The problem for you, is that I have fed you both lies and truth before. The decision lies with you.'

'I know more than you this time,' said the woman, adamantly shaking her head, 'I will make the pact, and then you will give me what I want.'

Akeon set his wine glass on the table and rose to his feet with deliberation, a treacherous smirk painted across his face. The woman knew how cleverly he played his games, she was unfazed by his expression and remained confident in her estimations. No, it was more than an estimation, it was a certainty with absolutely no need for guesswork. More fool him for making a fruitless deal.

'I trust that you do not mind that we make our pact

official, with a Gorothra?' Akeon enquired, though he knew she was sold, 'Good, then let us begin and I will take you to the Souls.'

x

Ataleka forgot the water flasks. When he sneaked back into the house for the third time, fortunate still not to have woken anyone and met Feletra outside with them, they were ready. Feletra was eager to make a start, the horizon to the east was already becoming a paler blue, although the starband still gazed down upon them for now. The starband was three bright stars in a long line and provided a measure of how far along the night was; the first star, Drenaas, would appear first, then Ilysehr, and lastly Astalien. It was common to use the term starband to refer to one night. Feletra glanced down at her thumb, it was a great deal redder than its left counterpart; she would bite on the tip softly whenever she felt anxious, and attempting to disobey her parents so plainly was no exception. The one thing they could not escape, however, was slinking back to the house without being noticed; their absence would be noted as soon as it was time to wake, and they could readily expect fury.

Feletra was taken aback when Ataleka began towards the stable. 'Where are you going?!' she whispered pressingly.

'I'm getting Banu, he can carry the load,' Ataleka replied, but Feletra had to quickly express her frustration at his time-wasting.

'Forget Banu. Too much noise getting him out, and he will slow us down. This is the only load we need –' she dangled a single empty canister in front of him, '– and I got the handcart out already, we'll share the weight coming back, it's time to go, now!'

She set the canister on the handcart, picked up the handles and marched off at an impressive speed, keen to leave the house in the distance and conscious not only of time, but also of how fast the day would come. Their trek would take them across the Plains of Nemenon, scorching hot flatlands of no more than dust, insufferable burning air and irregular serri trees with no nutrition to offer. There was little other life to be seen; dry reeds appeared in clumps and housed a few breeds of insect or bird, but the greatest predator on the plains was the Nova Snake. The Nova burrowed underground, a fast and highly opportunist serpent, any sign of a meal as fruitful as Feletra and Ataleka it would not hesitate to strike.

Once the house was almost out of sight, Feletra began to relax, though she watched the sunrise conscientiously.

'I still think you will regret not taking Banu...' Ataleka sighed.

'He is too old to walk this far now,' said Feletra, 'and it would probably just make Mother and Father worse when they see us.'

Banu was a horla, a creature of horse-like build, but larger and with a few other intriguing characteristics; horlas grew sharp horns from their skulls that curved inwards, they possessed large eyes that glinted black like oil droplets, and every fourth generation, a horla would bear a peculiar pair of tails from below each ear which stretched out double its length. Estra had always said the use of the tails was something dark and that men often hacked them off, believing them to be an omen or even killed the calf after birth to avoid terrible misfortune befalling their family. Banu had not been a bearer, nor had Nepenas, a second horla of the family whom Flior had formed a close relationship with; Nepenas was a fine specimen, far younger and fitter than Banu, his coat still glossy unlike his elder's longer, matted pelt and his muscles pronounced with youth. Six years ago, when Leao was born, Estra and Padryl struggled to provide with the strain of seven children, money was needed. A merchant offered a worthy sum for Nepenas and they were forced to accept, though Flior had felt the devastation like no other. Horlas had proven to be remarkable creatures and were well-established pillars of the history of Esilence, they had created faithful friendships with men and formed connections that were kindred and true.

It was nearly a four-league journey to the Sorpha and back, and bleak it would be. There was nought to avert their attentions or pique their interests in any way across the barren lands, save for the rise of Pytheria. The sun's first glimmer had passed once Feletra and Ataleka had reached half way, and now much of it shone brilliantly across the plains. *Mother will be rising now...*Feletra thought somewhat miserably, and she imagined Estra panicking at their absence, for imagining was all she could do; Estra was hard as a rock and remained calm in all scenarios, she never laughed or cried, even her smile was barely that and looked as if it gave her physical pain, and so she avoided that too. Padryl occasionally joked that it was the result of bearing the most unruly children in all of Elpura, much to their disappointment and they would throw jeers right back.

Suddenly, Feletra felt a rumble in the earth beneath her. Ataleka felt it too, and they stopped in their tracks, wearing matching expressions of vigilance.

‘Nova Snake?’ said Ataleka, disquieted.

‘I think so,’ Feletra acknowledged, ‘let’s keep moving.’

The chances of encountering one of the snakes was slim, but not unheard of. And neither was death. Padryl had been familiar with the beasts more than once; three he had managed to kill in defending himself, and a fourth he had had only one choice, to run, for its sheer size. But they were not to be underestimated, he had said, for they remembered people and knew family ties, thus if one of his children should ever face one, they best know how to fight it or how fast to run.

Feletra scanned the open horizon and wondered what else she could expect other than a river. She wondered whether she would be making for other horizons in the future, similar or wholly different to the one she gazed upon now. There was almost a sense of resentment, for she knew it was unlikely; she was not the travelling sort and there was something remotely fearful about stepping out into the world alone. There were lands that were foreboding, beasts that were strange, new people with frivolous cultures and erratic ways of living...and yet those very lands were inviting, those beasts were fascinating, and those same people were intriguing, interesting and eye-opening. She wanted to see it all, but there were more significant matters to attend to first.

‘Do you think it’s much further?’ moaned Ataleka, dragging his feet.

‘I’d guess about half a league. You’re not tiring, are you?’ Feletra grinned at him, the question had him straighten his back immediately.

‘No,’ Ataleka retorted. ‘Isn’t it funny, we walk all this way to a huge and nutritious river in the blistering heat, yet when we arrive, we cannot dive in or even drink the water?'

'And don't you be tempted,' Feletra reminded him sternly, 'we have our own drinking water, we do this for Leao and Leao only.'

'Yes, I know. What makes the Sorpha cursed anyway?'

Feletra rolled her eyes, 'You didn't listen to Mother's stories, did you?'

'Not much,' Ataleka confessed with ease, 'I was never interested in them like you. They wasted the time I could have spent climbing the aghaia tree or riding the horlas.'

'Well, the truth is, no one knows for certain. Some say there are sacred stones lying deep in the riverbed that give the Sorpha all its properties, others that the Eastern leaders cursed it with unnatural means as revenge when they lost the war, and some say that there were ancient deities that ruled Enphiah that were driven away by men, and that no mortal would find goodness in that which was too pure and only made for gods.'

Ataleka took it all in for a few moments, and then said, 'Interesting.'

Feletra sniggered at his simple reaction, 'What is?'

'You tell stories like Mother almost as well as you look like her.'

'Well, Ataleka,' said Feletra in a light sarcasm, 'for that remark, I think it's your turn to pull the cart from here.' She dropped the handles instantly and the canister rolled away with a clang. Ataleka chased it down and took over, chuckling as he watched her forge on ahead.

Feletra called over her shoulder to him, 'And back,' taking much joy in his sudden frown.

'Oh, that's not even fair...' Ataleka muttered under his breath.

The full circle of Pytheria glazed the clear azure sky, beating their backs with an immense heat they were only too used to, whilst Desporsa had already risen from the west horizon a calm royal blue, on her way to cross paths with Pytheria in the middle. The Sorpha then came into view, flashing and sparkling at them in the light, inviting them to its banks. They shared looks of delight and half-walked, half-ran the last stretch of land, smiling in relief at their achieved destination.

Standing upon the riverbank finally, Feletra felt overwhelmed: the river was even greater than she had imagined and more breathtaking than anyone could have described. The opposite bank was so far from them, and between the two a vast shifting sheet of water, enveloping swell after swell perilously, the current hastening forward with all speed and intensity, a great vessel of melted, flowing purity. ‘River of Lucrin,’ that was the meaning of the Sorpha’s name; lucrin was an immensely valuable material of the earth named somewhere between rock and metal, more coveted than gold, stronger than the foundations of mountains and lighter than silk. Since the end of the Nyvean War, the Luminors, great leaders of Enphiah, had diminished and retreated mysteriously from their duties to the lands, but their descendants lived on in Lor, Penthor, Setra, Chriah and Stura, and continued to wander in the shadow of false rule beneath the great halls of their ancestors, halls built and lined especially with lucrin, and liberally so.

Feletra knelt down precariously and gazed past her reflection; so clear, the depth of the river became unfathomable. She bent closer, drawn in by its beauty and without question, its temptress heart to lure in the mortals who would have their thirst quenched and their bodies enriched like never before.

'Don't,' Ataleka put a hand on her arm swiftly, and then handed her her water flask. Feletra pulled herself away from the bank and drank half enthusiastically.

'I wasn't going to touch it,' she told him, though she was not sure how much of that she believed herself. Ataleka spared her the reply, and they sat down to rest a short while.

Feletra cast her eyes away from the river and straight ahead; upon the opposite bank she spied something she had missed before. It appeared to be a small stone house or a lodge, standing utterly alone against the wilderness of the plains. The only detail she could discern at such a distance were a couple of shutters, closed as if the place might be abandoned.

'Ataleka, do you see that house across the river?'

Her brother shifted his gaze to where she indicated, 'Hardly a house, but yes.'

'Do you think it is being used? No one should be living this close to the Sorpha,' Feletra pondered.

'Surely no one is living there, no one is that foolish, are they? I think it's empty anyway, the shutters look like they're closed,' Ataleka said, squinting.

Feletra fell silent and continued to stare at the house with intrigue. She was curious all of a sudden, she wanted to explain its existence to herself. Never had anyone heard of any houses being built next to the Sorpha, but then she remembered something from the story of Nephele, the Lady of the Fire. A shrine was once built as a tribute to the Sorpha many years ago, and all came from far and wide to visit and pay their respects to the river to avoid a curse upon their families. One woman however, named Zenika, became so obsessed with the idea of the curse that she visited the shrine daily with her newborn baby, hoping that the place would protect them both, but ironically, she visited so often that she and her daughter both fell prey to the curse. Madness crept into Zenika, and when she realised that their lives would forever be a misery she set her baby alight and sent it down the Sorpha before stabbing herself inside the shrine. No one visited the place again since the incident, but the fate of Nephele, the daughter of Zenika, would be changed forever. The water of the Sorpha saved the baby's life, but also preserved the fire that had encased her; the river cast her onto the bank where she was found and raised in Thenigh. When she had become a woman, she returned to the Sorpha where the waters raised around her and enveloped her, and she emerged a being of eternal flame. Her immortality had been sealed within her since she was a baby, lifting the curse and for the rest of her time she would wander Esilence as the Lady of the Fire.

Feletra suddenly snapped out of her thoughts as she saw Ataleka bending down to the water, ready to fill the canister.

'Be careful!' she implored, and got up off the ground rapidly to supervise him. 'And don't take too much.'

'We do not know how much that is, Fel,' Ataleka replied, planting a foot hard against a rock in the bank so he could lift the heavy water up and out. He filled the canister with around two thirds, and then heaved it back up laboriously. Feletra could see the strain it placed on his shoulders and went to help lift the can from him onto the level ground.

'The tales are true so far, then,' Ataleka panted, 'how...how are we supposed to get that thing home?'

'Well, it's too late to go back without it now,' Feletra

said, reluctantly anticipating the journey home.

Ataleka rolled onto his back, and then became distracted by something tickling his forehead. He sat up and began pulling a cluster of orange-red grass until it yielded from the soil, the roots still dangling beneath it.

'What are you doing?' said Feletra, as if he was up to something. It paid to always be suspicious around her brothers.

'Don't you remember this?' he answered gleefully, 'Mother used to make the best stews with it, but then it grew out of our area. It's meftor, I thought I'd take some back with us. Who knows, it might sweeten the deal when they find out where we've been.'

'Are you trying to butter Mother and Father up?' Feletra laughed. 'We have the water, hopefully that will make them forget the rest when they see Leao well again.'

'You are confident it will work, aren't you?'

Feletra paused and looked back into the river, almost becoming mesmerised once more, 'No, just...trying to have a little faith, I think.'

'Alright, let's go home then,' Ataleka rose to his feet resolutely, but then something followed that stunned the both of them.

An echoing bang, like a clap of thunder, rang through Feletra's ears from across the river; she and Ataleka turned to see a growing white light issuing from every crack and gap of the abandoned house. They shielded their eyes as the light became blindingly unbearable, the shutters were thrown open of their own accord and despite the Sorpha careering away before them, Feletra felt sure she heard the sound of pottery smashing. The house appeared to be shaking violently now, and vibrations within the earth spread to where they stood like an earthquake. Feletra remembered the canister, and rapidly ran to steady it, conscious not to spill a drop. The white light then began to die back and the tremors ceased, the house appeared the same as before again, save for the open shutters, but Feletra and Ataleka felt lost for words.

'What was that?' said Ataleka after a few moments, 'Is someone over there?'

'I don't know...' Feletra could not tear her gaze away from the house. She began to hear more banging coming from inside; straining to see ahead, she saw the door fly open with force.

'Hide!' Ataleka grabbed Feletra by the arm and they ducked as low as they could into a cluster of grasses by a serri tree, though the cover was thin.

'Are you thinking what I'm thinking? Blackcraft?' said Feletra, and Ataleka nodded his head uneasily. Blackcraft was a dark practice that only certain individuals inherited from their forefathers or mothers, they had the ability to move objects with their will alone and access and utilise individual crafts or rituals that were forsaken. It was one of four kyms, powers created outside of Esilence that had long ago manifested within living beings and gave them unnatural capabilities. Feletra's knowledge on the area was limited, for Estra was always reluctant to speak of the kyms. She would simply tell them that kymic beings were wicked, their intentions evil and that they should be feared, for the morotehm (those with no kymic abilities) stood no chance against them.

They watched as two people walked out of the house, one a man, the other a woman, both appeared to be dressed as if preparing for attack; Feletra thought it unusual to see a woman in such bold and masculine attire, any other details were too small to discern.

Across the river, the woman looked out to the other side expectantly, though her expression was full of dismay and fury.

'I should have known,' she said fiercely, 'I should have known he would trick us like this. We're on the wrong side, I can see no one.'

'We need to go back, we should not have come here,' said the man, he had a hard look about him, full of history and burden.

'Not until I've done what I came here for.'

'Then what? We cross the river? You know as well as I the risks we run by staying here too long, he didn't lie about that.'

'We agreed this was the only way! Every other option we have exhausted, I cannot just throw this one away so lightly.'

'Using the Souls to begin with was a mistake –'

'Wait, what is that?'

Feletra did not know why, but she had felt compelled to rise from her hiding place in the grass, compelled to see these people, Ataleka had tried to keep her down but she would not yield, and now she walked slowly back to the riverbank, staring at the mystery man and woman. She could tell they were staring right back at her, and she had no idea how much danger she had just placed herself in, but she felt something more than intrigue for these people. It felt profound and wholly unknown, one half of her felt a whole world between them, the other no more than a needle head apart.

Though she could not hear them, the woman spoke softly

with awe, ‘Great Ilysehr above me, I see her.’

Ataleka could no longer restrain himself. Terrified for his sister, he leapt out of hiding and tried to grab Feletra, but the woman noticed the commotion instantly, and her expression dropped, ‘No, no, don’t –’ she said.

‘Ataleka! What are you doing?!’ Feletra exclaimed, fighting free of him.

‘Saving your life! They are craftsmen, Feletra!’

‘Stop!’ the woman called, and incredibly both Feletra and Ataleka heard her – they were too close to the river, Ataleka twisted one way, his footing was lost, and he fell into the vast swells of the Sorpha.

‘NO!’ the woman screamed, and her voice carried clearly to Feletra, who had fallen to the ground in an effort to pluck her brother out, but the Sorpha was too strong and too vast.

There was an intense flash of white light, and the man and woman disappeared within the blink of an eye. Feletra had no time to consider them, she could still see Ataleka fighting to stay afloat, and ran along the riverbank with him.

‘Ataleka!’ she thought there was no end in sight, there was nothing that could stop him or slow him down, until finally she saw a wall of rock debris protruding above the surface. There appeared to be no way around, he would hit the wall no matter what, but she knew the impact could also kill him, and he could barely see anything coming. Feletra was petrified of the water, it was foreign territory and she knew not how to swim, but she was overcome with the urge at that moment, and the voice that usually told her stay away to keep alive was gone, she knew only one thing – that she had to get Ataleka out of the water.

Her heart skipped a beat, and she jumped towards him into the river. It was a good aim, for she grasped his arm within a second and pulled him onto his back as they were hastened downstream like a swift breath lost on a hurricane.

'Put your legs forward!' Feletra ordered, and together they both outstretched their legs in time before striking the wall. It was no easy impact, but it was the best outcome they could have hoped for. Together they began edging their way back towards the bank, supporting one another to avoid submerging; Ataleka scrambled his way out first, and then helped Feletra onto the riverbank, where they both lay sopping wet and exhausted, feeling the weight of the Sorpha's waters lifting from them slowly but surely as it dripped off them to lay waste amidst the dust and sand. The gravity of their actions quickly dawned upon them.

'What does this mean?' Ataleka panted.

'Are you hurt?'

'Are we cursed, Feletra?'

'Tell me, are you hurt?'

'I'm fine! Except for the fact that my life is ruined, I have never felt better!'

Feletra paused and took a deep breath, she tried desperately to remain calm, 'We do not know for sure that we are cursed, it is possible we escaped it –'

'How? Look at us, we are dripping head to toe! If it weren't for those craftsmen this never would have happened, and what were you doing anyway? Why did you have to get up and stare at them? If you had just stayed down like I said –'

'I don't know, Ataleka! I don't know why I did it,' Feletra looked up and saw that Ataleka was staring at her as if still waiting for a real explanation, 'I just felt magnetised to them somehow, and that I had to see them properly.'

Ataleka sighed at length. 'Mother is the one who knows the most about the Sorpha, we should ask her what to do.'

'No!' Feletra disputed heatedly. 'She would never forgive us, and she would refuse Leao the water immediately.'

'You mean we're still taking the water back for Leao?'

'Of course! If we are cursed this will still not affect him, it will heal him, I know it. And I did not come this far to nearly drown in a sacred river only to go back empty-handed.'

Ataleka did not reply, he walked over to the canister, set it on the handcart strenuously and then looked back at Feletra, 'It's time to go home then,' she had never heard him sound so broken, and with such anger inside him. This was no juvenile antagonism anymore, but real, raw emotion. The worst part was that she could not even tell if it was directed at her, himself, or life for allowing fate to get its own cruel way.

The trek home was a solemn one, they said nothing the entire way and felt as despondent as the landscape was derelict. Feletra repeated the events at the Sorpha over and over in her mind, until her head began to hurt, or perhaps that was simply the heat. The blinding white light, the quake, the mysterious man and woman and the way they stared at her as if they knew her, and she had felt some sort of connection to them too, or was that truly just plain curiosity? It must have been, for she could not explain the former. And if it could not be explained then she must be wrong, or it must be the work of Blackcraft.

Feletra shook her head, *Now I'm beginning to sound like my mother,* she thought, and she hated that. Estra was the most intelligent and intuitive person she knew, and she had learnt much about the world and its dark corners, but she had chosen to close the minds of her children to the darkest of those places, and the worst stories of Esilence were not told. Feletra was no fool, she saw when her mother evaded the questions or omitted the finer details. It only fuelled her intrigue, fixed the allure and locked the captivation indefinitely...but had she gone too far? Should she and Ataleka have stayed at home? Were they cursed by the Sorpha's wrath? She did not even know how to find out.

Feletra offered to pull the handcart for the last half of the journey, she could see Ataleka slowing and the beads of sweat that rolled down his forehead, but he did not even glance at her, he grunted and carried on. She saw the resentment in him already.

They crossed the River Kestors, and after what seemed like an age of no more than silence, struggle and sweltering heat, home finally came into view. Feletra breathed a sigh of relief, though half of her did not desire to be there, she needed more time to collect her thoughts, but she could see her mother waiting within the doorway, rigid and presiding. She was only thankful that Pytheria had quickly dried up any evidence that they had been soaking wet.

As they approached, Estra took one look at them and then at the canister, 'What is that?' she said austerely. Ataleka did not know where to look, he often had been the one to let Feletra do the explaining.

'It's water from the Sorpha,' said Feletra plainly, 'it's for Leao.'

Estra looked between them, almost disbelievingly, 'Is

this one of your jokes?'

'No, Mother. Look,' Feletra lifted the lid off the can, and Estra peered inside. The surface glittered and shone radiantly, and she could see to the very bottom.

'Taking water from the Sorpha, what were you thinking? Do you realise what you could have done?'

Feletra couldn't bring herself to tell her the truth, and neither could Ataleka, who remained silent by her side. All she could think about in that moment was Leao's wellbeing.

'I know, but it will work, won't it? It will make Leao well again?' Feletra said anxiously, but she had never seen her mother appear to be at such a loss before, she could see she was torn.

'That water is both a blessing and a curse,' she told them, 'did you drink any?'

Feletra looked down and shook her head, she found it very difficult to lie, and was sure she must have swallowed some when she jumped into the river after Ataleka.

'I do not condone this,' said Estra, 'but I know why you have done it. I see that you have been selfless, and for that, we will try the water with Leao. But your father will still hear of this, and I cannot say what he will think. Is that understood?'

'Yes,' Feletra replied thankfully, 'can we give it to him now?'

Ataleka failed to break free from his moroseness, and walked away abruptly to the back of the house. Estra watched him go curiously.

'What is wrong with your brother?' she said sharply.

'He's alright, he's just exhausted. He carried the can all the way home by himself.'

'Better that he rests then. Bring the water inside, let's not waste any time.'

Estra only spoke the words she meant, and no time was wasted indeed in preparing a single cup of water for Leao, though the canister was so heavy it required a great effort from the two of them just to angle it perfectly without spillage whilst Bri was charged with holding the cup.

When Estra went to wake Leao, he was curled up as if shielding himself from the freezing cold.

'I'm not thirsty,' he protested, and pushed Estra's hand away, but she persisted.

'This is medicine, Leao,' she said, 'this is the medicine you need. Don't you want to play again?' she tried once more, and the thought seemed to encourage him enough to take a sip, then he drained the entire cup. Feletra stood nearby with her heart in her mouth, she prayed it would work. Something had to come right out of this day, it just had to.

Leao laid down his head and curled up again with his eyes closed.

'Does he need more?' said Feletra, 'How long does it take?'

Estra ushered her out of the bedroom quietly, 'I do not have any answers, Feletra. I have never used Sorpha water before to treat anything. We must be patient.'

Feletra stopped Estra before she could walk away, 'Mother, can I stay with him? Just to watch him.'

Estra nodded carefully, 'Alright, yes,' and Feletra hoped she could not detect all the fear she was radiating at that moment. Softly, she closed the bedroom door behind her and took a seat at the bottom of Leao's bed.

There was only suspense now, she did not know how

long she would have to wait, or what rules there were to drinking Sorpha water, but she would make the journey twice, thrice, a thousand times for more if he needed it. She would deal with Ataleka later, if he would even speak to her again, she wished he was there with her, waiting as anxiously as she was for Leao to start some endless conversation as he once did. He would begin a story as comical as the flies buzzing around Banu because they were his best friends, remind them about how Desporsa must love Elpura, because they never had any bad weather, or have a profound question, asking if any of them would return as better creatures like Byte or Banu when they died. Questions such as these would often take them all aback, for Leao's imagination and in particular, the depth of his mind, was remarkable for his tender age.

Feletra watched and waited all day, still he did not stir; the exhaustion of her trek with Ataleka began to hit her, and she laid across the bottom of Leao's bed, passing in and out of sleep restlessly. She lost most of the day to nothingness and all sense of time escaped her; it didn't matter, she was in the right place.

When she awoke next, evening had come, moonlight shone into the room brighter than usual, and someone had passed in and out to light a candle by the bedside. She recognised a change in Leao's position, and fear was the first emotion that struck her; she lifted her head awkwardly and looked towards him blearily, then her eyes opened wide.

Leao was sat atop his blankets, kneeling on the bed, and staring at his sister intently. His eyes were radiant, startlingly so, the same incandescent golden hue as Padryl's, and there was a glow to his skin like a fire reborn from the most sullen of ashes.

'I'm hungry, Feletra,' he said, his spirit fresh and crisp.

Feletra could not believe her eyes, she began to laugh, and then they laughed together.

Chapter 3
Eastern Allure

Leao could not be stopped. For seven days since he had been cured by the Sorpha, he would be the first to wake every morning and the last to sleep at night, his energy was boundless and infectious. Even Estra showed no sign of wanting to slow him down; beneath her dry, sombre expression Feletra knew she must have been rejoicing inside, for her son was saved.

Padryl rejoiced openly and spent all of his time with Leao when he was away from the fields. He quietly commended Feletra and Ataleka for bringing the water home, but equally did not forget the fact that they had disobeyed him, and so they missed one dinner. Feletra did not care, it was worth going hungry for one night. Ataleka still would not speak to her, and she became more concerned about him every day that he evaded her company. Worse still, it made her feel alone, Ataleka had never behaved like this with her before, and they had always relied on one another, but the rest of the family were blind to his downcast mood for the merriment of Leao. Every day was a good day, and Feletra slipped into the jubilant atmosphere well, until Ataleka returned to the house from the fields every evening, and she was heavily reminded of the events at the Sorpha...of the curse. If it were true, she knew they would not be able to hide their symptoms forever.

On the eighth day, Padryl came home early with Ataleka at his heel. Feletra had not seen them coming, she had taken pleasure in watching Leao and Bri listen to one of Estra's stories, it was a deeply comforting thing to see her brother back outside once more in the sunlight.

'Alright, one more. What story would you have next then?'

'The Horla of Fire!' Leao cried enthusiastically. Feletra smiled knowingly, this one was his favourite; the Horla of Fire was the beast that rescued Nephele from the riverbank and never left her side. When she became the Lady of the Fire, she imbued the horla with her power and immortality. It is said that to speak ill of Nephele is to invoke the temper of the horla, who will appear to defend her honour and smite all those who deliver contempt.

Feletra was startled when a wooden staff rattled at her feet.

'Pick it up,' said Padryl, Feletra did so and followed her father and Ataleka to an open space of land just beyond the aghaia tree. She had forgotten all about the agreement to learn combat with them, then noticed Ataleka carrying a sword rather than a staff.

'I don't get a sword?' she asked in confusion. 'How do I learn with just this?'

'You will learn the way I say you learn,' Padryl replied affirmatively, 'Ataleka is a little ahead of you, you need to begin from scratch. Stand there.'

Feletra did as she was told and tried not to argue, and she wondered if her father truly would teach her as much as her brothers if she proved herself. Ataleka stood apart from them, unsheathed his sword and practiced some swings alone.

'Hold out the staff like this,' said Padryl, demonstrating with his own, 'that's right, now I will take you through some basic techniques.'

They spent hours together, until Pytheria began to sink and the last auburn glow of the day was upon them. Feletra had performed steps, swings, thrusts and leans, but all the while she watched Ataleka and saw him move faster and aim better, and she began to feel the frustration, for her father had not even enacted a scene of attack with her yet.

'Father, how is this helping? It feels foolish, *I* feel foolish.'

'And why is that?'

'I have barely learnt anything, Ataleka already knows how to attack and defend and I am stuck with a piece of wood that can't even protect me.'

Padryl rubbed his chin thoughtfully. 'Come here,' he said.

Feletra hesitated a moment, and then walked towards him. Without warning, Padryl spun and swept low with his staff, knocking her to the ground instantly.

'Why would you do that?!' Feletra grumbled.

'It was a forceful attack, was it not?' her father said casually, helping her to her feet.

'Yes!'

'If a piece of wood can attack forcefully, do you not suppose it can protect just as much? Show me your pass spin.'

Feletra reluctantly held out her staff, and spun it between both her hands, passing one from to the other at a steady rate, but her focus was thrown out now. She stopped and sighed, 'What is this meant to prove?'

Padryl grasped his own staff, and began to spin, slowly at first, then faster and faster, passing it beneath his arms, above his head and back again at a phenomenal speed.

Feletra had never witnessed such skill before, she stood in awe before him as he came to a stop.

'Would you have felt safe to approach me just then?' he asked her simply, and she shook her head. 'Then a piece of wood can protect you more than you think.'

'But if I'd had a sword, I could have stopped you.'

'If you had a sword, you'd be slower, and don't forget, I command two ends of that staff,' he drew a circle in the ground with a line through the middle, 'that means that two parts of me are defended at any one time, you would have to know exactly where to step and where to aim to break my barrier. Timing is the difference between life and death, Feletra, that is why we begin with the basics.'

Feletra sighed in acceptance, and proceeded to practice a few more of the steps and turns, but all the while she felt detached from her staff, and she knew she should have felt more of its presence if she were to command it the way her father did. Padryl went to check on Ataleka's progress, and Feletra felt an even greater sense of incompetence just from watching them, the way they flowed and complemented each other, slow lunges, quick twists, then slow again. Padryl returned to her and immediately noticed her look of disdain.

'Do you wish me to stop teaching you?' he said.

'No,' she answered, she had half been expecting such a question that would give her license to go back to her old, dull house chores, 'it's just...I'm too slow, Father. I can't do it like you can.'

'It does not matter how slow you are, if you don't stop. And let me tell you, it took me thirty-nine days to conquer the staff, and years to follow to ensure that I remembered it. I did not stop.'

Feletra glanced at Ataleka again and his short sword, and Padryl followed her gaze, understanding her feelings of inadequacy.

'You are trying to run before you can walk, Feletra. I can give you as many lessons as you like, but you need to find the will by yourself, otherwise I am wasting my time.'

Feletra snapped to attention, 'No, I know...I'm sorry, I will. I'll try harder,' she realised suddenly the ridicule she would have brought upon herself if she gave up after the first lesson, and remembered all the fight she had put into obtaining them in the first place, but there was so much turmoil and unrest running through her mind that she feared her focus might be misplaced.

'I am glad to hear it. Come and have a rest before dinner, let's finish for today.'

'Call me when it's ready, I'm going to practice a little longer,' Feletra said resolutely, and Padryl appeared to appreciate her answer. He called Ataleka over to the house, whose eyes lingered darkly on his sister for a moment. She forced herself to ignore his glare, she must focus.

The night swept in cool, and the darkness was comforting to her, a blanket of concealment to soften her unease. Feletra was the first to hear a distinct sound, the sound of hooves in the distance, she stopped training and looked to the north, where the silhouette of a single rider came forth. He stopped and dismounted by the door to the house, and Feletra recognised from the green attire and horla tack that he was an ebrat. The ebrats were the messengers of Enphiah, the job was highly paid and revered; for all its simplicity, an ebrat took the duty to his heart and was expected to deliver every single letter he was charged with. Every day they risked life and limb against some of Enphiah's harshest terrains and most challenging environments. The ebrats were supported by creatures known as the hithri, or a hithre as one singularly would have been called. The hithri were small, brown, furry animals, no larger than a fist, with a great tail curled up inside them that resembled a broom head. They were the fastest creatures known, used only for high priority letters and by the wealthy, for they were few and far between and the price for their service was steep.

Feletra watched Estra accept the letter at the door before he rode off, a few moments followed and then Leao was running from the house excitedly towards her.

'Feletra! Feletra!' he cried, 'He's coming home!'

'What? Who is coming home, Leao?'

'Flior! He's coming home!'

Leao dragged Feletra by the hand and they found the others inside, talking feverishly between themselves. All but Estra, who handed the letter to Feletra to read with a look of mild satisfaction that presented itself as her version of smiling.

'Your brother returns to us very soon, have a read,' she said soberly.

Feletra opened the letter eagerly:

Dear Mother and Father,

I hope you all keep well. Penthor is serving me as I had hoped, I have found much support here in my endeavours. I will keep my letter short and expect to be with you all by the second day from you receiving this, when you can hear everything in person.

Your son,
Flior.

Feletra frowned a little, 'He doesn't know about Leao, does he?'

'Right now, no,' Estra replied, carefully folding the letter again, 'he will understand.'

Feletra said no more on the matter, she knew Flior would not be happy being the last to find out, but together they had all scraped what little money they had left to pay for consultations from the herra, little could have been spared to pay for an ebrat to send to Penthor as well.

They sat to dinner, Leao led the conversation as he once did, there was no silencing him. The effect of his miraculous recovery lingered with them still so that his animation was infectious, and his lack of ceasefire could not come close to irksome.

Feletra gazed down at the quiet Bri, who was busy writing in her notebook beneath the table.

'What story are you writing today, Bri?'

Bri was startled and rapidly snapped her book shut as if caught writing a love letter to an admirer, 'Nothing,' she murmured, though it had attracted the attention of the company.

'Is Bri writing in her diary again?' Skepreo teased, and Padryl tapped him on the arm discouragingly.

'It's not a diary,' Bri retorted in barely a whisper, she was incredibly bashful, unlike the rest of her bold and fearless siblings. Her hair fell soft and dark with red highlights like Estra and Feletra, and she shared their eyes, deep black pools that knew no end. She was a small girl and she enjoyed hiding in cramped and awkward spaces, there she would take her notebook and write her next story in privacy, or until Leao came and found her for a new game. She told no one exactly what she wrote, only that they were stories, but Feletra thought that they must be fantastical, outlandish and altogether romantic, for Bri was often found daydreaming into some other world, likely one that she had created.

'I think what Bri is doing is commendable, she knows her future already and is set on being a writer,' said Estra as if she was representing, 'her talents are hidden but promising, you should be encouraging of your sister.'

'I'm sure Bri writes some lovely diary entries, Mother,' Skepreo smirked.

Padryl sniggered, but when Estra threw him daggers he straightened up with his best attempt of looking genuinely stern, 'Enough of that.'

Feletra smiled half-heartedly, still she could not forget the scene at the Sorpha, and etched deeply into her mind were those two distant figures of the man and woman, enigmas that should have been intimidating but were instead a curious pair that were captivating and invited her for a better look...how she wished now she had stayed down.

When Flior finally arrived two days later, it was late afternoon and Feletra was busy practicing with her staff. Ataleka was still set apart from her, but she no longer let his presence affect her, she was determined to succeed. She felt that she had made little progress in the space of two days, but Padryl continued to support her. The lessons were put on halt for the rest of the day, however, for everyone gathered around Flior to greet him enthusiastically, Bri and Leao were the first to be at his side before he could even bring the cart to a stop.

'Stay away from the cart while it's still moving!' Estra called fruitlessly, the pair aimlessly ignored the three horlas jostling about before them as they were given the order to halt.

'Hello, you two!' Flior swung himself down off the cart in one fluid motion to embrace them both together; he wore a grey travelling coat that swept as low as his ankles, though he was closer to his mother's height than his father's, his face was long and he also lacked the olive skin of Padryl. He did, however, share the same golden eyes, and walked with a strong and dominant air about him.

'Always the carts,' Padryl commented, 'you still hope to find Nepenas, don't you?'

'Of course, and I will,' Flior replied, 'until then, riding another horla just doesn't feel right.' Flior was twenty-three years old and had lived away from home for five of them, in that time he had settled in Penthor, began a respectable career in cartography and the arts but had also quietly been searching for Nepenas; Flior was the highest-earning member of the family and had readily decided he would buy Nepenas back no matter the cost when he found him.

Feletra and Ataleka were the last to receive a greeting.

'What sullen faces we have here, have I aged that much since you last saw me?' Flior jested, and Feletra and Ataleka appeared rattled for a moment, unaware of how they might have seemed.

'Oh, no, we're just tired,' Feletra explained hastily, and Ataleka nodded along, 'we've been training.'

Flior was taken aback. 'Training? You continue to surprise me, Feletra.'

'It's not that surprising,' Skepreo interjected, 'Fel was always one of the boys.'

'Is that why I always beat you in a wrestle?' she retorted, and Skepreo slinked away from the procession of laughter that followed.

'I see nothing has changed here then,' said Flior.

'Actually, son, there is something your father and I should tell you,' Estra took Flior inside the house silently.

'Ataleka, Feletra, bring your brother's things inside, will you? Skepreo, get the horlas some water and into the stable,' said Padryl before following Estra into the kitchen.

Flior only had two bags with him, and one was crammed full of maps, Feletra overheard some of the conversation with her parents on her way to the bedroom.

'Why hadn't you told me sooner?' came Flior's voice.

'There was little you or anyone could have done,' said Estra in earnest, 'we had already tried everything.'

'But I could have brought with me the best herras of Penthor, it's no issue to me, Mother.'

'We know, Flior,' said Padryl, 'but we were very fortunate, nonetheless, it was a risk that we took with the Sorpha, but it seemed we had no other choice left.'

'And it was Feletra and Ataleka that brought the water home? They must have known it was serious or they would not have risked so much...I trust they have been acknowledged for their courage?'

There was a pause, Feletra was hidden behind the doorway and she imagined her parents must be shifting uneasily in their seats at that moment.

'They still disobeyed us, Flior,' said Estra, 'they went

without one meal, with hindsight what they did was reckless –'

'Madness, even,' Padryl agreed, 'they could have fallen prey to the curse and even Leao as well, we had no idea what to expect.'

'Your father is right, I agreed to give that water to Leao based on faith because that is all I had left, but still I was racked with doubt in doing so. Three of my children were put at great risk, you must understand that as a parent, Flior, our incentive is only to protect.'

'They were the only ones with a solution and to take action on it...' Flior disputed, 'and yet you punished them. You punished them for saving their brother's life. Forgive me for bearing a childless man's point of view but I feel that ingenuity should be applauded.'

Feletra smiled to herself, it was good to have Flior back, he stood for reason, balance, and gave others a voice when their own was strangled or had gone unheard. She heard a chair scraping along the floor and bustled quickly into the bedroom where Ataleka was crouched next to Leao, reading a book together. Ataleka noticed her presence immediately as she set Flior's things down by his old bed and rose to leave.

'Ataleka, wait,' Feletra stopped him by the door and lowered her voice, 'how long are you going to ignore me like this? I think we need to talk about the Sorpha.'

'There's nothing to talk about, Fel,' Ataleka stubbornly left the room, giving her but a moment's eye contact.

Feletra sighed in exasperation and turned to Leao. 'What's that book you've got there?' she said lightly, 'Do you want me to carry on with you?'

She knelt down encouragingly next to him, but Leao was

no longer reading, he was not even looking at the book anymore. Feletra followed his gaze, he was staring at the corner of the room, the very same corner by his bed. 'Leao?'

Was this a joke? This was not possible; the delirium should have been cured.

'What are you looking at, Leao? Do you see something?' Feletra clicked her fingers in front of his face, she waved her hand, he was utterly fixated and would not respond to her. She put her hand to his forehead, his temperature was normal, there was no fever, then what was wrong with him? The misgivings began to grow in the pit of her stomach again and she failed to understand anything that was happening. The Sorpha water should have cured everything...

Without warning, Leao blinked twice and began reading aloud again from the book as if nothing happened. Feletra was taken aback, she stopped him abruptly.

'Leao, Leao – listen a moment. What was that? What were you staring at?'

'I wasn't staring,' Leao replied defensively.

'Yes, you were. You were staring at that corner again like there was something there.'

Leao shook his head at her, 'No, I've been reading my book. You can read the next page, Feletra,' and he continued.

Feletra gawked at him for a few moments, then she stormed out of the bedroom and into the scullery where her mother was chopping vegetables.

'He did it again,' said Feletra uncontrollably, 'he's acting as if he is still delirious!'

'Who? Leao?' said Estra, her concern less prominent.

‘Yes, Leao, and it was exactly the same as before, it was something about that corner in the bedroom, he was just staring at it and I couldn’t break him out of it –’

‘He is a child, Feletra, and a lively one at that, I am sure there are all kinds of odd things he might do in the moments he decides to wind down.’

‘So you think this is normal?’

‘I think it is Leao being Leao, and I think you might be reading into things too far. You are still worried for him, that is understandable, but you have cured him, be at peace with that. And do not tempt fate, another illness like your brother’s is too ill a prospect.’

She brushed past Feletra into the kitchen, who felt suddenly dumbstruck at that moment, or the opposite, that her mind was cramped and stifled with too much information, she couldn’t tell. Tempting fate...what was that she once said? It had been years, but it crept back to her from forgotten depths like some old creaking cockroach rather than a fond memory, *a shift in fate.*

‘Are you alright?’

Feletra returned to the room, Flior was gazing at her worriedly.

‘I’m fine, Flior.’

‘You don’t look it. Why don’t you come outside with me? Get some fresh air, I’m about to set up my easel by the river.’

Fresh air sounded like an attractive idea at that moment, Feletra followed Flior out to the River Kestors, and she couldn’t help but be reminded that it ran off the Sorpha, that it wouldn’t exist without it, yet it was a good river. Less pure but giving without contract or obligation. No rules, just simple water, but Flior was quick with his eyes and he took note of Feletra's wandering into the gentle fluid crests.

'You haven't been the same since I came home, Ataleka neither. Have you two had a fight?'

Feletra hesitated, unsure of how she should respond, 'Just a minor disagreement, you know how it is.'

Flior nodded uncertainly, he was aware she was omitting a great deal of information, and she could tell he knew.

'Speaking of such,' Feletra continued hastily, 'it sounded as if there was some sort of discord between you and Mother and Father. Is that why you're out here?'

'No, I didn't really agree with how they felt you and Ataleka needed to be punished for helping Leao recover, but what is done is done. I am out here to be out of the way whilst Mother prepares dinner, the house gets too hot. Thought I'd take the opportunity to paint a few western landscapes whilst during my stay, they sell for more across the border.'

'You can afford paint?' Feletra leant in to examine a row of tiny ceramic pots that Flior had laid out. Paint was a luxury in Enphiah, and as such a finished painting was worth even more. Other luxuries included ink, wine, various spices and oils, and enna (a soft and silky material).

'I can afford quite a few things these days, I did try and send some money home, but Father would not have it.'

'Too proud.'

'Exactly, and I know we have never needed it much living off the land, but if they had told me about Leao there is a lot I could have done to help. Thankfully you and Ataleka did what you did, or we could have lost him.'

Feletra wanted to stop hearing about her courageous venture with Ataleka now, it had not felt courageous, it had felt desperate, and there was more evil associated with it now than goodness. The Sorpha had quickly become a place she desired only to forget, but would she be able to? It was a merciless illness, and you could not cure that with which you have been cursed. She thought back to Leao, was he even truly cured? Perhaps Mother was right, perhaps it was simply his short attention span, surely a common trait in highly animated children.

The day flew by quickly, Feletra watched Flior paint the river and the land beyond it in silence, with little and everything to be seen. He was meticulous with each brushstroke, and there was character expressed from every bristle, an artistic streak was dominant within him and he had Estra to thank for it. The attribute, with Feletra of course still yet to find her absolute skill, had escaped her.

By the time Flior had nearly finished, Estra approached looking for Feletra.

'Feletra,' she said, 'can you come sit with Bri and Leao a moment? I need to keep an eye on the food before it burns,' it was really more of an order than a request, and Feletra left Flior's side to take Estra's seat before the house, an eager Bri and Leao staring up at her for a story.

'Alright, is there a theme today?' Feletra said with a sigh, truly wanting to be elsewhere at that moment, for her heart was not in it, and her mind even less so, 'What tale would you like?'

'Mother has been telling us about the Great War,' Bri mumbled, and Feletra sighed again in defeat, and began. The Great War, or the Nyvean War, was perhaps the longest and most detailed story, for it was a true one. It began in Men. 21, following the founding of Enphiah in Men. 1, when three great explorers from across the northern seas discovered the prosperous land, they were leaders who brought settlers with them and were known as the Luminors. They divided Enphiah fairly between the three of them to rule for themselves, until the eastern leader, Sethra, argued that his region was not as yielding, and the resources poor. No one could understand his view, for it was clear that the east was in fact rich in prosperity, and many historians believed Sethra was driven by jealousy for the Sorpha. He declared war upon the Luminors of the west and the midlands when they refused to share rule of their own lands, which lasted for forty-eight years. In that time, the east had discovered preathins, foul creatures of the earth that they could set upon their opposition and deliver incredible damage, and the fadres also allied with the east, a long native race of Enphiah, though their reason for alliance was ever unclear and they were known as cunning and untrustworthy people. Sethra's right-hand man, Chrie, mutinied in Men. 34 to take opportunity of Pyra which lay forgotten in the south. Rukurehn and Nago, Luminors of the west and the midlands, experienced unparalleled devastation, until Sethra was finally defeated in Men. 69 and surrendered, begging to keep his land. His land was reduced, and he was mercifully granted a small dominion to call his own known today as the Eastern Enphiahn Region. The feud, however, had never truly been laid to rest, and the easterners were avoided wherever possible.

'Feletra, Briapora, Leao! It's time to come inside,' Estra was calling.

'But I want to hear the part about Chrie and Pyra!' Leao moaned, but Estra was persistent, and Feletra was glad to leave it there.

'You've heard it a thousand times already, Leao,' said Feletra, ushering them both inside, though it was not entirely true. She had read the history books, and there were numerous gruesome and unheard of details that her mother would have left out, too dark to fill her children's heads with.

Dinner was extravagant in honour of Flior's arrival, the sight of not one but two roast pheasants to keep their bellies full was enough to widen Leao and Bri's eyes out of their sockets. The table was as loud as ever, and much of the conversation centred entirely around Flior and his time spent in Penthor, the wealthiest land in the midlands. Estra subtly queried as to whether he had found a lady in Penthor yet, though he openly confessed his work had taken precedence during his time away, and any distractions of the nature would simply slow him down. It was impossible to tell whether Estra approved or disapproved, for her straight expression remained devotedly unchanged. The house was so isolated out on the plains that meeting anyone new was a rarity; only Lampaea had been thought to have found someone, a girl whom he had met collecting water one day by the Kestors four years past, until she returned every day to see him. Lampaea had been subject to the teasing and the jeering of his siblings, but when he would only roll his eyes and smile in return Feletra knew there was something real between them.

Once the table was cleared Flior spread his maps out and they gathered round to examine his fastidious work.

'If you were not my son I'd say you were lying,' Padryl commented, 'you say one of these fetches forty pieces?'

'That's right, and the demand is growing. There seem to be a greater number of travellers nowadays.'

'Is that so? Astounding.'

'There's Pyra!' Leao shouted abruptly, landing his index

finger firmly on the land that separated Stura and Chriah. Feletra noticed this was not the first time he had expressed a sudden liking for the place; for no reason anyone could find, Leao loved to hear about Pyra in stories and grew excited whenever he saw the name in books or on maps, but Estra disapproved greatly, for Pyra was home to the most malevolent and wicked.

'And what do you know about Pyra, Leao?' she said, right on cue, 'that it is full of the most hateful kind of people, craftsmen that would not hesitate to do harm to anyone with their fiendish and unworldly ways.'

'That's only Chriah,' Feletra found herself speaking up unexpectedly, 'the Sturans are a good people.'

'Yes, and those Sturans still must live in fear to this day, the Chriahks will never change. And Stura is nevertheless forever tainted with the evil of their neighbours, no one with any sense would remain so close to such villainy.'

Feletra smiled downwardly at Leao, who was silenced just as his mother had hoped. When Leao and Bri were led to bed Feletra decided she would join them, her busy mind was exhausting her and sleep seemed to be the only way to stop it from running away altogether.

'You're going to bed this early? Not even done any work today, have you?' Skepreo scoffed.

'Your brother is right,' said Padryl, 'and we've not seen Flior in so long, why not just stay up for one more drink with us?'

'Maybe tomorrow, I just think I need to rest early tonight.'

'It's fine,' said Flior understandably, 'Feletra did seem a little tired today. Go and rest.'

Feletra took her leave before they changed their minds,

she caught Ataleka's eye on the way out and noted his look of apprehension. She knew what he must be thinking, it was not true tiredness but a symptom of the curse creeping through. Perhaps it was, she had no idea, she immensely disliked putting yet more thought into the very notion. *Let him think what he wants,* she thought bitterly, *he's too stubborn to talk to me anyway.*

It was with a great sense of relief when she laid down her head and stared dully at the ceiling. She heard their muffled voices, laughing and exchanging stories merrily, though she remained certain that Ataleka must still be sitting there like a churlish mute between them all, she could not hear his voice amongst them. Wearily she cast a last look over Bri and Leao, they were already fast asleep. She lingered on Leao a little, but he did not move, there was no pointing or staring now.

Feletra closed her eyes, she allowed sleep to wash over her and fell deep into slumber, but it was not long before something awakened her again. Her eyelids fought her dimly in the dark, all the lights had been extinguished save for the moonlight streaming through the slats in the shutters and everyone slept soundly around her. That is, until she spied Leao, and she could hear him saying something, repeating it over and over. He was stood facing the corner in the darkness.

As Feletra lifted herself heavily out of bed to approach him, she came steadily closer so as not to wake the others.

'Leao,' she whispered, 'go back to bed.'

Then she began to hear what he was saying.

'Pyra...Pyra....'

Feletra thought he must be sleepwalking and dreaming about Pyra, it was hardly surprising given his obsession with the place, though he had never done this before. There was something strange at work.

'Leao?' she placed a hand on his shoulder, and without warning Leao spun around, his face eyeless and his mouth drawn like a doorway into an everlasting abyss.

'Pyra!' he screamed terribly, his voice sounded dreadful, chilling and not his own.

Feletra awoke instantaneously in a cold sweat, she was unable to control her breathing, it felt as if there was a madness swirling around her. Ataleka was by her side immediately.

'Calm, Fel, calm down, you had a dream.'

Feletra's eyes darted around the room, Flior was sat up in his bed looking over in concern, but Skepreo, Bri and Leao slept too deep to be disturbed.

'Leao, I saw Leao –'

'What, what happened?' Ataleka's soft tone was alleviating, he appeared to have forgotten about their altercation in that moment.

'He was...' Feletra looked over at Leao again, he was the same, healthy boy he had been before, 'nothing, nevermind. I just had a fright.'

'It was a dream, Feletra,' Flior reassured her, 'go back to sleep.'

Ataleka gave her a brief nod of comfort and returned to his own bed. Feletra laid back down and pulled the sheets up high, she continued to watch Leao for most of the night, unable to fall back asleep and always half-expecting him to change into some lurid entity. Was she overthinking everything? She must simply be worrying too much. Or worse, were these the visions that the curse had promised? Manifestations of her mind that no one else could see, whether awake or asleep. She began to feel separated from her family, alone, and afraid.

Chapter 4
Chains

The reflection did not smile. Feletra peered down at herself in the River Kestors, a troubled face stared back. For all the sun they received, her skin naturally failed to darken unlike that of her brothers, though neither was she pale, or her parents would have summoned the herra years ago. Her eyes were long, much again to the image of her mother, they reached out for her temples like the tips of an eagle's wings, the very shapes appearing as if slashed into her face for their acute lines. Her nose and lips did not follow this rule, and swept into position with deeper curves and steep bends, soft and trusted; her hair fell in rich waves just past her shoulders but there was too much of it to contain, Feletra hated how her thick tresses roasted the back of her neck every day.

'How are you feeling?'

Feletra was startled by Flior's voice from behind her, she stood up quickly, 'Fine, if you're referring to last night.'

'I am. Not just that though, Feletra, I get the impression this whole thing with Leao and the Sorpha is bringing you down somehow, and don't think I haven't noticed Ataleka either, he is a little more stubborn than you though. You know I am around if you need to talk.'

'I know,' Feletra dearly desired to say more, but it was not wise, she concluded, and they began to walk back to the house.

'It has been good to be home, seeing everyone again. I think I came back at the right time.'

'There's only Lampaea to complete us now,' said Feletra thoughtfully, 'he never even writes to us though.'

'Nor I,' said Flior, unsurprised, 'but that is Lampaea, he does not care for the small life and routine. He was ready to go his own way for a long time.'

No one knew of Lampaea's whereabouts or how he had spent his time away, it had been four years since he had left home, two years sooner than the more traditional age of leaving at eighteen, but Estra and Padryl would not have been able to stop him. Feletra would not have been at all surprised if she did not see or hear from her brother again for another ten years.

'How long are you staying?' Feletra enquired.

'Another week or so, I am in no rush for now.'

'And then where to? Back to Penthor, I suppose?'

'No, I have business in Liasis and the south-east first,' Flior gestured in the direction of the south-east from where they stood, and it was within that gesture that something clicked within Feletra, 'then I have to make a stop in Halprigh to see a buyer...have I said something?' Flior noticed the look of dawning upon Feletra's face.

'No, I mean, yes,' Feletra replied, and she pointed in the same direction as Flior had gestured, 'that's south-east, yes?'

Flior paused, 'Yes...why?'

Feletra took another moment to piece it all together, yes, it made sense, 'Can I borrow one of your maps?'

'Alright, but – Feletra!'

She had barely waited for a reply and tore off to the house and into the bedroom, roughly she grabbed one of Flior's full maps of Enphiah, Pyra and Orpegh and took it to spread out on the kitchen table. When Flior found her, she was already weighting down the corners with water jugs and spare utensils.

'What have you found that is so important we had to run like that?' said Flior, and Feletra traced a finger from where they were in Elpura all the way down to Pyra.

'Pyra,' she said resolutely, 'that's it, Pyra is south-east. That's where Leao was pointing, but why?'

'What? Ah, yes, Mother told me about that. I don't think it means anything, Feletra, Leao has always loved Pyra, after all.'

'But to know where south-east was like that? It's not normal, Flior, ever since he fell ill his behaviour has been too strange to predict, he is changed somehow.'

'But think, how long has he had this deep liking for Pyra?'

'I don't know, about three years,' Feletra sighed.

'Three years, long before the illness. There is no connection, Feletra.'

'Illness or not, he is still different! Why am I the only one to see this?' she charged out of the basin room and back into the bedroom, slamming the door behind her and fell onto her bed in frustration. After a few moments in which to calm down, she regretted leaving Flior like that, he simply did not understand. But who would? It seemed to others she was attempting to provide answers to questions that hadn't been asked, solutions to riddles that did not exist. On any other day Ataleka would have listened to her, he would have understood, but even he had his own unique quarrel with her now.

Feletra clasped her hands together in a distinguished fashion, her lips were pushing against one another stubbornly as she tried to digest it all. She glanced over at

Leao's corner, on the next wall from it were a couple of shelves of old books, and she saw a few about animals, plants, children's books...and then two or three about the lands. She collected these ones down off the shelves and beat the dust off a little, and began to read *The History of Enphiah, Pyra and Orpegh.*

Somewhere in the back of her mind, she remembered there was something unique her mother had mentioned about Pyra, and now the notion was eating away at her to know. It may have been nothing, but these books delved into greater detail than Estra could regale in her stories, and whatever she may have mentioned in those stories in the past was enough to pique Feletra's interest today. It almost felt as if she was unearthing something she was not supposed to, something that should have been left dead. And then a certain chapter caught her eye; after a couple of hours of uninterrupted reading, she came across a passage on a part of the war that had become blurred over time, conflicting views obscuring the full truth. It was told that Nago and his men discovered something that would cure any ailment, any wound and any sickness, even a curse. It was a cure to all, and Nago shared his bounty with Rukurehn; together their armies became unstoppable and were innumerably revived against Sethra's attacks. In Men. 64, however, the cure disappeared inexplicably, and rumours became rife that it had been stolen by the men of Chriah after Chrie had fervently expressed his desire for such a trophy. The cure was never heard or seen of again, and the story quickly became myth, no more grandeur than folklore and an object of children's tales by the fireside.

Feletra held her breath as she closed the book. The next passage had included an old rhyme about the cure that she and Ataleka used to recite together, she only remembered bits and pieces, but it was not important now. Why even read the history books? *I am overthinking,* she thought, her head beginning to throb a little.

The cure? A myth.

These were pieces that belonged to a different jigsaw puzzle, Feletra was no closer to deciphering her own perplexities. She replaced the book on the shelf carefully, just as her father burst in unexpectedly.

'Come on,' said Padryl abruptly.

'For what?'

'Training,' he threw the staff at Feletra which she caught just in time, and escorted her outside, 'what were you up to? Not feeling ill, are you?'

Feletra had to bask in the irony of his question for a moment, 'Just reading.'

'Good. Alright, show me what you remember.'

Feletra performed adequately with her staff, she found herself moving quicker and with increased agility, but still she felt further behind than her brothers had been at this stage. Padryl would tell her to pick up her feet, to pivot at the exact moment and to observe her full surroundings, not just straight ahead.

'You have certainly improved,' Padryl observed, 'how do you feel?'

'Quite confident,' Feletra lied, not even sure why she had, but hearing her own honesty might have dampened her spirits further than she could bear for one day.

'Well, that does make things interesting then. Ataleka!'

Ataleka was, as per usual, training some distance away from Feletra, and he ambled over to them upon answering his father's call.

‘Put the sword down, and take this,’ Padryl instructed, handing him his own staff, ‘we’re going to try a little one on one practice, I won’t assist unless I feel it is necessary.’

Feletra looked alarmed suddenly, ‘What? You want us to fight?’

‘That is what you agreed to for your training, Feletra,’ said Padryl, ‘I will be able to see how much you have both been paying attention, but no foul play, I want you to take this seriously. Find your starting positions.’

Reluctantly, Feletra took her position some paces away from Ataleka and faced him. He stood with his back arched slightly and reminded her of Byte when he encountered something with hostility. In his eyes were a web of silk shadows that veiled his feelings from everyone, reserved only for Feletra but obstinately preventing her from quelling the loneliness. Why did she have to fight him when he was like this? And she could not imagine having reached Ataleka’s level already, but it was too late to admit the lie of confidence now.

‘Begin,’ Padryl announced.

Ataleka moved in on her instantly, his attack was swift and agile and caught Feletra off-guard. She spun and ducked to dodge him the first time but forgot everything she had learned. There was anger in him, but was he truly using it against her?

Feletra attempted in vain to re-centre herself, but for attack or parry she was ready to deliver neither, for Ataleka charged at her once more with all speed, his staff struck the back of her knee and he spun on his heel to aim for her midriff – Feletra blocked his advance just in time and she vaguely heard Padryl comment in the background. It must have been a compliment but she knew it was pure luck, as

Ataleka regained his form within a matter of moments and became a swirling blur around her; with the staff he cleared her off her feet with ease – suddenly he became a swift silhouette against Pytheria that was looming down upon her, she braced herself against another blow with her staff, but her strength was no match for Ataleka's.

'Roll out, Feletra,' said Padryl, but it seemed impossible the way her brother was bearing down on her.

'I can't,' Feletra uttered with strain, and it was clear in Ataleka's expression that he would not yield to aid her.

'Ataleka, break off,' Padryl commanded, but Ataleka was not listening, 'Ataleka, now!'

Finally Feletra was released, but she had no time to catch her breath, as she rose back to her feet Ataleka flipped straight past her and knocked her staff out of her hands, he struck her back with unexpected force that even Padryl noticed, 'Stop, Ataleka!' and as Feletra met the ground once more she turned and like lightning Ataleka had trapped her, poised with his staff to her chest. It was over.

'That's enough. I said take it seriously, not personally. Feletra, you were not focused at all and Ataleka, you could have seriously harmed your sister. Training is finished until you two have dispelled your differences.'

Padryl walked off and vanished into the house in disappointment. Feletra swatted Ataleka's staff out of her face like a poisonous fly and stood up with a medley of emotion brimming inside her.

'What was that?' she demanded, 'I know you're unhappy with me, but it was like you *wanted* to hurt me. How long are you going to be like this with me?'

Ataleka did not give her eye contact once, he tossed his staff carelessly to the ground and left her standing there alone.

'You cannot be silent with me forever, Ataleka!'

Nothing would turn him, and Feletra had not as much complaisance as to follow him and pester. The misery set in, Feletra now even had the joy of missing her training to look forward to, all because Ataleka would not resolve things with her. Yet although she discovered it for the wrong reasons, she realised how overwhelming the training was, and how it was becoming yet another skill that was evading her. There felt nothing natural about it, she could not attain the flow that her brothers could, the flair that had been painstakingly clear with them was missing in her, and her sense of misguidance on the matter brought her dismay and added fuel to an already confused fire that she could not tame with Ataleka. The flames burnt blue, green, scarlet...all as unnatural as this curse would surely prove to be, and she could not help but deny it.

The following day moved slowly, Feletra had completed all her chores and wandered over to the stable. The air inside was stifling and hazy despite the fact that all the shutters were thrown wide open, it had the usual musty smell of dry hay and damp wood about it that she enjoyed. One that was less favourable was the sack of manure left slumped by the door.

Feletra filled the water troughs even though there was enough to last until tomorrow. Banu was watching her intently with his ancient, overcast eyes.

'Even you see more sense than some of us, Banu,' she said, patting his neck fondly, and he grunted in response the way an old man might, tired of the effort expected of conversation. Banu had reached an incredible eighty-six years of age, a feat worth noting amongst horlas as their average life span was usually sixty-five to seventy. It would be a sad day for the family when Banu passed.

'I can find you a job if you want,' Skepreo's voice from the stable door startled Feletra, 'I'm good at that.'

'What are you doing back?'

Skepreo grabbed the sack of manure cheerfully and heaved it over his shoulder, 'It's manure time! Come on, you can help.'

Feletra sighed reluctantly and followed him to the fields. Strangely, she somehow felt like a lamb being led to slaughter, not favouring the company of her father and especially Ataleka at that time.

'I heard about Father refusing to train you, that must sting.'

'I can't say as I really blame him,' Feletra replied honestly.

'What are you and Ataleka fighting about then? He's never been this quiet before.'

'We're not fighting, he just...won't talk to me. I don't know why,' Feletra quickly added this last part, much to the disbelieving gaze of Skepreo.

'Still a terrible liar, you know,' he said, and Feletra only acknowledged the remark with half a smile, enough to say he was right.

They approached Padryl and Ataleka by the wheat field, who were threshing the grain tirelessly. For this crop it was harvest time, but for many others they would be newly sown, or only half-way through their life cycle; the climate of Elpura was wonderful in catering for a wide diversity of crops and fruits in patches such as which Padryl had long taken advantage of for his family.

Skepreo set the manure down which caught their

attention, Padryl looked up with interest but Ataleka, spotting Feletra, continued threshing.

‘I sense a wanderer,’ Padryl commented.

Feletra shrugged her shoulders, ‘I’m jobless, it seems. How can I help?’

Padryl glanced over his shoulder at the unrelenting Ataleka with some subtle disapproval, ‘Alright,’ he said, ‘fetch the last few sheaves on the other side of the field for threshing. Ataleka, lend your sister a hand.’

Feletra knew he would suggest Ataleka join her, she no longer knew if she wanted to be around him anymore or not, for his mood was toxic and contagious.

‘I’m busy,’ Ataleka responded without stopping, and Padryl’s face fell suddenly.

‘Are you disobeying me?’

Ataleka then ceased his work, clearly hearing the tone in his father’s voice. He carelessly let his flail fall to the ground, ‘No,’ he answered quietly, and walked off to the opposite side with Feletra, keeping a fair distance. She thought him truly childish by now.

‘Don’t keep looking at me like that,’ he said suddenly when they were out of earshot.

Feletra was taken aback, ‘Like what?’

‘Like it’s my own fault for feeling this way, it’s not and you know that.’

‘No, of course not,’ Feletra responded coldly, ‘everything is my fault, you have made that quite clear. Have you forgotten that I saved your life?’

‘It would have been better to let me drown. Now I have nothing to live for, the curse is only here because of you.’

Feletra couldn’t believe her ears, she had never heard such hurtful things, and unwillingly it transferred into anger, ‘How can you say that to me? And how can you forget why we did this? We saved Leao –!’ Ataleka increased his pace to be away from her, but Feletra would not let him escape her so easily, it was as if he didn’t care, and she would make him care. Did he not share her emotion of joy upon seeing Leao well again? Or realise that they were in this together?

‘We share the same fate, Ataleka! We suffer this curse together! Stop and look at me!’

He wanted no more than to forget, since the day they had arrived home from the Sorpha he had tried to forget everything, but Feletra would not give him the chance anymore. He needed to face her, no more running away and hiding, her chains held him tight, unwavering, her will was rigid and she would bind him with it until he saw reason and became her brother again. They needed each other now more than ever.

Suddenly, Feletra stopped, for Ataleka had stopped moving just ahead of her. Had she finally gotten through to him?

‘Ataleka?’

He gave no reply and appeared immobile. He was a silhouetted statue from where Feletra was watching him, Pytheria shedding its last rays across the field and the sheaves they hadn’t quite reached. His feet seemed to be rooted to the ground, his arms pinned to his sides; Feletra approached him slowly, when his whole body began to then shudder uncontrollably, he emitted strangled sounds of pain from within.

Feletra was immediately alarmed, ‘Ataleka!’ she ran to face him, but knew not what to do – he was struggling against something unseen, fighting it; he looked down at her, his eyes were the only part of him he had any control over –

‘Feletra –’ he managed to utter, but there was nothing she could do. Whatever kept him in its grip became severe, for Ataleka’s elbows closed in further, his breathing strained and his clothes were tearing, exposing the tender flesh that jaggedly sliced into itself. Rich, viscous blood rushed forth and saturated the chaff-littered field beneath them.

Feletra felt her heart leaping out of her chest, ‘Father!’ she made to run back for Padryl’s help, but he and Skepreo heard the panic in her voice and sprinted across the field with all speed. Feletra thought it all felt like a dream, so slow with the resolve or destination not being reached fast enough. Ataleka was losing breath, he could exhale but gain nothing back, like a snake crushing him, but there was no predator to be seen.

Padryl and Skepreo were bounding through the wheat field towards them, and only arrived when Ataleka fell to the ground in a heap and drew in one huge breath.

‘Ataleka!’ Padryl called, skidding to his knees and cradling his son’s head in his hands, ‘What happened?’ When Ataleka could not answer for the need to regain that which took leave of him, he looked straight to Feletra.

‘Feletra? Tell me now.’

‘I don’t know what happened, I didn’t know what to do. He could not breathe, or even move.’

‘Why did you not call me sooner?’

‘I would have, it happened so fast –’

‘What of these wounds on his skin?’

‘I know none of it, Father, nothing. The wounds, the binding –’

'Binding?' Padryl repeated in greater alarm. 'How do you know this, Feletra?'

'I don't! It just looked that way, like something was holding him there, but I could see nothing.'

Feletra silently felt her fears of the curse coming to the fore, it had to be, she had never seen something so unnatural. It was beginning then, the journey of immortal suffering.

Padryl ran a hand down his face as Feletra stared at him helplessly, then he picked Ataleka up without hesitation. Skepreo was scanning the fields darkly, he seemed to be anticipating the perpetrator to appear suddenly.

'Back to the house, quickly,' said Padryl, 'we need to get your brother in your mother's care now.'

Feletra detected that his voice was coated in a fear she had never witnessed in him before, and a force that spoke of anger. She was afraid that anger might be directed at her, but how? Did her father truly believe she was involved somehow? She dared not ask. Estra had been regaling Bri and Leao with another evening tale just outside the house, but she flew to her feet when she saw Ataleka being carried from around the corner. Flior caught wind of the situation from inside where he was drawing at the table, as they hastily brought Ataleka inside he swept the table clear of his work and his brother was laid down precariously.

'What happened to him?' said Estra, darting about the kitchen to create a tincture.

'We cannot say,' Padryl replied, 'something unseen bound him, choked the breath out of him and broke his skin.'

Estra threw him a look of shock and question, 'Unseen?'

'Yes, Feletra saw it happen.'

Estra's expression evolved further, Feletra saw it, she and her father were exchanging glances as if they could immediately guess what was happening.

'I'm going back,' said Padryl resolutely, 'I will take Flior and Skepreo with me. You must lock yourselves within the house.'

'What?' Skepreo piped up, sensing there was something he was unaware of. 'Why?'

'Craftsmen, there could be someone out there,' Flior answered.

Feletra's eyes widened, 'You think this is the work of Blackcraft? Why would there be craftsmen in Elpura?'

Padryl was already leading his two sons outside, 'Lock the door behind us, Feletra,' and he was gone. Feletra was stood there aghast, she knew this could not be Blackcraft, but had nonetheless failed to consider the possibility, or indeed that her family would think this way.

'Hurry, Feletra,' her mother called, and she locked the door before rushing back to Ataleka's side, he took rapid shallow breaths and groaned in pain for the wounds. Bri was closing the shutters to all the windows and lighting candles whilst Leao stood watch anxiously from a corner, 'very good, Bri, we must make sure no one is watching.'

'Will he be alright?' Feletra asked nervously.

Estra's eyes shifted to her daughter with an element of uncertainty, 'He will. Though I do not know what I am treating, are you sure you saw nothing?'

'Nothing,' Feletra shook her head truthfully as her mother pushed a thick red paste into each of Ataleka's wounds, he winced from the touch. 'Mother, I don't think they will find anyone,' Estra peered at Feletra imploringly then, 'I do not think this is Blackcraft.'

'Do you not?'

Feletra hesitated, she had no choice but to explain herself now. Estra was already searching her with her soul-scraping eyes, she had not imagined how hard it would be to tell her what happened at the Sorpha.

'Feletra, if you know something that may help your brother you must tell me now.'

*But it won't help...*Feletra thought.

She was unsure of how to begin, 'I may yet be wrong. Mother, will you tell me again of the Sorpha's curse?'

Estra continued to stare at her unblinkingly, and her eyes seemed to shine slightly. 'What have you done?' she whispered, and for the first time, Feletra thought she might have noticed a spark of emotion from her. Queerly, it sent a shiver down her spine.

'Mother,' she persisted, 'what happens to one who is cursed? They will bleed with no cause, won't they?'

'They will bleed, yes, to what extent I do not know but they will bleed. Feletra, tell me the truth, does Ataleka carry the curse?'

There came a long, droning pause between them, Feletra would have given anything to be elsewhere just then. It was as though some unreal flash had appeared before them, and it was in that moment that their minds merged...they seemed to be discussing the rest of the conversation without words, even without thought. If only it were that simple.

'Both of us,' said Feletra finally.

'What happened at the Sorpha?'

Feletra opened her mouth to speak, then closed it again. For all the times she had replayed the scene in her head, still the words were not forthcoming and remained strangled somewhere in the back of her tangled mind.

'We fell in...we fell into the river.'

Estra did not stir, but Feletra knew she was fighting all the rules of outburst within her. All the shock, the despair, the fear, 'How did this happen?'

'It was an accident, I thought I saw something across the other side of the river, I tripped and Ataleka tried to pull me back, but he was the one that fell. I went in after him and brought him back to the bank. We were too afraid to tell anyone, afraid that it was true.'

And still afraid, she knew it. Afraid to speak of the whole truth, especially now, when craftsmen were feared to be around their home. The man and woman at the Sorpha were not bad people, how she knew this she could not say, but it was true without question, they had meant them no harm. But her family would never believe this, not now, not even Ataleka, best they remained in her memory, it was safer to keep them in the dark.

'There can be no doubt...' Estra said under her breath.

'We did not mean to waste the water, our intentions were selfless! To gather it for Leao only, but everything went so wrong –'

'Whether selfless or not, the Sorpha knows no different, Feletra, only that it was wasted! It does not matter what you do or who you are. There can be *no* doubt...the curse is with you both. I cannot cure this.'

Feletra felt tears began to well in the corners of her eyes, so much denial she had stored since the day it happened. It was real now, as real as her mother's words carrying that gravity as she heard them spoken, and it had taken form on the table before her, as Ataleka grasped at the thick, humid air surrounding him for more breath.

‘This is my fault, there must be something we can do?’

Estra was shaking her head, looking down into Ataleka’s closed eyes, ‘You should not have gone to that river.’

Feletra felt helpless, she unlocked the door and Bri watched her run to sit against the aghaia tree in solitude, her head in her hands.

Estra took a deep breath and began crushing an orange root with a pestle and mortar rhythmically that she would use to ease Ataleka’s pain, ‘Useful for so many things, meftor.’

Padryl, Flior and Skepreo did not return home until the later hours of the night, Ataleka had been moved to his bed, and Leao and Bri had also been ushered off to sleep. The men, as expected, had nothing to report, they found no one, nor anything untoward. Estra and Feletra had maintained a silence so deep that one of them might as well have been dead and unperceived by the other, but they stood to attention once the men had returned.

‘There is some cold food on the table for you,’ Estra told her sons, ‘I must speak with your father alone, don’t wait up for us,’ she glanced back at Feletra as they disappeared into the bedroom, who knew exactly that her confession would be repeated to her father, word for word. They hid nothing from each other.

‘How is Ataleka?’ asked Flior.

‘He sleeps,’ Feletra replied, ‘and his wounds have been treated.’

‘I don’t think I will sleep tonight,’ said Skepreo, ‘not knowing that there’s someone or something out there. Just because we didn’t find anyone doesn’t mean they won’t be back.'

'That's if it *is* Blackcraft,' said Flior, invoking interest for the discussion, one that Feletra did not wish to partake in.

'I am going to bed, it's been a long day,' she did not wait for her brothers to respond and made quietly for the bedroom. A candle still burned by Ataleka's bedside, she thought she would go over and see him, and then decided against it. What if he was still angry with her? He had even more reason to be now, he had fallen to the curse's grip first, and he had been right, it was her fault. There was nothing she, or anyone could do to save them from this now...she thought back to the book she read about the cure...*why can't it be real?*

In truth, sleep was the last thing Feletra wanted, but she would try if it meant laying the day's events to rest and forgetting it all just until dawn. She listened to Ataleka's steady breathing and the low voices from the bedroom next door as a warm breeze drifted in through the shutters, bearing with it the heavenly scent of spelethra, a rare flower found only on the Elpuran and Asirian plains. A common phrase accompanied the flower for those who caught the smell at night:

'The sweet scent at night
Plays change at first light.'

It was apt, of course, for Feletra knew there would be change, there already was. The scent was, in fact, somewhat late in coming. Flior and Skepreo made their way discreetly to bed as she mulled over the marks of the curse...bleeding, sickness, a loss of each sense, visions...it was not surprising people had taken their own lives. The woman on the other side of the Sorpha, she had screamed as if she knew the curse would befall them, she cared when they fell into the river, but then where did she and the man go? Feletra made a decision in that moment, she would return to the Sorpha the following morning, cross over at the Elpuran Bridge and go to that stone house that had captivated her so much. It all began from there, and the events were too strange and conspicuous to ignore; if the man and woman were still there, she might find some help, or at the very least answers.

Feletra dozed on the ideas and slept lightly, waking with a start every so often at no more than the rustle of bedsheets or the call of the night birds. She was roused again later into the night when there came a dull thud from across the room as Leao had fallen out of bed again. He moaned sleepily in protest when Estra came to tuck him back in before swiftly gliding out once more like a ghost.

Feletra was ready to reconcile the keepers of sleep for what she hoped would be the last time that night, when she heard her name uttered from the main room. It seemed Estra and Padryl were still discussing the matter of the curse, even at this hour. She went to stand by the door and listened attentively.

'Why had they not told us sooner?' came Padryl's low voice. 'They know we are here to help.'

'You must stand in their shoes, my love,' said Estra, 'realising they were cursed must have been terrifying, especially at their age. It may be that they even chose not to believe it until today, denial is not uncommon, it certainly explains why Feletra and Ataleka were behaving so strangely with each other. As for help, I feel there is little any of us can do. Even in the early stages, we both know there is no cure to be had.'

'What of the herra? Is there nothing he can do?'

'Padryl, the herra is powerless. This is no common illness, Feletra and Ataleka will be besieged by the curse for the rest of their lives.'

'If only the stories were true...'

They had Feletra's full attention.

'What stories?'

'Of the cure.'

Estra sighed in exasperation, 'Do not start on fantasy when your son and daughter need you. No good will come of false hope.'

'It remains but a myth and I know that,' Padryl conceded, 'but I feel the desperation already, Estra, the wretchedness that will destroy them. This will change all of our lives,' there was a short pause, and then Padryl spoke again, 'I will see the herra nonetheless tomorrow and ask his advice.'

'By my hand, you shall not. Should but one person hear of this and the word will spread to all who would lend an ear, the small-minded will think it evil and catching and there shall be no ebrats or merchants come to us. There are seasons when we rely on the merchants for trade just to survive, we cannot risk our livelihood. Moreover, Feletra and Ataleka would be known and exposed to all in Enphiah, we cannot attract the wrong attention, no one can be trusted, Padryl.'

'Then how do we help our children?'

These last words sounded strained and full of sorrow, and Estra did not answer immediately.

'Help is beyond us,' she finally said.

Feletra returned to her bed, she felt numb to their words, her parents were crying out for a miracle that could never be. She felt that perhaps she had thought so much of late that she should surely have not the strength to think now, Bri's dark shape was the last thing she saw before plunging into her own dark and ambiguous world. The light sleep that had plagued her before was being repaid as she began to fall fast and deep, her body heavy as if she were composed entirely of water from the Sorpha...further and further down she fell, through earth, water and mist...

There was a noise that came sharp and grating behind her somewhere, like a knife on slate, and then it faded away into a haze...the fog began to shift, and outlines of objects and people came into focus. She saw her mother sat in her chair outside the house, was it the next day already? Feletra, Bri and Leao were sat on the ground before her, waiting...yet when Mother spoke, it sounded distant and spectral.

'Well, what story would you have today?' she asked, and Feletra found herself answering quite unexpectedly and with the enthusiasm of a child.

'The Dalpha Alliance and the eastern wrath!'

'No, the Horla of Fire!' cried Leao.

Feletra's suggestion was defeated as Mother began on the majestic flames of the legendary creature's mane and tail and how Nephele, the Lady of the Fire, was the only one he would obey.

Footsteps could be heard behind them, and Feletra was suddenly horrified to see Ataleka staggering towards them as though possessed, his skin a gaunt and deathly white like a corpse and his eyes rolling in their sockets, glazed in a pale film.

‘Ataleka!’ Feletra exclaimed, ‘You should be resting! Mother, we need to take him back inside!’

‘Leave your brother alone, Feletra. He will manage,’ she replied, with not a care about her.

‘How will he? He is fatally ill!’

‘Feletra, listen to the rest of the story. Ataleka, back to bed, you are interrupting us.’

Ataleka began to bleed from sunken lacerations in his neck, his arms and from his abdomen, he coughed and vomit and mucus spilled out of him lazily, but Estra simply continued with her story. Something was wrong. She, Bri and Leao had barely noticed the situation, this was not them.

The shapes began to merge again...the colours became grey, dull and ashen...and then the greyness formed rock, great boulders, a cave loomed before her. There was no greenery here, no plants, no trees, no good...the place was invaded with men who each held weapons ready, they appeared to be guarding something. Every one of them was tall, broad and ruthless-looking. Feletra felt a chill somewhere, like how one would react to a brisk sea breeze, but then her blood was churned to ice in a jolt when she saw the entrance of the cave. The opening was lit by torches, and she was dangerously drawn to it. And it connected...it was connected to her, or was it Ataleka?

And then a boy crossed her. She hadn’t seen or even felt him, but she knew a boy had intertwined with the vision before her and was gone again in the blink of an eye. Suddenly, images moved too quickly for her to keep up, convulsing and simmering like spasms of the sky and horizons undulating to the meander of snakes in the sand...and the haze gradually seeped in again, what flashes of light...an image slowed for one glimpse to show fire, burning wood, a forest choked and drowned in the smoke and ash...the images blurred again, faster and faster, the sound of sword clash, and the thunder of the earth beneath horlas' hooves...

Her eyes stung cold.

Feletra was sat upright in her bed, and knew what to do. The dream, no – the vision. The vision told her what to do, somehow. She had to find those caves, they hid the cure to the curse, it was the only way to end it. She had to end it, for she and Ataleka were cursed.

Chapter 5
The Green Thorn

Shortly after Feletra had woken, a man far from her home in Elpura cursed and glanced resentfully at a pair of empty shackles on the wall. He was tall, he moved with deliberation and exuded an air of prudence deserving of others who might have shared the room within which he walked. They would have given him much space, for there was a power about him that demanded assiduity, vigilance and an apparent hierarchy, of which he mounted.

He gripped a wooden table before upturning it in anger. Wine and water spread across the cold stone floor, following the cracks and edges of each tile like lost rivers. Across the room he scraped books from their shelves and cast them everywhere so that they lay scattered like colourful insects. When this did not satisfy him, he did something quite extraordinary, and outstretched his hand at a grand crystal vase which stood proudly upon a black stone mantlepiece. The vase burst and shattered where it stood.

He took a deep breath and slowly made his way over to the foyer where a door hung wide open in the night, he spied a figure in the darkness, vanishing into the trees.

'You'll return to me,' he said quietly to himself. 'When you are ready, and you feel the need, you will return.'

x

Feletra wasted no time and gathered clothes, food and other

essentials as quietly as possible. She had barely put any thought into what else she might need, even the socalled essentials seemed scarce in her little pack, she added a loaf of bread and a spare flint and steel. There was no way of knowing where to find these caves, but that did not stop her. She had already decided to return to the Sorpha and would still cross the bridge to the house first, but from there she did not know how to find her destination. Perhaps those caves were the Lucrin Caverns? For they were known to be heavily guarded, like in her vision.

The moon was low in the sky, and it would be long before Pytheria rose again. Feletra thought of leaving her mother and father a message, but...what would she say? The truth that she had left to find some cure for Ataleka and herself despite that she had no idea where to go? And she remembered earlier, when she had overheard them saying that there was no cure, yet now she knew there was. Not even the wisest could dissuade her from the belief, the vision was more than just a dream and had come to her for a reason. It commanded her and she was determined to listen to its message. There was hope.

She took one last look around and tried not to think of all the panic and disarray caused by her disappearance in the morning.

Reluctantly she made for the doorway and out, but as soon as she stepped outside her heart sank, for there, by his cart, was Flior.

‘Feletra? What are you doing?’

Feletra remained silent, Flior moved closer and spied the pack slung on her shoulder.

‘Are you...? Are you leaving?’

It was pointless to avoid him.

‘Please, keep your voice down,’ Feletra sighed, ‘yes, yes I am.’

Flior’s eyes widened, ‘What? What’s this about? Why?’

‘I can’t tell you, Flior, you wouldn’t even believe me. Please just let me go.’

‘I will not let you go anywhere until you tell me where you are going and why. It doesn’t look as if you are going to return in the morning,’ he indicated the crammed pack she was carrying.

‘I’m sorry, I cannot tell you.’

‘Why?’

‘You know I have always looked to you for advice, Flior, I have always respected your words, but this time, I know something that you would never believe to be true. I cannot have you calling me deluded and using it as the excuse to try and keep me here, it won’t work.’

Flior thought for a second, ‘Is this about Ataleka?’

Feletra did not give him eye contact, but he already knew.

‘I myself do not know what happened out there on the fields,’ he continued, ‘but it seems that you do. Tell me, is Ataleka in danger because of this?’

Feletra felt her answer would be heavy and difficult to part with, but she trusted Flior.

‘I have found a way to c –, to *help* Ataleka. It can’t be found here though, and no one else was meant to find out.’

‘If you won’t tell me everything, then at least let me come with you. You don’t have to be alone.’

‘No!’ Feletra exclaimed, they heard someone stir in the house, and waited until it was calm again, ‘You mustn’t come with me, nor anyone. I’m a part of this, let me fix it.’

‘You know Father will come after you.’

'I know. That's why I must ask you to stay here for me, delay him as much as possible. But please, Flior, you must not tell anyone what I have told you here tonight. I'm trusting you.'

'I cannot lie to them.'

'I'm not asking you to lie, just to keep quiet, and when I leave, go back inside and do not look back out until Pytheria rises.'

Flior frowned uncertainly, 'I thought you trusted me?'

'I do, but it helps if you never saw which way I went if you're going to be as truthful as possible to them. I can at least take some of that guilt off your shoulders.'

Flior began to pace aimlessly, then he stopped and stared at his sister for what seemed an age, she could see the torment in him.

'Can I be certain you will be safe?' he said finally.

Feletra knew not how to reply. Safe? How was she to know? She had never set foot outside of Elpura.

'I have to go,' she murmured.

'Wait,' Flior turned back to his cart and rummaged around for something, he returned carrying a thick folded piece of parchment and handed it to her. She already knew what it was, a map of Enphiah, Pyra and Orpegh, an item which would serve its value when her path was clear to her, but she was grateful for it, 'take it. I hope you are not going far enough to need it, but...'

'Thank you.'

'And take one of the horlas,' Flior added. He led her into the stable, unbolted one of the stall doors next to Banu's and the horla within awoke to the noise, 'he's strong, he will give you a good start.'

'Don't you need him?' Feletra said, quickly preparing

the tack.

'I have two left still, and I don't suppose I will be going anywhere for a long time. Mother and Father need support with Ataleka...why am I doing this?'

Feletra was startled by the question, 'Doing what?'

'Letting you go so easily. Letting you go at all. You are my sister and even I know you are too young and unprepared to ride out alone.'

'But I ride out for Ataleka, this isn't like Leao, it's something far darker. I know I can help him.'

'How do you know?'

Feletra hesitated, 'Something...came to me in the night, I can barely describe it, but it was powerful...and it told me what I need to do. Just please understand that you cannot come with me, Flior. I know what I'm doing is right, I promise you.'

Flior looked down at the hay-strewn flagstones in resignation, 'Very well, I will ensure your trust in me is not misplaced.'

They led the horla outside where Feletra mounted, she may not have completed her training in combat but she was grateful that she knew how to ride from an early age.

'Flior,' said Feletra suddenly, 'what were you doing before I found you?'

Flior smiled listlessly, remembering why he was awake and outside, 'I was preparing to go down to the fields and wait for dawn, paint something colourful for the house, raise the spirits a little. I know how early it is, I couldn't sleep.'

'There is still time,' Feletra reassured.

'No, I have to go back inside, as you asked.'

Feletra nodded solemnly. 'Thank for you for helping

me.'

Flior acknowledged the sentiment and walked away towards the house, when he stopped and looked back, fear and entrapment in his eyes, 'There is no way I can keep you here, is there?'

Feletra met his gaze, she felt the burden of his heavy heart, having to turn his back and walk away from her, but she responded to the strength she had in herself at that moment, the determination, no one would stop her.

'No,' she answered confidently, 'look after them for me.'

Flior said nothing and returned to the house in silence. Once he was gone, Feletra took one last look at her home, the house, stables, her family...everything was still, there was no breeze to quiver the leaves of the aghaia tree, yet she thought she heard the screams of every inanimate object to stay. She shared the blood of this place and felt accused of tearing apart a once peaceful and joyful life, *but I have to...*she thought, *I have a chance to cure us.*

Gently, Feletra nudged the horla on and set off at a canter heading north towards the Sorpha. It was exhilarating to be riding again, the last time she had ridden on horlaback was several years ago when they had Nepenas; she remembered how to ride well, Padryl had even taught her without reins. She inhaled the scent of the spelethra and sped on to a gallop, the warm air that beckoned to a dawning of change whistled through her hair behind her, the wilderness and the night belonged to her.

Once Feletra had reached the Sorpha, a strong sense of foreboding came over her. Beautiful, and yet so quietly savage...she tried to cast the thought aside for now and focused on finding the Elpuran Bridge. The enigmatic stone house rested there across the water, motionless and serene, however as she looked up and down the river, there was nothing else in sight; recalling that the bridge lay east from home, she reached for Flior's map to confirm and continued her trek across the Plains of Nemenon, estimating the bridge lay around six leagues away, though she would need to return westward again after crossing if she were set on journeying to the house. She realised that time was of the essence, her father would be racing out after her to bring her home as soon as dawn broke over the land, her disobedience would be considered reprehensible, not even Lampaea left without persuading his parents first. If she had any hope of helping Ataleka and herself, she needed to act quickly and with stealth, for Padryl would not easily give up the chase.

When Feletra slowed the horla down to a trot for a drink from her flask, she was given a jerk and lurched forward slightly, noticing that the horla had tripped on something.

'You did that earlier as well,' Feletra pondered, looking about the ground in vain for conspicuous signs, 'what is your name then, I wonder? Did Flior not give you one?'

There were two brown lines that ran the length of its black horns, a sure trait of the males. Not convinced, Feletra dismounted and took a closer look about the creature's hooves, but he appeared to be in exceptional health. She pulled the horla forward for a short walk until he stumbled again, and then wondered how she had missed it before. It was the tail, so long and untamed it was a wonder they had made it this far.

'So that's the reason you've been so clumsy? I think I've just decided on your name,' said Feletra, taking a band from her own hair and using it to contain the horla's unruly tail instead, 'Steptail. How do you like it?' The horla appeared to jerk his head in some approval, 'Steptail...' Feletra repeated to herself as she mounted and set off once more, content with his reaction.

Pytheria graced the land sooner than anticipated and splashed a rusty orange dawn across the dust and the river, Padryl would have woken by now. Feletra was running out of time to get away. Worse, she was about to turn around in the opposite direction back towards home, for there was the stone Elpuran Bridge ahead. Her breath caught in her chest when she saw it, for this bridge looked ancient, disused for many years, hazardous beyond rationale. She approached the end and saw that many of the stones had fallen from their place, indeed some still lay in the river itself. The relief of finding the bridge rapidly became uncertainty, could they cross safely? Feletra looked around fruitlessly, as if expecting some other solution to appear, she could continue on to the Drohan Bridge, but that was at least another thirty-five leagues east, and more back. Moreover, it left the window for Padryl to find her dangerously wide open, she simply could not justify the extra travel.

Without warning, Feletra felt a shudder in the ground below her. She glanced at Steptail's rear, thinking his tail had come loose and he was tripping on it again, but no, it was not Steptail. The horla sensed the change as well, and became notably uneasy, pawing at the ground. The shudder came again, closer, thunderous and imminent.

Feletra knew it could be only one thing. A Nova Snake appearing now could not have been worse luck, she even had no weapon, and felt the dread rising deep from inside her gut. She watched the earth beneath her with alarm and tried to steady Steptail, she couldn't have the snake feel the vibrations from his hooves, but the fear took hold of him and he could not be calmed – the ground rolled and spun, until the snake burst through before them, spraying earth all over them.

Steptail cried out and reared up on his hind legs in terror, Feletra gripped hard with her calves to stay atop her steed –

'Hold fast, Steptail!' she yelled, and she beheld the great beast before her for the first time in her life, overwhelmed as she instinctively scoured its face for a pair of carnal eyes, but there were none, yet it regarded her accurately where she and Steptail stood – the snake took one great inhalation through its narrow nostrils, steeped in greed and – yes, Feletra saw it with dread, familiarity – there was no better prize than the offspring of Padryl, slayer of three Novas, but Feletra, though she was almost paralysed with fear, was not ready to end her journey and fail her brother this soon. She took one look at the snake, grey and green scales like armour made of bark but harder than steel, raining particles of dust and sand, fifty times greater than Feletra and Steptail combined, and she knew she was not prepared to meet her end there and then. She had a place to be, and time was limiting.

As the Nova thrust towards her with its blunt head and opened jaw of a thousand perfectly lethal fangs, Feletra pulled Steptail on towards the bridge, 'Move!'

The snake pounded straight into the ground just as the horla moved in time – Steptail raced onto the bridge and instantly the stone slabs beneath them shifted precariously and abruptly – Feletra urged the horla onwards desperately, the Nova was directly on their tail, full of fury and pent-up revenge.

Steptail hesitated when another stone was dislodged under their weight and fell into the Sorpha below.

'Go, Steptail! Go!' Feletra cried, but the Nova Snake was shifting its way closer to them from the riverbank, curling the length of its entire body about the bridge, Feletra looked back and screamed at the beast like a warrior warning its opponent of the fight it could face if it dared – the snake recoiled a little, she remembered her father saying that harsh and coarse sounds abused its senses. The beast grew impatient and snapped at them again, a narrow miss that threw Steptail off balance and into the wall of the bridge – stones crumbled everywhere and Feletra was nearly launched into the river once more.

Steptail panicked and struggled to move on but he was strong and persevered, Feletra encouraging him with every passing moment.

They neared the end of the bridge when the snake made one last strike with its tail – its aim was precise until Feletra fought it with her voice one more time and bellowed, it missed them but the bridge was finished. The last stronghold of the structure gave way and collapsed like a stone storm into the Sorpha, the snake was caught between the wreckage and trapped, unable to reach them as it snapped and hissed but only fortified its grave further as the stones sank deeper into its scales. Steptail had leapt for the other side, only too late for the bridge had trapped him too in its disintegrating tomb, he whinnied in pain, his hind leg caught directly between two of the slabs.

Feletra carefully dismounted and balanced herself amidst the stone remains to examine Steptail's leg, she glanced over at the Nova Snake and felt safe in the knowledge that it was unable to attack them.

'Don't struggle, Steptail, just be calm,' she reassured her companion whilst trying to calculate how she could free him, for she had not the strength to pull the two great slabs apart. She spied a gap between them and noticed a cluster of smaller stones clamped together on the underside of the bridge. She lowered her body down as slowly as possible so as not to cause another collapse, although Steptail and the Nova appeared to be providing the obstructions that were preventing it, and through the gap she pulled and pushed at the smallest of the stones first, then another came loose, and another...

One of the main slabs shifted dangerously and Feletra quickly dived for the edge of the bank at the end of the bridge, grabbing Steptail's reins as she did so, the horla's leg winched free as the slab fell into the river and he was pulled hastily onto solid ground again. The snake remained trapped and hissed wildly at them, sensing they had escaped.

'One day I will come back to this place,' said Feletra indignantly to the Nova, 'and the only bridge over the Sorpha here will be your bones.'

The snake growled at her as if it had understood her words. She turned her attentions to Steptail, his leg was cut deep and bleeding profusely; Feletra extracted the water flask from her pack and spare cloth, after thoroughly cleaning the wound she bandaged the leg gently and encouraged the reluctant horla to stand.

'I'm sorry you came into this, Steptail, this should never have happened.'

Steptail appeared to have calmed down a little but still pawed the ground nervously at the presence of the Nova

Snake, Feletra would have left him at the bridge to wait for her if the snake were not there but she could not guarantee his safety that way now, he would have to walk with her.

'I know it's not ideal, I am sorry, boy, but if that snake escapes and hurts you I couldn't forgive myself. You'll have to walk on the leg at least half of the way to the house, then I will do the rest myself and come back for you, alright?'

Steptail nodded his head towards the Sorpha for a drink, but Feletra led him away from the bank, too much grief had already come from those waters. She withdrew her water flask and a cup and filled it for him, she knew it was a pitiful amount for a horla but she began to fear how little water there was left even now. Together they trekked back westward along the Sorpha, and Feletra was grateful when the savage sounds of the snake finally disappeared into the distance at her back.

Steptail did well to limp as far as he did with little complaint or resistance, it was clear he trusted Feletra, but after two leagues she exercised a long-awaited pity on him and took advantage of several serri trees in one patch that provided a little shade, albeit mediocre. She made to tie his rein to one of the branches, then thought better of it, sensing he was a loyal companion to her.

'I will be back for you in a while, then. Stay here and rest that leg for now. Oh, and no drinking from the river, understand?' she wagged an authoritative finger at him before leaving him in the shade alone. She felt counterproductive walking back the exact same direction from which she came, the only difference being that she travelled along the other side of the river. She felt alone again, but above all she felt alert like never before; the vast openness of the Elpuran Plains left her vulnerable to danger that could appear from any direction. The closer she came to home the keener her senses became, as she grew ever more fearful of her father finding her, and in such a lifeless environment there was little she could hide behind, ironically the Sorpha provided her the best protection until she was clear of it, and that time could not come soon enough.

Indeed, she had in that moment dubbed her homeland 'lifeless,' save for the Nova Snake paying them a rare and unwanted visit, and then she stopped abruptly in her tracks and thought she may have to eat her own words. As though it had appeared instantaneously out of nowhere, upon the serri tree before Feletra perched the most magnificent eagle she had ever seen. The flick of his crest lay flat against his proud head and his glossy brown and scarlet wing feathers were primly tucked into his sides. Yet there was something very different about this bird, and Feletra could not tear her eyes away from him. He was not apprehensive of her at all, he had not the motions typical of other birds, such as the jerking of the head place by place to follow her wherever she dared move, and was so still he could have been mistaken for a statue. His eyes of blazing gold were lively and fiery, and as Feletra moved, so did they, but he gave her the eerie feeling that someone was concealed inside of him to watch her.

Feletra slowly approached the serri tree, until she stood directly below him, still he did not move. She whistled to him.

Nothing.

Her curiosity of this unusual behaviour grew tenfold, and she walked on past the tree. Once she was a few paces ahead, she turned suddenly on her heel with her arms outstretched and stamped her foot hard.

'Ha!' she shouted, expecting a quick scare to cause some normal reaction in the bird, but she was met with even more peculiar behaviour. The eagle was no longer simply sitting; his wings were spread wide in all their grandeur, with one razor-sharp taloned foot in front of the other almost bracingly, his noble head held high with crest fanned out. What made the situation even stranger was that the eagle stood equally as still as before, and made no noise whatsoever, though his beak hung open as if in challenge as to her next move.

Feletra decided she was wasting time again, this bird was too perplexing to figure out and distracting her from her cause. She continued walking, leaving the eagle poised as he was; she glanced over her shoulder a few times to capture some movement, all in vain for nothing had changed, the great wings remained outstretched, beak half open.

You surely belong in some far-off dream, she thought to herself, *or perhaps I am just stuck in one.*

The stone house came into view and appeared exactly as she had last seen it in the daylight, with its shutters wide open. She suddenly felt a reluctance to come any nearer, what if it was dangerous inside? Were there craftsmen? Or something too dark for her to even comprehend? Feletra pulled herself together, she just survived an attack from a Nova Snake, she was not about to let an old deserted house remind her of fear now.

The door was left slightly ajar and appeared ready to fall off its hinges, and so Feletra conscientiously slipped through the gap to avoid pushing it all the way open. The place truly was as small as it looked from the outside, but it was no home to anyone; there was no bed, no stove, no basin or pots or anything that would have suggested so. Instead it was crowded with strange artifacts – vases, rings, necklaces and pendants, charms, bottles and tapestries were littered everywhere, many of which simply depicted the Sorpha, whilst others portrayed cracked and decaying images of people kneeling before the river or deathbeds of both adults and young children, sickness and expressions of despair. There were even small ornaments of various animals, some carved out of wood, others a material that Feletra had never set eyes on before, but she knew it could only be lucrin. She held a lucrin statue of a horla as long as her arm and expected the weight to pull her down, but it was unnaturally light, lighter than any other metal in Enphiah, it shone oddly between silver and a dynamic blue.

The centre piece stood at the far end of the room, an arch of white stone draped in enna, the fabric turned feathery from the wear of time. Inside the arch was a single candle, the wax almost fully depleted and coated in dust. When something crunched beneath Feletra's feet she looked down to find small shards of pottery scattered about, and then she immediately remembered that day, when she and Ataleka witnessed the white light, felt the earth quake beneath them, and heard the sound of pottery shattering into pieces...

She looked around, the realisation dawning on her. This was the shrine of the Sorpha, it was still here, after all this time. And this is where...

This is where Zenika killed herself.

Feletra desired greatly to stay no longer. There was no sign of the man or woman, she had gleaned no more information that could have helped her decide what to do and where to go. The caves she saw could have been oceans away, far from Enphiah or on some other map she had never laid eyes on, but she had to keep trying, she could not simply ignore the message she had been given.

It was time to leave this wasted shrine, the foreshadowing prospect of doom seemed to hang thickly around everything here, as though the cobwebs had caught it, the dust absorbed it and the very air long dead and suffocated with it. Feletra began to back away from the arch, but then felt something else under her heel. Less than a second later she quickly withdrew her foot, suddenly feeling heat, as though a flame had been ignited, but when she looked down there was nothing burning, only a tiny figure of a wooden horla, far smaller than those on the shelves and tables. She turned it in her fingers and examined it curiously, it felt rough to the touch and a little warm, a dainty little thing. Carefully she wrapped it in some of the enna cloth and stowed it in her pack, wondering if it might bring her some good luck.

As Feletra headed for the door, she heard a strange sound behind her, a scraping noise as if from a blade on rock. She turned and gasped, unable to breathe for the sight that beheld her. A woman, crouched before the wall by the white arch in a filthy and torn white dress; thin, black unruly hair spraying from her scalp and clearly chopped in places or pulled straight from the roots, the loose locks still caught between the live strands. She dragged a knife down the wall, over and over, her hands were white, the skin adorned in a marbled pallor that not even the grave could justify.

She stopped. Feletra could hardly move as the woman

began to turn her body towards her, sensing the presence of another. It was then that Feletra noticed the blood stains on her dress, trailing all the way down from her chest to her naval, she was gripped in terror and began to back away towards the door – in the commotion she bumped into a table and tripped over more artifacts that smothered the floor and her eyes were torn away from the woman in that moment, when she looked back up she had disappeared.

Panic-stricken, Feletra's eyes darted about the entire shrine for the entity, and when she did not reappear she ran from the house with all speed and back along the Sorpha, not looking back once. She briefly recognised the serri tree that the eagle had perched in, its branches were now bare and the bird was gone. She was quickly reunited with Steptail, who had stayed and waited for her as she had requested, and relief flooded her just to be with him again, a friendly face no matter if he could not share a conversation with her.

'You have no idea how happy I am to see you, boy,' she said breathlessly, and walked with him back past the Epluran Bridge, where Feletra observed the Nova Snake lying dead across the stone remains, tongue lolling out of its wide open mouth. *There is already so much they wouldn't believe at home...*she thought, reviving the scene at the shrine. That was not the woman she was seeking, she had never seen anything like it before, but whoever or whatever she was could not have been affable. It was a fell place, a darkness impregnated it like a parasite feeding from the inside out, a rotting core at its fetid heart.

'You're still limping badly,' Feletra observed in Steptail, 'I'll take you to the nearest village where you will have to stay for now, that should be Betharanei in Otra –' she whipped out Flior's map and checked it. She was correct, Betharanei was the closest village but the journey would be long and arduous, especially at walking speed, it would take them the best part of the day, though Desporsa offered them a little breeze today, a welcome sensation against the heat. Feletra pulled up her hood as together they headed north-east for Otra.

A serri tree was nothing to catch the eye at. Their branches were few, and they never grew foliage, leaving them dull and ugly. However, this particular serri tree made a mark, a red flag had been tied to it, bearing the symbol:

It was the symbol of Otra, Land of the Silent, and marked the borderline into the land. Feletra felt the relief wash over her to have finally reached the land, her water flask was running on dregs and Steptail was in desperate need of help with his leg. She carried on past the mark and painted on the other side of the rag was the symbol of Elpura, Land of the Blood:

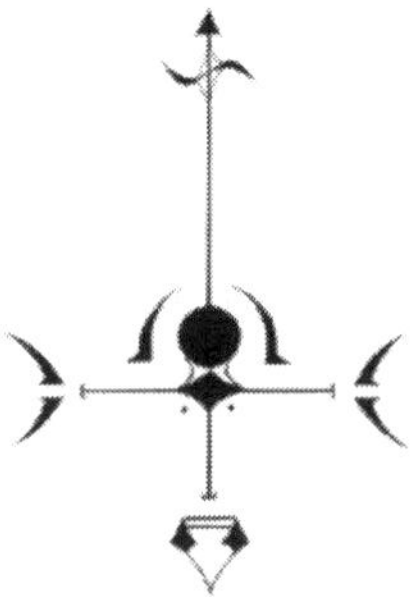

Signs such as these would be placed repeatedly along the border to inform those crossing it. Every land in Enphiah had its own emblem to represent it; when a traveller passed from one land into another they were likely to find a sign similar to the one Feletra passed, however they were not always a rag tied to a tree. Many took advantage of the location of the borders and might have etched an emblem into a log, painted on a rock or cliff face or even created a wicker symbol from straw and leaves.

A little further into Otra and Feletra began to see houses in the distance, houses of Betharanei. She followed the path into the village eagerly, and almost instantly the people who normally went about their lives stopped and stared at the young girl with her horla. It was not an unwelcome stare, but it became clear that they rarely received visitors. The houses were neatly constructed, rooves not of straw and reed like Feletra's home but entirely wood, she noticed a stable at the end of the main road, twice as large as her family's and quietly made a beeline for it.

Other horlas could be seen carting goods around, one man ushered a couple of pigs along with his son, children chased each other playfully, weaving in and out of their vexed parents as they attempted to maintain interrupted conversations with the neighbours, and a group of old men sat outside beneath a veranda playing a game with tokens on a circular board. It was a jubilant, merry place, where a villager knew every other and significant values were kept close to the heart.

A woman appeared to notice Steptail's injury and rushed off to the stable. Feletra glanced down at the horla's leg, the bandage was beginning to unravel and she hastily bent down to retie it.

'Excuse me!' a voice interjected above the hustle and bustle, Feletra stood up and identified the man that had called her outside the stable, next to him waited the woman who had ran off to fetch him, 'We can help your horla, come into the stable.'

Feletra obeyed without question and led the aching Steptail into the cool stable, it smelt fresh and clean, there was no musky scent like her stable at home. There were six other horlas basking in the shade in their stalls, with room for another eight comfortably. Steptail was not yet granted a stall however, as the man beckoned them over to the middle of the aisle.

'Bring him over here,' he said gently, he had a mature look, but his face remained youthful, in his twenty-seventh or eighth year, Feletra guessed. As he bent down to examine Steptail's leg a ray of sunlight penetrated through the beams and highlighted his rich golden locks. His eyes shimmered a deep sea-blue, there was warmth and affection in them. He had a typical stableboy strength about him, arms and hands that easily handled wild animals, operated pulleys and levers, lifted heavy loads and a knowledge of all things bolts and nails. Feletra sensed the difference between this man and her brothers immediately and received a fair impression he would have no idea how to swing a sword, that again was a particular sort of strength.

‘This wound has been dressed well,’ he observed, removing the bandage.

‘I did the best I could,’ Feletra replied timidly.

The man raised his head and smiled at her, ‘You are very young to be travelling alone, are you on some errand for family?’

‘Suppose you could call it an errand,’ Feletra said after some hesitation, ‘but yes, it is for my family.’

‘It sounds important, I will ask no more. I hope you do not have to travel far though?’

‘Oh, not far, no,’ Feleta replied, trying to remain as inconspicuous as possible, ‘I am only crossing the border into Halprigh from here and then I can return home.’

The young man looked at her again, confused and somewhat suspicious, ‘There is no border from Otra to Halprigh, perhaps you mean Thenigh?’

Feletra paused for a moment, ‘Oh, yes! Thenigh! I often become confused between the two, I meant Thenigh,’ she felt her cheeks burn slightly, but it soon flushed away when he was smiling again.

‘Forgive me, you have had no introduction. I am Emmet, and the woman behind you is Halemer, a good friend of mine.’

Feletra had forgotten the woman who had called Emmet out to help, yet there she stood patiently by the door, her hands cupped in front of her and an aging smile about her round face. Her tight blonde curls were swept messily into a low bun and she wore an unobtrusive evergreen dress that covered every part of her but her head. She was a relatively large woman, motherly looking, and indeed desiring only to be motherly, lines dipped and bowed around her eyes suggestive of sincerity and an innocent frankness.

'Good day to you,' she said vivaciously and walked forward into the stable as if the invitation had been long awaited, 'what is your name?'

'Feletra,' she saw no harm in it, and felt incredibly at ease with these people.

'Well, Feletra,' said Emmet, having finished Steptail's new dressing and leading him to his own stall, 'welcome to Betharanei. You and your horla may stay as long as you need. Do you plan to stay the night? Or must you leave today?'

'Oh, Emmet, do not plague the poor girl with questions now,' said Halemer, taking Feletra by the arm and leading her out, 'not when she is weary from such a walk. Come. Come into my home and we will fetch you something to eat. You as well, Emmet, you don't eat enough during the day as it is.'

Halemer's home turned out to be very similar to Feletra's own, there was the same stove, clay oven and basin, but it was decidedly smaller and had but three beds in the adjacent room. There was a pot of vibrant red and blue flowers on every windowsill that brightened the house with a sunshine of its own, and Feletra suddenly thought her own home was lacking in this energetic, colourful aura, perhaps because so many boys could not be trusted around pretty things.

'Sit there at the table, and I will see what I have.'

'I think she would rather rest for now, Halemer,' said

Emmet, having caught them up, ‘evening is closing in, the Valley House will be serving dinner soon, why don’t we take Feletra there instead?’

Halemer stopped rummaging about her pantry and looked at Feletra to confirm or decline.

‘I think I will wait till later to eat something, and rest a while for now,’ she said.

‘Of course! And you will have one of my beds then, there are two spare, I live alone these days. And when you wake later you will be ready to sup with Emmet and myself. You will enjoy the Valley House, I promise you, it’s where we all gather in the evenings for food, drinks and merriment.’

‘I look forward to it, and thank you for your hospitality.’

They said no more and left Feletra to sleep, though peace was still hard to come by. She felt apprehensive of closing her eyes after her vision, hoping never to see Ataleka like that again. And the woman that appeared like a ghost at the shrine by the Sorpha, if she visited her again, whether in her dreams or not, she would not know what to do. She could not even say who she was, but a wild thought crossed her mind that she may have been Zenika, the madwoman, mother of Nephele. But she lived centuries ago...that could not be possible.

Feletra allowed her weariness to grow stronger, her eyelids fell. She was safe here, she had to tell herself that. Her breath swelled in her chest slowly like a fog passing in and out of her, she saw a green thorn in the dark.

Chapter 6
The Valley House

Feletra woke to footsteps outside. The night had come. Quiet voices came in pairs or threes interrupted by peals of laughter as they passed by the house. Some footsteps were quick and light, owned by the children and their high ringing of shouts of excitement.

She left the bed without the help of one child knocking on the shutter and his mother scolding him.

'Leave that shutter be! Have I not told you before?'

Halemer and Emmet were nowhere to be seen; Feletra merged into the throng of people outside and assumed they too were migrating towards the Valley House. She was led into a building, a large establishment that eclipsed all of its smaller neighbours in the village. Large white candles in brackets gave the place a dim haze and the air tasted delicious with hot food being carried to tables in every direction. She felt certain this must be the Valley House.

'Feletra!' came a voice from behind, she turned to find Emmet walking towards her enthusiastically, 'I was going to come and fetch you later, but it looks like you have beaten me to it. I think Halemer has already arrived.'

And Halemer had indeed already arrived, for it was not long before they found her deep in conversation at a table with two friends, but she immediately noticed them, said something brief to her companions and rose to greet them.

'Come. Let's have a separate table.'

Feletra and Emmet followed her to a small secluded corner where the deafening sound of laughter and drunken singing was dimmed and unobtrusive.

'Now –' Emmet began.

'Hold your tongue Emmet!' Halemer commanded, 'This girl will not answer anything you have to say until she has had something to eat! Now,' turning softly to Feletra, 'what will you have?'

'Oh, I don't mind. I am quite happy to share something?'

'An excellent idea. Stay here, I will see to it,' she left the table to order the food, while Emmet brought three empty flagons and a jug of water over. As he poured he suddenly stopped.

'I'm sorry, I did not ask. Would you like something stronger?'

'Stronger? Like what?' Feletra asked.

'Well, wine, ale?'

'Oh, no thank you,' she replied submissively, but Emmet smiled knowingly.

'You have never tried wine or ale, have you?'

'Well, my family never keep such drinks in the barrels. And they are an expensive luxury.'

'Expensive? Not if you can brew it yourself.'

'That skill does not run in my line, then. We keep to what food and drink we are granted.'

'You are not from a village or hamlet, are you?'

Feletra shook her head.

'Our house stands alone, out on the plains.'

Emmet resumed pouring the water.

'I once lived that way,' he said, 'but when both my parents died, and my brother was still young, I had to support him in every way I could, and living away from people was not the answer, and so we moved here, to Betharanei.'

'Is your brother joining us?'

'No, he does not come here.'

'Where is he?'

But at that moment Halemer had returned to them with a large brimming tray of food. She had brought roast chicken, lamb, potatoes, bread, fresh tomatoes, sliced watermelon and a cooked plant which Feletra was sure she recognised, but thought it better to ask in case she was mistaken.

'This plant, is it spelethra?'

'It is, yes,' answered Halemer, 'how did you know?'

'I grew one when I was seven, it didn't grow very tall though.'

'I think that's about the same age my parents taught me about plants and how to care for them as well,' said Emmet, 'I'll never understand why such a tradition came about.'

'I recall when Halemedra also grew a spelethra at that age, it seems to be a popular choice amongst children,' said Halemer.

'Halemedra?' Feletra inquired.

'My daughter. She has left Betharanei now, to make for the east of Acro, I believe. She has always wanted to travel since she was small. I wish she had not left so young, though; at eighteen there is still much to learn about the world, but then I suppose there is no better way to do just that,' despite Halemer speaking so positively of her daughter her eyes looked distant and her lively smile faltered, then she blinked as if waking from a sad daydream, 'try the spelethra though, Feletra. I find the taste is as beautiful as the smell!'

Feletra peered down at the slinky plant on her plate that had been cooked to a crisp, dark green. Breaking off a small part of the stem, she found it strong and potent, but it had such a sweet after-taste that she was happily inclined to finish it all.

'So, Feletra,' said Emmet when most of the food had been cleared, 'how did your horla become injured like that?'

'Steptail? We were crossing the Elpuran Bridge over the Sorpha, a very unstable bridge already, when we were attacked by a Nova Snake, we managed to escape but some of the stones gave way and trapped his leg; I managed to help him out again and bring him here to safety.'

There followed an unmistakeably long pause of awe from Emmet and Halemer, they looked at each other as if they had both heard incorrectly.

'Did you say a Nova Snake?' said Emmet disbelievingly.

'That's right. It was just bad luck really, sightings are quite uncommon.'

'Bad luck?' said Halemer. 'My girl, it is a miracle you are still alive! How in Esilence did you escape?'

'More luck, if I am honest. All we could do was run for the bridge, when the bridge started to collapse it trapped both the snake and Steptail, but the snake died soon after.'

'Incredible,' Emmet marvelled, 'I have never heard of any surviving an encounter with one of those things, and you even managed to kill it, I truly am amazed, Feletra.'

Feletra maintained her modesty and decided not to mention then that her father had dealt a far greater blow to the beasts in his time, they were so impressed with her story that Padryl's might have overwhelmed them entirely. She would have thought it more commonplace to have heard of men slaying the Novas but now it appeared she had wholly underestimated her father's skill and courage.

'You are indeed the bravest girl I have ever met,' said an astonished Halemer, 'but it must have been a terrifying ordeal.'

'Yes, it was,' Feletra replied shortly, still ingesting the compliment of bravery that she had never been awarded before, it was almost confusing and she didn't know what to do with it.

'Oh, I saw to your horla while you were sleeping,' said Emmet, 'and I am afraid he cannot leave here until he is fully recovered, that wound will need time.'

'Actually, I was hoping to ask you, if I could leave Steptail here. I know he is too weak to carry on with me and it looks as if he will be well cared for in Betharanei.'

Halemer sat up in her seat. 'But you are most welcome to stay in the village as well until he has recovered?' she suggested openly.

'I would, but it's very important that I set out again as soon as possible. I will miss Steptail's company, but my family are depending on me.'

'Where is it you are going?' Emmet asked, but Feletra did not answer immediately and she looked down uncomfortably at the table.

'I...I cannot –'

'I'm sorry, it was no right of mine to ask.'

In the short silence between them they heard the conversations of others, laughing, calling and the scraping of chairs along the floor.

'Of course, we will tend to Steptail as best we can,' said Halemer sympathetically, 'and keep him here as long as you need. There is no better hand in the village with horlas than Emmet. Do you know when you will return for him?'

Feletra shook her head, 'I'm sorry, I don't,' she replied

dismally, 'do not expect me at any time, treat Steptail as well as the other horlas.'

'You will stay the night though, won't you?'

'Only if I am no burden, then I can leave at dawn.'

'Of course you are no burden!' said Halemer, yawning, 'this day has been a trying one for me however, I think I will take my leave. You remember which is my house?'

Feletra nodded in reply as she rose from her seat and bid them goodnight, leaving her with Emmet. A young woman came to retrieve the empty plates on the table and a man with a grey beard sat down behind them with a grunt, he retrieved a pipe from his shabby black coat and lit it carefully.

'Evening, Emmet,' he said in a brusque tone.

'Good evening, Amanyl,' Emmet replied with the friendliest of smiles, everyone must trust him, Feletra thought.

'Man from across the border has just arrived in the village.'

This was unexpected, Feletra was automatically on high alert.

'Another newcomer? That makes two today,' said Emmet, glancing at Feletra, 'what is his business?'

'He wasn't clear on that. He had no cart though, no supplies even, just himself and a horla. Looked very worn; must have come quite a way across those plains.'

A man from across the border, with next to nothing? Nothing but a cause, Feletra thought, fear striking every nerve in her. She tried with much difficulty to remain calm in front of Emmet, but her eyes darted about unstoppably, from corner to corner, table to table. Her hands kept fidgeting and her heartbeat grew louder in her head.

Emmet's face grew serious with concern.

'Are you alright, Feletra?' he said, but she barely heard it. All at once the man known as Amanyl opened a pair of shutters and leaned on the sill.

'Here's the man, Emmet, coming in now,' he called. A quick gust of air blew in from the window and extinguished the candle in the bracket above them.

The doors of the Valley House opened once more, and in walked Padryl, his stride prouder than a king's. Feletra sank lower and lower in her chair with dread as he looked around the place. He will search everywhere, she thought. She had to leave Betharanei.

'Emmet,' she said, 'is there another way out of the Valley House? Other than the main doors?'

'What's going on? Do you know that man?'

'I have no time to explain! Is there another way out?'

Emmet hesitated, looked at Padryl warily on the far side, then back at Feletra.

'There is one I know of. This way.'

Feletra carefully slipped off her chair and followed, keeping herself hidden behind Emmet at all times, although weaving between so many tables and chairs made it a difficult task. They were moving towards the opposite end of the house, where Feletra could make out the dark outline of a single door with a heavy bolt just behind the bar, but on nearly reaching it she glanced so often at her father that she walked straight into a small table and tripped over something on the floor. She ignored the stares from the people around her and prepared to rise again, but Padryl had been alerted to the commotion, and Emmet crouched down beside her and quickly stopped her from standing up again.

‘That man,’ he informed her hurriedly, ‘he is now coming this way, if you get up now he will see you.’

Feletra looked about frantically, and saw what must have tripped her: a thick black circular ring on the floor which formed the handle to a hatch door.

‘Where does that lead?’ she asked desperately.

‘I don’t know. A cellar, perhaps, it must be. But there is no definite way of knowing if there is an escape out of there –’

‘There is nowhere else to go,’ Feletra said firmly, and crawled as quickly as she could. Together they lifted it open; Feletra descended first, but before Emmet closed it on them he pulled the nearest table to, so that it covered the door (much to the disagreement of those who were dining at the table).

As soon as the hatch was closed above them, they were immersed into pitch blackness. All that they heard were their own shallow breaths against the muffled voices from above. Hastily Feletra felt about with her hands and placed them on the cold, narrow walls either side of her for balance; her foot edged forward, but the stone steps were so steep she almost slipped down them.

‘Be careful,’ Emmet warned.

Slowly but surely, they made their way down in the dark, with each step becoming steeper the further they went. A man shouting was faint in the distance, and Feletra tried not to believe it was her name being repeated over and over, Padryl calling her in vain. Above them, footsteps thudded to and fro, and beneath them a soft wet substance like mud thickened under their feet, then there came a dripping noise further down somewhere.

‘This is no cellar, Emmet,’ Feletra observed ominously.

He made no reply. The stairwell seemed to go on forever, and then an unusual smell became apparent as all sound from the Valley House passed away.

'What is that? Do you smell it?' said Emmet.

'Yes, metallic almost. Like iron.'

'No, burning. It smells like cinders.'

It seemed to be a combination of the two, though neither of them could say what it belonged to, but it was, nonetheless, becoming stronger.

'You say burning,' Feletra said, 'I say metal; could there be a blacksmith's down here?'

'Betharanei already has a blacksmith's. And what would be the convenience of one down here?'

The stronger it became, the more they were unable to name it, and when such a high-pitched, grating cry echoed up the stairwell to them they tried suddenly to stop in their tracks, but Emmet lost his footing and slipped on the muddy stone steps, pushing Feletra down with him as they cascaded down faster and faster, fruitlessly trying to take hold of something and stop themselves, but the walls were equally as wet as the steps and their fingernails scraped painfully down them. Finally, Feletra's hand caught something which felt like a corner – the wall here broke off and must form another passage to the left. But it was a fleeting moment of hope as she failed to keep her grip and fell faster than ever.

'Feletra!' Emmet shouted – she knew he had held onto that corner and was safe, but he could not help her.

The pounding of the steps into her back all at once disappeared and it became a smooth sliding as the surface beneath her became mud alone; suddenly she stopped and plummeted face down into the same watery sludge.

Clumsily she rose to her feet again and wiped her face but there was no light down here, and something moved in the dark nearby.

'Who's there?' she said shakily, and it moved again, not a shuffling noise but a scuttling one, and it was on the walls, circling her quickly from one wall to the next, even above her.

'Feletra! Can you hear me?' Emmet called, but she dared not answer. The creature whose presence she shared immediately inhaled sharply in a low breath and released it in another bone-rattling shriek. She heard it as it leapt down from the wall and landed before her. The stench of burning flesh and raw metal was now so thick it was like a smoke she could have choked on. Something snapped loud and dull like a bone breaking.

Feletra was not prepared to wait for this thing to hunt her like prey, and blindly sprang for the narrow passageway from whence she came. Instantly she felt a firm bony-fingered hand grab her ankle and tighten its grip. Effortlessly it pulled her back down – she kicked and screamed wildly but it fought just as hard, if not harder. Emmet's calls of despair were faint to her ears and continued as one hand on her ankle became two on her head. Swiftly she kicked out and managed to find its stomach while her fist slammed into what felt like a windpipe, the creature emitted a strangulated noise followed by an enraged howling and something warm and wet spattered across Feletra's cheek – once she was free again she returned immediately to the passage and dug her fingers deep into the mud in desperation. She rose higher and higher and Emmet's voice came clear again. By the time she reached him tears were streaming down her face and she was hysterical with fear, but there was no time to wait around in the dark – together they ran aimlessly down the new set of steps, the creature's wails at the loss of a meal taunted Feletra and made her move twice as fast.

The staircase did not last long before they hit flat stone and came to a door. Emmet fumbled for the bolt, found it, and they were out.

A cricket chirped somewhere while they breathed deeply and Feletra tried to come to terms with what she had just experienced.

The stairs had led them outside, at the back of the Valley House where a few large barrels stood. Feletra stayed quite still for a moment, eyes wide whilst the moon glared at her, not knowing what to do anymore.

The door creaked open behind her and the blackness faced her again. She slammed it shut and barred it.

'What was that? Did you see it?' said Emmet.

'I saw nothing,' Feletra replied in almost a whisper, 'only felt...and heard...'

'What happened down there?'

She failed to answer, brought her hands to her face and felt all the dirt still clinging to her skin. Emmet noticed something, and he walked over to her slowly, staring at one side of her face.

'What? What is it?' she said, and Emmet gingerly touched a finger to her temple. What came away was like oil, jet black and gelatinous, he stretched it between his finger and thumb with disgust.

'What is that?' said Feletra, turning around to the barrels and trying each tap until she found water to wash it off.

'I don't know, I've never seen anything like it before,' Emmet rapidly wiped his hand against the ground as if it was infectious.

Suddenly Feletra remembered that her father was in Betharanei, and that she had to leave.

'Emmet, where did I leave my pack?' she asked in a dazed tone.

'In the stable...but what about –? Wait, Feletra!'

Feletra tore off round the Valley House and through the village with Emmet in tow, amidst the confused stares she received, past the real blacksmith's, and into the stable.

A stable boy who had been forking bundles of hay jumped in fright at her entrance.

'It's alright,' Emmet reassured him, 'go home.'

The boy gladly obeyed and left.

Feletra's pack had been hung up on the wall, and once she had it down again she went over to Steptail's stall.

'I do not know when I will see you again, but Emmet will be your new master and he will look after you. Goodbye Steptail.'

Steptail had believed that he was going with Feletra when she approached him, as he pawed the ground anxiously and pressed his face against her arm as she stroked his mane. Reluctantly, she drew her hand away from him but he continued to try and reach out to her and knocked at the stall door with his hooves.

Suddenly the noise outside grew louder. People ran by the open stable door in a frenzy, shouting to each other. It was eight or nine men, and they seemed to be chasing after something. Feletra was worried that her father might have learnt that she had just left the Valley House, and was on the hunt again.

Emmet turned to Feletra, 'I will lead you out of Betharanei, towards the east.'

Quickly Feletra took out Flior's map and unfolded it.

'And then into Thenigh,' she decided.

'No,' said Emmet unexpectedly, seeming to doubt the decision. 'There are many villages over the Thenin border. If you truly wish to escape this man that hunts you, you must take the path on the right where it splits for Droha.'

'But what is wrong with the villages? And the Thenin road?'

'Do you not see? You will be expected to stop at these villages for more supplies. So, make for Droha, take the bridge over the Sorpha and from there leave the road, into the wilderness.'

Were she not desperate to leave Betharanei as quickly as possible at that moment she would have stopped at hearing about the wilderness. She was not trained for it, knew not the terrain nor what to expect, or even where to find food if she ran out. But even as helpless as she might find herself off the road, it was not the time to think of that now. Now was the time for flight, and Emmet, though he had known Feletra for less than a day, appeared to be more than ready to help, and in Feletra's eyes, had proven himself a faithful friend in answering her needs. Tonight, the black clouds that obscured the white of the moon were another friend to Feletra. To make an escape across the open plains she had to be stealthy, quick and defy every hold of weariness to make her way unseen, she had to take advantage of the late engulfing darkness that was prepared to cloak her.

Taking one last look into Steptail's abandoned eyes, she hastily followed Emmet away through the village. They kept within the shadows of the houses and crept quickly through the narrow passageways of the back streets rather than the main road. Suddenly Emmet halted Feletra with his arm when they were at the back of a market stall, just around the corner came the low voices of three or four men. While Emmet stood, Feletra crouched down and tried to listen, but they were almost whispers. She peered around the corner: there were four of them, but when another four came darting breathlessly from the front of the house she withdrew swiftly. They spoke frantically as the others tried to quiet them.

'We did not see anything – we could not –'

'Keep your voice down!'

'...could be anywhere by now...'

'We cannot stop searching! We must go out and look again!'

'No. The people are already starting to suspect us.'

'Are you certain the door was left open?'

'Yes. It had been unlocked from the inside.'

Immediately Feletra seemed to recognise one of the voices, it belonged to a man with a grey beard, to –

'Amanyl...' whispered Emmet.

There was no time for Emmet to express his disbelief, as the resound of another man's call so close struck Feletra deep with fear.

'Feletra!'

It was her own name, and her own father calling it. The eight men scattered at it, feeling their discussion was no longer safe, but it was Feletra that felt the greater peril: she was deadly determined not to return home without that cure, especially with her father.

'Emmet,' she said, 'what if he wakes Halemer? She will surely tell him everything!'

'I know. I must get back to her, but not before you leave. This way.'

Quicker than before, they wasted no time through the maze of houses, until eventually the way was clear, and the Plains of Nemenon faced Feletra again. Emmet beheld the girl he had known for less than a day and failed to convince himself why he so readily wanted to help her, he knew nothing about her nor her hunter. It felt right somehow, he sensed her helplessness was genuine and that only he could provide her with an escape route.

'You remember which way to go?' he said.

'Yes, the south-east road to the Bridge of Droha, and then make my way into the wilderness.'

'But before that Feletra, watch yourself. There is no road from Betharanei and you must keep your head straight for the east if you want any hope of finding that path that you need.'

'Alright, thank you, and Halemer. I wish there was more time.'

'As do I, but there is none. Go quickly, I have to find Halemer.'

Feletra made one quick nod and they separated, but then Emmet turned around once more and called back to her, 'And Feletra, the terrain of Droha is different to Otra. Be ready for it.'

And then he left her alone again, sprinting back into the warm homely lights of Betharanei; the same dim, swimming lights that had initially welcomed her into their Valley House, and now bitterly rejected her into the cold, dusty dark of the night.

She had been staring transfixed at these haunting lights when she should have been running, but she found herself craving them. To be back with her family, because the moment Emmet left her and vanished she felt the most small and lonesome than she had ever felt before. Her shoulders were hunched and her fingers grasped tight around the single strap of her pack as if it were all the possessions she had left. The lights seemed to become brighter the longer she looked at them, and they were everything, they were home...

No.

Home was her father.

Betharanei was her father, waiting for her. Suddenly the grip on the strap loosened and Feletra stood straight with her shoulders back. Turning away from the village, she faced the vast eastern plains, black and daunting before her, and without warning even to herself, she ran. With great speed and haste, she found a new energy inside her that could be released and felt as though she could almost spring away in her escape. She was not fazed when her name rang out in another despondent cry from the village.

When the moon was unmasked, and Betharanei long behind her, Feletra stopped to rest and drank from her leather flask. She was still in Otra; it would be a while before she reached the road. She knew that she was also still in flight, and did not stop long before careering away again, hoping to create as much distance as possible between her and her father.

After an age, it seemed, Pytheria finally broke over her skin. Rising directly from the east before her, it slowly blinded her the higher it rose. She slowed to a walk from exhaustion and wandered from her course every now and then, finding it difficult to keep her track straight. Looking back to the west, Feletra noticed that Desporsa was catching up in the daylight hours. Surprisingly, there was no rider on a horla that should be her father that could have made an appearance by now. Perhaps Emmet had managed to divert him? It was at least an encouraging thought on such a bleak walk, ironically enough, at the expense of Padryl. On and on she trekked; the heat from Pytheria was incredible, burning silver like a melting disc of ore and glistening in ripples against its opponent, Desporsa, the sun who would grant no blissful breeze today, each of them battling to have Feletra strive for the forked road ahead in disputes of fiery touch and a merciless rule on the day. Meanwhile the Black Dwarf sat in his still throne and mocked, seeming to doubt Feletra's strength and stamina, but she defied him nonetheless, in her slow but determined stride.

The longer the journey went on the harder the ground beneath her feet became. Sharp stones began to accumulate and crunched at her heels. Before long, small rocks could be seen among them, gradually increasing in size. Many were embedded in the earth, and Feletra found she had to be constantly looking down just to avoid tripping over them.

When Pytheria and Desporsa crossed courses directly over her head, Feletra caught sight of a house in the distance, away to the north. For a moment, she thought she had in fact led herself home, but then the absurd idea subsided as she carried on and a woman holding a baby emerged from inside, staring at her in some surprise. Once that house had disappeared another came about, this time to the east and smaller than the last with a quaint stone well stationed by a meagre vegetable patch, there was no life to be seen or heard and she would not have stopped even if there had been. Having looked down at her feet and the protruding rocks for most of the walk, Feletra failed to immediately notice the great rock formation that now loomed before her like layered sheets and came to an abrupt peak without a true point. She stood for a while under its dull yet overwhelming presence, squinting against the sunlight to meet its magnificent heights. After then deciding to walk about the formation and averting her gaze to its shade-soaked depths, she stepped into the shadows on the other side and found a couple of shallow pools of water, cool and clean from the cape of darkness.

Ahead of this Feletra spied a narrow space between two smooth walls of rock. Just large enough, she squeezed through, filling the gap that felt as though it could close in on her at any moment. The passage led to a small sheltered cove in the wall, withdrawn from the open skies. Beyond it the passage ended leaving a jagged crack, before it was just visible to see where it opened again further down, narrower still than what she had come by.

Seizing the opportunity, Feletra decided to spend the night. Leaving her pack within the cove, she made her way back through the narrow passage to fill her flask from the water pools, looked about the plains, then returned. Although the serri trees made a good source of firewood, she thought it wise to remain inconspicuous, and realised in that moment that had she remained at home, she likely would have been taught survival skills in the wild once her combat training was complete. No matter, perhaps she would have simply failed at that too. There was still time to fail in the real world, out here, where no one would find her slowly perishing in the blistering heat.

She was alone on the dry desert plains, beating the heart

and breathing the breath unto it that the place so desperately lacked in. No breeze of the air conducted itself to shake any leaf of any tree, though serri trees had nought to shake in their state of lifeless, twisted and charred bones. The night preyed on the weak remaining day, teasing the playful sweeping shadows that flitted quickly like bats' wings through grainy stone cracks, between deformed boulders and across dappled coves. As the faithful servants of the darkness, the shadows did their master's bidding and crept about, above and below every area of the landscape like demons whilst the nocturnal creatures were tempted to accept the invitation of awakening; to descend upon the bleak world as a mark of timid life.

Feletra did not bring a travel cloak with her, but now wished she had – anything to wrap around her against the new cold that came seeping into her small body with an unwanted dread from afar. Afar seemed to feel like a land that was breaking under its own foothills with corruption and evil, the land she had already stood upon in the vision, but mostly, the land she was trying to reach. As she brooded on this her head began to droop and she fell into a deep sleep, dreamless but not without the ever-repeated question of *Where are they? Where are they?* How would she ever find those caves with no lead? It was indeed a deep sleep, but such unexplained questions made it an uneasy one.

Feletra woke late into the mid-morning when Pytheria and Desporsa had risen before her. She was happy to leave such an uncomfortable rest place where her bones had pressed and ached from the hard rock. Having not planned to sleep so late into the morning, she now hurriedly ate a small breakfast of bread and cheese, washed her face in one of the pools and was ready to set off again. It was not, of course, without being careful, however the plains currently saw no other life. The only sound that emitted was from that of her footsteps, and so she felt confident enough, despite the eerie deathlike atmosphere of the land that exuded from the very air surrounding her. Feletra was walking along somewhere off the outskirts of the Plains of Nemenon, but Otra, Elpura, Asiri, Lor...what was the difference? She only hoped with anticipation that Droha was somewhat more of an eye-opener.

Feletra had no idea how long she had been walking for anymore, nor where she was, until the crumbling stones at her feet came at once to an end; that is, they had split and now broke off in two different directions. She looked down and around. It was the stones that had formed a path the whole time, and that she had in fact been following the very road she was trying to find for at least a few leagues. Now becoming surprised and aware that she had reached the fork in the road already, she took the path on the right as Emmet had told her. Just a few more leagues, and she had found the border of Droha. At the side of the road the symbol, or emblem of the land was carved deeply into a large rock –

Feletra crossed the border somewhat warily. From that point onwards she spent several days on the wearisome journey to the Drohan Bridge, becoming accustomed to the creatures that surveyed her suspiciously in the day and inspected her while she slept in the night, scuttling or slithering away in a whish when she moved. She grew into a habit of routine that suited her, sleeping late and waking early, thereby wasting no time that she could use for walking. Her supplies kept well and she managed to ration the water, as there would be no river until she reached the Sorpha, but even that water she must refuse, after swearing to herself that she would never again touch that cursed river.

And yet with each day that passed she could feel the increasing lightness of her flask and panicked a little more every time she drank from it, once spitting it back to save for later; and all the time feeling the effects of the dryness and the heat weighing her down, dragging her feet and straining her neck just to keep it up. The silence of the plains seemed to accentuate her senses, particularly her hearing, and on the twelfth or thirteenth day since crossing the border, when Pytheria could not possibly have burned any hotter, she heard something. It was difficult to make out, but something was moving towards her from the road. Soon she could see that it was a cart, and on her instincts spun on her heel and raced ahead in fear. The thinning of her shoes over the days left her feet now the most painful they had been so far as the stones dug in razor-sharp against her soles. The rest of her body did not fare any better; her muscles ached, her head was spinning and the cart behind her was approaching closer and closer.

Briefly she looked up and what strength of mind she had

left registered that the bridge was not far in the distance now.

And then she gave out.

Collapsing to the ground as clouds of dust and earth curled about her, the last thing she saw was a wooden wheel coming to a stop by her head, the spit in her mouth all but gone and taken for granted as much as the breath in her lungs as the aridity drained insatiably into her airways, yet at least there was no more silence.

Chapter 7
Breaking Fear

For all those days that Feletra spent on the plains with nought to accompany her but the wilderness itself, she had developed an air of solitude, the type that enabled her to bar the desire to depend on another. And in that same space of time, Emmet, who had been delving blindly into dark matters that were beyond him since Feletra had left, seemed to have acquired something of the same quality, despite his own isolated living for some years now.

The night that he had left Feletra standing alone and staring into the lights of Betharanei he had then bolted for Halemer's house. Padryl had still been calling out for his daughter when Halemer awoke to such unfamiliar commotion and Emmet had just caught her as she opened the door. He had been forced to explain everything in a hurry, omitting the attack under the Valley House, although she became very confused and he had to repeat three times for her to understand. Eventually it came clear and she agreed to keep quiet, albeit still looking somewhat perplexed, but Emmet did not stay with her and quickly left to intercept Feletra's father. He managed to convince him that a girl by the description of 'dark waves of hair' and 'deep brown eyes' had been seen leaving in haste that night for Lira in the north. Padryl left in a flash without replenishing any of his supplies.

But these were not the dark matters that Emmet had already thrown himself into. He did not look Amanyl in the eye when greeted by him after overhearing the conversation of the secret gathering he was a part of, and no longer returned with enthusiasm towards him. It did not take him long to realise that the discussion was linked to whatever was being kept beneath the Valley House, and he and Feletra becoming involved had sparked a fear among them.

Emmet became intrigued and fearfully eager to unlock the conspiracies that some of the villagers were members of. He began to seclude himself more and more to his house and visited the Valley House less at nights, until his visits ceased completely and he lost all feeling of trust and safety he once had for the place. He even reduced his time with Halemer and left the stable boy alone more often to tend to the horlas. Within the security of his house, he drew out plans and possible explanations that might fit, burning them once memorised to dispose of evidence. After much thinking, he was able to identify every one of the eight men that had been talking together by matching the voices exactly and recording their actions and locations over the days.

Emmet had become stealthy and careful around each of them, trying not to give anything away. After his discovery of them all he returned to a cheery conduct towards Amanyl to maintain being inconspicuous. If they were going to be false to him, so was he to them. His investigations then led him to the main issue, which meant discovering the actual secret they were keeping, for he could tell it was a dangerous one, and decided that the only way was to figure out what the creature under the Valley House was. He knew it would be difficult without Feletra to tell more clearly of her experience, but he was determined, and searched desperately through all the books his parents had left him and his brother when they died. Yet they only told of domesticated creatures, horlas, sheep, cats and the likes, nothing that could have matched the shriek he had heard. After a day or two he informed Halemer that he was going to ride out to Aphlicohn in Lira, a city well known for its libraries and extensive teachings from scholars, although he refrained from telling her that he would be attempting to seek out a deadly predatory creature, but then Halemer had said to him:

'You mustn't spend so much time indoors as you do, Emmet, or you'll become as much a recluse as a preathin.'

'A preathin?' Emmet questioned, bewildered.

'Do not tell me you have not heard what a preathin is before?'

Emmet shook his head, his education had been lacking since the death of his parents, and he had focused on bettering the life of his brother. Halemer sighed in exasperation and fetched a book of her own from a shelf.

'I am surprised you have not heard of them,' she said, handing him the book, 'they were used against us in the Old War. The Setrans were the first to discover them. Terrible, malicious things; the very spawn of Blackcraft I would say. Killed many a great man in Mid Enphiah. We saw the last of their race die out, though; still, makes me shiver just to think of them.'

Emmet had been flicking through the book all the while as she spoke, pausing on some disgustingly illustrated pages and drawings of haunting deaths upon men.

'Halemer,' he said slowly, 'may I borrow this book?'

'Of course; are you still going to Aphlicohn?'

He stopped short before the door and turned around again.

‘Er, no. Maybe some other time. And thank you.’

Emmet read every word without fail and consulted the book every day, making notes from some passages and trying to link them to his subject. There was nothing he did not analyse on the creature, how it ate, where it lived, everything. And all the time he felt more and more confident that this was the thing lurking below his beloved Betharanei. But why was it there?

Emmet thought that he knew every person of the village in the fifteen years he had lived there, but now understood that even the friendliest of smiles could hide a whole history of deception, and that he did not truly know the people he once thought he did.

x

Feletra opened her eyes instantly. She was lying down but was no longer outside on the plains and her body was wrapped loosely in bedsheets. She felt refreshed after becoming so drained from the walk, but now the confusion began to set in. As she sat up properly, she saw that she was in a small, soft bed with holes in which feathers were bursting, and that someone had brought her to their house. She thought for a moment she was back in Betharanei, but then she noticed the skin on her forearms; her hairs stood on end, detecting an evening chill, this was not the pleasant, temperate air of Otra. It was no larger than Halemer’s house in all other respects, and was just as homely; a fire shone and crackled strongly in the hearth, the late eventide sunlight poured in through all the open shutters to illuminate every corner, and a most inviting smell of roasting vegetables, if not to accompany some meat, was drifting in from the second room where Feletra could not see the chef but only observe the billowing steam that issued forth.

Feletra thought she had better meet this person that had taken her from her trail to their home. As she left the bed, as comfortable as it was, to stand before the doorway, she observed a man with his back to her as he bustled to and fro busily in such a small kitchen to tend to two large pots and three smaller ones above a line of fire, some simmering gently while others boiled dangerously. The man was rather portly and round in stature, although Feletra thought that if he stood next to her, he would likely tower above her. His head had little hair to speak of and appeared to be receding from age, while his feet were clad in thick leather boots with broad soles, yet he somehow manoeuvred them about the floor in a quick and spritely fashion. Settled that it would be more wise and thoughtful if she did not disturb him at that point, Feletra decided she would wait in the other room, however she gave a start when she turned to find a small girl stood there, no older than Leao. Feletra thought of what to say, but then the girl spoke first.

'You were the girl sleeping on Themson's bed.'

Immediately the man in the kitchen turned towards them, and as he beheld them his eyes lit with a broad, cordial smile.

'You are awake!' he said in a light and airy voice. 'And in good time for dinner as well. We are just about to sup.'

But Feletra had expected more of an explanation before accepting an invite to dinner from a man she knew nothing of.

'I'm sorry...' she said slowly. 'Where am I?'

'Ah! Forgive me, I am Gheor. I was on my way home

when I saw you on the plains, although I should not have known exactly why you began to run away...ah, it is not my place to ask perhaps! Nevertheless, when I saw you then collapse I could not have left you there simply to rot in the sun! And a girl of your age all the more!'

It appeared that Gheor spoke all too slow at first, and then far too fast, for Feletra was still dazed.

'Am I...still in Droha?' she asked uncertainly.

'Yes, of course,' was the reply, 'and my children and I are Drohans true to heart! You are in Fawntree of Droha. Now, I feel the best thing for you is to now restore your strength, would you please sit –?'

'Wait,' Feletra interjected, 'I am in Fawntree?'

'Yes, this is where I brought you,' said Gheor patiently.

'How long have I been here?'

'Well, you've been asleep for an entire day, your energy was utterly spent. The Plains of Nemenon are not to be taken lightly.'

Feletra turned away for a moment, trying to take it all in. She knew where Fawntree was, only felt amazed at how far she now was from home. And a whole day she had lost? That was precious time in which she could have been found by her father, though fate was thankfully thus far in her favour. Meanwhile, Gheor carried on past her to where a table had been laid for eight people.

'I will have to quickly fetch the children in,' he explained in a bumbling manner, 'but please, have a seat for the moment.'

He beckoned her to a chair on the end, which she accepted gratefully as he left the house. The small girl that had addressed Feletra before did not follow her father but drew up a chair next to her and stared without speaking for a time.

'What is your name?' Feletra asked to break the unsettling silence between them.

She stared for a few more seconds, and then said, 'Atrika.'

Feletra was about to reply when Gheor suddenly returned at the door, closely followed by a flurry of five children, shouting and calling excitedly as they flitted about taking their seats at the table. The eldest was a boy with rich auburn hair and small bright eyes in a fair face, his frame a slender one. He looked mature for a boy who was at least one or two years younger than Ataleka, as he calmed down the three sisters and one brother who had entered the house with him to sit in their places. Atrika continued to stare at Feletra, while Gheor brought plate after plate of food to the table, but none of the other children seemed to have noticed the presence of their guest yet and began to tease each other or fight over seating places. Finally, Gheor sat down at the opposite end to Feletra and managed to settle the others.

'Now, listen to me,' he said to them all, 'give your respects tonight as we have company.' At that moment, all eyes turned to Feletra. It appeared they had already acknowledged her being there after all.

'Have you a name that we may call you by?' Gheor politely asked.

Feletra gave them her name, and then Gheor answered by circulating the table with each of his children's names. Inyenaphe, Plineah, Petra and of course Atrika, who was also the youngest, were the girls. Themson and his brother Renon made up the six of them. Themson was the eldest.

'Now understand, Feletra,' Gheor began again, 'you may

stay with us for as long as you need. But I must know, where are your parents?'

Suddenly Feletra was stuck for a reply. She could not possibly tell him, or he would take her back to Elpura. Naturally he would ask after her parents like this, he was one himself, and was devout to the idea of responsibility.

'I...never knew my parents,' she lied, 'I lived with my uncle but he recently died.'

There was some silence at her unexpected story, and then Plineah spoke.

'But why did you leave home?' she inquired.

'Plineah, can you not understand?' Gheor interrupted. 'The girl was clearly grief-stricken!'

'I am sorry that you lost your family,' said Themson genuinely.

Feletra would have said thank you but it felt terrible enough lying to such an extent without accepting pity on her part.

'In that case, you truly may stay as long as you need,' said Gheor, his heart warm and full of love, 'I will make it so that you feel entirely welcome in Fawntree. We would not normally share it so openly, but we as a family, understand more than anyone in this village the pain of loss.'

Gheor stopped for a moment and looked down. Themson continued on his father's behalf.

'Our mother died with our sister two years ago, in childbirth.'

'I am sorry,' said Feletra, feeling even worse for her deception.

The dinner proceeded rather solemnly after that, but the night passed on quickly as another phase of darkness took the land and candles shone like burning eyes in dim grey corners. It was not long before five of them were asleep and Feletra, Gheor and Themson were left awake. Feletra had sat outside the house by herself and gazed in deep thought down a narrow road of Fawntree. The houses were all of stone; they looked sturdier than her own back in Elpura, yet also more clumsily built. What they did not have was the same homely atmosphere though, and the village was far quieter than Betharanei.

Feletra fell asleep instantaneously, slumped in her chair on the veranda. She slept peacefully for several hours undisturbed, little realising she was about to be awoken to a great frenzy of fear. Her eyes snapped open just as quickly as they had closed, and she found Gheor shaking her and urging her to stand up.

'Come, Feletra! We cannot stay here –'

'What is this...?' she replied drowsily.

It was still dark. Becoming slowly aware of the situation, the first thing she heard were the deafening screams of men and women and the wails of children. One after the other, either in groups or alone, the villagers streamed by the house, driven by sheer fright of an entity Feletra had not yet come to hear of. Gheor had remembered her pack and shoved it into her hands as he pulled her away from the house and they all made down the same road. Themson and Renon were a few steps ahead, leading the way with bright torches in their hands. The girls were crowded close to their father and Atrika held on tightly to Gheor's hand. In the confusion Feletra allowed herself to be dragged onto the main road of Fawntree where there was an even greater number of people, all pushing and running in the same direction, although Feletra still was desperate to know what they were running from.

‘What is going on?’ she managed to ask, but the commotion was all too loud for either Gheor or anyone to hear her. Suddenly the crowd parted for a second and she spied a young infant, a boy crying and alone on a doorstep. Drawing her hand away from Gheor’s hold she weaved her way over to the child. Gheor had felt her pull away from him and looked about, calling her name, but with the others urging him forward and his children in tow he had no way of stopping.

Feletra kept her eyes peeled for the parents who might come for the boy, but when the intensity of fear amongst everyone increased and no one appeared she lifted the child in her arms and joined the other villagers once more, deciding he would be safer with someone. She did not travel far with him though, as a woman could be seen battling her way in the opposite direction of those who fled, towards Feletra. She recognised the boy as her own immediately and took him off her. No time was given for either of them to speak, the woman was gone with her son in a flash, and Feletra was left alone again. The people were like a vast sea that she was caught in the tide of, forced along unwillingly. None of the houses were lit anymore, all light save for that of a few torches and the moon had been extinguished. As she carried on down the road it seemed the ground began to slope downwards on a hill, causing all upon it to go faster.

Not far down from Feletra, a young man who had paused within the flow stopped to view the situation, and in the thick of bodies that moved frantically about her, Feletra banged forcefully into him. He turned quickly as she looked up at him, and at that moment her heart beat rapidly, her mind whirling in a frenzy. They came to stand in a frame of time separated from the rest of the town, as she locked her gaze with a pair of striking dark eyes in the face she knew only too well.

'Feletra?' he said, astounded.

'Lampaea!'

In the midst of everything, Feletra felt as if her brother were not really there, standing before her.

'What are you doing here?' he said after some hesitation, but it appeared that Feletra was at even more of a loss. She had been woken a short time ago to the cries of despairing villagers and now she had been reunited with one she thought she would not see again for a long time to come, but there was no time to stay where they were at that moment.

'Come on,' Lampaea took action and pulled Feletra away off the road and back through the houses. He was so fast she struggled to keep up, but eventually he led them to the edge of the town and they came to a stop.

'I cannot believe I am seeing you here, Feletra!' he said at last, 'But...why are you away from home? Why are you in Fawntree?'

Feletra's words were choked, she knew not what to say, but she could not lie to her own brother. It was too late for that.

'Do not send me back,' she said finally, barely audible.

'Send you back? You mean you are here alone?'

'Yes. I left.'

Lampaea paused and stared at his sister as if she had grown to be older than him suddenly. The circumstances seemed all too foreboding and he could sense it strongly in her.

‘Has something happened at home?’ he asked.

Feletra did not answer straight away. The last cries of distress from Fawntree were carried away on the wind.

‘I left home to help it...’ she replied shakily, feeling Ataleka’s pain return to shoot through her again. Lampaea studied the change in Feletra’s expression and voice, and decided to ask no more at that point.

‘Come with me,’ he said, leading her around the outskirts of the town until they came to an area with a fenced-in yard. To one side was a house, and to the other was a large stable. As Lampaea jumped the fence Feletra stayed and waited while he disappeared into the stable. Moments later he reappeared with a horla, opened the gate on the far end and circled the yard back to her.

Silently he gestured for her to mount.

‘Lampaea, you cannot just take someone else’s horla!’ Feletra exclaimed.

Lampaea sighed. ‘The people here make their living by lending horlas to travellers. Why do you suppose the gate and stable were open?’

‘Shouldn’t you leave some money then?’

‘Feletra, I have no money, and the people, like all the others, have fled. And coming out of that stable it looks as if we were not the only ones to have taken a horla tonight. It is a long way to where I am staying, so if you will help me make use of this horla we can at least make a start.’

Feletra mounted the horla reluctantly. ‘What about you, though? We need two.’

But then Lampaea helped himself up to sit behind her and took presidency of the reins.

‘Not necessary. Besides, this was the only one left.’

As they rode away Feletra was unsure of which direction

they were leaving in, and after a while she only felt tiresome again. The journey was very uncomfortable, and as the next dawn lit the white clouds a cold morning wind whistled by and stung her eyes; it caused her to close them all the time, until eventually she chose to keep them closed. Lampaea kept watch over his sister.

x

Feletra felt as if she might become unwillingly accustomed to a new habit of waking to find herself in new unfamiliar places after every sleep. The location she woke to observe this time though was perhaps the most unexpected so far. It was quite a change from the feather bed in Gheor's house; she found herself curled up against a tall tree, and then looked down, seeing she had been sleeping on dry, bare earth and covered with an old, thin blanket that was frayed and had gaping holes. Birds above her sang and called loudly and insects spoke in bright buzzing voices to taste the sweet honey-scented air.

As she sat up a thick protruding root pressed hard into her lower back and she stood up to absorb the picture of a dense forest surrounding her. The trees were some she had never befallen eyes upon before; they were very straight, the trunks were not as thick as an aghaia, nor as thin as a serri tree. The ground was more soiled, darker in colour and softer than on the plains. Although there was no breeze there did seem to be a clear, airy feeling to the place. There were toadstools and mushrooms growing in thick clusters, some taller, others stouter. Feletra did not know what they were, but was intrigued all the same, as well as everything else she could spy that was new and strange.

And then she remembered she had found Lampaea the night before; he said he would take her to where he was staying. But Feletra could see no opening between the trees, no house, and could tell she was directly in the depths, if not the middle, of a forest and a forest alone. What was more, there was no sign of Lampaea himself, and she began to wonder if she had dreamt of him instead. The great chase in the town too, perhaps. She had forgotten all about Gheor's family from everything happening so fast, and so that came as a second shock.

She took a step forward within the magical place that looked as if it was an illusion from a fairytale.

'Where am I?' she muttered to herself, but then was startled to hear a voice answer.

'Elenia Forest,' came the reply.

Feletra spun rapidly on her heel and saw Lampaea staring down at her from a small elevation in the ground, relieved to discover it had not been a dream after all.

'Lampaea!' she exclaimed. 'You were in Fawntree last night! I didn't dream it.'

'No, you didn't,' he replied as he descended down the hill to her, 'but you must have dreamt something. A person does not sleep that long without remembering at least one dream, do they?'

'Why? How long have I slept for?'

'It is gone afternoon. Pytheria crossed Desporsa a long while ago.'

Feletra felt surprised she had lost most of the day to sleep, and not for the first time; this quest was draining her more than she had anticipated.

'It feels like morning,' she said, 'I thought you were taking me to where you are staying?'

‘I did,’ said Lampaea indifferently, ‘you slept in it. You stand in it. This is my home.’

Feletra looked about her once more. ‘The forest?’ she inquired disbelievingly, ‘Is there not a small house then? Or any sort of shelter?’

‘The forest is my house, and the canopy is my shelter. Come.’

She followed him as he darted back up the hill and disappeared over the other side, and sure enough, as she came to the top, she beheld a large clearing that Lampaea had inhabited to mould to his own living area. Or tried to. At the far edge a heap of clothes and sheets had been dumped carelessly next to a thick wooden bowl, while others on the tree nearby rippled and danced in the light breeze from a branch. There was a ring of sharp rocks arranged rather out of proportion in the centre of the clearing, enclosing a set of small logs, many of them burnt black from the previous fire. Above them a spit had been positioned, stained deep red from the blood of a number of unfortunate animals. Beside the spit a larger seating log had been left, and to the opposite edge that faced the south-east trees there was a small collection of wooden spears, some laid down and others plunged into the earth so that they stuck up like a crooked fence. In addition, there was also a coil of rope and a cage-like contraption comprised of sticks and draped in web-like fibres between the open spaces that sparkled even in the shade, as if it emitted its own white light.

The lack of cover from the canopy above meant that most sunlight entered, and the ground was slightly drier than the surrounding forest. From where Feletra stood upon the border of the clearing and following it round, the ground sloped down again so that it dipped to give a formation something of a bowl or basin resemblance. Lastly, an untidy stretch of blankets was laid where the ground came flat just once, with a very torn and scratched pillow at the head, white feathers bursting and being carried away on the wind.

'Is this where you have been staying the whole time?' Feletra asked as she made her way down the hill.

'Since I left home? No. I have been travelling around Enphiah; to Penthor, Ferin...I stayed in Beltro for a long time, and even went to Mereta for some days.'

'Mereta?' Feletra repeated, 'That would be Eastern Enphiah! How did they allow you past the border? I heard there were guards?'

'There were. They questioned me some; who I was, where I was from, but I posed no threat. There was no reason not to allow me entry.'

Feletra sat down on the log, wary of it rolling away, but it remained steady.

'But what have you been doing?' she asked.

'Just travelling mostly, and...well, yes, travelling.'

Automatically Lampaea turned away and knelt down beside the spit, preparing a fire for them. Feletra had not noticed before but on his back was set a quiver of arrows, and he had managed to secure the bow next to it. His dark hair complimented the soul-searching tone of his eyes, rather like Skepreo's did, although Lampaea's was somewhat less unruly and well kept. It was that air of independence and trust that bestowed strength to his character, and despite that he had failed to impress the greatest sense of maturity on Feletra's childhood, she felt very safe to be with him. Yet now it seemed the world had raised him above his previous station; his face and body had become weather-beaten, and hardened from rain, earth, stone, wind and tree. Having now reached his twentieth year it became as clear as the Sorpha that those past ages with his family had been spent in restlessness. Even Estra had recalled that Lampaea's entry to the world had begun in screaming like no other and with his eyes open, claiming that he had cried out for release and his eyes eager to devour the life before him with sights and smells and tastes. Although it may also have been the matter at hand, the matter in which his sister had appeared before him on very suspicious terms, that encouraged his expression to be so grave.

'And what?' said Feletra inquisitively, sensing from his conduct there was something he was not telling her. 'What else as well as travelling?'

'There was nothing else. I just travelled,' came the reply.

'You were travelling in search of something, perhaps? I know your eyes when you hide away, Lampaea –'

'And I know yours!' said Lampaea, raising his voice unexpectedly.

Feletra was slightly startled. 'What?'

'You are hiding more from me than I am from you, you cannot expect me not to notice it. Did you want me to forget that I found you in Fawntree? With no explanation?'

There came a long, droning pause from both parties. When Feletra averted her gaze he returned to the spit.

'There is some natsa and bread over by that tree,' he said, gesturing without giving eye contact. As she slowly made her way up the opposite side of the clearing she came across the base of a tree that formed a large cove between two uplifted roots, large enough for Lampaea to store most foodstuffs there, like a pantry, and at the forefront Feletra extracted a parcel neatly wrapped in cloth. As she sat down atop the hill and began to unfold it she watched Lampaea at work intently. He had managed to sustain a small flame that now grew steadily and spread to lick the dry tinder logs hungrily.

'You said this was Elenia Forest?' said Feletra after what felt like an age.

'Yes. Around eight or nine leagues west of Fawntree to the forest front. Although we are at least twelve from there. The heart of Elenia.'

'I remember reading about this place, how so many admired its beauty, I can see now what they meant, reading about it is not enough to appreciate it.'

'There are few who do, I have always thought this forest is sorely undervalued,' replied Lampaea shortly, his mood clearly affected by his sister's stubbornness to divulge.

Feletra looked down at the bread and natsa she was eating. The bread was sweet from being kept close to the fruit yet retained the soft wheat texture. To flavour bread with natsa was a widely-used delicacy in Enphiah and popular at breakfast time or late supper.

'Why did you choose to stay in a forest? As beautiful as it is, it doesn't seem entirely convenient, Lampaea.'

'I enjoy being out of doors and am capable of making my own space this way, with no rules but my own and no one to peer over my shoulder.'

'You were going to tell me something before,' said Feletra pryingly, 'what was it?'

'Whatever news I have, I should think that yours has twice as much interest.'

'That may be,' answered Feletra staunchly, 'but I would

rather hear of yours first.'

Lampaea stood up and looked at her.

'Very well,' he said rather carelessly like their father, although Feletra was too curious at that moment to have noticed. He crossed over to the spears and withdrew one from the ground; after checking it was suitably sharp he passed by Feletra who was finishing the bread and continued without a word into the trees behind her.

Feletra watched him over her shoulder.

'Yes, then?' she called, expecting him to stop, turn and speak to her, but when he did not and walked further and further away she rose from where she sat and ran after him.

'Where are you going?' she said, irritated at being ignored.

'Hunting,' he replied. 'Go back to the clearing and watch the fire. I may be a long while.'

'You said you'd tell me –'

'Later.'

But then Feletra stopped and looked at him sceptically.

'I promise,' Lampaea said to reassure her, 'now go back.'

Feletra then ceased following him and observed as he drifted silently between the noble and tall trees, until he disappeared into the fruitful undergrowth like a shadow, his movement and sound all immediately unperceived. When Feletra returned to the clearing she sat down upon the log and sighed. Picking up a stick she twirled it idly between her fingers before throwing it away.

The fire blazed in a dance that twisted or weaved to form strange and unfamiliar shapes, caught quickly once in the cage of her eye and then gone again. All in what seemed to be a moment extended, Feletra captured the flickering image of a beautiful horla, draped in flame and burning powerfully. In the same instant that it was gone, she heard the cry of the creature, although it came from behind the hill of the clearing. Leaving the log and the fire, she darted to the top of the hill and looking down saw that a narrow stream wound its length through the trees and trickled down white rocks.

Beside the stream a horla was tethered to a tree. She removed the loop of rope from its neck and stroked its mane tenderly before sitting down at its hooves by the stream. The water ran by as if it had a life and voice of its own, speaking softly in free whispers that glided peacefully like the quiet morning birds in flight, just beneath the pink clouds. Feletra admitted to herself that the water was not as beautiful as the Sorpha, and perhaps it never would be, but what she did know is that just watching this stream made her feel content inside and at ease, whereas the Sorpha never evoked such emotions of tranquility, even before the curse had begun.

There she stayed for a long time, sighing every so often as the breeze touched her warmly and passed on, while Pytheria slowly sank lower and lower and blinked at her dark-lashed eyes through the swaying open gaps of leaves. The horla had wandered about during this time, never going far, eating this and that off bushes, nudging Feletra affectionately on occasion, sipping from the stream until, when dusk was settling, it had ventured further away, under where the canopy had grown thicker. Feletra noticed just in time before the creature had vanished entirely from sight.

As she set off to bring the horla back, she took note of how dark it had become, and Lampaea had not jested when he said he would be a long time; Pytheria was now blocked by the density of the forest. She did not want to lose the clearing, and so looked back all the time in an attempt to remember the way she had come, although the closer she thought she was coming to the horla, the further it appeared to be from her. She did not realise how very like her the beast was, curious and eager, but always in the wrong time and place. As she sped up and ran the last few paces she finally caught hold of its mane and tried to steer the other way, but the horla did not comply, instead it stood stock still, and did not even blink as its eyes were fixed on some dark shrubbery ahead. Feletra strained to see what might be there; the breeze came again, but not warm as it had been by the stream. Cold yet light, it swam uneasily through the trees and bristled the black undergrowth like a knife slicing mercilessly into the air.

Then she saw that something was moving within it; a front leg extended outwards, and what appeared to be a head followed. Once her presence had been detected it fixed its steely gaze forward on her.

Feletra and the horla remained frozen as the creature before her slowly began to lower its head as a predator would, and then emitted a menacingly deep growl.

At that moment, the horla reared up on its hind legs and fled back the way they had come – Feletra had no choice but to follow and raced after it. Not once did she look back.

As the edge of the clearing and the stream approached she managed to stop the horla and then looked about nervously in every direction. After a while, when it felt safe, she guided the horla back to the stream and replaced the rope about its neck. Together they were still wary and eyed every tree and bush with suspicion; and when Feletra peered down into the centre of the clearing she noticed that the fire had gone out, a few wisps of stray smoke escaping into the air.

Feletra observed the sullen remains of the fire and incompetently attempted to rekindle it, but to no avail, and so she resigned to the log once more and stared into the ashes. As Pytheria left the day behind, Lampaea finally returned, carrying the carcass of a female deer with him.

Feletra rose to her feet abruptly.

'Why is the fire out?' Lampaea asked initially, setting down the carcass and sighing as he took up the flint and steel to start a spark again.

Feletra hesitated.

'I saw something further down in the forest,' she said.

Lampaea looked over his shoulder at her.

'You left the clearing?'

'I had to. The horla was wandering off.'

'What? Did you remove the rope?' said Lampaea, then quickly checking to see if the horla was tethered again.

'It was just for a short while, I was sitting beside the stream when it started walking off –'

'She. The horla is a female,' Lampaea corrected.

'Yes, well I followed her to bring her back and that was when I saw something,' said Feletra as Lampaea managed to encourage a small flame.

'What?'

'I don't know what it was, an animal of some kind, but...strange and fierce; we ran before it could do anything, but for sure it could have had us both in a second.'

'There are many things in Elenia, in any forest in fact. Though you most likely saw a wolf.'

'I have seen what wolves look like, Lampaea, and even in the dark I know that was no common wolf. It was much bigger.'

'We shall leave it to be guesswork then,' said Lampaea coolly as he began slicing into the deer carcass with a knife.

'Aren't you afraid that something like that could attack us in the night?' said Feletra worriedly.

'For the time that I have stayed here, nothing has attacked me.'

Feletra did not know what to say; she felt vulnerable, yet at the same time safe because she was with Lampaea. On watching her blank expression, Lampaea said, 'There is a common saying for those who live in a wood: "In the morning, your skins will thank your ears if danger is by."'

'What does that mean?'

'It means...' he began, adjusting the spit, 'that we will always hear the creatures we fear before we see them. Often there will be a prominent or unfamiliar cry that we hear, and so our ears will prepare us, and save us. This only applies to forest animals of course. As it is, there has been no such cry that I have heard in this forest.'

Feletra returned to sit back down on the log; she knew inside that what she had seen was dangerous but felt unsure whether to fear the prospect of it or not. Nonetheless she chose not to pursue an argument over it, as Lampaea would frequently win them bluntly and quickly, and that was a clever, witty little attribute from their mother.

'Will you tell me now?' said Feletra.

'Tell you what?'

'You know what. Before you went hunting you said you would tell me what else you had been doing beside travelling this past year.'

Lampaea glanced at her and paused; after leaving the flank cut in a set position on the spit he sat upon the ground opposite her.

'Do not think that I left home not to travel, for I did, and have enjoyed every moment of seeing Enphiah. I did however, try to find something, and I am still searching.'

'Searching for what? A treasure of some kind?' Feletra asked.

Lampaea smiled a little.

'She is to me.'

Feletra stared at him in surprise and intrigue.

'She? It's a girl you've been trying to find?'

'Yes, but I have had no luck thus far.'

'But who is she?' Feletra questioned eagerly, 'Do any of us at home know of her?'

'I think you should do. Do you remember not long before I left, the girl that kept coming to the River Kestors?'

Feletra's eyes widened in realisation.

'She is the one you are searching for then?'

'Yes. The times when she always appeared outside our house was when she visited her aunt and uncle, the couple that live not far north of us, although she told me that her home was in Betharanei. We both had a desire to travel, and agreed that we would go together, and so when I left at sixteen I went to Betharanei to find her, but she was already gone. Her mother said she had left unexpectedly, and had left me a note. I still have it with me.'

He dipped a hand into a front pocket and withdrew a letter that he handed to Feletra to read

My Lampaea,

Forgive my leaving sooner than what was planned, I was

drawn into East Acro, near to Saph Nehn. Come find me there.

Halemedra.

'The note...it's so short,' said Feletra.

'Yes, I too was surprised at that. We've exchanged letters before, and they were always long and full of enthusiasm...I felt that something might have been wrong, as she didn't even give a reason why she left, so I set off immediately for Acro and searched all around Saph Nehn as she said, but there was no sign of her. No one had seen or heard of her. After that I did not know what to do; I travelled around and after staying in Ferin I decided to return to Betharanei and made back west, which is why I'm here now.'

'So, you are returning to Betharanei to see if she went back home?'

Lampaea nodded. 'If she's not there either...I think I'll have seen enough to know that something is not right. But I'll not stop looking for her now.'

Feletra gazed back down at the note, re-read it once more, and then stopped this time as her eyes rested on the name. She knew there was something she had heard about it not long ago.

'Halemedra...' she said aloud to herself. Lampaea looked up expectantly. She felt a strong familiarity to the name and stared hard at the paper as she struggled to remember.

And then it came to her.

'Halemedra – of course!' she exclaimed, 'Halemer's daughter!'

'You know her mother?' said Lampaea in some shock.

'Yes, I do! Halemer befriended me in Betharanei, she allowed me to stay in her house, and in the Valley House was where she told me of Halemedra –'

'I don't understand, what did she tell you of her?'

'Just that she was making for the east of Acro as the letter reads, but the fact is that Halemedra has not returned home to Betharanei as you think she has. She was not there when I was anyway. If you went to Betharanei now I think it would be a wasted journey.'

Lampaea looked resentful of the whole situation and almost for Feletra's confirmation, he was at a loss. 'Perhaps she means to avoid me.'

'No, I do not believe that, although I do believe your first guess, that something is wrong. Think, Lampaea. Her letter was far too short and it gave no reason at all to her actions. And she has made for East Acro, and you must remember that Acro borders Eastern Enphiah, Setra of which shares the greatest stretch of leagues. Do you not suspect anything?'

Lampaea looked at her gravely over the fire.

'It seems a little far-fetched, Feletra...' he said steadily.

'But it is possible, don't you think?'

'It's possible, yes...but I would need more to believe that Setrans were involved in Halemedra's disappearance, and why would they target her if that were true?'

Feletra fell silent. Lampaea was right; as much as their reputation was against them, the Setrans had little motivation for taking a travelling girl captive, although the poor likelihood of that notion only provoked further thought of her whereabouts.

When the deer was ready the two of them ate quietly and without discussion. The night was a cold one as there were no clouds above them and the stars blinked down in the circle of sky that the clearing permitted. White eyes in a black, absorbing face, they sat and peered out from under the dark blanket while others seemed to sway in it, next to a moon hidden somewhere under the youth of oaks and elms. Down upon the ground there was also life; the black widow scurried across the earth on quick dark needles, away from the flying sparks of the fire in loathing of it and back home to the white silk in the ivy bush, where important packages and deliveries needed to be sorted. On her way, the field mouse tiptoed by with caution, ears pricked to the quick little darting noises of the night and glinting black eyes that shone white and burning in the firelight. And every so often a black shape or two could be seen creeping on rapid wide wings to block the stars; they would feel so very close, and made no sound.

'What are they?' said Feletra, looking to the skies. Lampaea followed her gaze and watched as another shape flew by.

'Bats,' he replied simply.

'We have bats at home, they're not *that* big!'

'They are here. The forest bats are always larger. Although I have seen other creatures on wings at night, not bats and larger than those.'

Feletra looked at him uneasily.

'Don't worry, nothing will attack us!' said Lampaea, laughing slightly at her anxiety.

Feletra tried to observe the obscured white moon, reduced to blinking at her, 'It's late.'

Lampaea only acknowledged, but Feletra no longer felt the fatigue; Elenia Forest seemed to awaken her, to lift the tire that her eyelids were plagued with before. It may have been the sudden contrast she was presented with, moving from a deathly, exposed barren land to a lively and colourful forest. Alternatively, it may merely have been due to seeing her brother again. The relief and fright that had flooded her heart on suddenly finding him in Fawntree was an odd mixture. And then she recalled the event in the town, realising she was still perplexed.

'What happened in Fawntree?' she said. 'When everyone was running from something?'

Lampaea looked up at her with his deep-set eyes and wondered how he should answer.

'There was a scare,' he said finally.

'A scare of what though?'

'A preathin. They thought there was one in the town.'

Feletra recognised the name somewhere in the depths of her memory, there was some sort of tie to the old war, but she was otherwise dumbfounded. Lampaea guessed she might have been.

'A what?'

'Preathin. You don't remember, do you? Many people don't like to think of them if they can.'

'I last heard about the war stories in length from Mother when I was ten or eleven, I know she told us about the preathins but I don't recall. I have never seen panic like in Fawntree, they must be very feared to clear an entire town.'

'What emotion they evoke goes beyond fear,' said Lampaea, meeting her gaze once more.

'But what are they? A race of men?'

'Men? No. Even men do not have the capacity for evil such as theirs.'

'Creatures then?'

'Yes, although I know that men have used them in the

past, unleashed them even, as I don't suppose it would be easy to control one preathin, let alone thousands of them.'

'What men? The Easterners?'

'Yes. They used preathins and bred them as part of their army. The armies of the West and Mid Enphiah had never seen them before, they thought they were strange and weak, when in fact they were far more powerful than anticipated, forcing our soldiers that were initially stronger and greater in number, to be pushed back for several years. The preathins caused incredible devastation on more than one occasion in the Nyvean War.'

'How did our armies overcome them?' said Feletra, listening intently.

'Ah, well figuring out how that could be achieved consumed a fair portion of the entire war really. Through much toil and death. The east continued to use the preathins, more so than their own men. There were five major battles in which they continued to slaughter us relentlessly, from which the Five Graves were named. Do you know them?'

Feletra shook her head, and so Lampaea went on.

'The Five Graves are the deathbeds from those five battles of our men. The first is in Penthor, the second and third in Beltro, the fourth in Acro and the fifth in Delica. There are no settlements built on any of them, no houses or villages, and some say the spirits of the preathins still prey on those of the dead soldiers and torment them.'

Lampaea's eyes were so distant it was as if he were speaking of his own brothers.

'The west and the midland were known for their strategies,' he said in procession, 'and they did not hesitate to try new ones when others failed, yet of course they were never any of them a strong enough match for the preathins, and so after those five battles there was a great meeting of minds between our lands, conducted by the two great rulers, Nago and Rukurehn, that was named The Lloriad Web. It was in that meeting that the men of Ferin made the decision that the only way was to capture some of the creatures and discover what made them such a powerful enemy. It was eventually agreed upon, and some Drohans and Beltrorns would help the Ferinians to bring back at least one preathin.'

'And they succeeded, yes?' said Feletra.

'Yes, they managed to capture two without the eastern army knowing.'

'And what did they find?'

'It took a very long time, the Ferinians seemed to be the ones who knew what to look for in them, and so it was left up to them. And then they began to notice patterns in certain behaviour. The preathins were kept caged and always if someone was close enough their behaviour was erratic and menacing, and whenever they had finished studying them for a day, one soldier would stay there as a guard. Yet there was one guard who fell asleep, and the preathins calmed down. They became...almost stationary. The guard was caught by another who viewed the scene from afar, and reported the change back to his masters. The Ferinians deduced that the preathins detected prey by feeling desire from others.'

'Desire?' said Feletra, bewildered, 'I don't understand, how does that fit with the sleeping guard?'

'The mind is shut off when a person sleeps,' Lampaea explained, 'therefore they feel no desire, except during the dream state. So, as unhelpful as it proved to be, one was only safe from a preathin in dreamless sleep.'

Feletra's imagination began forming many an image from what she had just been told.

'What do they look like?' she asked.

'That, I cannot answer, and I hope I never can. I wouldn't like to face one.'

'Wait, I think I'm starting to remember more of this story, were the preathins not all killed? We won the war, I thought they became extinct?'

'People *like* to think that, yet there is no reason not to suspect otherwise, in my opinion that is. There has not been a preathin scare in any land before now, and although word will spread of it from Fawntree, I am also certain it will not be believed that one has been sighted.'

'Why? Surely it's a serious matter –'

'Yes, it is, very serious. And that is why its rumour will not last long, because people don't want to believe it. In this age, everyone seems to hear what they want to hear; whatever doesn't adhere to that is blanked out. Informing these people of anything remotely threatening is like spilling water on ice to them; they can't really see it, but it's still there, spreading and solidifying without them even noticing. Such is the ignorance of our age.'

Feletra fell into deep thought after that and tried to picture in her mind what a preathin might look like, shuddering at the thought of meeting one, feeding off her own desire...she wondered how she had come to forget about this race so easily, she could always recall her mother's stories so well, especially those that were true. Perhaps she had fallen prey to the ignorance of the age, as Lampaea had suggested so cynically, blocking out the undeniable details that were considered all too monstrous and frightful to admit. Or perhaps Estra had taken the consideration into her own hands, shortened the story at this point so they would all sleep better at night.

'There is much I've told you tonight, Feletra,' said Lampaea, 'now will you tell me your side?'

Feletra stared at him through the dying fire.

'I will tell you that the next night.'

Chapter 8
The Student of Elenia

A normal awakening from the comforts of a bed familiar to her once involved Feletra opening her eyes in quick succession (as well as irritation) to Lampaea dripping cold water from squeezing a wet cloth onto her face. Therefore, it was with some surprise when she awoke in the same fashion after coping gratefully without it for the past years. His laugh followed as it usually would have done at home; his was the type that was infectious, his victim would always laugh with him, and immediately forgive him.

For her breakfast Lampaea had cooked Feletra something which he appeared to have forgotten was not seen or grown back in Elpura.

Feletra looked down at what she had been given and prodded it curiously.

‘I think I have seen these growing somewhere nearby but...what are they?’

Lampaea turned and smiled.

‘Mushrooms. Try them.’

Feletra did so and found no complaint. Throughout the morning and into the afternoon there was very little to do. She washed in the stream, lay about wherever there was sunlight and when Lampaea was busy she would spend time with the horla, which she named Elpura to remind her of home, and removed the rope to allow her some free roaming. Feletra kept a closer watch on her this time, although it seemed that the fright of the previous night had had an effect, as she did not wander far from Feletra.

In the late afternoon Lampaea was equipped with his bow and arrows again, and also carried the cage draped in white fibres that Feletra had noticed before.

'Are you going out again?' Feletra asked, eyeing the cage in his left hand.

'Yes, just for extra. I won't be as long as last night.'

Feletra hesitated, and then said, 'Can I go with you?'

Lampaea glanced her up and down once, smiled lightly and shook his head.

'No,' he said bluntly, but Feletra became adamant.

'Why not?' she demanded.

'I need as much quiet as possible when hunting. That becomes less likely with two people.'

'I can be quiet though! And I can give you space.'

'Why do you want to come?' said Lampaea.

'To give me something to do. And I should like to see you hunt.'

Lampaea stopped to consider briefly, and then sighed in resignation. 'You can come, but *please* try to be quiet,' he said reluctantly, and Feletra beamed with triumph.

'Should I bring anything?' she asked.

'Are you hunting?' Lampaea answered.

'No.'

'Then you don't need anything, do you?'

Feletra only smiled in reply, still happy he allowed her to accompany him. He led her deep into the forest, far away from the clearing, where the canopy grew so thick that the afternoon could have been mistaken for evening. Feletra noticed there was much more movement and rustling in the undergrowth around this area, and that the further they traipsed the more insects she could spot, each one more elaborate than the last.

'Is there good reason for choosing this part of the forest?' asked Feletra quietly as she batted away another fly.

'Yes,' was the reply, 'the canopy gives greater cover here, so it's darker and the prey is less likely to see you immediately. Also, there are more animals moving about, and so they create a diversion to any noise that we might make. And, you may have noticed that the tree trunks have become thicker as well, that means easier hiding for the hunter. Not only that, more prey will be found where there are thick trees, for the same reason, to be hidden.'

Feletra was taken aback at how much thought he had spent on it.

'A true predator if ever I did see one,' she said admiringly.

After a time Lampaea selected a suitable spot and they squatted down among the bushes and weeds.

'Now what?' said Feletra.

'Now we wait.'

Feletra anticipated correctly what turned out to indeed be a rather long wait when the hours of dusk unfolded, or so she thought, it was all too difficult to tell the time of day in this area of the forest. She tried her very best to remain as still as possible, although it became increasingly difficult and unbearable not to scratch where the insects landed on her or flick them away. And yet all the while Lampaea did not waver, sitting poised in the very same position like a statue. He threw looks of disapproval at Feletra's constant fidgeting.

After what seemed like an entire age, Lampaea spied a rabbit in the distance; it was close enough to strike. As he slowly raised an arrow to the bow, Feletra became alerted to the situation and attempted to peer over the bushes, but

Lampaea could see she was too easily seen and gently pushed her back down. Instead, she tried forming a gap in the leaves to see, but now she made too much noise, and Lampaea was forced to stop her.

Feletra glowered at her brother and sat down as he silently instructed her to. As she watched him prepare to release the arrow, she picked some blue flowers nearby and twisted them about in her fingers.

Lampaea was ready at that moment, when – ‘Ahh!’

The arrow was given, but the rabbit had already darted off. Lampaea turned to Feletra, but then saw that the flowers she had picked were edging and pushing their way beneath the skin in her wrist, blood trickling out where they made entry.

Immediately he knelt down and yanked them out. Feletra gasped at the pain and held her arm shakily as he tore a strip off his hood and wrapped her wrist in it.

‘Come on,’ he said calmly, leading her back to the clearing.

‘But what about –?’

‘It’s getting too late for that now and your disturbance would have us waiting till midnight for another sighting.’

‘I’m sorry, it’s just –’

‘I know.’

Quick footed as they were on the way back, it did not take long to reach the clearing. Lampaea knew it would be darker when they returned, and so had purposefully left the fire burning before they had left. Setting himself down on the log next to Feletra, he removed the bandage to examine the damage.

‘How was I to know a flower could be so dangerous?’ said Feletra.

'You should not tamper with what you don't know,' replied Lampaea wisely.

'And what was it then?'

'Wypnon; once touched it will try to squeeze under your skin entirely, and then into the bloodstream. As soon as they are completely in, there is no coming out. After around a week the colour of the affected limb is lost and turns white, and all feeling is gone, rendering it useless. You should be fine though, just keep it covered for a few days.'

Feletra complied by replacing the strip of material from Lampaea's hood, only too thankful that he had been there to help, when she thought of the consequence in which her arm was close to resulting in nothing more than a pointless, swinging dead thing at her side. From that point, she felt desperate to know more of the unknown, for if something as meagre as a small flower was so dangerous then she shuddered to think what other living things, in the forest or not, were capable of, such as the menacing creature she had faced the other night with Elpura, and then she remembered the even more traumatising situation under the Valley House in Betharanei; the long and thin bony hands that had grasped her tight, the great shriek in her ears. The images of it flashed by in her memory, but they were just flashes of darkness...

'Lampaea,' said Feletra, purposefully trying to stop thinking about the Valley House, 'could you teach me to hunt?'

Lampaea stared at her, uncertain of whether she was serious or not.

'Teach you to hunt?' he repeated with some doubt.

'Or to defend myself even, or both! Father taught you how to fight, he started my training too but then I left before

I could finish.'

'Father trained you to fight?' Lampaea laughed in disbelief. 'How did you manage that?'

'That doesn't matter, what matters is that I never finished, but you know it all, you could teach me. Please, Lampaea,' she said earnestly.

'Why do you want to know how to defend yourself?'

'Because...because –' but then Feletra faltered, and Lampaea formed the words for her.

'Because you are not returning home in a hurry, are you?'

Feletra did not answer, but maintained her gaze with his, understanding what he was to say next, yet fearful of how much she should tell him, for it was inevitable that the conversation and questions would soon come to pass.

'I think,' Lampaea began, 'that it is time you tell me your story, Feletra, and exactly why you are here.'

There was a deathly silence that had frozen between them, and Feletra would have wished for anything, a light wind at least, to steal over her at that moment, anything to suggest that life still existed in this penetrating stillness that she so loathed. At the thought of exposing her secrets, there was a coldness that came so suddenly that the very flames of the fire might have iced over. In her hesitation, which felt more like a year, her mind had never worked so rapidly, flicking through a thousand images and words before comprising a suitable answer.

And then she looked into Lampaea's patient face once more, understanding that, in all fairness, she owed him some sort of explanation.

What will he think? Would he send her back home after all? Will he even believe her when she tells him what has happened? It had been years since she had last spent any time with Lampaea, she had no way of knowing how he would react to such news, he was clearly more grounded now, he viewed the world as a man, not a child anymore. Feletra was unsure if such a change would work in her favour or not, but she could not ignore him forever.

'It began with Leao, he had fallen prey to an illness like we had never seen before,' she said, surprised at the confidence in her tone.

'What? I had no idea he was sick.'

'You wouldn't have done, we had no way of sending an ebrat to you, no one knew where you were. Leao was close to death.'

Lampaea looked downcast and hung his head in what appeared to be shame, 'And now? Please say he is well again?'

'He is well, but only because Ataleka and I brought him water from the Sorpha –' Lampaea's expression instantly turned to one of alarm, 'wait, don't judge us, we had no choice. If you had seen him you would have understood why our hand was forced. But…there was an accident at the Sorpha. Lampaea, I am responsible for something terrible.'

'What happened? Tell me everything.'

And so she proceeded to tell him everything, as he asked. From the very start with Ataleka and herself sneaking out to the Sorpha, and even Leao's unexplained behaviour, she unfolded every little detail as if they were tiny pieces of paper, each enclosing her next sentence. Once she had begun there was no stopping, leaving Lampaea barely any time to question in between, although he made certain that he listened intently. The moon passed through its phases of the night just as quickly or as slow as Feletra passed through those of her tale. She had not forgotten any of it, she spoke of the mysterious man and woman outside the house, the strange attack that Ataleka endured, and then delved into the events that occurred once she had left home. It disturbed her the most to relive the memory of the Valley House and the thing lurking beneath it, and Lampaea noticed that her speech became quieter and slower when she described it, but she knew that the only way of going forward was to tell him and confess all.

'I did not expect to find you in Fawntree though,' she said once she had finished, 'what were you doing there if you are staying here?'

'I missed the taste of bread and some other foods, and so went to get some supplies. When the town descended into a mass panic I stopped to try and see if there truly was a preathin, not that I knew what to expect if I did. But enough of me. Feletra, why are you so sure that you and Ataleka have the Sorpha's curse?'

For a moment, Feletra felt as if nothing she had said had been taken in by Lampaea at all. 'I've told you!' she cried in frustration. 'What else could have caused that to happen to Ataleka on the fields? And my vision was even more certain!'

'But the way you describe what happened to him, it sounds nothing like the curse. You remember what Mother said it entails, and binding the body, or crushing, whatever it was, is not a part –'

'But what of the unexplained bleeding? That *is* a symptom; and what if this invisible binding is the cause of it being unexplained?'

Lampaea stopped to think, for she had made a valid

point.

'It's possible,' he accepted, 'but then, why haven't you suffered anything yet?'

It was Feletra's turn to think now. She tried remembering back, and realised that nothing had happened to her like Ataleka.

'I don't know,' she said slowly. 'I haven't felt anything...Mother said the curse involved the gradual loss of the five senses, but mine have only improved.'

'When you were on the plains?'

'Yes, I could feel it. Everything was clearer and more sensitive. And yet it doesn't make any sense...perhaps it does not happen straight away; because the curse extends life, it may be that it hasn't had any effect on me yet.'

'Or...it may be that you are not cursed at all,' said Lampaea reasonably.

'No Lampaea, I know I am,' Feletra replied indignantly 'why else would the vision –'

'The vision, Feletra. You are certain this was telling you what you have to do? And not just a dream?'

'I have never been more certain about anything, and it was *not* a dream. Far too real to be a dream, yet so indescribable. It was a message.'

'What if it was Blackcraft?'

'What do you mean? How could –'

'Craftsmen can be very powerful. With enough strength, they can penetrate a person's mind, manipulate it.'

'Then, why me?'

'I don't know, but it is a possibility nonetheless. I will not deny that you received that vision for a reason, as I know you wouldn't have left home if it were a mere dream. As for the Valley House, I cannot begin to imagine what creature it was that attacked you. I do not think I will ever feel the same again the next time I walk in, knowing that.'

'I could never return there,' said Feletra, 'not knowing what lay beneath me.'

'I'm glad you met Emmet, I also know him.'

'You do?' Feletra replied, although not too shocked, having known that Lampaea visited Betharanei more than once. 'He is a good friend, he said he had a younger brother though, did you see him when you went?'

Lampaea suddenly looked uncertain and he pondered on a response.

'Emmet's brother died, Feletra, fifteen years ago when he was thirteen. His brother was only eight.'

At these words, Feletra slowly looked aside distantly into the dark trees, feeling terribly foolish and thoughtless for speaking to Emmet before as if his brother had been alive and in Betharanei with them.

'He did not tell me,' she said, 'but how?'

'Lack of nutrition; eventually he became fatally ill and could not stomach anything. Even now Emmet believes that he failed him and has felt nothing but guilt.'

Something suddenly dawned on Feletra. Emmet's situation with his brother was not so different from her own with Ataleka. And the thought of failure to him had never crossed her mind until now; it seemed unbearable. So badly she did not want to fail him, for although she was hunting for the cure for both of them, she only ever thought to attain it for him, it was his life that was the more significant.

'I know you are thinking of Ataleka,' said Lampaea, interrupting her thoughts. 'Never think you will fail him, or yourself.'

'Lampaea, do you believe me?' asked Feletra, and her

brother looked fixedly into her eyes without blinking. He tilted his head slightly.

'Yes,' came the reply, 'every word.' And Feletra smiled warmly, as if she had fallen into a safe cradle. 'I think that if you had wanted me to believe a lie, you would not have made it as elaborate or have given so much detail. Not to mention, you could never lie as much or as well as me or Skepreo.'

Feletra snickered briefly, it was a fault she could live with. Suddenly she greatly appreciated the support and security she felt with Lampaea, if not also the simple sensation of happiness that she had so missed since the curse began, but then her smile faded again as she thought of an invisible journey ahead.

'How am I supposed to succeed for Ataleka when I have no idea where to go?' she said helplessly.

'You mean the cure?'

'No, I know where the cure is. It's in those caves I saw in the vision, but the caves themselves...'

'Tell me about them again. You said they were guarded?'

'Yes, all wearing thick clothes, and they had weapons.'

Lampaea shook his head, supposedly trying to piece everything together.

'The only guarded caves I can think of are the Lucrin Caverns.'

'The caverns!' said Feletra, her eyes widening. 'What if the cure itself is lucrin?'

'No,' Lampaea replied bluntly.

'Why not?'

'If it were then people would be using it liberally.'

'But it's all guarded, nobody is allowed to take any.'

'It is guarded because it is expensive and the wealthy

would have its source protected. I just don't think it can be lucrin; the cure is believed to be a myth, whereas everyone knows that lucrin is as real as you and I. The properties of lucrin have been measured over and over for thousands of years, if it were a cure that kind of discovery could never have been kept a secret with how frequently it is used elsewhere.'

Feletra looked downhearted and sighed. The fire before them seemed to have become smaller. She stared at it in disappointment as another long silence was absorbed by the trees and swept over them. It was like a motionless wind with a biting cold, when suddenly, Feletra beheld with her own eyes a crystallised layer of ice feed upon the fire to spread from the logs below to the very tips of the flames. It held momentarily as Feletra almost gaped in awe before disappearing again, released to a sway of movement once more.

'Did you...?' she said vaguely to Lampaea, who looked up.

'What?' he asked, but then Feletra shook her head, now unsure of whether she imagined it, and she said, 'Nothing.'

'Wait,' said Lampaea suddenly, Feletra expecting that he had seen something after all, 'what was that story?'

'What story?'

'The story Mother used to tell us; it was about a cure, there was a rhyme to it.'

And then Feletra also remembered; there had indeed been a rhyme, although it had been so long since she had heard it that it was difficult to recall. The history book she read back home – it had detailed the same thing, Nago's cure. The story from the rhyme itself had involved the great gathering of Sturans that were named The Men at Dusk, who marched into Chriah to the caves alleged to hold the cure and finally dispel the secrets kept from them by launching an attack. The Chriahks however, were merciless and slaughtered them savagely, those few that survived were taken prisoner for life and tortured.

It then all became clear to her.

'It's Pyra...' said Feletra, almost aghast. Lampaea gave her a swift look to encourage her continuance. 'I remember now,' there was a second in which she basked in her own revelation, and then recited:

'Down in dark'd Chriah
Slept deceit and mystery
Dead be the thought
Hers the black history
Served they a limb
And served them a life
To the nameless men
Sworn blood by knife
Sank deep her stone home
In villager's mind
Yet high rose Lucrin shield
Greed a'festered bind
The Land of the Hidden
Bound true to name
For beneath the black roof
Sat miracle to shame
Cure to the wound
Cure to the age'd
Yet lightless and legend
Kept still and cage'd
Still darkness boxed

Blind of fox and wren
Dead be the thought
Down in Leohreten.'

'That was it. That was the rhyme,' said Lampaea, clicking his fingers, 'they say the Sturans recited it over and over in the Chriahk dungeons from the insanity of their torture. What if a myth of a story could have been truth? The part about the cure that is.'

'Well, I think these must be the caves, Lampaea,' said Feletra, 'everything makes sense. The rhyme even mentioned the cure itself! Do you think they'll be shown on the map?'

She reached over to her pack and withdrew Flior's map, unfolding it excitedly, but as she scanned Chriah, there was no sign of any caves.

'They're not on here,' she said, dispirited, but Lampaea spared no surprise.

'They wouldn't be. This only confirms our suspicions, that the story is not a lie at all. If the Chriahks had nothing to hide then why aren't the caves on there? Mapmakers must, after all, comply to the land laws laid down by Lor and Penthor; in other words, maps are not accepted unless they display all landmarks and are completely accurate. No other land is obliged to have power over that law.'

'So how did Chriah get around it?'

'I imagine they would have sealed off the area reputed to hold the cure. They might not have power over mapping laws but they still have power over their own land and can do what they like with it, so even Lorahk and Penthoran officials cannot enter where they are not allowed. That is just a theory, of course; I'm sure there are other possibilities why the caves are not shown on the map.'

'Unless...it truly was nothing more than a myth.'

'I know you do not believe that, Feletra. Your vision, remember?'

She nodded and then lowered her head to the map again, this time spotting something else in Chriah that gave hope.

'Leohreten,' she said slowly, 'this at least has a place on the map. And the last line of the rhyme: *"Down in Leohreten,"* this place is related to the caves, it must be. I think it is close by to them; if I could go there I might find some answers.'

'That seems the best thing to do.'

As Lampaea looked at Feletra he seemed to remind himself that not only was she too young to travel alone, but also that the matters with which she was involving herself were incredibly deep and dangerous. For him, it seemed readily decided that his course would now alter in the direction of Pyra, whether with or against the will of Feletra. Not even pure naivety could claim to the idea that she would not have made the slightest prediction of Lampaea's proposal to accompany her.

He was aware she had rejected Flior's companionship, and a rejection of his maturity and experience left little in the way of hope for him, however she had had her reasons, and Flior, he thought, was more submissive and less persuasive than he. Nonetheless he decided to leave these skills until the day when they were necessary, feeling that she'd be more likely to accept the idea that way, for he knew her stubbornness.

After an absence of conversation Feletra fell asleep and Lampaea carried her over to the scantily-made bed. Although he wanted her to rest, he wished she had stayed awake a little longer now, for he had forgotten to say 'yes' to her request.

Feletra discovered his decision quickly enough the next day when a bow was tossed at her feet. The majority of that day was spent away from the clearing, in the depths of the forest as Lampaea began a new teaching session. In the beginning, it was difficult for him to adapt to the role and pass on his own knowledge, and he expressed his impatience at Feletra on more than one occasion. After a time though, he thought of his father's methods, and how these proved to be effective in his own training. He soon became thorough in exploring the skill with her, and it was important to recognise where her weaknesses in it lay.

Feletra had an excellent aim; this could be seen in her poise and her eye-line alone, however it became noticeable to the trained perception that the target, when beheld by her mind, was always somewhat shaken, and Lampaea knew that this had all too often been the same downfall for himself in the past. The trouble was believing. If Feletra could not believe in the ability of the bow then she would never achieve perfection, therefore Lampaea adopted a particularly significant technique of Padryl's. It was a strange one, and only when he started using it himself did he understand how effective it proved to be. He asked her questions, only every now and then, sometimes before she released an arrow, sometimes after.

If a bow is a root, what is an arrow? he would say. A flower, she would sensibly reply. And if it was required, he would say something else, perhaps reminding her that although there was the flower, the stem should not be forgotten. The aim of such a practice was to imbue a sense of power and belief that should be divided equally between the bow, the arrow and oneself, for each was necessary. Thereby from achieving this the mind was able to work in conjunction with the eye.

'Why are you asking these questions?' Feletra asked finally.

'That is not for you to know just yet,' came the reply. It was important that the student was not informed of a reason, and how it helped them, as the mind became overpowered by it, and far too conscious of its effect, causing a steady focus to falter immediately. It had not been for a long time, until Lampaea was fully confident and could aim as a natural archer, that their father had revealed the secret behind the questions to him.

As the week wore on, so did Feletra's training. Lampaea thought it wise to begin with archery, as it was a light skill to learn, and as much as he tried he could not envisage his younger sister wielding a great sword with unquestioned talent. The idea of it was almost comical, if he was being honest with himself.

Her talent with the bow however, became incredibly defined with each day; the sharper her perception grew, the harder the questions became. Lampaea also began asking them at more awkward moments, mainly in the second just before the arrow was released, so as to test her accuracy.

'The bow is the heart. What is the arrow?'

'The blood.'

'If the arrow takes away the seed, what does the bow bring?'

'The wind.'

'If the bow is inside you, and the arrow outside you,

what are you?'

'I am nothing.'

At the same time as answering this question, Feletra had released the arrow; it had pierced the very centre of a flower that Lampaea had pinned to a tree for her. The flower was no larger than a thumbnail.

Lampaea smiled broadly as Feletra flexed the string on the bow, surprised at her own outcome.

'Now what?' she asked him.

'It's complete.'

'What is?'

'Your training with the bow.'

'What? How? Are you sure?'

'Never more certain. Your accuracy seems to be flawless, Fel.'

'But we have only spent a few days on it.'

'And you need no more. You've achieved in little over a week what others take months to perfect. What skill would you have next?'

As they conversed Lampaea went about collecting the arrows that Feletra had shot, with she tagging along behind him. For Feletra, her completion with the bow seemed to have come very fast, but she chose not to argue if her teacher was that certain that she was ready. Nevertheless, the sheer contrast to her training at home was incredible, she was utterly amazed with her own capabilities, the fact that she could finally be good at something.

'So I thought some use…with a sword, perhaps?' she said rather tentatively. Lampaea stopped and stared at her very gravely. She knew her success to learn the sword at home had dwindled to nothing more than a pipe dream, but things could have been different now, there was no Ataleka for competition, no desperately trying to prove every inch of her worth.

'A small sword even?' she knew herself that it was an ambitious thing to ask.

'I'm not trying to make you a killer, Fel. And we both know that swords aren't used for hunting. At least the bow can provide you with both defence and food.'

'Yes, I know. And I am no killer, it would just be for extra defence, like the way Father taught you. If he had enough faith in me then surely you can?'

'You must have been persuading him for a long time. This is sword wielding, it's dangerous.'

'Exactly, if someone drew a sword on me what chance would I stand to defend myself?'

'Who's going to be drawing a sword on you?' Lampaea said dubiously. 'And even if they did what reason would they have to attack a girl of sixteen who is no threat to them?'

'I'm going to Chriah, Lampaea. The very place I would avoid at all costs if I could. I've never met a Chriahk, but their reputation is strong against them. I would never feel safe confronting any one of them if I weren't prepared; who can know what they are capable of?'

It was true, inside Lampaea knew it, and by teaching her the secrets of the sword he was her best source of protection. It seemed he would let Feletra believe that he had no safer option but to teach her the defence, for still she did not appear to have considered the possibility that he would join her to Chriah. Yes, there was no way she stood a chance of protecting herself against those people, she needed him and she barely knew it yet. Lampaea gazed in thought at his sister; a stubborn, adamant girl, he knew that. If he could show her the stamina needed and just how fragile life became at the edge of a blade, perhaps she would feel more inclined to accept his help nearer the time of her leave.

‘Alright,’ he consented, ‘just the defence though, not direct attack.’

Although the day’s fatigue sat with her after the archery training, Feletra grinned all the way back to the clearing, though when they did reach it, Lampaea set aside his bow and quiver, retrieved his sword, and tossed a smaller short sword at her feet.

Feletra almost looked perplexed.

‘We start now?’

‘Yes. Pick it up.’

‘Why though? Can we not rest for tonight and start tomorrow?’

‘Do you think your opponent would adhere to that?’

Feletra picked up the sword a little reluctantly and held it out before her with her feet apart. Lampaea wanted to laugh. She even looked ridiculous with it.

He walked casually over to her and knocked the weapon out of her hand with little more than a flick of his own.

‘Now what are you going to do?’ he asked her.

Feletra made to retrieve her sword but Lampaea then held his by her throat.

‘There is nothing you can do, you would be dead,’ he answered for her, and although Feletra couldn’t see the blade, she could feel it hovering there by her flesh like some lethal animal, pulsating a hot blood that hungered to taste hers. This approach felt vastly different to Padryl’s, real and raw.

Finally, Lampaea withdrew.

'The enemy will not be giving you any chances, you cannot let them take the advantage,' he handed her the weapon again. 'Try and disarm me this time.'

Feletra edged forward towards him a little at first, Lampaea stamped his foot and she flinched. Then she made a charge. Her sword was held too low though; Lampaea bore down on it – it struck the ground and he kicked it away with ease.

'Never flinch or hesitate. Your opponent will be looking for that and use it against you,' he said as she picked up her discarded sword once more, which may as well have been rendered a plaything by Lampaea.

'I know,' Feletra said.

Her brother tossed his weapon to the floor.

'Try and attack me.'

'You said this was defence only?'

'I know, but just try. Don't worry, you won't hurt me.'

Feletra obediently made a second charge and felt more confident this time knowing she had the benefit, but it seemed this again was not the case. Lampaea hit the flat underside of the sword, casting it, as well as the arm wielding it, towards the sky, leaving him safe as he violently spun her round and pulled her in, grasped the hand around the hilt tightly and immediately the blade was at her throat again, cold and threatening.

Feletra gasped in fright at the sudden turn of events; held in the jaws of a human vice, she was instantly rendered helpless and immobile.

'Can you see,' said Lampaea, 'how there is never any power in the weapon itself, but only ever in the user? You were confident you could take me down, because you thought I could do nothing for myself. As the sole attacker, you thought only of yourself, and not of my reaction. Don't. You must always anticipate a reaction, a defence of any kind, even when they seem unaided.'

He released her. She touched her throat as if trying to feel her pulse still beating.

'You didn't give me a chance,' she breathed.

'No, I didn't. And I won't be giving any after this, either.'

'Why? How am I supposed to learn anything?'

'Trust me. There will be something you will learn.' Lampaea said this more to himself than to Feletra, perhaps in his high hope that whatever Feletra learned would only dissuade her from the sword, rather than encouraging her towards it. Although it may have been that Lampaea had forgotten some of his sister's determination, for the lesson continued into the early hours.

The next few days became weeks, all focused on the wielding of a small sword and hunting. Although Feletra made sufficient progress with hunting, her profession with the bow was not to be confused with that of the sword, for she still made little headway with the latter. Whilst she complained that her brother must be teaching her very differently to how their father would have done, Lampaea maintained that this was not the case and that she had a natural flair for the light and quick-handed nature of the bow; it was simply that she knew not how to meet the heavy demands of a sword duel and manage to combine this with agility.

Feletra was disheartened but did not let this show. Her skill for the hunt grew more pronounced with each day, she used this talent as a distraction, and enjoyed using the ship, which was the cage-like structure she had spied before. The web fibres were obtained from a particular spider known as the recorhix, as the web's scent was appealing to small animals, and it then acted as a sleep-inducing poison which was painless. Lampaea reassured Feletra that they themselves would be safe from the fibres; it required a much greater amount of the web to have any effect on them. He had learnt how to make a ship from other hunters he had met, although it was a rather slow method of catching a meal, and why it was called a ship no one could say.

For the coming days Feletra felt a turn in the wind and knew that she would soon have to leave. She warned Lampaea of this, who would only nod in response. It pained Feletra to turn her back on Elenia Forest, after becoming so accustomed to it, and she now began to look over Flior's map each night, planning her route. Lampaea then realised that Feletra was indeed not aware that he was also joining her, or perhaps she could have relied on him to direct her without the map. He sat down opposite her, and decided that it may be best to inform her early of his intention.

'Feletra –'

'Yes, I know what you're thinking,' she interrupted, 'the real route won't look as smooth as it does on a map and all that, but I am aware of that.'

'No, I was going to suggest that I come with you.'

Feletra's head was instantaneously lifted from the map, but before she could say anything Lampaea quickly continued:

'I know you don't want this and feel this is your fault to correct but the truth is, it's not. If you go to Pyra alone I am sure you will not return alive.'

Feletra crossly re-folded the map, a stony expression

marched forth across her young face, her eyes declared the battlefield ripe, 'Just because I am your sister, it doesn't mean I need protecting all the time!'

'Why can't you just stop being stubborn and try to see that you are vulnerable, whether you like it or not? I've already shown you how easily you could be killed.'

'I'm not like you, Lampaea,' Feletra retorted, standing up, 'not all of us cause enough trouble to risk death. What's more, no one has any reason to attack me, they'd just think I was a young girl travelling around Pyra.'

'No one your age travels around Pyra, they'd know that. And you're the worst liar there is. Chriahks see through everybody; you'll be at the height of suspicion.'

'Why can you never give me a chance to prove myself?'

'Chances get people killed,' said Lampaea, raising his voice, 'especially in Chriah. That land is not as pretty as it appears on a map and you need to realise that.'

'How would you know what it's like? You've never been there either.'

'Which is exactly why you can't take any chances!' Lampaea shouted. 'You have no idea what's out there and it's childish to think that you do!'

Lampaea's voice echoed around the clearing, but Feletra was silenced from retaliating as a deep and strange cry rang out across the trees from the west. It tickled Feletra's skin coldly as a group of bats emerged unexpectedly nearby and flew off towards the east.

'What was that?' Feletra said, though it was remarkable that Lampaea even heard her, as it was barely a whisper. Without knowing it, she had taken a step closer to him.

'I don't know,' said Lampaea, his previous anger all subsided, 'I've never heard that in Elenia before, yet I've never had to argue or shout in here before either; I think our voices may have alerted it.'

'*Our* voices?' Feletra repeated, 'You were the one shouting.'

'Feletra, don't start.'

'How are we supposed to sleep now knowing there's something out there?'

'We don't. At least, not the whole night; I'll stay up the first half of the night, and you the second.'

Lampaea made it clear in his tone that he was in no mood to listen to any more of Feletra's grievances, which she ascertained successfully without the need for further dispute, and let it rest. No amount of pride was worth alerting the beastly creature she had encountered weeks before to their presence now. She felt certain it must be that which she had seen with Elpura deeper in the forest, and wondered if Lampaea had since forgotten her account of the incident.

Despite the sinister cry, nothing approached the clearing as the night wore on. Feletra found it difficult to sleep whilst Lampaea watched, and when it was Feletra's turn to keep watch, it was no effort to wake her.

The winds seemed to have strengthened now, and it caused her to fetch a blanket for her shoulders. Lampaea, like the rest of the forest, slept silently, there was no sound from the morning birds as the dawn crept forward. The fear of the animal that shared Elenia with them enabled Feletra to remain wide awake, an onlooker peering into the clearing might have regarded her as some sort of small animal protecting its territory. She even felt small at that moment, and repeated her argument with Lampaea in her head. He had called her childish, and on reflection, perhaps she had been. It was time to start seeing what made sense, even when it might damage her pride or disagree with her opinion, it was time to start *listening.*

I rejected Flior, and look how much trouble I've ended up in already, she thought. She looked back at Lampaea, and smiled at how thankful she was just to have received his offer. The journey would be easier with her brother at her side, she was even surprised at her readiness to adopt humility, it felt unusual. She found herself now looking forward to telling him, he would be relieved at her change of heart.

Although it couldn't be seen through the trees, Pytheria had risen faster than expected. The sky above them was a fading pink, and then there came another distant cry.

Feletra jumped to her feet and Lampaea was immediately roused. The scare scrambled their rationale for a moment, believing it belonged to the same creature as the night before, but once they had sharpened their senses again they realised it was the sound of a horla. Sure to this assertion, the pounding of hooves became apparent, until they entered the clearing and a large black and white horla cantered forward before coming to a halt with another loud whinny.

Elpura had been greatly alerted to this call from the stream and they could hear her disturbing the water anxiously. Feletra and Lampaea were forced to step back and duck for the erratic behaviour of the horla, it appeared to be driven by raw fear. Lampaea calmed the fearful beast as best he could, but still it shifted its head this way and that and pawed the ground relentlessly.

'Where has it come from?' Feletra asked, keeping a safe distance.

'Nowhere amicable. This is Halemedra's horla, Fitaeba, I'd know him anywhere,' said Lampaea. He noticed a belt had been loosely tied around its midriff, but then saw that a piece of paper had been wrapped around the belt, held in place by a fraying piece of string.

'He's been sent to us,' Lampaea said lowly.

'What?'

'Look there, there's a note on him.'

As Lampaea edged forward towards Fitaeba's body, the horla watched him with wide eyes. He moved slowly closer, until he could place one hand on his neck and use the other to quickly detach the letter from the belt. Fitaeba grunted in hostility at him.

'Don't you recognise me, boy? It's me,' said Lampaea, an unsettling mix of comfort and confusion in his voice. Feletra stood eagerly before Lampaea as he unfolded the dirty paper and began to read.

He spent but a moment to scan it, and then looked away with an expression of horror. His hand dropped to his side with the letter still in it.

'What is it?' said Feletra, becoming deeply concerned.

He handed her the letter aimlessly. She quickly read:

Lampaea,

Come quick to Setra. I am thrown. They blackened me with oiled pits, they bled me on Setran soil, I bleed till you find me. Maliste, the new one.

Come quick to Setra.

Halemedra.

Lampaea sat holding his head on the log; he seemed to be debating with himself to the point of facing a crisis. Halemedra's disappearance had finally been solved; Setrans had taken her, though for what reason was still a mystery.

Feletra suddenly realised why Lampaea sat looking so lost instead of immediately galloping away on Fitaeba to Setra to find her. He was now faced with a terrible decision, either to find Halemedra and leave Feletra, or to accompany Feletra and leave Halemedra. Feletra acknowledged the severity of the situation, her plight was nothing at this moment compared to Halemedra's, it seemed her moment to tell Lampaea of her need for his companionship to Pyra had been missed. She readily made the decision for him.

'Lampaea,' she said gently, 'you must go to her.'

Lampaea looked around despairingly.

'But I cannot leave you to go to Chriah alone.'

'Yes, you can. I am making this decision easy for you. Please, go to Setra.'

'How can I?'

'Halemedra needs you more than I do.'

Lampaea paused. Feletra looked down at the letter again.

'What is Maliste? She says it is the new one of something.'

'I don't know,' Lampaea answered despondently.

'Well, whatever it is, she's in danger. I did not think the Setrans were still like this.'

'I don't think any of Enphiah knows it. If it becomes public knowledge Eastern Enphiah may pay for it dearly, it could easily upset the balance of peace which Lor and Penthor had fought so hard to maintain. This is serious.'

‘Which is why you have to go there,’ Feletra finalised.

‘Feletra –’

‘No, you will go to Setra straight away. Lampaea, there is no choice to this, she could be dying.’

He had to admit this was true. Halemedra may, in fact, already be dead. After walking to and fro in the clearing, and deliberating a little more on the matter, Lampaea took Feletra’s advice and quickly began to pack for Setra. Yet he worried now about the road that Feletra would take out of Elenia towards Liasis. It was crucial that she knew about the wood in between.

‘Fel, if I leave you to go on alone, will you be able to avoid Whiteblind Wood?’

‘Of course, I just follow the road. It leads straight past the forest front, I’ll be fine.’

Lampaea suddenly stopped packing as dread for his sister’s welfare overcame him. She had absolutely no idea.

‘No, the road disappears just before the wood appears,’ he explained, ‘do you not know the rumours of Whiteblind and why it is called that?’

‘No, do I need to?’

Lampaea sighed and proceeded to tell her.

‘Yes, you really do. Every path that is laid out to lead around Whiteblind disappears as if it were never there. No one knows why but the stories of if being some sort of haunting are most people’s guesses. Nearly all travellers that take the road from Elvanoh stumble into that wood unintentionally, and many do not know or remember how it happened. Once in the forest, there is only half a chance you will come out again. From inside, there is only one way out, and it is by luck if you should find that. It is made all the more difficult by the fact that the whole wood is downhill, because that one road of escape is north and uphill. If, however, you miss it, then you will continue downhill, further and further, until you reach Dead Man's End.'

'What is Dead Man's End?' Feletra asked, a daunting feeling tight in her throat.

'It is the end of the wood and, effectively, the end of you.' Feletra thought he could not have been more blunt. 'Those who were unlucky enough to take the wrong path will arrive at this point, raised high as the cliff above the sea, although it's so sheer and hidden that no one ever sees it. The downhill slope towards it becomes so steep that you see nothing until it's too late. The fall takes you.'

'And why is it called Whiteblind Wood?'

'Because you are as good as a blind man walking through there.'

Although Feletra feared the inevitability of approaching this wood, she tried her hardest now not to let Lampaea see this within her, for he might be put off leaving for Setra.

'The best chance you have,' Lampaea advised, 'is to trek the undergrowth and fields between here and Liasis; that way you will cut across the road and hopefully rejoin it after it reappears at the wood. Just be careful you rejoin it *after* the east side of the wood, and *not* before.'

Feletra listened to everything he told her, so much so that she found it easier to simply memorise his voice in her head. Soon the two of them were ready to part their separate ways, each to help someone they loved. Feletra was equipped with a short bow, a quiver of arrows and a small dagger. She felt odd carrying weapons, as if marching to a battle, and they did present an extra burden, yet nevertheless they increased her sense of confidence and she felt safe. She was also obliged to take Elpura with her, as Lampaea would be relying on Fitaeba to lead him straight to Halemedra.

Once they had both prepared themselves with supplies and tidied the clearing, they stood facing one another and Feletra found it a strenuous bidding when she was forced to say goodbye to her brother yet again, feeling that it may be another year or more before she saw him again. Perhaps even never, if he too was caught by the Setrans, though she hastily pushed this thought aside.

Lampaea walked with Feletra to the edge of the forest and showed her the way south-east that she would be taking.

'Do not forget what I told you about the road.'

'I won't,' she assured him.

'I will send you an ebrat once I am in Setra. Take care of yourself, Fel.'

'And you.'

She mounted Elpura.

'Remember to never trust a Chriahk.' Suddenly he slapped Elpura's haunches, setting her and Feletra off at a fast canter across the dry Drohan fields. Feletra looked back over her shoulder at her brother, but he was already gone. He was never one for long goodbyes.

Chapter 9
Sleepless Whiteblind

Ataleka sat cross-legged by the River Kestors. It was a safe river; shallow enough, a slow current, and clean. He liked the way the water lapped so steadily over a protruding rock, like a cat's tongue licking its paw. A light wind brushed by, crumbling some more of the dusty bank into the river. It raised the hairs on the back of his neck. His stomach felt empty, though he was not hungry; without Feletra his youth already felt spent.

Bri and Leao no longer shouted or ran about the house as they used to, it was terribly quiet. As he sat there, Ataleka wondered where his sister was at that moment; he didn't know whether to think ill of her or not – a part of him said she had left for a very good reason, another part that she had been thoughtless in leaving when he fell sick. Either way, he awaited her return anxiously with each day, as well as his father's.

His back was to the house. Estra had approached only a few paces away from him, calling his name repeatedly to come inside for dinner, but he could not hear her.

x

A last cluster of lights began to disappear gradually in the west like stars losing the will to live. This was Elvanoh in the near distance, and the night was ripe for its slumber. One light had remained, high above the others, just a single flame. A quick glance at the navy skies reaffirmed that the stars were still with her, and in abundance. Areas of the southern skies were painted a deep but sickly purple, as streaks of clouds stood before the stars here and blotted them out. Back in Elpura Feletra saw clouds only around five times a year.

Visions of every family member had been knocking on the doors of her mind since she had left Elenia Forest. By sheer self-control she had kept these doors well locked, and reminded herself that this particular trek required all the concentration she possessed. If she could avoid Whiteblind Wood it would be the next positive step of her journey after being with Lampaea, and she wanted to prove to herself that she could achieve this.

By the morning, she and Elpura slowed to a steady trot as the wood came into view. Feletra had remained awake throughout the night ride to this point, and so had been able to observe the light that still crept warily between those trees. The Elvanohn road to the woods had been found, a wide and shallow groove set in the moist Drohan earth, studded with smooth stones and devoid of vegetation. Tufts of lazy green grass became more abundant in this southern region, spotted with brown, and there were also less serri trees; instead what was left of these were interspersed with clusters of trees which Feletra had not the recognition for. They were taller than a serri, and exhibited small arrowhead-shaped leaves, which bristled like a cold shiver when a breeze passed through them.

Feletra stopped to ponder the situation. She gazed at the wood through tireless eyes, and saw how it spread out towards the east, and then there was the road next to her. Everything was laid out. How was it so difficult to avoid Whiteblind? There was a vast plain and open, rolling hills in which to do this; it all seemed far too simple.

She continued onwards, safe in this knowledge, and passed by the forest front with ease, despite the fact that Lampaea would have considered it too close, no doubt. The trees of Whiteblind appeared very fat and stout-looking, with a relatively flat and un-branching canopy, and predominantly dark green foliage painted the scene. There was a unique feature which might have been viewed from a further distance: great tangled spurs of leafless wood poking out of the canopy in an ungainly fashion.

The protrusions rose tall above the other trees as if they were pale arms of the elderly reaching to the skies; they were thick and had stood against many an age, an oddity being that they were entirely white in colour.

Elpura's canter had reduced in speed due to the increasing steepness of the coming hills. Feletra had for a while been so intent on seeing the back of the wood that she had only looked southwards, now to realise she was directly on the forest front itself. She felt bewildered at how she had managed to come so close and tried to steer Elpura away. This might have seemed an optimistic attempt to Feletra, though her horla seemed to know better, and struggled evermore to fight the approaching dark trees. The outer hills rose higher before them. The undergrowth thickened significantly beneath them; dry grasses grew long enough to reach Feletra's feet.

She stopped again, more abruptly this time. The winding forest line had blocked her so that it had curled around her path to loom unfavourably before her now.

'What...?' Feletra murmured to herself in perplexity.

She became anxious and looked about her blockade at every angle as it now partially encircled her like some waiting trap with an open jaw. She was also in the shrubbery before the trees, and knew how spontaneous the forest front was, if it could be called as such, but failed to understand how her firm focus had evaded evasion itself.

It made no sense.

Feletra peered now into the depths of the wood that seemed to emit a sour and unwelcome essence of hostility. They were black. Nought could be discerned; the darkness was unfaltering like a starless night captured in a sealed vessel. The longer she gazed into its black pits, the more she felt she was being drawn inside.

She looked away, and Pytheria's light about her seemed to be blinding all of a sudden. After a few blinks, she tried once more up the hill opposite the wood, though even the hills would not sympathise. Feletra's agitation in navigating around the outskirts of the trees caused her concentration to waver, and before she had permitted herself a moment to distinguish where she was heading, she had entered Whiteblind itself. It took another few minutes for her to accept this turn of events.

Once again, now amidst the darkness, she stopped.

Is there another way out? I'm only at the edge, it shouldn't be difficult to quickly turn back now...

Despite the vain attempt to govern her thoughts with some miniscule degree of sensibility, she continued to look about frantically for the best direction out of the wood, and out of the predicament she had now besmirched herself with. But everywhere appeared the same, and she failed to identify where she had actually entered. The entire place was stood in a death-like silence, with only the dimmest of pale orange light penetrating the canopy; it danced in a pretence of smoke across the leaves and between twigs.

The ground was littered abundantly with dry leaves and other dead matter, and the air was thick with warmth and humidity.

Feletra had tried her best to remain calm, but she could feel the rising panic within her, and a pulsing heat increasing in her head, made worse from the stifling atmosphere. Just as Lampaea had described, the whole wood was on a great slope of a hill, and she now careered uphill with Elpura in tow in a bid to find an exit again, though the task seemed to be an impossible one and went on forever. After recognising the same sequence of trees five times, Feletra was sure she was going round in circles. Her breathing became heavier in exasperation and her chest began to feel tight. She noticed that Elpura appeared to be feeling the same effect, and observed worriedly that her eyes were glazed over with a faint purple sheen. And then in horror, Feletra saw within them the reflection of her own eyes, mirroring the same glassy glaze. The horla's head wobbled uncertainly and dropped every so often as if being taken by the desire to sleep.

Feletra did not cease the strife to escape, but she now panicked more, her feet stumbling and her mind drifting further away from logic and reason. After wandering around in so many circles to this point, she appeared to have reached closer to the heart of the wood, as it was even darker and the air even more suppressing.

She took a step forward again; she lost the balance on one foot and grasped the nearest tree for support. Suddenly she blinked and the whole scene before her became blurred. The weight of her body felt heavy, and the tree she was so desperately clutching to might have been slipping away beneath the sweat of her fingertips. She inhaled the musky, pungent air but it did not seem to be exhaled afterwards.

Feletra moved again, as if in a dream, releasing the rein on Elpura without knowing it. Then every sound became unnaturally loud. Eerily clear to her ears, her footsteps on the dry leaves crackled with a volume that was incredibly startling, as if the entire forest was cramped inside her head. The sound of her breath was no different; it was like a forceful gale inside her lungs.

It was too much to bear. She looked down at her hands and they were shaking. Her vision faded into darkness, her head pounding like a drum. The seconds shortened to that one aching moment of nothingness that materialised. Her entire body quivered now, and then the silence hit her.

In deafness and blindness, Feletra fell to the forest floor.

x

'Gentlemen, welcome. Crafstmen of Chriah, Setra, Delica, Depra, Mereta and Fliir, you know why you have been sent to me.'

A tall man enrobed in a rich and power-instating red with glaring and merciless eyes stood to address ten other men who were sat in a circle around a heavy wooden table, all waiting patiently for their host to begin. Most of them were still and prepared to listen intently, though one of them was a relatively young individual who was etching lines into the table top by moving his index finger back and forth, but his finger not once made contact. Another was leant forward and throwing glances of anxiety about his peers, eager for what he was about to hear. His hair was thin and greasy, his face sallow-skinned and gaunt, with large bulging eyes that were fit for a frog. On the wall behind their host, a vast collection of knives, daggers and other assorted weapons hung or rested.

'As I am sure you are all aware,' their host continued, 'Chriah is moving fast in conjunction with our friends, Eastern Enphiah. Now we simply wait. However, Chru has requested that I combine the powers of the strongest craftsmen that we have to offer, lucky for him the Sabrine already exsited then. Together, we each have Blackcraft strong enough to form a Liquis. Not only will that make us near impossible to defeat when the time comes, but it will also allow us to create the necessary upheavals prior to that. Subtle benefits, if you like.'

'Akeon, there is something which I am sure you must be aware of yourself,' an older man of the circle spoke out, his small blue eyes ready to question his host and bright against a white, wiry beard, 'there are only eleven of us here – we need twelve to create a Liquis, and that extra member cannot be any old craftsman who knows no more than how to boil an egg, every member must be truly powerful.'

'Wisely pointed out, Sernehr,' said Akeon, 'and indeed I did have a twelfth member, but he has escaped me. For now. No matter, he is returning to me as we speak.'

'He abandoned matters like this which urgently need to be discussed?' said Sernehr. 'Are you sure he is the right man for this?'

'Yes, I am certain. I can easily persuade him; his power is undeniable, and I refuse to miss the opportunity of harnessing it.'

Sernehr nodded and said no more.

'In the meantime, we need to use what we have to build the foundations of an age that will never be forgotten, a new and vast kingdom that will bring the ongoing feud with our neighbours to an end when they finally answer to us. We must also...*persuade* others. The simple folk. You all know we have ways to which they cannot say no.'

The man who had been leant forward and listening eagerly withdrew his shoulders in excitement and smiled like a child who had just won a particularly difficult game.

A young man who looked uncannily similar to the one that had been rhythmically etching into the table now rose to attention suddenly. They wore the same navy blue robes and sported the same wild black hair.

'What are you suggesting, Akeon? Persuasion by force?' he said.

Akeon immediately sensed the air of disagreement in his voice and looked at the youth sternly.

'Yes, Methen. Our Blackcraft is greatly valued, and it shouldn't be wasted at a time like this.'

'But it's blackmail! You're referring to families – women, children, the elderly – people who don't even deserve this –!'

'I have no place for a craftsman who is too blind and idiotic to realise his potential for such a great opportunity as this. You are either with me or not.'

'I can't condone this, or be a part of it,' said Methen firmly. He rose from his chair and faced Akeon directly

The young man next to him known as Bedaraan ceased his artistic carpentry in Akeon's table and also stood to attention.

'I apologise, Akeon,' he said, 'my brother does not know when it's best to stay silent, nor what is best for him.'

'I know exactly what is best for me,' Methen said through gritted teeth, 'and I won't find that in torturing the innocent. This circle is sick, if this is what we reduce ourselves to.'

'Sit down!' his brother commanded, and Methen was forcefully sat back down with Blackcraft. Bedaraan had needed no more than to fix his gaze upon him. But this did not dissuade Methen, he stood up once more and with a flick of his hand the chair was thrown backwards and shattered against the wall.

'I'll not join you.'

Akeon watched for a few seconds as he began to walk towards the door. He sighed shortly, and then the doors slammed shut before him. Methen turned around to face the rest of the circle, and before he could have seen it coming a knife had flung off the wall behind Akeon and plunged into his throat. It was an accurate shot and the tip poked out the back of his neck.

Methen crumbled to the ground as his brother looked on in less shock and sympathy than was expected.

'To walk away from this without allegiance is not accepted,' said Akeon, unyielding and disconcertingly calm, 'know your place, and know that it's Chriah.'

'Akeon,' said Sernehr, 'what of our eleventh member now?'

'I am never without my ideas, Sernehr. Bring me Korsthr.'

x

On her awakening, Feletra's bodily state felt the very opposite to how it had been before her collapse. Everything seemed much clearer now; she would have almost felt refreshed were it not for the grim and ominous ambience of the wood surrounding her.

There was still a faint orange glint in the forest light, suggesting that she had not lain there for too long, though it was decidedly cooler.

She lifted her head from the ground, then steadily rose to her feet again. Elpura was still with her, and had been waiting patiently for her to awake. Although her vision and hearing had returned, Whiteblind was still silent and appeared to host no life; there was no birdsong, no typical forest rustle in the leaves, nothing. And yet Feletra felt that unmistakable notion of being watched constantly.

Slowly she turned her gaze to her left, where there was thick shrubbery growing. Within it she spied a small glow of white that seemed to flash every few seconds.

She *was* being watched.

The creature moved slightly to reveal another white eye, glinting like lucrin in the woodland shadows. Feletra sensed this thing was not alone, and carefully looked over her shoulder – there she spotted another pair of white eyes fixed on her, then a third pair next to these. They were the same eyes as the creature she had faced in Elenia, and she now attempted to walk away quietly with Elpura, pretending she had not seen them; she hoped with all her heart that this would prevent them from racing after her. She withheld her breath, and every step felt more cautious, if not pointless, as she felt certain they were following just as stealthily.

Feletra jumped a little when Elpura gave a sharp tug on her rein, followed by a few more. Her rider recognised this reaction of fear all too well in horlas and tried desperately now to calm her without raising alarm. The horla however, would not yield, and began to rear on her hind legs, pulling

Feletra backwards to where she had lain.

Finally, the commotion sparked a response in their stalkers, as one of them gradually stepped forward into the light directly within their view; Feletra watched something white moving closer, though had not the time to see its face –

Elpura had spotted their predator and the pounding sense of danger overcame her as she pulled free of Feletra and galloped away downhill in terror.

For one brief moment Feletra stood rooted to the ground facing the creature that had emerged, and in that moment she rapidly matched its image to that of the Elenia beast: larger than she had first guessed, with broad shoulders and slender forelegs, a thick and heavy coat of tangled and knotted fur. Its great wide face was dominated by a huge jaw inside of which Feletra dared not imagine such a set of weapons, and those bright eyes that had calculated how worthy she was of being their prey.

'We've met before, haven't we?' Feletra whispered. The enemy growled threateningly and Feletra shot an arrow at it – the tip had barely scratched its skin.

She had only one choice, and ran.

Feletra raced ahead with as much speed and energy as she could muster, nothing else mattered but the will to survive; she looked back just momentarily and saw that all three of them were chasing her – they were exchanging deep echoing cries to one another as her breaths grew shallow and her heart felt ready to explode in her chest. She could feel her thighs burning; she felt there was a madness in the air, for nothing could ground her nor her mind, it swam as rapidly as the trees would blur on by and she leapt blindly ahead, each step a lift greater than the last.

Without warning one of the creatures had caught up and was closing in on her left, and then she saw, with great despair, a second on her right; they had signalled to encircle her.

Where they ran alongside her, again came the flashes of white to either corner of her eyes, whatever this may have been, though in her whirl of panic she thought she could discern the white shapes as something that extended from their backs.

Further and further downhill she careered, quickly realising amidst the horror and confusion that running away would nevertheless only lead to her death, as it brought the famous Dead Man's End ever closer. Suddenly Feletra felt her knees develop an abrupt weakness at this thought and the effect seemed to ricochet around her body.

The power in her leg muscles faltered and she slowed – the wolf-like creature to her left took advantage and came close enough to make one gaping bite at her arm – as warm spit dashed across her skin, it narrowly missed her; she yelped a little at the attack, lost her initiative and tripped on a creeper vine along the ground.

Thorns and twigs tore at her hands. She spun onto her back – one of the wolves pounced above her.

She kicked its jaw from beneath it and scrambled rapidly to her feet again – but the wolf was faster. It advanced at her again and managed to pin her down this time with incredible strength. Feletra fumbled quickly at her waist for her dagger as the creature's hot breath doused her face in sickly clouds, and drove it into its foreleg.

Her attacker howled in pain and she was momentarily released. Another was immediately on her tail though; she quickly spied a hollowed-out log and forced herself inside without hesitation. She crawled into the weak, rotting cavity infested with maggots as the last two of the beasts were tearing the moist and crumbling wood apart about her with all the force they could summon. As she watched her poor, sodden sanctuary being torn down with wide eyes she listened to the sound of them sniffing her scent from the outside, preparing for a mighty strike.

Then she saw the one she had injured appear at the opening of the log. As it stood staring at her with vengeful eyes for a moment, Feletra could see everything now. The flashes of white she had caught before were great white protrusions, sprouting from the wolf's back as if growths of Whiteblind Wood had commandeered their bodies. They were woody in appearance, mangled in shape with an old and crinkled texture, exactly like the enormous protrusions of leafless trees that reared their attention seeking heads above the canopy of Whiteblind.

Suddenly a claw pierced the log above her, and the one Feletra had fixed her gaze with now charged at the opening with all speed – she cried out and struggled backwards on her hands, a trio of dark, intense snarls emanating from the pits of their stomachs, lusting for her blood.

With the dagger still tight in her left hand, she did not anticipate there being a drop at the other side of the log. Before she could stop herself, she had reached the end and fell not into earth, but into water. It was a deep, clean pool.

Something strange then happened; Feletra saw a burst of flame before her, near to the surface. As fast as it had appeared, it was gone again. In the panic of everything she could only assume it was a person, but before she could move towards it something else had entered the pool; to add to her devastation, it seemed her predators were also aquatic, as one now approached her with an open jaw, its eyes even brighter beneath the vividly clear water. There was a perilous hunger in them.

Feletra tried to swim to the surface, but a swipe was made at her leg, and caught it. She emitted a silent scream in agony and became trapped – the breath slipping away from her body.

In a last effort, with what remaining strength she had left, she plunged the dagger deep into its white eye, dying the pure water crimson about her. The creature still advanced on her and she attacked it again, tearing at its throat this time, until it finally became motionless and sank further to the bottom of the pool. She clawed her way to the surface desperately, using the rocks to push against. The nail on her middle finger snapped back and ripped off but she had no time to spare the pain for that now.

When her head reached the air she inhaled so deeply she thought the shock might cause her to pass out again. Across the way, the other two wolves stood beside the pool, one drinking the stained water, but when Feletra had heaved herself out and faced them both, the drinking ceased and the two of them stared at her in silence. They looked from her to the pool a few times, then turned and walked away.

Feletra felt bewildered, but did not stay to watch them go, and sprinted off uphill in the direction of the flame. She did not know how long she ran for between the trees, but the evening was quickly closing in and the fear was still in her. She constantly expected to find someone, the person that had created that fire, but found no one.

And yet...had the flame not been underwater?

The immeasurable notions in her head were running faster than she was. Then she remembered a similar impossibility. In Elenia with Lampaea, a layer of ice had enclosed the fire in the clearing. *What was significant about the fire?* she thought. *Does this only happen around me?* Then she thought that the Sorpha's curse might be responsible, perhaps Ataleka was experiencing similar things, strange visions that would have otherwise been treated as insanity.

She cleared her mind again, desiring to keep her wits about her this time and not clouding everything with immediate judgement.

Before she knew it, and by some miracle of following that direction of the fire, she was out of Whiteblind, but still she ran onwards, breathing in the fresh air of the hills around her now. She did not know how she escaped the woods, and did not look back at them once, she just kept running towards Liasis in the east. As Lampaea would have said, she was 'lucky' to have found the one path that led out of the wood, though Feletra felt strongly that it had nothing to do with luck. She knew that whoever had made the flame had aided her, and shown her the path to escape.

She spotted a small overgrown hollow straight on and headed towards it.

x

Emmet jumped at the knock on the door. Ink spilt across the papers on the desk before him. He cursed a little before throwing the sodden writings into the fire. It was nothing important. Sighing, he heaved himself from the chair, but then stopped short by the door.

'Who is it?' he said.

'Emmet, it's me! I'm sorry to bother you, I've just

brought you some fresh bread.'

Emmet quickly returned to his desk, gathered up any significant papers and hid them in a draw.

'Come in, Halemer.'

She entered the house bearing a wrapped loaf. Emmet found it so uncomfortably alien to be feeling a sense of paranoia, hostility even, towards Halemer, though he was further compelled to it when she so easily glanced about the inside of his home upon entry.

'Will that be all?' he asked as she laid down the bread on a nearby table. She nodded in some surprise of such rapid dismissal, and then turned to the door again.

'Alright, thank you,' said Emmet, watching her go. Suddenly it felt as if she was a symbol of his trust, and it was drifting further and further away with each step she was taking. She was just a middle-aged woman, such a person could not be involved with evil deeds...but then, he had assumed Amanyl was no more than a middle-aged man, also seemingly going about his daily life. *Stop*, Emmet thought, *she is your close friend.*

Almost as soon as he had thought it, Halemer stopped before leaving, and faced him again.

'Emmet, please,' she implored, 'what is this?'

'What?' he replied.

'All this hiding indoors, constantly disappearing then reappearing at the Valley House, now reading strange and dark books. You've changed so much, and ever since Feletra left. Tell me, is there something happening? Something I should know of?'

'No,' Emmet responded simply, 'there is nothing happening.'

Halemer looked at him with a stern but compassionate

face. Only she could pull that expression.

'And...and you?' she said. 'Are you alright?'

'Yes, I'm fine.'

Halemer blinked a few times and swept her hands down her dress in a gesture of resignation, 'Alright. Come back to the Valley House soon then,' she traced a finger across her brow. 'People miss you, and are asking after you.'

'I'll see.'

Halemer made her way out. Before the door closed on her, she said to him, 'If you need someone to speak with, remember where I am.'

Emmet smiled and nodded, and the door clicked shut. He locked it, then decided something as he watched the embers glimmering in the fire. Immediately he sat back down at his desk, picked up a quill and began a letter.

Feletra,

I trust you are keeping well on your journey? I understand if this letter may seem unexpected to you, since we were in the company of one another for but a short time. In spite of all this, I felt that you were entitled to know the current state of events occurring in Betharanei, given that you were subjected to the same situation as I that night, under the Valley House. Or rather, that it was you who provided the crucial evidence for me to begin some investigations into the intentions of a number of villagers living here, each of which I have known as friends. For it is these investigations, you see, which I have been conducting ever since you left. I have been tracking the actions of those eight men that we overheard that night, and have established for sure that they are part of plans beyond Betharanei, and far beyond Otra.

There was a night in which I followed two of them, and overheard 'Chriah' mentioned throughout the conversation, they also spoke of playing 'a waiting game,' now I am most aware, as I assume you also are, the dangers surrounding the land of Chriah, not least because of their past. Knowledge of this 'waiting game' has brought it clear to me that there are dark affairs in motion abroad and within Enphiah, affairs of a scale that we have no power over. But something is coming. I can feel it greatly now.

I have been trying in vain to identify your attacker from the Valley House, as it's clear there is some link of this matter to that creature. Nothing is certain, though my studies have led me to believe that it may be a preathin. Tonight, I will do something that may seem rather bold to you, but I plan to return to the Valley House, and confront that creature. I must know, you see, else everything I have done will have been for nothing. There are dark conspiracies that need exposing, and in doing this I may at least piece some part of this puzzle together, should I succeed, that is.

Be not alarmed by me, nor think that I am merely writing to you so that you may be an outlet for me to vent my thoughts on. I write to you, Feletra, because I feel you are the only one who I can truly trust at this point. Betharanei will never be the same for me again, unless I can restore its purity and 'cleanse' it, if you like, of its deceptive residents. My last word to you is to please steer well clear of Chriah, as the danger may now be far more immense than you imagine. Should you find time to reply to me, do not use an ebrat. I would not trust them with the content of our subject.

Your friend,
Emmet.

Emmet pored over the letter for a second. He then sealed it within an envelope and stowed it in his coat pocket, having disregarded the dribble of hot red wax across his fingers.

Confidently he strode into his small, cramped kitchen, and gazed at a knife made of pnapsor before hiding this next to the letter in his pocket. Pnapsor was a cheap but common metal in Enphiah, he hoped it would be enough to serve him. He had a slightly more unconventional method in mind of sending his letter to Feletra, it was a private, unseen method.

When the letter was sent on its way and the village lanes were cleared of life, he made his move and crept through the sleeping Betharanei to the Valley House, just as he said he would.

x

No. You can all wait till tomorrow for the next part of the story. It is a long one, after all.

...these words were so familiar...oh yes, they are what Mother would say.

Feletra had been vaguely thinking about it all.

Now, hers was a story she might have preferred to listen to at home. Was it so very odd that she was living it instead? Well, yes. And there came Estra's voice again. What Feletra had seen with her own eyes was most likely unfathomable to her family.

Liasis was very far from home, but Feletra now thought it wasn't far enough. In that instant that she had arrived at the small town, after nine hours alone on the road, she wanted only to be in Chriah, to find this cure and have everything over with. Although rather quaint and welcoming in appearance, Feletra failed to appreciate this about Liasis due to the intense heat that day. She was thankful it was a cooler climate than the Plains of Nemenon, but without Elpura, who had disappeared entirely since Whiteblind, the walk had been arduous and unforgiving.

There was barely anyone to be seen about the place, and only faint voices were heard. She hated that. A burning heat mixed with a quiet hush, when there should have been laughter and the sound of falling water to cool everything down. She had limped through the town and emerged at the outskirts facing north-east, and resided in an unused barn for the night. The smell inside reminded her of the stable back home, that scent of moist wood and the primitive musk that horla and cattle left behind.

Feletra carefully unwound the damp bandage from around her thigh, partially desiring not to see what was beneath. The wound was greatly discoloured at the edges to a deep and angry lavender, and the pain was far from gone. She quickly replaced the bandage before she began to pity herself too much, and peered at her nail-less finger and sighed, caring not a jot for it.

Ataleka was with her again that night, in her dreams. He was a flickering image, standing tall on an outcrop of rock above an ominous cave opening. He was staring down at her with an austere expression set upon his grey but youthful face, and holding something in his left hand, something that dripped rubies...it was the brightest thing she could see, as the rest of the harsh, dire scene was painted in monochrome, even herself. Even Ataleka, who squeezed tighter at the hanging flesh he grasped.

Feletra was watching him, calling his name over and over, though her own voice was silent and strangled to her.

Finally, Ataleka took the flesh in both hands, and wrung it out like a shredded wash cloth, twisting it upon itself as the blood was excreted and splashed onto his bare feet a little. He kept his eyes fixed on Feletra below him, but then had suddenly appeared directly before her; his eyes were covered by a hood over his head and his mouth was slightly open, as if ready to speak, or release something.

His parted lips, held so firmly in place, were like the cave opening behind him, a narrow gap, still and foreboding. Would he not but indulge in the sweet satisfaction to lick his lips at that moment? To quench everything a little, for they were cracked and dry; a desert canyon at nightfall, devoid of a tongue to caress its empty riverbeds.

Slowly he began to lift his head; Feletra watched as the image of him began to flicker again, but when he revealed his face, it was not Ataleka, but someone she had never met before. It was another boy, a young man even, who looked into her eyes now just as steadily as Ataleka had done. He held out his hand to her, but as she was about to take it, she could feel hay suddenly, and then a bird cry nearby made the transition for her back to reality.

The dream was gone. And so was the boy's face, his identity was lost to her. Feletra sat up instantly. There was a light cold sweat on her brow, then a second bird cry caused her to jump; she looked up in awe to see a great eagle perched above her, watching intently with its wide, golden eyes. It then swiftly thrust out its wings and gave one last high-pitched call before flying out of the barn again, leaving the soft hushed echo of its proud feathers on the air in its wake. It was like another ethereal sound that should have belonged on the plane of dreams.

Feletra sat watching the doors of the barn for a while before attempting to sleep again. They were ajar, with no movement, and she thought there might be the possibility of the eagle returning at any moment. She eventually lay down on the hay again, thinking of her dream and the bird. The eagle had been exactly the same as the one she had stumbled across on the plains in Elpura; she remembered how that time it had reminded her of someone watching her. No one had any reason to be watching her though, only she and Lampaea knew of her business, and the thought that an eagle could be following her did seem a little foolish perhaps. Feletra did not dispose of its strange coincidence however; Enphiah was not the home of the eagle, and she was sure few could have come across two in the space of time that she did.

She could not return to sleep for the remaining hours after that. She tossed and turned and was no longer comfortable anymore. As soon as Pytheria's light leaked through the slits in the barn walls to greet her, she left the quiet Liasis behind her, and was glad to. When she had another ponder over Flior's map whilst on the move, she saw with some despair how far Xenor was, as this was the closest port that would take her to Chriah. She estimated a good forty-five leagues.

Along the way there were quite a few people that crossed her path and sped on ahead to Calaben or Xenor, or further.

It seemed to be a more commonly used road than any she had walked along previously, or it might have simply been the fact that she was using the marked road at all, unlike the way she had trekked the undergrowth through the centre of Droha. But this path to Xenor forced her to use the road; the surrounding environment was far too overgrown everywhere else to make any headway. The forests and woodlands of the south were certainly becoming thicker and more prominent – this was Enphiah's link to its neighbour, Pyra: Pyra was the Woodlands, Enphiah the Desert lands, and Orpegh the Water lands.

Feletra kept her head down whenever there was another passerby, she was aware there was still a risk of her father using the same road. People glanced at her briefly as they overtook: ebrats, families, merchants, but Padryl did not appear amongst them at any point.

Then a man with a cart transporting sacks of vegetables stopped next to her and offered her a ride.

Exhausted from walking, she gratefully accepted. The man seemed friendly enough to trust for this much.

'I can take you to Calaben. Is that where you're heading?'

'No,' said Feletra, a little crestfallen, 'I'm going to Xenor. Will you be going there as well?'

The man shook his head, 'I will be stopping in Calaben only. It's your choice.'

After another quick look at her map. Feletra decided to take his offer and climbed up onto the cart to sit amidst the rolling vegetables. She had a better chance of saving energy for the walk from Calaben to Xenor this way at least. It became a rather bumpy journey, though she cherished the opportunity to admire the magically touched scenery of the trees that fanned out brilliantly at the tops, and the pale white and yellow blossoms of some of the shorter ones that were so light and fragile they glided on the breeze when breathed upon and pecked her cheeks occasionally.

A few times she sat dozing with the sunlight soaking her face and the seasonal heat seeping into her skin as the jolting and wobbling of the cartwheels became almost relaxingly rhythmic. She could smell the refreshing scent of salt drifting from the South Sea of Dalpha every so often; it was quietly satiating and soothing when she inhaled it deeply; the very taste of that unseen, creeping ocean spray, with its lenient and meekly tiptoeing aromatic kiss, was like a long-anticipated drink to quench her thirst.

By late evening the man decided they would make a stop and sleep for the night. Despite the mass of food he was carrying, he miserly did not offer Feletra anything to eat. She counted her blessings she had managed to obtain any sort of transport however and contented herself with some mushrooms and berries from Elenia.

Feletra took advantage of the extra sleep she could treat herself to laying in the back of the cart to when the man awoke before Pytheria's dawn and set off again. She still had her eyes closed when the cart came to a stop. When she opened them again, hearing the busy voices of townsfolk around, she acquired that tired, heavy feeling on her eyelids that one gained after slumping about on a hot day for too long. The man was standing at the back of his cart, looking at her.

'We're here,' he said, 'do you have some sort of payment for me?'

Feletra stared at him for a second, trying to recall if he

had requested this of her before she had accepted the offer.

‘Payment?’ she repeated.

‘Yes. Something small will do, like five pieces. Or a trade, if you like. But I don’t often bring people to towns for nothing.’

Feletra looked away awkwardly as he began to unload his vegetables. She had no money, and nothing else to give him that she didn’t already need. She felt angry at the man for not mentioning before that he would be expecting something in return, rather than just helping someone in need. *It’s not as if he wouldn’t have been making the journey anyway...*she thought bitterly.

‘Can I stretch my legs around the town first?’ she asked lightly, hiding the friction and jumping down from the cart.

The man looked at her suspiciously.

‘Just for a short walk,’ she added, ‘and I will leave my things here so you know I’ll come back.’

‘Very well. I have to drop these off at a few doors,’ he gestured towards some full sacks, ‘so make certain you’re back when I’m finished.’

Feletra nodded compliantly as he heaved two sacks and made off down a busy lane. She walked away in the opposite direction but made a point of watching him disappear at the same time. Now she tried to think quickly, for there was certainly no way she could pay him. As she continued to walk slowly down the stony and sloping streets of Calaben, she looked over her shoulder where the cart was still visible through the mass of darting people.

The man had returned already for his second load, clearly he wasn’t walking far to drop off each sack, and could keep a good eye out for Feletra returning for her own pack and then fleeing with it. That at least was one idea she had, though if he caught her there were plenty of people walking about to help stop her running away on foot; she imagined him shouting, 'Thief!' would be enough to spark such a reaction anyway.

She sighed miserably and stopped to lean against a wall set in the shade, then began to wonder how Ataleka was now, wondering if the curse was acting as slowly on him as it was on her. She had in fact forgotten that she was also to suffer the same ailment; she wanted to help Ataleka more than herself, more than herself and him put together. But how long would it take? The walk to Xenor would just be another tedious part of the journey, a part that could be done faster. And then she looked up again at the cart, still stationed quietly in an open square of Calaben as people bustled around it ignorantly.

Suddenly, Feletra began to greatly consider the bold move. It was wrong, and it truly was theft, but it was a way out, wasn't it?

In the square, there were a few troughs set around the edge, one of which the two horlas that had pulled the cart were busying themselves with, bending down with their slender and muscular necks. Feletra took a step towards the cart, then stopped.

The man returned again for another load.

She hid behind a small wall when he looked around, and pretended to have dropped something to avoid any stares. Once he was gone again, she casually but swiftly approached the horlas and patted them so they were aware of her presence.

She saw that the cart was empty save for her bag, the rest of the vegetables had been unloaded and were laid on the ground ready.

*Well, at least he'll lose no trade...*Feletra thought in a doleful way to redeem herself.

After a last look around, she rapidly lifted herself up to where the reins had been laid and gave them a sharp crack. The horlas were immediately stimulated into movement and set off down the lane ahead.

Right on time, the man reappeared from around a corner and sprinted after her.

'Stop! What are you doing?! Stop the cart!' he shouted.

Feletra's heart was racing. She desperately urged the horlas on faster –

'Come on, come on!' she called.

'Stop her! Somebody stop her!' the man yelled continuously.

The people of Calaben watched in awe as a young girl raced away aimlessly down narrow streets. They dodged to the sides in terror as the horlas cantered relentlessly towards them.

Feletra saw with dread a dead end straight on – there was an incredibly tight right turn there, but she couldn't stop now.

She roughly pulled on the reins to make the turning; the horlas whinnied in surprise, and the right-hand cartwheel caught on the corner firmly – the horlas pulled it free forcefully, causing it to splinter a little as shards of wood littered the ground behind them. The whole thing jostled about even worse now with a damaged wheel, but Feletra's main concern was how to escape Calaben altogether.

As she looked behind her the man was still on the chase. And then she saw another cart materialise ahead of her on the next lane; it was on the move as well (albeit at a soft trot) and was full of wooden crates labelled: *'Xenor*

Merchantry.'

Instinctively she followed it and overtook, thankful it had been a wide enough road. Sure enough, the road was a main one through the town and led her out.

As Feletra made her galloping escape into the wild once more, the man could only stop and watch his horlas and cart become a small dot in the distance. She looked back at him one last time and laughed at the sheer thrill she was feeling. She felt alive as the wind rushed through her hair.

Xenor would not be far now.

Feletra thought Calaben had been fast-paced enough, but when she arrived in Xenor, it was by far much busier. She had made the journey to the town within the day, though the atmosphere had turned rather grey for the early evening and both Pytheria and Desporsa had been overshadowed with thick clouds that rolled endlessly about the dull sky.

Feletra had wasted no time in selling the horlas on to a new owner, now that she was to cross the sea. When she had asked around, a woman recommended that she see a man who lived in the heart of Xenor. Gladly he purchased the horlas for ten pieces each, but said that the cart was worthless due to its damage. He did however, offer her to leave it outside his home for someone to collect and disassemble it. Since it was secretly not her property, Feletra accepted without any qualms, and almost felt somewhat relieved inside that the evidence of her theft would be destroyed.

There appeared to be no main road directly through Xenor, as it was made up solely of narrow and twisting lanes; clearly one had to live here in order to know an efficient way of getting around, for every turn that Feletra took looked the same as the last. The fact that all the lanes were either sloping up or down from incredible heights rather than just flat was also a hindrance and an irritation amidst the confusion. People bumped into her when she was on the move and stepped on her toes when she stopped, too busy going about their own errands to apologise or acknowledge her.

Just prior to the peak of her frustration, she finally reached the port itself and was glad to see the back of the cramped and winding streets. Instead she received a breath of fresh air; there was a brisk wind gliding across from the Sea of Dalpha, mingled with the pungent smell of raw fish.

What she beheld with her eyes however commanded her primary attention. Rows upon rows of huge and magnificent ships, lined side by side like great warriors awaiting the call to charge on the front line before a battlefield. Their pale white sails were their flags, blowing about madly and uneasily below wrathful dark clouds that edged in further over Xenor to encase the town. The waters around the port grew restless and teased the calm ships, causing them to dip and rise steadily, secreting a little more majesty with each sway on the impatient waves upholding them.

Feletra stood in admiration of them for longer than she realised.

'You look as if you've never seen a ship before.'

Feletra jumped and turned around to face a very tall man, a grey wiry beard poking out stray strands in all directions, and small brown eyes peering in wonder down at hers. He smelt of old battered leather and overly burnt tektra, a commonly smoked weed in Enphiah.

‘In honesty, I haven’t,’ she replied with a smile.

‘Is that so? Well, you’re not the first. And here in Xenor is one of the best places to see them for the first time; here lays home to the best shipbuilders around and all along the Pyraihn Shore. I take it you’re looking for a ship to Pyra?’

‘That’s right, as soon as possible, actually.’

‘Ah, well luckily for you I am the right man to see about that,’ the man had been concealing a large well-used book beneath his cloak and brought this forward now. Swiftly he opened it and flicked through thick pages until he found the correct one.

‘Yes...there are two leaving for Stura,’ he confirmed, tracing a finger carefully across the page, ‘one for Demelor, departing very shortly, and the other to Varehna in the morning.’

‘I’ll take the one to Demelor, please.’

‘Certainly…’ the man snapped his book shut and whisked it away under his cloak again. As he began to reel off a list of details about the journey, Feletra noticed behind him a person shrouded in a dark aura of their own and withdrawn into the shadows of a stone alcove, their face completely hidden beneath a black hood.

The person was as still as death.

Naturally Feletra could not see their eyes, but she felt almost certain they were fixed directly on her.

‘...the crew manning the ship will be happy to provide something though...’

‘What?’ said Feletra with much delay, and the man paused and stared at her.

‘W-were you not listening?’

‘I’m sorry, which ship is it I take?’

‘The Weeping Dove, can you remember that?’

‘Yes, thank you,’ said Feletra, glancing yet again at the stranger behind him, who still had not moved.

The man smiled and hid his impatience well.

‘Alright then,’ he concluded, ‘oh, just bear in mind it’s about thirty pieces to secure a place, depending on how many passengers the ship has already accepted.’

Feletra was left unable to reply as he left her standing there with a whisk of his exaggeratively long cloak, and instantly engaged himself in addressing another individual requesting his assistance.

When she had located the Weeping Dove she discovered that entry and transportation were indeed thirty pieces from a portly member of the crew who was accepting the payments.

She paced about the port in irritation, having only twenty on her, with which she did offer, to no avail. She was almost laughed at for presenting such a meagre offer, and was informed that the price would increase should many more passengers step aboard.

She decided to think whilst taking a solemn walk beside the grand ships, wandering the length of them three times, and came up with nothing. But on the fourth, as she approached the Weeping Dove once more, the man who had originally rejected her offer now beckoned her eagerly.

‘You there! Young lady!’

‘Yes?’ Feletra said, half-expecting him to be calling some other girl.

‘Welcome aboard,’ he said simply, and stepped aside for her.

She stared at him as if he was an idiot.

‘I haven’t paid; I’m sorry, I can’t find ten extra pieces.’

‘All expenses have been paid, you may come aboard,’ he

reassured.

Feletra walked over uncertainly. ‘Paid by whom?’

‘He did not say his name. I couldn’t even see his face; he wore a hood and a black cloak.’

Her curiosity had come to a peak; she knew who he was describing, though why this person had paid for her to sail to Pyra was indeed another mystery altogether.

She paused before the man with an expression of utter confusion, and then stepped lightly onto the Weeping Dove. As she passed inside, there were three steep steps leading back down to main ground level. The air inside was cool, given the limited space which would only admit one person for the width down the walkways. She was rocked gently with the sway of the ship, feeling less than comfortable walking upon such an unpredictable surface. There were short bursts of cold air from somewhere, raising the hair on the back of her neck, and creaks in the woodwork from above and below.

She came to a man who stood behind a tall wooden counter.

‘Good day to you. You’ll be needing this,’ he handed her a long heavy key with a label attached reading *‘23,’* ‘your private cabin has all been paid for.’

‘Oh. Thank you.’

This hooded stranger had paid for a cabin as well? It was all becoming more and more suspicious, and Feletra wondered if it were a wise idea at all to stay on the ship, for her own safety. But then her curiosity kept her there – she wanted to find this person, whip back their hood to reveal their face. Ask them endless questions. This was under the assumption the stranger would be sharing the voyage with her; there would be no point in paying her fare and room if not.

She wasted no time in making her way to the deck; this is where all passengers were congregating, so she expected to find the hooded mystery amongst them. She soon realised this was a naïve venture, the idea for them was to stay hidden, after all.

The breeze was so fresh up on deck. She leant against the bulwark in some resignation of it and watched the busy port from above. She hadn't noticed until a few moments later, but there was a boy next to her, also just leaning there. He caught her glancing at him, and smiled.

She didn't know what it was, but something in his smile had lifted her feet from the deck for that second. It had an almost narcotic effect on her, but in the most pleasant sense. She could not describe it as calming however; it had been striking, his eyes seemed to darken as it occurred, like two horizons punctuated by a brilliant burnt carmine sky that fell prey to sleep under an over-powering instant nightfall, held by the obligation to bow down beneath that crescent moon of a smile.

'You're trying to escape from something.'

She turned to look at him, though not face-on, not expecting to be spoken to. He had not moved any closer to her. There was room for three more people between them, Feletra was somewhat glad of the distance.

'Escape? What makes you think that?' her reply was not as steady-sounding as she would have preferred, for the statement had been rather ominous coming from a stranger and had taken her aback.

'Stura is...beautiful. Who wouldn't want to escape there for a while?'

'Oh, yes. Exactly.'

His voice was relatively deep and smooth for his age. He could not have been one or two years more than herself.

He looked back out to the port, and Feletra decided to steal a longer gaze at him without appearing too obvious, to properly identify who she had been talking to, of course.

He could not have been from a background too dissimilar from her own, for his clothes were just as drab and dishevelled, though his were incredibly filthy as well. He also appeared to be drowned in pockets; wide ones, shallow ones, deep ones, buttoned ones, and the majority of them sewn on clumsily. No doubt by himself, she thought. She could spot a man's touch easily.

His shoulders were broad and well-rounded, though the rest of his physique was hidden under all the folds and flaps of the pockets. His hair was very short, the colour reminding her of roasted chestnuts; it was tended to about as much as a gardener would cut grass for grit. This worked for him.

For someone who lived in a hot and dry environment where Pytheria shone almost constantly, Feletra's skin was still paler than his. He looked very healthy, and Feletra believed you could have pierced the skin on his forearm for some depth before he bled, his sizeable hands seemed to reinforce this.

Suddenly he drew away as if something had pricked him. He passed a hand over his arm, looked up at Feletra with such force behind his eyes, then walked away down to the lower decks.

She looked down briefly and found herself exhaling a deep breath, as if she had been holding it the whole time he was there.

'Excuse me,' came a foreign voice behind her.

She spun around to a very tall and skinny man with watery, distant eyes.

‘Yes?’

‘You have been invited to the banquet tonight. I have been told to inform you that you should not miss this for anything, and are greatly expected.’

Chapter 10
In Safe Hands

Motivation was hard to come by. But Lampaea had some, and he cherished it. His was in the form of a face, the most beautiful he had ever seen. The full lips, the pinched blue eyes, and the longest, most graceful fair locks, of Halemedra. The image may as well have been etched into the inside of his skull, for there was not a day that it did not haunt him since her letter.

As he arrived closer to Felisten, the capital of Ferin, and hoped with all his heart that Halemedra was still waiting for him, a young man only a few years older than himself drew past upon a large dray drawn by four horlas. He looked down at Lampaea with cold grey eyes as he passed.

Lampaea continued warily, and looked on. The content of the dray had been concealed by a tightly-held sheet of black leather. He thought he spotted something move beneath it, then blamed the wind.

He stopped. There was no wind.

But just as he was beginning to suspect something, a great white horla came galloping towards him from the east, its rider wielding a huge sword in plain sight. Only his eyes were visible, the rest of his face hidden under a black bandeau emblazoned with a white symbol.

He rode straight past Lampaea as if he were not there, towards the dray instead, and sliced at the black leather covering. There, lying helpless, bound and gagged, were nine or ten individuals, children included.

The man responsible for them cursed and withdrew a

crossbow. He brought the horlas into a gallop now whilst aiming poorly at the rider, who kept attempting to edge closer.

Lampaea gave the signal to Fitaeba and he rode to the scene with haste to help free the victims, though he struggled to catch up. Quickly he fumbled for something he had acquired in Elvanoh; it was a long thin chain with a wide hook at the end – with some skill he tossed it and managed to catch the rear wheel. A sharp tug and one of the spokes was broken. As he suspected, poor craftsmanship, and the wheel could not sustain itself – it spun off and the left side of the dray splintered, the wood scattering in all directions.

The rider played this to his advantage, adeptly replacing his sword, and withdrawing a crossbow from nowhere.

His target was within range – and shot down in the forehead.

The horlas could sense their master's passing, for they slowed to a stop soon enough. The rider, as mysterious as he was, jumped in his place and disappeared from view for a few seconds.

Lampaea, as he now approached the cart, dismounted and had marvelled at his skill and agility, for the man was huge in stature. At least, from a distance.

Suddenly he reappeared again upon the cart, as if from thin air, standing tall and straight with his great crossbow directed at Lampaea, who stopped abruptly.

His eyes were piercing above the black mask, hard and deep set like a rock carving against low, dark brows. The look, a fierce and tenacious one. Lampaea began to wonder if he were not the real enemy, and felt for his own bow.

The rider jumped down, maintaining his defence. He

was still huge, if not more so now.

'Who are you?' the man demanded, or beast, Lampaea thought, standing entirely in his shadow.

'I'm an Elpuran,' Lampaea answered in his rather reasonable tone.

'What's your business?' his questions were succinct and direct, but not hurried. He gave the impression that he had all the time in the world should he apply it to the process of beheading Lampaea, who in turn would not have doubted his sincerity on the act.

'I am on my way to Setra –'

But it seemed this answer had struck a nerve, for the man had moved closer, his arrow within close range.

'Why? Are you a trafficker? Have you come to intercept me from freeing these people?'

'I just helped you free them!' Lampaea shot him a lasting glare and walked over to the captives, who had still been whimpering from aches, impatience and confusion. With a short dagger he released them all, and then faced the man once more, who was still on his guard.

'I'm not your enemy, and I have a good feeling you're not mine. Lampaea,' he held out his hand.

A pause followed.

'Bren.'

He grasped Lampaea's hand in response, who somewhat wished now that he hadn't offered it, for Bren's grip, or tackle as it might have been described, was as firm as everything else about him.

Lampaea flexed his fingers in the detection for residual life when Bren wasn't looking.

The rider removed his mask, which Lampaea had recognised as bearing the emblem of Beltro.

‘I too am heading for Setra, in search of two people who were taken from me, and to raise a storm against those Setrans, for whatever sick deeds they hide from us. I will purge them and their country.’

In his deep and fluent growl, there was a hateful malice brimming with revenge and unstoppable passion.

‘Then we are both looking for someone there,’ said Lampaea as the two of them helped the captives down and gave them some water to share out. ‘But I feel as if you know more than I do. What did you mean about trafficking? What exactly is happening?’

Bren looked over the people.

‘Rest for a moment,’ he said, ‘you are safe with us.’

He then took Lampaea by the shoulder until they were out of earshot.

‘Eastern Enphiah is planning something. For how long it has been going, I cannot say, but I have caught wind of this in Beltro, my own land. People disappearing, loved ones, friends, and now my own family too. Taken, they were, from Ahone in Thenigh. I have been on their trail ever since –’

‘And you thought they might have been with this trafficker?’ said Lampaea.

‘Yes. Though they were not. No matter, these people were clearly being transported for the same reason. Oh, I have stopped every suspicious traveller like him on my way. Many have been carrying no more than fruit and vegetables or hay. But I must be sure. He is the first trafficker I have caught.’

‘How do you know these people – the traffickers – are going to Setra?’

‘There have been others, Beltrorns that I know, a couple

of Acrounians, who have kept watch along the Eastern Border, all reporting the same thing. Carts bound with black leather. Hands pushing against the sheets. Shouts from men, cries from children, and the drivers calling back to be silent. Some of my men have been as bold as to follow them. We believe they were all led to Maliste.'

Lampaea's eyes grew wide.

'Maliste!' he said urgently, and hastily felt around for Halemedra's note.

'Keep your voice down – those people are frightened enough by this ordeal,' said Bren. 'What are you looking for?'

But then Lampaea had found it.

'Here, here – look! Maliste. This mentions it too; the girl who wrote me this is the one I'm searching for. She's in trouble –'

'She'll have been amongst those taken captive. How long has she been missing?'

'Long enough...' Lampaea tried to hide his solemn thoughts from appearing too obvious. The more this pieced together the more pain he felt.

'Were you there when they took her? Did you see them?' asked Bren.

There was a short silence and now a new emotion took Lampaea powerfully. Guilt.

'No...' he said slowly, 'I wasn't there.'

Bren looked him up and down once, seeming to understand where and why the hammer had struck. He looked down at Halemedra's letter, then handed it back to him. Lampaea stowed it away as if it had been momentarily stolen from him.

'You can thank her though, that letter,' said Bren airily,

'it eases my nerves tenfold.'

'Why?' said Lampaea as they returned to the people, he failed to read past the despair in Halemedra's cry for help.

'Firstly, it confirms what we believed about Setra, that everyone is being taken to Maliste. Second, it has proven that you are genuine, and someone I can trust. I hope. You do not want to be someone I can't trust.'

Bren tended to the captives, and his strong expression did not crack.

'And what happens now?' said Lampaea, handing out some bread from his supplies. 'Where will these people go? Home?'

A child of eight or so looked up expectantly at the mention of home. Her mother, too, held her tight and appeared hopeful.

'No,' Bren said shortly, 'they can't go home. Not yet.'

'What?' the mother with her child piped up. 'Why not? We are free now.'

'Yes, but you are not safe,' replied Bren bluntly. 'They will return to your villages for more no doubt or, if they want you specifically, and discover they do not have you, you will be hunted. I cannot say for sure, because I don't know what the Setrans are doing, or why. But I can provide somewhere safe, keep you all hidden until we know, so I will take you to where I stay with my own people, in Olonath.'

'The forest?' an old man said.

'But what of our own people at home?' came the woman again. 'The rest of our families – they could be taken next, and we can't even warn them –'

'Go home, if you wish,' Bren said coolly, 'but you will not have the protection of I or Lampaea on your way back.

We also have some food and water. I have seen more and more of these carts crossing the wilderness. If you want to risk you and your children being captured again, say now and be on your way. If not, follow me.'

On that note, Bren turned instantly on his heel and strode off in the direction of Beltro, south-east. He made a clicking sound and his horla caught up to him. Lampaea stood awkwardly where Bren had been beside him, though luckily it took the others little thought for persuasion to start moving, as they already felt vulnerable without his large presence.

Lampaea let them walk on first, and smiled a little as he released the four horlas from the cart, which were later used to carry the children and elderly members of their party. He caught sight of the man that Bren had killed, his eyes and mouth still open slightly, and tried not to think of how many more would end that way. He then shuddered to think what was happening to Halemedra, how they might have treated her.

His fists clenched.

And then he thought of Feletra. What if she too had been taken by one of these traffickers? Well, then he would fight to free her as well. He would fight anyone, anything. No one would hold them there. Setra was not prepared for a battle, but he was. And so was Bren.

x

Feletra was a little naïve at times, but even she was no fool, and had a decent degree of foresight.

She felt the white cotton dress delicately, examining some of the enna trimmings, and then stood and held it against her for size.

She had been presented with it an hour ago, by the same watery eyed man who had informed her of her invitation to the banquet. He seemed to be someone's lackey. And that someone was clearly her admirer. Although approaching her through some servant would not do his cause any justice, in Feletra's eyes. The prospect of a mystery man might have been romantic and excite the most fanciful of other women's hearts, but Feletra could have laughed at the idea. Probably because she wouldn't have known how to react to romance. In fact, the very thought of someone proclaiming an adoration for her seemed highly improbable, let alone amusing.

Perhaps it was because she had grown up with five brothers and a hardened mother. Or that she had lived off the land, helped to work for her own food, played simple games and would not have recognised things more valuable than bread. Her life was not a decorative one.

*I have certainly never worn a dress like this before...*she thought. *And it would be rude to turn up without it now.*

The dress was in no way Feletra's motivation for accepting the invitation however. No, she was greatly curious to meet this person. After she was through questioning them, it would be highly amusing to hear why they had not set their eyes on a woman of higher calibre instead of herself. Unless there was an ulterior motive, which she also planned to unearth.

When she was dressed, she took a few moments to smooth some non-existent creases down the front, sighed, and made for her cabin door.

Then she stopped, and began rooting through her pack, remembering something. It had been pushed to the very bottom, but was still in perfect condition, when she withdrew the carving of the little wooden horla, and tucked it into her garter. The skin where it touched felt warm for a second.

Was that going to rub?

She padded the side against her thigh with a cotton cloth and made out, locking the door behind her.

She wasn't sure why she took the ornament with her; it simply brought some familiarity in the form of a possession, she supposed, since her pack would be left behind in the cabin.

Upon finding the correct room, she discovered there were seven others sat round a cramped oval table. They all looked at her as she entered, one very thin woman sneering at how young she was to be joining them, two of the elder men rising from their seats in respect until she was sat, and one slim and somewhat drab-looking man at the head, smiling at her rather eerily.

'Welcome,' he said in an equally eerie tone, 'I am Vitry, the captain of the Weeping Dove. Please, will you share your name with us?'

The captain of the ship? He could not have been older than twenty-five. Thirty at a push.

'Feletra,' she replied quietly.

The captain smiled again and nodded to himself as if to say, 'I should have known.'

'And forgive the abrupt invitation,' he continued, 'I am sure you are a little confused by it, but your beauty drew me in so that I could not pass on the opportunity to meet you.'

Feletra laughed briefly through her nose. No one else laughed.

She looked up again in composure.

'Oh...really?'

'A woman of modesty! Now that is...truly admirable,' said Vitry, beaming.

He wanted to share his enchanted mood with his other guests, but they each appeared far from interested. After all, the food was waiting in front of them, and it had been dire enough having to wait for their eighth member, let alone becoming involved in the captain's personal delivery of affection.

'A most magical scene,' interjected the sneering woman, abandoning the obligation to suppress any sarcasm, 'but Captain, I must insist that now we dine, and save any informalities for after.'

'But of course,' replied the captain amicably and raising a glass to Feletra, who half-heartedly returned the gesture. The sentiment had not even founded a slight blush for its ridicule.

The dining experience passed by rather quietly. A male grunt here and there, a whistling sniff, an unappreciative passing comment on the tenderness of the beef, the chink on glass as no guest was left without wine for a second.

Feletra soon discovered she was no fan of red wine, and felt awkward when she politely polished one glass only for it to be targeted instantly for a refill.

The whole affair felt awkward. There were the stomach-churning bedroom eyes of Vitry, the bitter glances of the only other woman. The silence. The small room. The swaying of the ship. The delicious food spoilt by the company.

And there was an open window, which swung and creaked with the ship's motion. Feletra was sure she had seen something move outside a couple of times.

As the meal came to an end, she saw it again – there was a small creature, not much larger than a rabbit – it had darted past on the deck and now sat on the ledge, peering in on the banquet with curiosity. It had a fat little belly and black round eyes. Its ears were large and wide, with wire-like lashes fixed at the tips which whipped about delicately when the ears flexed back and forth.

Many of the other guests had not noticed and were now deep in their own conversations.

'Feletra,' Vitry had suddenly drawn up a chair next to her. She looked at him in astonishment, then back at the window. The animal had vanished.

'Now then –'

'Captain,' said Feletra, 'do you allow animals on your ship?'

'A-animals?' he looked at her in some confusion. 'That would depend on why they were being transported. Why do you ask?'

'No reason,' she took a sip of wine gingerly.

The captain resumed his creepy smile. That perfectly trimmed thin, black moustache crept along his upper lip like a trail left from some unfavourable insect.

'I think you've had too much wine, Feletra...'

Or not enough, she thought.

'No, I'm quite fine.'

'Tell me, why is it you travel alone? It's not something you often see, a girl so young...'

He had leant forward on his chair. She remained straight in hers, still clasping her glass. It was a barrier, a weak distraction. Something to look at, something to hold and drink from, rather than focus on him.

‘I enjoy travelling alone. There’s more freedom.’

‘I admire your independence,’ said Vitry, his eyes widening, ‘that confidence. But are you not even a little afraid?’

‘What is there to be afraid of? Everywhere I have been in Enphiah has been an enjoyable experience for me, I do not see why Pyra should be any different.’

Feletra thought that must have been the best lie she had ever told. She was almost proud of it.

‘Intriguing, but why Chriah? Why there in particular?’

His hand had sneaked round to the back of her chair at some point. He was staring intently into her eyes now.

Feletra stopped to reassess the situation.

The wine?

No, I have not had that much. This is not *my mistake.*

‘I... did not mention Chriah,’ she said firmly, and put her glass down.

Vitry’s smile faltered and he blinked a few times, then attempted to regain it.

‘Ah, but you did, not a few moments ago –’

But it was too late.

‘No, I did not. Excuse me, I have stayed too long,’ Feletra stood up as if she had somewhere more important to be. The other guests ceased talking and all eyes concentrated on them now.

As she made for the door Vitry grabbed her hand.

‘Please, I think you misunderstood –’

Feletra snatched her hand back and walked out into the corridor. She had not lost her wits to the wine. At no point had she mentioned Chriah; he knew more about her than he should have done. This explained the mysterious invite and all her passage fees being paid for – whether it was him, or someone else, she was being followed.

She was but half way down the corridor when without warning, the captain had her again – she was pinned forcibly against the side and her calls stifled to a murmur –

'Don't struggle, Feletra – I said *don't* – I don't want to harm you, but I will if you continue –'

Feletra felt terrified. For all her previous evasion, her eyes could not look anywhere but into his now – he was far stronger than he looked, holding her in a grip that would not yield – she longed for her dagger, of all times that she did not have it –

'Now, I will ask you something once, and I hope, for you, the only time – why are you looking for the cure?'

As he slowly removed his hand from her mouth for a reply, she fixed him with a look of pure bewilderment.

How could he possibly know this? Well, he would learn no more, and she spat in his face with loathing.

All of a sudden he looked murderous, and Feletra was deep in fear once more.

'If I can take no words from you –' he said slamming his hand back to her mouth – 'then I will take something else from you –'

He began pulling at her dress, it was animalistic – up rose the hem, his moist palm now travelling sickeningly up her thigh – his eyes seemed to brighten more and more with excitement, hers with dread – she tried wildly to escape, to flail, to bite, anything, but nothing would come of it.

She felt his aimless fumble at her garter, and suddenly he recoiled from her, screaming and holding his hand in pain –

'What is that –!' he exclaimed.

She saw what appeared to be a deep burn across his palm

before attempting to run – no good – the captain would not give in.

But just as he had caught her again, something had come to her aid – amidst everything, the creature from the window ledge had appeared now to leap atop of Vitry's head, and with huge claws dug them severely, fatally into his eyes.

There was no room for screams this time, only shock, as Vitry staggered backwards and slumped to the floor. His whole body began to shake and he gaped openly as blood drained into his mouth.

The creature was not alone, and sprinted back to its master, who was marching towards them with a dagger in his hand.

Feletra could not have mistaken those pockets, nor those striking features. It was the boy she had met on the deck.

As Vitry feebly raised his fingers to his eyes and began to howl, the boy knelt swiftly by his side and slit his throat, as if he did this every day. Carelessly he wiped the blade on Vitry's sleeve, and then picked something up – the wooden horla had fallen from Feletra's garter.

He looked at her instantly and she made an involuntary gasp.

'Yours?' he said.

'Yes.'

He tossed the ornament at her.

'It's very warm, interesting,' he spoke so calmly, whilst she felt on the verge of collapse. 'Go and find some crew members. Tell them you witnessed a murder.'

He turned on his heel in the opposite direction, his furry companion tagging along in haste before leaping for his shoulder.

Feletra had been struck with fear, relief, and now wonder. She looked down at the body before her.

'Wait!' she called, and ran after him.

The young killer stopped.

'That's it? I –' she felt breathless, and words could not be formed before him. Then she composed herself. 'Thank you.'

He paused before her for a second, and then said, 'I don't deserve that.'

And he was gone again.

She wanted time to think. There was no time. If she stayed there much longer someone would find her and name her the murderer.

She stood there for a moment with a smattering of blood across the white dress, a wooden horla grasped loosely between her finger and thumb, and heard that sickly creak of the ship all around her.

Then she ran, jumping over the still legs of the dead Vitry and turning one corner, two, three, until she found someone. She led two of the crew to the scene of the captain's death, and explained what happened, omitting certain facts such as the attack on herself. There was no need to indicate any motive that might incriminate her instead. As for the killer, he was a hooded individual who she had not spoken to, and disappeared as quickly as he had arrived.

He may have been brutal and savage, he may have been many things, but he still saved my life, she thought.

Feletra was feeling somewhat shaken, having been harassed then watching a man's life be taken in the blink of an eye, therefore the crew were easily convinced that she was simply some poor damsel in distress in all this, and instructed her to return to her cabin in case the killer returned.

She did so, and locked the door. Moments later a horn sounded, used in urgent meeting of all the crew.

Feletra looked around her room warily, as if a man with a creepy smile might emerge from under the bed or creatures which she didn't recognise with huge pointed ears might spring at her from the top of the wardrobe. Then she saw that she was still wearing the white dress, and desperately changed into something else. The little horla was returned safely to her pack.

The hours of the night passed by sleeplessly. Images and every small detail in them plagued her, but mostly of him. Her saviour. Never was one more curious than he. It was likely he was simply passing by and came to her aid as anyone would have done, but Feletra had felt something poignant about him, as if he had meant to be there. And that strange animal of his that had watched everyone at the banquet. A coincidence? The questions were mounting but she was receiving no answers. She had thanked him – why had he not deserved it? Who was he? And who was the captain, who appeared to know her business? Were they both involved in spying on her?

He must be following me as well then, she thought. *He must have known the captain; perhaps he just killed him to stop him taking the information from me first...*

Feletra dared not leave her cabin that night, but swore she would find him in the daylight. There was nowhere you could hide on a ship.

'Get off me! I'll kill you! *I'll kill you!'*

Feletra could feel his broad hands against her shoulders, immobilising her. She tried frantically to reach her dagger – she had it this time – she wouldn't make the same mistake twice –

'Stop, Feletra – be still.'

She ceased and looked into his dancing green eyes, listened to his smooth voice, and smelt the scent of bloodshed and cinders from his hair.

'How do you know my name?' she said helplessly.

He looked at her steadily.

'I'm going to get you out of here.'

He walked away, seemingly into – the sea? For a crash of waves had come to greet and envelope him.

She should have followed, she wanted to follow. But her body could not move –

She was shaken into this world – the world of ghastly unknown things, of easy kills, of unfair curses. The dream was over.

Feletra sat up calmly in her bed. The blankets were strewn across the floor, and everything was cold.

It had been three days since she had attended the banquet. Three days in which she had been unable to locate him, and in which every sleep since he had haunted her dreams. Sometimes he was alone and silent, sometimes he was with Feletra and spoke short and profound words to her, and other times he stood still amidst a heaving crowd, reminiscent of those at Xenor. But he was there again last night, and so was Ataleka. It had been a brief and simple dream; Ataleka turned away, turned back, and had transformed into him. And that was it.

Feletra wished there was more to say than 'him' or 'he.' She wished he had a name. It would have given her more comfort, to then know that he too was another someone, going somewhere, doing something, rather than just a faceless entity. But his name had escaped her, as did he, it seemed, for she had searched high and low on the Weeping Dove for him. It became apparent that you could hide on a ship after all; there was no sign of him or his small companion.

She took a shawl to wrap around her shoulders and peered out of the window, a shiver snaking down her spine. They were far out to sea; the waves had become aggressive with gales sweeping in from the south unmercifully, and land was not to be seen anywhere.

Another wearisome day was passing by; all passengers but the children were feeling this now. As a dull twilight rolled in Feletra had engaged herself in teaching a little girl how to sew, when she saw it – a reddish coloured furry something dart past on the deck like lightening. She left the girl to continue her patchwork and immediately tried to follow it, round corners – up and down staircases – through railings – eventually it had stopped on one of the lower decks adjacent to the stern, sat on the railing and tugged tentatively on its master's sleeve. Feletra, out of breath, looked upon them both and edged slowly towards them.

'I want to know who you are,' she said strongly. She cast her mind back quickly – did she bring a weapon? Yes.

He was facing away from her. There was a pause as he looked at the creature next to him and said quietly, 'You need to stop giving me away like this, Afax.'

The creature bowed its head somewhat apologetically.

Feletra came up beside him.

'Do you speak? Or are you as few of words as you are of places?'

He turned to her sternly, and Feletra wished for a second she had not spoken so boldly to him.

'Maybe I want to know who you are?' he replied airily.

'You seem to know enough about me already.'

'Do I? Remind me of your favourite colour then as I appear to have forgotten.'

His dry humour was lost on her as she grew more frustrated.

'I'm not playing your games. Why are you following me?' she demanded.

'I'm not following you.'

'You're lying! I saw that – thing of yours –' she pointed at the creature, who hissed back at her – 'looking in on the banquet to spy on me –'

'He's not a thing, he's a giptern, and his name is Afax.'

'W-yes –' she said stammering, unhappy at the interruption, 'and then who should happen to be at my aid when I am attacked but you –'

'Are you complaining?'

'No! Of course not, but you must have been listening to the banquet by that window. I just want to know why you were there at all, and…why you helped me.'

The wind whistled in cold from above and the ship rocked dangerously.

'Alright, yes, I was listening. And yes, I came to check on you when I heard you leave.'

'But why?'

'I was concerned for your safety. I knew Vitry, and I knew how he could turn.'

'But...you don't even know me.'

'Is that a good reason not to help someone in need?'

She paused, and felt herself softening all for his good

deed. She then shook herself inside. *No,* she told herself, *liars like this still existed, he could still drive a knife into your throat, too.*

'So, you knew the captain,' she said slowly, 'you have been working together then. Following me from Enphiah, haven't you?'

He gave a crooked smile, and Feletra was flooded with a momentary forgiveness. But she did not smile back this time.

'Good on you, for being so suspicious of strangers,' he said, 'but I'm not a stranger you should be worrying about. Whoever you think has been following you, it is not me. I don't know a thing about you, except that you're sailing to Stura. Or so you say, because now I think you have a lot to hide.'

'On the first day that I met you, you said I was trying to escape from something, and now after all this, do you really think I wouldn't suspect you to be a liar? Who says that to a person from just looking at them?'

'That was just a sense I got from you. I wasn't wrong though, was I?'

'You don't need to know why I'm going to Pyra,' she said with tenacity.

'You're right. My apologies.' There was no tone in his voice.

'But if you knew the captain,' said Feletra pressingly, 'then you must have an idea how he knew so much about me?'

'I knew him. I was not his friend. What was it he knew about you?'

Feletra sighed in exasperation.

'He...he knew part of my reason for travelling to Ch – to

Pyra. He wanted to know the rest.'

The young man looked down and nodded. It began to rain lightly.

'So why are you going to Chriah?' he said, looking up at her once more, and Feletra's eyes were ablaze.

'I *knew* it! You *are* involved! You knew about my journey to Chriah all this time –'

'Calm down. Of course I didn't, you're simply a bad liar. You don't think enough before you speak, and nearly uttered the word yourself. And some advice, if you're trying to conceal these things, do not openly admit the truth the next time someone guesses correctly.'

Feletra sighed heavily again. She did not know whether or not to trust him. On the one hand, he had been a murderous spy, on the other, he had supposedly done it all for the right reasons.

'What are your reasons for being on this ship then, for going to Pyra?' she said, 'Would you have been involved with the captain once this journey was over?'

'I do not think that is very fair, you being obliged to remain silent on your business yet I am expected to share mine. And no, Vitry would have gone his way, and I mine. I do not enjoy his company.'

'Then why associate yourself with him?'

He stared at her with interest.

'What is your name?' he said. Afax jumped upon his shoulder nimbly.

'Atrika,' she said defiantly. 'And yours?'

He moved towards her.

'That's a lie,' he said, and began to descend the stairs behind her. 'Nerehr, but I prefer Nil.'

Nil disappeared from sight with the giptern, leaving

Feletra alone again. She felt no desire to follow him this time. Some of her questions had been answered, and she believed he had been (at least mostly) telling the truth. Moreover, he'd seen how careful, how stubborn she was, and wasn't going to let on about himself until she did, there was no point continuing the conversation. She was not prepared to let her guard down, and why should she? Not to him. There was no benefit in telling him anything; he had done his part by helping her once, but now he had nothing more to do with her.

Feletra returned to her cabin and requested an extra blanket from the crew along the way. The rain had become heavier.

x

There was not one of more dominance than the other between Lampaea and Bren. And although their party felt certain there would be a clash of male power and leadership soon enough, the two of them appeared to have invested their own pre-eminences into a secure collaboration. There was a mutual respect here, and they had recognised their priorities as being the protection of the party, finding few things on which they disagreed.

Lampaea would have gladly fought the Setrans with Bren at his side.

The plains had been empty since they had begun their journey to Olonath; the spirits of the rescued had increased as the days went on, whilst their two protectors felt forever cautious that more Setrans would appear for the escapees, and even a little apprehensive that not even a merchant had crossed their path.

They had already crossed over the River Spelonas and were approaching the Well of Oxena in Beltro; the road they were on was usually a well-used one. The lack of passerbys was disconcerting.

Lampaea wiped his brow and felt inside a pocket for Halemedra's letter, checking he had not mislaid it. He then looked back at the people he and Bren were escorting; they grew lax and lagged further behind with each day.

'We will set off again immediately, Lampaea, once these people are safe. I promise you,' said Bren, noticing his anxiety.

'What?' said Lampaea.

'To Setra. I know you are impatient to be there, and maybe even considering leaving the party early to go there now. You feel as if time has been wasted.'

'Time *has* been wasted, and continues to be. She could be dead.'

'Have faith.'

'I do, but it wanes the longer I abstain. It's the only thing that's kept me here. And the people are better protected with the two of us.'

Bren nodded in agreement. 'We're almost at the forest front now, once inside things will be easier. Then we find my camp, gather some of my best and head north. There is strength in our numbers, and we can make up for lost time on foot by taking a horla each.'

Lampaea's heart felt lighter for Bren's positivity; he had to remind himself that he also had close ones to find and rescue from Setra.

'Bren,' he said, 'who is it you've lost? And how did it happen?'

Bren's eyes darkened upon the memory. His expression

suddenly had gone from aggressive and tenacious to one deserving of sympathy.

'My cousin, Phebet and her aaron. Our families have always been close, and so I grew up with Phebet; she then moved to Ahone, and I paid her a visit every so often from Beltro. We have never lost contact. I had just arrived there again seven starbands ago, when Phebet's neighbour ran to me and said she and Kolhr had disappeared just the day before. Their house had been ransacked in the night. I was told that angry, cruel voices and the sound of horlas could be heard as it had happened; I set off immediately to try and find them, and I knew it had to be Eastern Enphiahns.'

Lampaea shook his head in disgust.

'I think the time has come, Lampaea,' Bren continued, 'for the Enphiahn armies to reassemble. The Lor Nimh Ring and the House of Demata need to be alerted. Only they can bring all of Enphiah together. We must teach our neighbours once more what they will answer to. It seems their stubbornness and greed know no bounds, even after all these years.'

The Lor Nimh Ring and the House of Demata of Penthor formed the two greatest authorities of order between the Western and Mid Enphiahn regions, situated accordingly in Lor and Penthor. They were created following the end of the Nyvean War, when the regions were divided and the people demanded a dormant protector to watch over them. The line of the Luminors vowed to forever defend Enphiah, but with this as their sole duty and the people free to govern themselves as desired over the past two thousand years, the responsibilities of the Luminors seemed to wane to a vague memory and the gravity of their very presence faded. The descendants of the original Luminors however, continued to serve to the present day.

They had arrived at the Well of Oxena, which was incredibly huge, renowned for being the most impressive to be found in Esilence, and for its coded language of escape deep inside, everything painted and crafted entirely by Beltrorns. The unnecessary work of masonry appeared surprisingly intricate for its beastly creators and altogether beautiful.

'Just give me a time and place,' spoke the eldest of their party, a man named Yemhica who had been listening to their conversation intently, 'I may be seventy-three but I would gladly crush the Setrans with as much spirit as fifty young warriors. You should meet my grandson, Wariken, his skill is formidable.'

Lampaea smiled at the old man's patriotism before turning back to Bren in an undertone.

'The Luminors would not listen to us,' he said bitterly, 'they would avoid war at all costs with the east, for they have grown weak in power. They have forgotten how to lead. You and I alone could better round an army. No, without the proof they would laugh and employ us as their jesters.'

'Perhaps you are right, perhaps –'

But at that moment, the two men had both seen something in the distance.

Four, five, six horlas all racing towards them. At the sight of their guides having stopped, the party too came to a halt behind them and looked ahead with worry.

Lampaea squinted against the sunlight. He could make out dark clothing, some with cloaks – hoods – one held his arm aloft –

The others followed suit – there was the sound of metal

removed from sheaths –

Lampaea and Bren withdrew their swords in unison.

‘Easterns!’ Bren cried.

‘Get on the horlas!’ Lampaea called. ‘Go!’

The party scrambled about in fear; there were tears and crying instantly from the children as their mothers and fathers almost threw them onto the horlas in despair.

Horlas carrying as many as each could muster were galloping towards the forest of Olonath one after the other, whilst others ran on foot – some continued to panic and were moving far too slow –

Lampaea and Bren braced themselves. An archer shot at them and struck the well –

‘Lampaea, here!’ said Bren, taking his shield for the two of them as they crouched behind it.

‘No, the well is better protection –’

Bren quickly followed Lampaea until they were before the thick stone wall of the well. One of the elderly men of the party had not desired to flee and knelt down beside them poised with a small knife of his own.

‘Yemhica – what are you doing? You can’t stay!’ said Bren.

‘You two need help,’ Yemhica replied, ‘I heard what you said about the Setrans – I’m not letting them take me and my family away again!’

Lampaea looked helplessly at him. ‘No, Yemhica, you have to –’

But the riders were already upon them, there was no time to persuade anyone otherwise –

There were flashes of metal – animals moving too quickly for them – cloaks of black and navy blue sweeping past –

Lampaea and Bren were no amateurs though, and already had three of them down and one horla; perhaps Lampaea had grown too confident at that point, for his blade had swiftly claimed another of his enemies, when he took a blow to the head from behind – he heard Bren take care of that one for him – and as he lay face down temporarily upon the dry ground, he saw one of the riders had split from his comrades and headed for the innocents –

Shot. An arrow to the head of a woman on foot.

Lampaea rose to his feet again and turned –

Stabbed. In one side and out the other, Yemhica was silent when he fell to the ground.

Lampaea charged the assailant through with his own sword.

This left one in their midst, and the other who had made for their party was now returning to the well.

But even the one by himself – he was fast. *Very* fast.

He fought both Lampaea and Bren together with ease it seemed, a sword for each hand – was he even looking at them? For he was hooded and they could barely see his chin, let alone his eyes –

He pushed them further and further backwards, until they were up against the well – the other rider had arrived and engaged himself with Lampaea now. *You're easier*, he thought, coming away from the well and making the advance.

But Bren had never seen such speed before, and struggled to match his opponent's techniques – he tried to sweep one heavy blow to finish it – but it took too long – a slice was taken to his shoulder.

Being a true Beltrorn, Bren barely uttered a sound at the pain, but he was in some shock at being stricken, and then further shock as all at once his enemy pulled back his hood in an instant and smiled hideously at him.

The face – not a man – was all Bren could think, for the visual jolt was enough to momentarily immobilise him, and he was kicked firmly in the abdomen into the wall –

He tried to steady himself – reached out – and fell backwards into the well –

He grabbed onto the side – Lampaea had seen him.

But Lampaea's distraction was too long, and suddenly he was disarmed – but he left his weapon on the ground and swung into the well to take Bren's arm, who was slipping away, his weight twice as much as Lampaea's – they heard laughter above them.

'I can't keep hold!'

'Don't fall with me, Lampaea! Let me go and stay!' said Bren.

The shapes of two heads, one hooded once more, came to blot out Pytheria on them and looked down. Then one of them kicked his heel at Lampaea's knuckles before Bren could shake him off, and the two of them could only watch the daylight shrink away and darkness ensnare them.

Chapter 11
The Dove That Wept

The common folk hadn't noticed, but the messenger system in Enphiah was disintegrating. The ebrats, in particular, were slowly disappearing from the Western and Mid Enphiahn regions, whilst the hithri were being kept by those of wealthier status and only used sparingly. The East were gathering them too, and they did not let them out again, save for messages sent within the Eastern Region itself.

It was with some relief then, that Emmet could rely upon a different form of vector to carry his letter to Feletra. Horlas were, and always had been, remarkable creatures. Their memory was unquestionable, their loyalty infallible. And no one quite knew what it was about horlas, that gave them that efficacious gift of sensing and locating an individual whom they had served in the past. Steptail had recovered rapidly in Betharanei since his accident at the bridge; he was ready to venture out again. But this time, he had been sent out alone, and Emmet was depending on him to have the letter reach Feletra in time.

Some horlas who had not bonded well with their rider were incapable of finding them again, and the sense for their trail was weak. But Emmet had to believe that this was no barrier for Steptail. He knew very well the taste of her presence, the signature of her personal aura, surely he would find her with ease.

It was on that night, after sending Steptail off into the Plains of Nemenon, that he had made his way to the Valley

House and slipped into its underground passageway once more. The building was always unlocked; thieves were unheard of in Betharanei. He lit a torch, and carried with him the short knife of pnapsor, a grappling hook he had previously stolen from the blacksmiths on a supposed social visit, and a small brown leather satchel slung across his shoulder. He could see the steps now, and how they were gradually becoming the black oily slop that he and Feletra fell victim to; when he felt the slope was too slippery to stand upon, he dug his hook firmly behind a crack in the wall and tugged on it before lowering himself down carefully.

He reached a low-set stone chamber, with another, narrower pitch-black passage leading off to the left.

There was silence save for an irregular drip. The stench of raw metal and burning was intense, and served as an acute reminder of the last time. His feet were nearly sinking into the viscous black substance which layered the ground heavily.

Emmet touched the spherical wall cautiously, and his fingers pulled away whole thick strings of the peculiar oil; it seemed everything was covered in it. He wiped his hand hastily on his coat.

The silence then ceased, and sniffing could be heard; Emmet was still, and listened.

He went to face the second opening in the wall. A slipping and wet grasping of flesh on cold stone could be heard from inside. And then the most distinct sound of all amidst this arduous wait: Emmet screwed up his face when it reached his ears. A very dull clicking and cracking as the thing moved along closer to the chamber. No bone in its body was stable; it was like its entire frame must reassemble with every movement.

Of all his research, Emmet was suddenly reminded of a very poignant quote:

'Out of my Esilence, I saw –
A spirit spat out of the deepest and most unwanted corners of the Artrysiptic.
An eyeless being that did creep towards me,
A poor beast only, that did seek my flesh and mind with such untamed thirst.
"Look not now, comrade," said I, "for its lust wanes not."
Those bones – Those bones!
That then shifted upon one another and snapped and moved and had rotation.
An ill thing –
That did scream at me until I might have bled for a given!
What noise I had lived without till now –
From it my very soul dragged into black earth and fire from whence it came.
And my comrade was set upon with haste.
No more the fortunate, I.'

It was a piece that had been recovered from a soldier in the Nyvean War. Emmet now felt as if he was seeing things through the eyes of the soldier – the light of his torch flickered disgustingly across the creature's feeble body, it almost appeared human – only he had no comrade to overshadow the intense desire that now filled the chamber –

'Preathin: A creature of the earth, blind and frail, and

seeking their prey on the presence of desire.'

What desire was he feeling now? *My mind is crowded,* Emmet thought. The desire to escape, to see the thing properly, to achieve what he came for, to be brave...

But he felt his bravery slipping beneath the claws of fear the more this thing moved before him.

Swiftly he placed the torch in the black substance on the floor and held the knife in front of him, ready.

And then every illustration from every book Emmet had researched began to emerge from their pages, but none more horrific than the image that he beheld now, the one that moved as it had been described to him, skeleton snapping and pausing and snapping again. The one that drew back shallow breath over its teeth to sense him head to toe deliciously; the preathin tasted the air that it planned to no longer share with Emmet, turned in his direction, and unleashed a chilling screech that had his blood and breath freeze as ice would commandeer a lake.

'So, everything I suspected was true...and I only had to come here to find out...'

But the preathin, the very creature that Enphiah's ancestors thought they had buried, could not hear his words. It heard only his desire, and sprang for him.

Emmet had been poised – and charged into the thing, struck its midriff with the knife, and immediately felt bone enclose around it. It was the most unexpected thing to occur –

Emmet suddenly found himself shielding his face with his arm as the preathin now had him trapped against the wall, biting and snarling and spitting that black fluid all over him whilst elsewhere it flowed freely over his hand from the wound.

He couldn't believe it – he pulled with all his might but the knife was stuck fast, until finally –

All at once it was free again, but there was a new problem now.

There was no blade left – what remained was a pockmarked scrap of metal and a hilt. Emmet panicked – the preathin's strength was beyond expectation and he was running out of ideas now that he had no weapon –

The preathin was fighting hard against his resistance – its pale grey face edging closer to his fresh and youthful one – fibres of black sludge stinking and dripping from its mouth and firing from gaping craters and valves in its skin, the crusted rims crackling as they expanded or depressed in size –

Emmet decided there and then that this would not be the end of him. He looked into the shallow concavities of thin flesh that would have formed its eyes, and with all the force he had left to summon shoved it to the ground –

The preathin flailed its limbs in its own filth for a moment – in a last resort Emmet removed his satchel and wound the strap about the creature's wasted neck from behind.

And pulled.

And pulled.

And pulled.

Excess black fluid ebbed away as the preathin fell still.

Emmet wiped his face of the stuff and stepped back. The fire of the torch was fading away; he looked at his knife in the dying light. It had disintegrated even more since he had last looked. But then he heard something else, and feared the preathin was still alive on first thought. But it had come from the slope he had used to enter the chamber – a sliding sound, until suddenly a man halted at the end and looked him squarely in the eyes.

It was Amanyl.

‘Of everyone in the village, I knew it would be you I’d find down here, Emmet,’ he said, and then withdrew his own knife. ‘I’m sorry, boy. You know too much about this.’

‘You’re wrong,’ said Emmet, ‘I’ve only just begun,’ and he darted for the opening the preathin had emerged from.

But the tunnel he had taken led somewhere that merely worsened his plight, as an even greater chamber lay at the end and he was confronted by huge cages, each enclosing several cramped and squirming preathins.

There were men too, observing them from the outside, some writing things down whilst others climbed atop the cages to feed or tease them.

And there was a separate area – it was open; there were five men all pulling on ropes and operating pulleys that were anchored to something unseen in the exposed earth. It was a slow process – whatever they were pulling out was incredibly resistant. And then one came out – they were unearthing more preathins, these ones were white all over, smaller than the others and inactive.

Emmet could not believe his eyes. They were being bred like livestock.

There was an echoing laugh behind him. He turned to see Amanyl stepping down from the tunnel mouth.

‘Surprised?’ he said. ‘I’m not so sure you are. You’ve been keeping a close eye on us, haven’t you, Emmet? And all since that girl came to the village. She left fast, I see. What’s her part in all this?’

‘Irrelevant,’ said Emmet as convincingly as he could.

‘She was just passing. I’m the one you need to worry about.’

They had begun to slowly circle each other, despite that Emmet no longer had any form of defence.

‘I do not think I will have to worry for long about you; you’ve spent your life shoeing horlas, Emmet. Do you think you can even handle what is happening here?’

‘I’ve come this far, haven’t I?’ Emmet replied, and he sounded almost like a child seeking approval from his senior. ‘I know this is all in league with Chriah, and soon the whole of Enphiah will know of it.’

Amanyl laughed again.

‘I don’t think you quite know...’ he said, ‘just what Chriah can throw at this wasted land.’

But as he finished his sentence, Emmet had circled back round to the tunnel, and suddenly scrambled through with all haste. Amanyl launched his knife at him, but upon a miss it clattered to the ground, and he called some of the men over.

‘Go! Get through and kill him!’

Emmet landed with his feet sinking into the black substance again in the first chamber. It was harder to move when he attempted to run, and he had to wade through, pushing the dead preathin aside and then he began to hoist himself back up the slope using the grappling hook.

There must have been about four men on his tail, but Emmet was hopeful for a gap in time between them when he heard them cursing and struggling up the slope behind him.

He reached the same corner as when Feletra had been with him, removed the hook and exited the Valley House from the side door. In a flurry, he ran into one of the water barrels outside, and then raced towards the stables.

The streets of Betharanei slept soundlessly; Emmet wondered if his pursuers would maintain the silence to avoid the attention.

There was one horla awake, and he looked at Emmet as if he knew and had been waiting. There was no saddle ready, nothing. There was no time.

‘Get ready, Syndrex,’ Emmet whispered.

He snatched a bushel of apples and mounted.

Then there was a scurry of footsteps by the stable door, only to be opened by one of the men from the Valley House.

‘I have him!’ he called smugly.

But Emmet boldly gave the signal to Syndrex, and the horla, brimming with energy, charged ahead with all speed.

Calling his bluff, the man did not move.

‘You’re trapped, Em –!’

He was cut short by a swift strike of the horla’s hooves to the face, and Emmet rode off with haste across the vast plains, to Lor.

The sound of stressed horlas was at his back.

His enemies followed on.

x

Feletra had forgotten how many days had passed now since she last spoke to Nil. The mood of all aboard the ship was depreciating quickly, and everyone began to notice the carelessness of the crew.

Since Vitry’s death, they could be heard singing drunkenly every night, bawling crude insults at passengers on the deck and frolicking lewdly with the women, making it well known to all that the captain had ‘selfishly kept them all for himself' when he was alive. Moreover, many were apprehensive concerning the knowledge that they shared their voyage with a murderer who had not been caught, though there was a general consensus that members of the crew were responsible, and steered as well clear of them as possible.

Their negligence had led the Weeping Dove astray and the Pyraihn gales rushed north, unbeknown to the passengers.

The swaying of the ship grew more and more severe, and when it grew so intense that Feletra was almost tossed straight out of bed one night, she was stunned to see water swilling back and forth on the cabin floor.

Almost instantly afterwards, there came a swift banging on her door – she reached for her small knife kept under her pillow, anticipating it to be one of the crew rousing her with vulgar intent.

'Open the door, now!'

It was the voice of Nil. Somewhat relieved but still sensing trouble afoot, Feletra rose to answer, but as she did so the entire ship began to rock to one side and she was thrown against the far wall. That was when she realised there were screams emanating from the neighbouring cabins, blending into the fierce whistling wind outside.

As the ship came to, she ran for the door and grasped the handle. Nil was there, as sodden as a drowned rat, his giptern seeking refuge up his sleeve.

'You have to get out. Get dressed,' he ordered, marching in.

Feletra hastily threw some more appropriate clothes on, though it was difficult to stand still with the ship's indecisive motions.

‘What’s going on?’ she said, slinging her pack over her shoulder and checking she hadn’t left anything behind, but her bow and quiver had slid out of sight beneath her bed. ‘Is it a storm?’

‘Yes. And the crew have abandoned us. All the boats are gone; would you believe they’re still intoxicated?’

Then there was another rock, sharper, steeper than before, and all too suddenly the entire ship was thrown in the opposite direction onto its starboard side – Nil flew first across the cabin – Feletra flew into him, and the door slammed shut on them.

With the force of the impact seawater was now managing to creep in through all manner of broken panels and crevices, and Feletra immediately became conscious of it.

‘The water –!’

But Nil was not interested; he wrestled Feletra off him and beheld the door, now horizontal to them. He tried the handle, but it was sealed tight against the water.

Then he yanked and cursed and twisted at it every which way he could. Nothing.

‘I can’t open it,’ he said to a horrified Feletra. ‘No one will come for us either. If we don’t get out now, we’ll be trapped and drown.’

The water was already knee-deep. Feletra turned pale and was shaking her head in disbelief as she waded over to the door.

‘No...no, this can’t be – there must – there must be a way out!’

She desperately tried the handle herself – she banged on the door and yelled at the top of her lungs for help.

The splinters adorning the poorly fixed door handle gave

way and burst; the handle shot out with ease and seawater flowed through freely. The pair looked at each other. They were at waist-level now, and the door was almost submerged.

Feletra banged even harder on the door and Nil ducked underwater to investigate something.

There was a loud creak between all the panels, and Nil suddenly reappeared –

'Stop doing that! Didn't you hear that sound? This door won't hold for long –'

Feletra wouldn't cease, and then Nil took hold of her arms –

'I said stop!'

'I cannot swim!' Feletra cried. She was undoubtedly reminded of the time she leapt into the Sorpha to save Ataleka, undoubtedly reminded of the irony of the whole situation and missing logic. But this felt different, this was slow, this was a drawn-out death, this was the water seeking her rather than her seeking the water; she feared it terribly and could not summon the same courage as she did that day.

Nil paused.

'Then you'll have to trust me,' he said calmly, 'I will get you out of here, but you must hold onto me as tight as you can when this door opens –'

'But it's stuck! We're trapped in here –'

'I think there is something I can do to help, but you have to stand back a step.'

Feletra didn't care what it was he had in mind at that point, she wanted out, and did as he asked.

He plunged beneath the surface once more.

Without warning he had grasped her ankle – a dull

shooting sound muffled by the water – and then Feletra was struck hard as the door was freed –

She barely had enough time to draw in her breath it had all happened so fast – but there she was, floating about underwater like a poor piece of lone seaweed whilst Nil had kept hold and anchored her. Then she saw it on the far side of the cabin, her bow and quiver drifting about aimlessly.

Nil pulled her over swiftly – took hold of her hips and pushed her up to the surface.

Feletra gasped – a second later there was Nil as well, undeniably calm and assuming control of the situation. There was only enough room to surface their heads and shoulders and the ceiling (or wall, rather) was beginning to restrict them.

'Put your arms around my neck –' Nil said, 'don't let go. Take a deep breath.'

'Wait, my bow –'

'Leave it! There's no time.'

Feletra took a breath as deep as she could muster, and then Nil led them down again and through the open doorway successfully. He was a good swimmer and stronger than he looked, but Feletra was too busy trying to stifle the panic rising in her chest to notice; every second she spent with immobile lungs was another closer to death – and Nil was still battling his way down the corridor for them.

Through some of the other cabin doors Feletra saw a couple of lifeless floating bodies.

She closed her eyes. Ignorance truly was bliss.

There were twinges in her throat – she could feel her heartbeat, drumming a melancholy plea to her to reach the air now.

She dared not open her eyes, in case they were still no closer to the upper decks. But then sounds about her ears changed from a blunt and distant hush to acute, clear running water, running fast.

Nil had found the right staircase; they were higher up – and then emerged. Both of them drew in breath sharply.

'Where are we?' Feletra asked in a fluster and blinked repeatedly for the salt stinging her eyes.

'We're in the galley.'

'The galley? I thought we were higher, why did you bring us a deck down?!'

'We are higher, the cabins on the starboard side are under, the galley lies on the port, and has a direct route up to the main deck,' Nil answered, confidence still in his tone and expression. 'Look up there,' he pointed to what appeared to be a small square door, 'that's the only hatch left we can use – it leads onto the deck, climb the steps to it and hurry.'

The steps were narrow and on their side as with everything else aboard the ship, challenging their escape. Nil grabbed with agility at the highest rung he could reach, then climbed his way up the last few to the hatch, as Feletra watched on and gripped onto the bottom rungs to prevent herself sinking or drifting.

The water level began to rise rapidly all of a sudden in the galley and the hatch was refusing to open – Nil had been thrusting his weight against it with his shoulder for the past few seconds.

'The water's rising, Nil!'

Nil tried harder.

Feletra watched the water chasing them with horror and struggled to anchor herself to the wooden steps against the buoyancy that began to lift them from below.

'We're running out of time!' she shrieked.

Nil repositioned himself and gave two forceful kicks – the hatch finally gave way.

In poured more water from outside – Nil scrambled out and managed to pull Feletra out after him.

But there was nowhere to stand or gather themselves, and they were together thrown to the wind as the ship dipped submissively to the elements – they were fortunate and were able to grasp the rigging of the shrouds; Nil had more bearing, and he was hanging on tight to Feletra before swinging her onto the ropes with him.

Feletra held something back in the pit of her stomach – it wasn't vomit, just dread circling around continuously and a severe tightness in her abdominal muscles that were preparing her with the inevitable contact with the sea.

There was no mercy to the storm – a woman screamed from somewhere as the force of the gales and the smattering rain pounded them, to which they were but two straggling stray feathers caught in a spiderweb.

But Nil had not let go of Feletra once, and not she of him; they each had an arm for the other, but it was difficult to know where to turn now.

'We have to let go of the rigging!' Nil shouted above the crashing of the waves and the wind in their ears, 'The ship is going down –!'

'I can't! I can't let go!' screamed Feletra – her inability to swim tightened her muscles even further, her mouth and throat were drier than ever with only the bitter taste of salt to comfort her, but her grip on Nil's arm loosened a little as she feared he would take her down into the depths of the ocean with him.

'You have to or you'll go down with the ship! It *will* pull you down!'

Feletra could only shake her head at him helplessly. The sea would absorb her, it would destroy her.

Then Nil took one look at her with disdain and suddenly drew a knife at her throat. He let go of her arm and she fumbled for the ropes clumsily – in doing so the blade tip was felt upon her skin –

'The wind can have my hand slip at any moment,' said Nil.

Feletra all at once was left with no choice – she felt a lurch in the ship's movement coming and let go.

Nil then followed suit – miraculously he managed to find her hand as the cold desolate water enveloped them once more. With much difficulty he pulled both of them free of the ship as high pressures tried in vain to suck them under with it.

They grabbed at a round table top floating past as the Weeping Dove sank further into the marine abyss, sobbing to the stars for the last time.

Feletra looked on and thought of all those who had not escaped, feeling all the more powerless, and thinking that if she had known how to help herself, she could have helped others. The storm continued to jostle them about and it felt endless, Feletra dipped in and out of the water between the fierce rolling of the waves and had never felt such aching in her arms before, but the desperation to grip the table top was all that spurred her on. After what seemed an age, the storm died down and moved on, leaving them surrounded by an eerie calm.

'Do you have your things?' Nil said after some time.

'Yes,' Feletra replied with some hesitation, briefly lifting her sopping pack; she felt lost without her bow and arrows.

'Are you a good archer?'

Feletra shot him a coy look, 'I'm decent, yes.'

'I can believe that, since you're bad at everything else.'

Feletra opened her mouth in defence but decided against it, no one else she knew had ever been so bold as to sum up her innumerable flaws in one breath. She thought to change the subject.

'Your creature – the er –'

'Giptern. He's safe. And very aquatic, fortunately. He's under the table top.'

Feletra's eyes moved down and she held onto the mouth of her bag with her free hand in case the giptern swiped something.

'So, what do we do now? We're in the middle of nowhere,' Feletra sighed.

'Not quite. If you look carefully there's land over in the far distance,' Feletra looked over her shoulder and could make it out clearly with her sharp eyes, 'also, I am sure that is one of our boats over there.'

Nil whistled. When there was no response, he called Afax up, who came to perch upon the table. His master gestured towards the boat and Afax unleashed a high-pitched, crisp bird-like call that rang unpleasantly through Feletra's ears.

'If they don't hear that...' Nil mused, but the survivors in the boat did hear, and after some time found them.

It was upon closer inspection that Nil's expression dropped; the boat was comprised of nearly the whole crew.

'Do you have a weapon? A small knife?' said Nil in a hushed voice.

'What? I-yes, I do, but –'

'Keep it on you, and keep it hidden.'

'Well, well…' said one of the crew as they approached, highly amused at the stranded pair. He leant forward to lean on his knees and Feletra could see the moonlight dashing off a series of intricate designs inked into his bald head, a black symbol had been etched deep into the notch where his collarbone jutted, though she could not recognise its origin. 'If it isn't our favourite traitor asking for help.'

Nil lifted himself up further on the table top and looked at them darkly.

'Listen to me, I don't know what I've done to offend you all, but this is not the time or place. We need your help.'

'And spit on Vitry's grave?' said the marked man. 'No. We do not take kindly to murderers and traitors of the captain.'

Feletra looked at Nil for his response, and also thought it rich of them to speak so audaciously of their captain, when she remembered how they expressively slated him once he was dead.

But Nil hesitated.

'I didn't kill him,' he said.

The crew laughed in a murmur and shared quick glances.

'I'm not sure why you play us for fools, boy. You're the only one that made a deal with Vitry, and when he had what you wanted, you killed him for it.' They all looked at Feletra then, who appeared bewildered and once more looked to Nil for answers.

He could not give her eye contact.

'What are they saying? What deal?' said Feletra.

The marked man sat back and smiled crookedly, his sallow and yellowing skin stretching as he looked from one to the other.

‘Look at him, girl. You sit in the ocean with a man of guilt, lies and blood on his hands. You ought to be careful...I think he has further plans for you...’

‘I had no plans for her!’ Nil interjected with irritation.

Then the marked man suddenly reached forward and took hold of his collar roughly. They were face to face.

‘Then why did you kill for her?’ he said maliciously.

‘I had good reason,’ Nil replied somewhat proudly.

‘I’m sure you did. But it’ll not get you on this boat.’

‘Fine. Then take her, take her to land. I can wait it out.’

He released Nil slowly and laughed again at the pathetically heroic gesture.

‘Let’s go,’ he said to the others, then faced the helpless twosome. ‘Leftovers from two wars gone without conquer. It’s a stale offer.’

The boat drifted from them until they were out of earshot.

There was a long pause as the dawn broke over them and stained the water’s surface with delicate blinking light.

‘Care to explain?’ Feletra said directly.

Nil finally turned to her, but his expression was sombre and there was anger suppressed beneath it.

‘No,’ he replied with distinction. ‘Start moving towards the island. It’s not far.’

Feletra was taken aback as Nil and Afax began to swim towards the land, dragging Feletra on the table top.

‘No? Whatever they were talking about, I was involved. So I deserve to know –’

She began to help in the pitiful swim, all the while grasping desperately with her right arm to the debris. The lack of any surface to stand on she found immensely disconcerting.

‘What makes you think you were involved?’

Feletra gave an exasperated look.

‘I’m not to be taken for a fool either, you know. The “plans” for me, the way they all looked at me, and referring to me as “leftovers.” What would you believe?’ she said bitterly.

‘I believe men like them are not to be trusted.’

‘Then I believe you should join them.’

Nil stopped abruptly and turned to face her. Wisps of that anger were seeping through his stony expression like smoke escaping from the cracks of the earth.

‘You are not familiar with appreciation of those that make a habit of saving your life, are you?’ Strangely, his voice had a dead tone to it.

‘Perhaps you had “good” reason, just as you did for killing Vitry.’

Nil stared at her for a second, then returned to the swim without a word more.

For the rest of their struggle in the Sea of Dalpha, Feletra kept as silent as he, deciding her main priority now should be to reach land where she was more able. But if she provoked Nil enough to abandon her now, her lack of swimming ability would leave her stranded. Feletra thought Nil had appeared more intimidating than perhaps he had intended and made the wise decision to avoid a confrontation in such a volatile and unfamiliar setting to her.

The island was beautiful and alluring; everything about it seemed completely natural, untouched and free. Feletra could feel that purity wash over her skin as they approached the tranquil shores; it was mixed into the clear water, sewn into every grain of sand and slept in the core of the mountains in the distance.

There was a thick forest before them and a few channels of seawater wound clumsily to the front. Pytheria shone strongly, but despite this only a minimal few shafts of weak light entered the forest – everywhere else inside was dark, ominous and tinted in a grey hue. There was nothing exotic about the place, but still heaving with life, many various small crawling and flying animals crowding both the beach and between the trees. There was a freshness here, yet Feletra had to tread carefully for all the native insects that littered the sand.

She sat down heavily, sopping wet and exhausted, wishing she had dry clothes to change into.

Nil chose to stand and squeezed at some of his pockets in an attempt to wring them out, whilst Afax poked at moving things in the sand and jumped up with a swipe when something buzzed over his head.

Feletra stared out at the sea moodily. Nil glanced at her and spared her some empathy.

'I paid for your entry onto the Dove,' he said, 'and your cabin.'

She looked at him slowly as if she already knew.

'Why?' she said with demand.

Nil pushed his bottom lip into his upper and raised his eyebrows.

'You were a trade piece,' he put simply.

'A trade piece? In what?'

'As I said before, I knew Vitry. He saw you from the deck before you had boarded, and thought you worthy of his bed. I had been trying to get some information from him, to which he refused. Then he saw you, and said if I could get you on board somehow, he would give me the information in exchange. When I noticed you were trying to board anyway, it wasn't so difficult a task for me.'

Feletra was at that point in which her mouth had opened in preparation for numerous curses in his name, but was so livid she could not decide on which would be most fitting, and it took a few seconds for any response to pass her lips.

'So I was as good as bait?! Just a product of desire to be sold so you could have your peace of mind!'

'Well, yes, but –'

'Why am I even still here with you – in your company as if you were so honourable!'

Feletra rose to her feet without hesitation, her straggly bits of soaked hair flying everywhere about her face.

'Atrika, let me speak –'

Feletra stopped short with a brief confusion spelt in her eyes, and Nil looked on coolly at her.

'Forget your name already?' he said.

But Feletra had stormed off towards the forest that fringed the beach. Nil sighed calmly and followed her.

'Let's think fairly here; yes, I did those things for ill purpose on your part, and I am sorry. I did regret it even from when the agreement had been set down between him and I. But I saved you from him, didn't I?'

'Yes, to the extremes of murder!' Feletra retorted.

At this, Nil halted. Feletra sensed she had struck a nerve in him and also stopped. Nil was no groveller.

'You don't know what he would have done to you, if I hadn't stepped in,' he said gravely.

Feletra began to believe that Nil knew far more than any other average boy she could have stumbled across. But he was so vague about it. About who he was, what he knew, his plans, his intentions. For this she felt frustrated beyond comparison, and refused to handle this mysterious demeanour of his any longer. It built up inside her more and more as they stared at each other, then she could look at his face no more and walked away again, onwards through the thicket. She withdrew her dagger and slashed at growths that obstructed her path as Nil remained still, watching her intently.

Then there was a high-pitch ringing sound – Afax was calling from nearby, and Nil went to investigate.

But as he approached the undergrowth where Afax had led him, he saw something that had certainly not been there for much longer than they had.

There lay the body of one of the men from the crew, three skinny arrows protruding from his chest. None of the crew carried a bow, and the arrows, he noticed, were adorned with the thorns of franchyn. A trademark plant that only grew on one island.

Then he looked to the tree upon which the body graced – sure enough, there was the symbol he was expecting, carved fresh into the bark, the dark orange ink still wet and glistening.

He ran to find Feletra before she went too far.

'Atrika! It's Ira! We're on the Isle of Ira!'

Feletra heard him, but only became more agitated at the sound of his voice, when suddenly there came a noise of splitting wood. To her left, one of the trees was falling in her direction – to her right, another straight after it.

Nil saw the danger ahead, and raced on to the scene in a bid to reach her in time. The two trees shook the earth as they collapsed to the ground, one to the front of her, the other behind her, incredibly both just missing her.

'Atrika – are you alright?' said Nil, as he and Afax

appeared before her.

But Feletra had no time to answer, as a third tree was following suit towards them, then a fourth on its way down, and a fifth; Nil jumped the one that separated her from him, took her hand firmly, and they ran further into the forest as more and more of the trees toppled by themselves behind them. After what seemed like eleven or twelve huge felled trees, the danger ceased, and the two stopped to gaze upon the damage.

'Were you doing that?' said Nil.

Feletra stared at him in perplexity, almost waiting for the joke.

'Me? Are you insane?' she replied, her frustration having peaked with him again at such an idiotic question.

But there was no time to consider the phenomenon, for there were quick and invisible movements in the shrubbery around them, and instantly, before either of them even knew where they had come from, at least fifteen men had encircled them.

They seemed to have appeared from nowhere. Directed at the newcomers, each held a spear aloft, save for one, who hung upside down from a bough with a crossbow.

Then a woman appeared, unarmed, from between them. The most elegant and ethereal woman Feletra had even seen, she could have been the image of dreams.

'Atrika...' she said with soft intrigue, 'is not her name. It is Feletra.'

Chapter 12
The Well of Oxena

Steady drips from Feletra's clothes fell to the ground and quenched the upturned soil as she stood there sodden before them.

Birds flocked above her and gave distress calls in the despair to find new homes.

Her gaze was fixed on the woman and her expression was shaped aggressively. But the aggression was not true within her, it was only to hide the fear that resided inside, a fear of the unknown, whilst more and more strange people learnt things about her every day, things they had no way of knowing.

'How do you know my name?' she said shakily.

But the woman behaved as if she had not heard.

'But you are something to be feared...' she said, mostly to herself, only her eyes moving as they swept the scene of the fallen trees. They paused upon the ground, and then flicked up to Feletra suddenly.

'Bring them.'

Without warning the men were upon them, the woman disappeared into the thicket like a ghost.

Feletra and Nil had their hands bound in an unusual substance – it looked and felt like a filthy, thick spider's web, and stung a little.

Feletra twisted her wrists about in discomfort. The stinging only increased.

'Don't. It will just worsen if you resist it,' Nil said.

Feletra exhaled through her nose shortly.

‘Forgive me for actually wanting to be free,’ she said with indignation.

‘Your friend is right,’ said one of the men to Feletra, ‘this is the web of chrysana. Like spider’s web, but unbreakable to all kymic activity.’

Feletra looked him straight in the eye, understanding a little better why the woman may have taken interest in her, albeit mistakenly.

‘I’m not kymic,’ she said to him quietly.

‘I did not say that you were,’ he replied in short, and led the group deeper into the forest.

Feletra kept an eye on him from behind and watched where he was taking them, he appeared to be their leader. A wooden charm dangled from his waist. He sported great brown boots with tangled laces and there were two hoods that hung down his back; the inner one was in fact a mask that could be pulled over and down to the chin with sweeping eyeholes. A couple of the other men were still wearing theirs as they followed and secured a perimeter.

Suddenly, at least, it was sudden to Feletra, a large grey bird with impressive red tail feathers perched upon their leader’s shoulder. No one else in the group had found this out of the ordinary. The man looked at the bird, tapped his temple with his index finger once and the creature took off again.

The forest looked untidy, there were cluttered vines that had no sense of direction and couldn’t decide what to spiral up next, all types of trees were muddled together – short and portly ones nestled into their taller peers with low sweeping boughs, whilst the others were all in contact with each other: headbutting, winding, fraternising. And there were more pitfalls and steep ditches than Feletra cared to count. It made the walk all the more arduous and shed no light on her mood. She and Nil had reached that uncomfortable stage of existing perfectly between sopping wet and bone dry, and with nought more positive occurring to distract them, the feeling of damp was all too tedious and heavy upon them.

They came to a steep incline, and at the top there was a huge wooden bridge leading over a high-current river far below. At the end of the bridge was a wide, flat dirt path that led straight into a small settlement.

The muddling of all the different trees no longer appeared so useless and unkempt; the tribe of people here were using them for everything. They had practical use, storage, decoration, and homes were stationed everywhere; on the ground, there were those made with wooden poles, some were merely holes dug into the hill on the far side, whilst others were in the trees themselves, dotted about at all levels. As Feletra looked up past all these she could see a platform at the top of the tallest tree, and wondered what lay up there.

They were led under a wooden shelter that looked out onto the settlement where the chrysana web was removed and two of the group stationed themselves at the entrance.

The leader of the men faced them both squarely. Feletra noticed he sported a long scar that ran the length of his hairline and down past his temple.

'You're free to move, but there is no way of escape past the bridge; we have eyes everywhere. You'll stay here until we know more about you. Try not to worry, we don't consider you our prisoners – prisoners wouldn't be treated as fairly. My name is Mathenhis. If you need anything, ask.'

'Yes –' Feletra said quickly, 'I want to speak to the woman.'

'Adrenache will speak to you on her terms, not yours.'

Mathenhis left them swiftly before Feletra could object.

She glanced at Nil, who returned the look indifferently. She began to pace slowly to and fro; that feeling of helplessness was gone – she couldn't pin when it had happened, but it had. Where once she would have felt so hopeless and vulnerable, now there was independence and power. She felt in control. It wouldn't last forever, she knew this, and she knew of the things out there that made her quail. Perhaps this is what made her stronger then. And it may have been all that seawater that cleared her head, for she was already planning the best route of escape from her prison, whatever Mathenhis wanted to call it, as it was a prison to Feletra whichever way they looked at it.

She peered through the slats between the wooden beams and out the open entrance as she paced.

'You won't find any way we can escape,' Nil cut in to her thoughts, standing perfectly still.

'You're right, because there is no "we",' Feletra replied testily.

'Well if it means anything, thank you.'

'What for?' she threw him an irritated look. It seemed to add to her dislike of him every time he said something she didn't understand. His persona was too vague for her as it was.

'If they hadn't found something interesting about you, we'd both be dead, just like the crew.'

'There wasn't anything interesting...they've just got some insane woman for a leader. Probably been licking too many of those crabs off the shore.'

Nil smiled.

'Insane? Don't you know who these people are yet? They're Efordrads – descendants of the Artons.'

Feletra stopped pacing.

'Artons?' she said.

'Yes, you know –?'

'Yes, yes – I know who they are. My mother told me all the stories. But I thought their descendants were said to be scattered and unknown.'

Suddenly she forgot about her frustration, her schemes to escape and her dislike for Nil, and she sat across the way from him, eager to hear about the gaps in history she had been misinformed on.

'Some are still scattered, mostly in Stura, a rare few in Beltro. But the rest stayed together and became the Efordrads.'

'But I thought the Beltrorns owned the Isle of Ira,' said Feletra.

'They do. They allowed the Artons to seek refuge here.'

'It makes sense,' Feletra nodded. 'They had nowhere else to go once the Chriahks had pushed them out.'

This was the Chriahks' first notable act of malice as an independent movement. It was against the native Sturans – the Artons. This came in Men. 42, when the newly-born Chriahks had seized Pyra eight years before; they acted under the power of Chrie, a man previously serving Sethra as his right-hand man, before betraying him and forming a secret army of his own. Chrie recognised that Pyra lay forgotten in the south due to the three warlord's greed to have Enphiah, but Pyra was a rich and rewarding land that was not to be overlooked.

But whilst the eastern side of Pyra was wild and

uninhabited, the west was not, and the Artons were met with violent threats to leave or be killed. There was passion in everything the Artons did, especially in their king, Notenyll, and so they fought hard to keep their land, but the Chriahks were too strong. Upon his deathbed, Notenyll ordered his daughter Illeno to gather whoever of the Artons were left and flee to the Isle of Ira. The Chriahks' victory came at a price however, as it is rumoured that Illeno blessed her homeland before she left; its plants and crops would thrive for any but the Chriahks and their lineage. As it was, crops failed and Chrie's men began to contract mysterious diseases, forcing them to move to the east.

Feletra sat in wonder for a moment, then looked curiously at the guards.

'I've always wanted to meet the Artons,' she said, 'see how they lived and how they used the Artrenium.'

'I don't think they do use it anymore. They're a changed race,' Nil said.

'That's not something you just stop using.'

Feletra then suddenly rose to her feet and went to face one of the guards at the entrance. Nil watched with interest from inside.

'I have a question,' she said in a very queen-like manner.

The man was tall and he looked down on her without a flinch.

'Ask away,' he said in a deep voice.

'Your people, you still have the Artrenium, don't you?'

'That is a myth.'

'What?'

'It is widely held that our ancestors possessed this gift, this Artrenium, but it is simply folklore. They were no more gifted than you or I. Don't believe children's stories.'

Feletra stared at him in disbelief and then swiftly returned to Nil.

'They're not Artons,' she said passionately.

'No, they're not,' said Nil, 'they're Efordrads.'

'They can't be the descendants though. No Arton would speak that way. The Artrenium made them who they are –'

'But I told you, they've changed. It's been nearly two thousand years since they came to Ira. A lot can happen in that time.'

Feletra was quiet and wore a passive frown. The Artons had formed a vast part of her childhood, her mother had told her and her siblings all the stories there were to know about this magical race of people. They had a kind touch, all life thrived around them, synchronised with nature, and they were fiercely loyal to their kind; everything they stood for must be protected without fail. These are the things that nature rewarded them for, and they were bestowed with the power of the Artrenium, a gift instilled in each one of the Artons and restricted to their line only. With it, their flowers bloomed bright, fruits awakened with a healthy glow from under the shadows of their parent stem, and trees grew so tall the mountains cast an envious eye over them. But there was more. The Artrenium blessed the Artons with the ability to heal; no leaf was left wilting, no member left to bleed.

But these were not the Artons...were they? Feletra was sticking with her stubborn beliefs. Either they were the descendants and did have the Artrenium, or they were a different race entirely and did not. And if they were…could they heal her and Ataleka of the curse?

'What are you thinking?' Nil asked.

'I'm thinking that there is no connection between these

people and the Artons.'

'They are still the descendants,' said Nil fairly, 'even the guard said that.'

'In my opinion, they just think that. It's nice to grow up knowing that your ancestors were this great race of people. It's almost tempting to call them imposters. But since they show no signs of the Artrenium and even call it a myth, I don't think there is any link there. It's not something you just lose or forget about.'

Nil sat back a little.

'This is something you have a lot of passion for, isn't it?'

Feletra felt surprised. It wasn't something she'd noticed before.

'Yes...I suppose it is,' she replied sheepishly.

'I'm learning more and more about you, I think,' Nil continued. 'The way you are so passionate about everything, even what you learn from children's stories. You're family-oriented. I'd say you were travelling in the name of a close one; I think it's for something very important, else you wouldn't have left home alone. I'd even go as far to say that you are from Elpura.'

Feletra made no reply. She was watching what she said this time, but Nil already knew he was right. And she knew that too.

'But I prefer to listen to all sides of a person's story before making an assumption about them,' Nil said.

'You won't let this rest, will you?' Feletra said calmly.

'Well, you intrigue me. I won't lie.'

'Oh, but you already know so much about me, don't you?'

Nil smiled at the luke warm sarcasm.

'No. I'm just using logic,' he replied succinctly.

Feletra said nothing. She chose to allow his words, his incredibly sharp intuition, to wash over her, and successfully so this time. For the escape took hold again.

An impulse was born within her. It was straight, streamlined, it knew its destination. In that moment, she felt unstoppable, fed the impulse, and rose to her feet without a word to Nil. She was not as comfortable as he to remain captive like this.

Full pelt, she ran to the bridge, and hoped that Nil was utterly astounded.

x

Upon each of their awakenings, Lampaea and Bren were wrapped in darkness save for the distant circle of light above that almost mocked them more than the enemies that had imprisoned them there. The impact of their fall had not been without pain, but on the descent Bren had managed to slow them down when he had dug a long knife into the wall.

In a rage, Bren had already ploughed a fist into the dry stone floor of the well. He seemed unscathed.

'Fadres!' he exclaimed. 'I should have seen it coming.'

'Fadres?' Lampaea repeated, confusion at the term.

'Yes. They're the ones that attacked us.'

'I thought they were just Setrans? Men?'

'In essence, they are Setrans, but they are a different race to men. They have always lived alongside us, and were here long before men came to Enphiah.'

'Then why don't I know of them?' Lampaea asked.

'Because they are a "shadow race". They do not wish to be seen, heard or thought about. They'd rather be disguised as common men, which they did in the Nyvean War. There's joy to be had in a playful mystery, in watching a man steeped in curiosity and stupidity for knowing nothing of them.'

'I don't understand.'

Lampaea saw Bren's silhouette move in his direction.

'Think of them as the parent who is still a child themselves,' he said lowly, 'and you as the offspring. They take pleasure in watching us "grow up" and try to understand. And let there be no doubt, their knowledge of Esilence is forbiddingly extensive, they make us look rudimentary.'

Even in near pitch black, Lampaea could read Bren's expression at that point. It was the dark face all over again.

But right now, it didn't matter what the fadres were and where their history placed them, Lampaea thought. What mattered was getting out.

'We both know about the Well of Oxena. There is a way out, isn't there? And only a true Beltrorn would know how.'

'I know what you're suggesting, Lampaea,' said Bren, 'but I wouldn't know where to begin. And if there are clues in the stonework, there is no light to see them.'

'But there never was light,' Lampaea reasoned logically. 'Beltrorns built the well expecting no one to need it.'

Bren had paused for a moment after to think, and concluded they had nothing to lose. He thought a little longer – the darkness was good for this. Then he gained some intuition from nowhere, and it directed his blind eyes to land on a stone in the wall ahead. He could not say where his mind had dragged the idea from, but perhaps the Beltrorns could prove their worth after all in a situation that demanded brain over brawn. A faint glimmer from above bounced off Lampaea's belt.

'Alright,' said Bren, 'behind you, there is a crack in the wall. Try doing something with that.'

'How can you see the crack?'

'I can't.'

Lampaea walked in a straight line to the stone, and indeed found it immediately; the surrounding stones were smooth.

Whilst there seemed to be hope in Bren's gut feeling, Lampaea could gain nothing from it. There was no effect in pushing, pulling, tapping, knocking, sliding, nought hiding there. Then Lampaea turned away with a smile, despite his expression being blacked out.

'I think this is your job,' he said finally.

Bren could be heard shuffling his huge feet forward.

'Must I do all the hard work for you?' he said, and Lampaea laughed shortly.

There was a pause. Then a sudden and quick grating noise between the stones occurred.

'What happened?' asked Lampaea eagerly.

'The stone just shot inwards half-way. All I did was trace the outline of the Beltrorn emblem.'

Bren sounded half amazed, half expectant. Lampaea needn't have squinted anymore, for there was light now seeping out. A dim, glowing scarlet, it ebbed away carefully from between the cracks and edges, and proceeded to drip to the ground.

'Is that...blood?' said Bren slowly.

'I think so,' said Lampaea, feeling excited that he was witnessing the legend of Oxena's creation.

There were many theories passed around about the secret of escape from the Well of Oxena. The most popular was that one must shed his blood in order for the well to recognise the person being of Beltrorn descent. The idea was then that a Beltrorn would never share the secret once free, or the well's purpose became invalid. Lampaea had other ideas though. Oxena was driven by fury of the Ferinians' jesting that the Beltrorns were worthless in matters of the mind and good only for swinging a sword, and so with the insult he took to building a cryptic well, one that only true Beltrorns could escape from. The Ferinians, known widely for their astute and calculating minds, accepted the challenge and failed repeatedly, unable to crack the puzzle.

As the luminescent blood crawled up and around the rest of the well in thin, cracked lines to light them in the darkness, wherever it was coming from, Lampaea kept his eyes fixed upon the stone where it began and now shone brightest. There was a faint sucking noise, a deadening silence – and then the stone flew away from them – backwards it shot with such force into more stone and earth, gone within an instant. A long tunnel was left in its place, shining weakly with the same blood smeared around the sides.

'Lampaea – look, the walls –' said Bren.

The glimmering blood had curled around patterns in the walls now. All was lit and waiting to be deciphered – symbols, diagrams, words, riddles, odd shapes and sentences in an unknown dialect.

'Do you know any of this?' said Lampaea hopefully.

Bren wore a faint look of recognition suddenly.

'The words, yes. It's in Old Beltrorn, or Fadic.'

As easily as he had uttered those words, Bren found himself drawn to a particular cluster of symbols not too high above them.

'Yes, these look familiar...' he said languidly, as if recalling a lost memory.

The symbols were entirely different to the typical Enphiahn ones. Lines of them, all joined together, they seemed to flow effortlessly.

'Can you remember how to read this?' Lampaea enquired curiously. The strange letters and curved shapes shone bright into his eyes.

'Yes. I was taught much of this as a boy, but back then I was arrogant; I saw no point in learning a dead speech. So I have forgotten some of it, but the basics are still in this...' Bren touched the lower lines of the text with his fingers and softly traced them within the grooves as if each angle would bring back another moment in his past of those vital teachings.

'What was it used for? The language?' said Lampaea.

'Scripts had lain written within Olonath since the Valistehn Period, said to be the language of the beasts, for when the men of Beltro learnt it, they could converse freely with the animals. There were few creatures who couldn't understand or respond. But the Beltrorns also taught it to the remaining Artons, who fled to us as refugees. Beltro was unsure as to how the rest of Enphiah would react to us so easily giving away the Isle of Ira to an unknown race of people during such an age of mistrust and hostility, so sharing the language was a way to communicate in secret, and our allies were kept in the dark for the time. But more importantly, so were the Chriahks. It meant the Artons were safe and hidden from all but the animals.'

'Soft hearts beneath hard shells then. Try and interpret it, Bren. It may be our only way out of here,' said Lampaea eagerly.

Bren turned back to the wall.

'Ferin know of this language also,' he muttered. 'They tried to learn it like us, but could make no sense of it. And yet still they mock us.'

He then said something under his breath, something foreign and beautiful, there was a river of Ls and Ss', struck by soft riverbed stones of Bs and Ds.

He trailed off.

'The rest is not important,' he said, 'but I think this is the passage we must pay attention to. It was not as difficult as I thought. Would you like me to translate?'

Lampaea nodded slowly, and Bren continued:

'Bleed unto me, Beltro.
Through your veins be your walls
And no day sees your falls
Speak unto me, Beltro.

See me not, see my blood
Swipe the walls, spy you I could
In my hole that light despair
I'm in the well, I'm in my lair.

Heed words unspoken
Speech written by beasts
Your escape has not ceased
Till the well be broken.

Bleed unto me, Beltrorn
Begin my stone storm

In the crease at your feet
Utter my favour, "defeat."'

He turned back to Lampaea.

'Poignant. But I'm not sure I understand what it's telling us to do,' he said in a bewildered tone, yet his face appeared enlightened.

'I don't think this is as difficult as it sounds,' said Lampaea, 'read it to me again.'

Bren recited the passage twice, and Lampaea began to piece things together.

'The first part – it simply describes the heart of a true Beltrorn. The second hints at the thing that will help us escape. And since this is the speech "written by beasts", I think it might be a beast that will help us. It lies somewhere within the well.'

'That might explain why there are no remains down here of those that did not make it out, clearly this thing likes to keep its home tidy. And this is its blood upon the walls,' Bren realised.

'Yes. The creature is testing us, and we passed the first part when you touched the cracked stone with Beltro's emblem.'

'Then the last instruction must be in the final line of the passage.'

'"In the crease at your feet..."' Lampaea repeated. Then he looked about the floor where Bren stood near to the inscription. Sure enough, at the line where the floor and wall met, something was different. In this 'crease,' there was an indent in the stone, in which lay a small box, though it was kept in the dark and not highlighted by the glowing blood that adorned the walls, seemingly deliberate.

Lampaea picked it out carefully with a scrape; it had not been moved for many years.

'Well, tis your language, and your word to give,' he said, handing it to Bren.

Bren opened the lid gently with his brutal-looking fingers. Inside there was an old folded piece of parchment, Bren removed and unfolded it carefully. It showed a bloodied handprint, not one, but three, each overlapping the previous. There was a rustle somewhere above.

'Only three have ever escaped Oxena's Well,' said Bren gravely, 'this is the beast's evidence.' He took out his dagger and made a thin cut across his palm, leaving it to bleed some within his fist and then opening his hand to leave his mark upon the paper, atop that of the last survivor.

He then returned the parchment to the box, brought it to his lips, and into it muttered the single word for 'defeat' in the ancient Fadic tongue:

'Peteha.'

Lampaea and Bren braced themselves, but there was nothing. They glanced at each other in the dim light in perplexity. What else could they have missed?

'Perhaps you were not to leave your mark there,' Lampaea suggested, but Bren shook his head adamantly.

'No, the mark must be left. There must be something else.'

Lampaea pondered on a possibility. 'Evidence, you say? A hand for each who lived and escaped?'

'Yes, the first I believe must have been the mark of Oxena himself.'

'Well, then. We have been slow,' Lampaea branded his own dagger now, cut his own flesh, and held out his hand ready to make his mark.

‘What are you doing?’ said Bren in confusion as Lampaea took the parchment out again and pressed his splayed-out hand into it firmly.

‘I plan to also live and escape from here. The beast needs his proof, no? Now he has it. I think he is watching, and knows very well there are two of us down here.’

‘Then let us hope this is all he needs,’ Bren wasted no time and repeated the Fadic word once more into the open box with the paper returned.

All at once, the ground shook, the walls began to crumble suddenly and something was awakening from deep within the well. The box snapped shut of its own accord and fell to the ground. Lampaea did not know where to stand that was safe, for he fought to keep his balance, yet could not grasp the walls to steady himself.

A strange rattling noise could be heard, and Lampaea drew his sword.

‘No –’ Bren warned, ‘the creature is here to help us. We cannot jeopardise our chances if it feels threatened.’

Lampaea withdrew a little reluctantly.

‘Do you know what it is?’ he shouted, for the stones crashed heavily about them now.

Then some of them began to twist inwards on the west side – the pair struggled to see what was happening through all the dust that rose about them in plumes – the glowing blood faded away in flickers – the stones then proceeded to burst out of the walls and Lampaea was caught on the arm as they attempted to shield themselves.

And then something emerged in a last violent crash of earth, stone and showers of dust.

They looked upon it with difficulty, squinting through the earthy clouds as everything stung their eyes and smelt of rough and natural prehistory.

The dust cleared and the beast had not moved.

‘It’s a rembrorhg,’ Bren said thickly.

Whatever its name, Lampaea had never seen nor heard of such a thing before – the length of it was sprawled across a third of the well as it eyed them both suspiciously out of two small yellow beams of eyes on either side of its head. Its skin looked as if it was made from the earth – so dry and flaky, scraps of it detached and fluttered to the ground as lightly as snow. A long and delicate tail was poised so carefully as it wound up the wall around them – Lampaea was reminded of the tiny lizards they used to play with back in Elpura.

The rembrorhg quivered its flat, streamlined body and moved forward on its stumpy four legs.

It sniffed the air and snarled in their direction, teeth bared.

‘Are you sure it will help us?’ said Lampaea doubtfully, taking a step back.

‘Try not to move – and yes, yes I am sure it will,’ said Bren.

Sure enough, the rembrorhg began to ascend the well effortlessly – by the top it stopped to inspect a stone piece with dense patterning, the ancient language was scrawled so finely upon it.

The creature edged its head forward so carefully, as if there was something greater and more foreboding that lurked within and might spring upon it unexpectedly.

Lampaea struggled to see what was occurring or even guess what was about to occur.

Bren beckoned him over where he could see – the rembrorhg delicately pushed its long and slender tongue into the stone.

'How –?' Lampaea breathed in disbelief, for the stone melted away around it in molten servitude, like a moth that had finally succumbed to the deadly seduction of a flame.

And then something emerged from the molten opening as the rembrorhg drew its head back – a wooden pole, juddering outwards – they could hear the rotational mechanism echoing from within the stone wall.

The rembrorhg then descended slightly in an agile crawl – flakes of skin and dust from its body rained down upon the trapped men – and repeated.

The same process continued further and further down the well until there were around thirty or so of the wooden pegs protruding aimlessly.

The rembrorhg bared a remarkably well-hidden set of teeth in a final roar at them as if to commence their challenge, and then settled quietly upon the floor to watch them, ironically more like an obedient dog.

Lampaea studied the creature with Bren for a few moments before they felt content that it would not attack. For all its hostile conduct, it did appear to conform wholeheartedly to the rules set down by Oxena. Despite this, Lampaea could not say whether or not the beast would have struck him were he not in the presence of a Beltrorn.

'I have a fault to pick,' Lampaea announced as they gazed up at the disjointed ladder. 'Those pegs are not exactly in a straight line.'

'True,' Bren acknowledged, 'an escape route designed by a determined Oxena would never be easy though.'

The glowing blood from the walls returned and began to extend into the pegs themselves. At this the rembrorhg gave a short warning cry to them – then Bren said something back in his old language, and the rembrorhg jerked its head in response.

'We have to move – now –' Bren ushered – but then Lampaea noticed something upon their earthy friend when it had moved – a deep lesion within its neck. The blood that had spread about the entire well was indeed that of the animal itself.

'What is it?'

'Once the blood reaches the end of the pegs, they will disappear,' Bren explained. 'We only get one chance, I think the blood is keeping the well stable for us somehow –'

And then he took hold of the lowest pole – it involved swings onto the next ones for they were so randomly placed.

Nonetheless – Bren swung his great mass towards it with tenacity –

And fell with punctured dignity.

'I told you it was a fault...' said Lampaea openly.

'First attempts never go to plan,' Bren replied, and he climbed the obstacle course once more – this time reaching the fourth – and this time falling again.

'This wall is near impossible –' Bren panted, his energy had waned almost as quickly as his positivity on the matter.

Lampaea tackled it next – twice he fell, then tried again, yet he successfully reached a peg higher every time.

Bren was less agile – Lampaea was nimble and quick on his feet. But the more Bren watched his companion's desperate attempts the more he had time to think.

He glanced at the rembrorhg. It sat silently watching Lampaea with an intent gaze.

'You know something, don't you? Something we're

missing...' Bren muttered, though the rembrorhg seemed to have heard him, for its eyes alone shifted to him. And then it too muttered something back, the deep tones gently shuddered the stone rubble about them.

One of the wooden pegs dropped off suddenly and fell to the floor, still glowing with blood.

'Bren, come on – follow me –' Lampaea called laboriously – he was hanging on precariously to the sixth peg, eyeing the seventh that was so far from him. Before the next swing he looked down again.

'That's it...' said Bren, and he began to approach the rembrorhg, which grew more anxious the closer he came.

'Bren – what are you doing?!' Lampaea exclaimed.

Closer still – the rembrorhg growled with intimidation. It stood feet wide apart and then padded at the ground a little.

Another two pegs fell, and then Lampaea felt his own weaken – to fall from this height now was not something he could afford.

'You've been expecting this all along,' Bren murmured to the rembrorhg. There was a glint in the beast's eye.

Lampaea watched in despair.

'Bren –!'

But Bren then launched himself at the rembrorhg to land squarely on its back – the animal writhed and snapped at him as it twisted its head this way and that.

And then Bren managed to take charge – he ordered something in Fadic again and suddenly the beast was in his command.

The peg was about to snap as the mysterious blood swept under Lampaea's fingers – he could feel it – Bren was not hesitant and drove the rembrorhg up the wall, slithering with all speed through the disordered ladder –

Just as Lampaea felt his weight slipping away, he had been snatched up again and now rode up the well hanging from a great dweller of the earth – his breath had left his body for a moment. He had been taken so fast he only then realised that it was the beast's tail he was clutched in. With such haste and skill the rembrorhg had dodged every wooden peg, even the ones that fell to the bottom – the inside of the well was crumbling all around them, the blood had run out – and then they reached the top – no longer a distant circle of light that was unobtainable.

They had spent so long figuring out how to escape that the light of Pytheria blinded them, and it was turning evening.

The rembrorhg set Lampaea down surprisingly gently and met the ground for Bren to dismount. *Not a clumsy nor impolite thing really,* Lampaea thought.

It did not wait for thanks though, and whipped away in a second back into the broken well from whence it came.

'Care to explain what happened to our original plan?' said Lampaea casually.

'Simple,' Bren replied. 'The original plan was impossible. Always had been. No one could have climbed the well the way those pegs were laid out, and especially not with the blood running through them. It was a test.'

'One that I failed then.'

'Of course you did. You're not a true Beltrorn. The rembrorhg spoke to me in the language of the beasts. It said, "think like a Beltrorn." So I did.'

'And you came to that? Ride a fierce, untamed creature to safety?' said Lampaea in amusement.

'Exactly.'

Lampaea paused, then laughed at his friend's raw mentality.

'Remind me not to venture into a forest with you too soon,' he commented, 'I'd rather be prepared for teeth, claws, tails and whatever else.'

Bren smiled lightly.

'Beltro is one with nature,' he said, walking off to the east, 'I should have known sooner it was the beast itself that would save us. Beltrorns think quick and they act quick!'

Lampaea looked after him as he strode off proudly.

'Nor do they waste time standing still apparently!'

Chapter 13
Salvation

In the heart of the Arc Mountains, there was always a quiet hush. Padryl had discovered this with some awe, and even more so when he stepped inside a small, desolate house upon the mountainside.

For inside it was as hot as the Plains of Nemenon, yet there was but a feeble fire burning, and outside the skies continued to snow.

There were sticks of all shapes, sizes, scents and colours burning – the air was thick with it. Homemade scrolls and scraps of paper hung from the walls and ceiling reading several unknown and complex languages, others with lewd or prophetic drawings.

A strange smell seemed to rise above that of the scented sticks, and struck Padryl with some pungent intensity.

In the middle of it all was a small man. He was sat upon a faded blue rug. And before him lay a set of scattered pebbles and a pile of dead ants, though where he had acquired them from in such a harsh environment Padryl could but guess.

The man's eyes were still closed when he swept the ants and stones to one side, and then he opened them to view his visitor; they were deeply bloodshot.

'The work you have put in to find your daughter is worth that of ten thousand ants. And your love, is second to none.'

'You saw me coming?' said Padryl. 'I am not surprised.'

The man's name was Dorsyn. He was one of the most famous craftsmen in Enphiah, though his immense powers for helping those in need had acquired him many followers in the past, until it wore upon him too greatly for their petty needs and in some cases, pure greed, and he retreated to the Arc Mountains where few, if any, would follow again.

'But it is you that surprises me a little,' Dorsyn replied.

'Why is that?'

'You have travelled so far already, yet you know that your daughter does not wish to be found.'

'She knows not her mind. She ran off without talking to me or her mother, thinking she knows best. I need to bring her to sense, to home, where she belongs.'

'And if she belongs elsewhere now?' said Dorsyn, his eyes glinting in an ugly smile as he took a handful of the ants.

Padryl studied the strange man for a moment. Without barely trying, Dorsyn had already given him cause to view the situation in a new light.

'What do you know about Feletra?' he said calmly.

'That she is and will be far greater than you know. But come, that is not what you came to ask me.'

Padryl knew the old man's game – to entice him with information; no doubt there was a price for such a leisure.

'I want to know where I can find her. If my daughter is as great as you say then she will show it to me herself, not just proclaim it, so I have no interest in hearing that from you.'

Dorsyn sucked the air in through his teeth.

'She moves to the east, to Pyra, though something currently delays her. All your journeys through Western Enphiah have been wasted steps.'

'She made an accomplice in Betharanei then, for I was told she was heading for Lira.'

But it was now as Padryl had feared, she was on her way to Pyra instead.

'She could be hundreds of leagues ahead of you by now,' Dorsyn commented, almost teasingly.

'No matter,' said Padryl resolutely, and he turned on his heel to leave.

'Wait –' said the craftsman, and when his visitor turned around he saw that he was being handed a beautiful dagger.

'When you find her, give her this.'

It was an unusual shape, and swung out left from the central blade to form a second; in combat it would easily drive a second blow to a perpetrator, perhaps more fatal than the first.

The blade no longer shone and was dull from past wear, but the leather-bound handle looked strong and fresh.

'A weapon of a craftsman,' said Padryl with some disgust, 'why would I expose her to such a thing?'

'You stand in the home of a craftsman!' laughed Dorsyn. 'What's more, you deliberately sought out a craftsman, to the very extremes of crossing the Arc Mountains. I think it is a little late to turn down a gift of good will.'

'Craftsmen know no good will,' Padryl retorted stubbornly. 'I came here only to benefit of your power, not to forgive you for it. I needed direction, I was desperate.'

Dorsyn seemed to have heard this all before from simple family men like Padryl, for he simply smiled and cast his insults off like dust from his shoulders.

'Your traditional beliefs of Blackcraft will be a fence to what matters most to you. One day, however, it will become a gate. If you will not pass the dagger to Feletra, take it for yourself. You have come this far.'

He did not wait for Padryl to extend his hand this time,

and pushed the handle into it firmly.

Suddenly Padryl did not desire to let it go or give it back. He hesitated in his desire to return it to Dorsyn but he no longer had the will for it. After he had wound it in some spare cloth, he continued to clasp it at his side, and subsequently strode out of the warm house once more into the snow.

As Dorsyn returned to his faded blue rug, he opened his hand and a cluster of live ants were unleashed, crawling into all the cracks of the floorboards.

x

Feletra was miserable. And uncomfortable. She sat in a huge hand-crafted cage which hung from the shortest tree.

Much to her embarrassment, her daring escape plan had failed spectacularly. Mathenhis truly did have eyes everywhere, for she had been snagged before she had even reached the bridge, and almost gagged, for her mouth would not cease upon capture, though she eventually settled for just the threat and fell silent.

One of her captors described her as 'a fiery one' when she kicked and cursed and even ventured a bite.

She had been left to reflect in her real prison for hours until darkness had set, and Mathenhis appeared beneath her.

'Adrenache will speak with you now. And your friend.'

'What if I don't want to listen?' Feletra said in reply obstinately.

'Then we will listen instead,' Mathenhis reasoned.

Feletra opted to be silent from thereon and was soon reunited with Nil once more, who could barely suppress a jeering smile when he saw her. Feletra was less than amused, and refused to make eye contact.

The nights here were beautiful. Outside there were orange and violet-flame lanterns everywhere; strange haze clouds could be seen in their light and floated about in tranquillity like waltzing ripples upon a hushed mountainside lake.

There were birds still awake, great and small, and tinny-sounding insects that made courtship and sang in the haze. Day and night, the island was very humid; the tribe seemed unfazed – all their clothing was heavy and looked stifling with thick leather.

It appeared Mathenhis was leading them outside the settlement; they trekked a narrow winding path uphill through the forest, until a large house came into view – it was grander than anything they had left behind. Great beams rose from the foundations and were shorn off roughly at the tops, and there were enormous birds upon the roof that stared down at them in stillness as they approached, whilst bats like Feletra had seen in Droha edged their way about the sides for a better look.

Inside the house, the smell was sweet, like a sickly, burning honey, and the air intoxicating and more humid than outside. Feletra disliked it intensely. Nil also pulled a slight face of discomfort upon entry.

There were no chairs or tables; a small fire contained within a glass lantern adorned with delicate wooden framing burned steadily in the centre of the floor. Three of the Efordrads were already sat in a circle around it, one of them was Adrenache at the head, her hair flowed unusually around her, with clear streaks of shining silver in between shafts of dark braids. The other two were not known to

Feletra and Nil. They were two men, one elderly and the other thick-set and shaped like a warrior.

Mathenhis stood to address:

'Feletra, Nerehr, please sit with us.'

They did so, unsure of what to expect. Feletra noticed that Adrenache closed her eyes for a few seconds when they had joined the circle; she looked at Nil and he returned the acknowledgement.

'This is Stenahn,' Mathenhis gestured to the old man, 'he is our most knowledgeable member, and his son, Raneao, the best of my forest eyes. They will be staying with us for the discussion. And you have already met my sister, Adrenache.'

There was a moment of silence, and then Stenahn spoke.

'We have come to understand that you are no ordinary visitors to our shores,' his voice was laboured, as if his words got caught between the wires of his pale grey beard before they escaped, 'and have decided, for everyone's benefit, that your gift should be discussed, Feletra.'

Feletra looked back at them all as if she had been struck round the head.

'What gift?' she said plainly.

'Adrenache felt something powerful arrive to Ira,' Mathenhis explained, 'and she feels it mostly from you. She is the only one among us who can sense these things so accurately, and has never yet been proven wrong.'

'Well, I am none the wiser than anyone else here,' Feletra replied, 'I don't have a gift. I think you may have been mistaken.'

There were some shifts in movement at this; the Efordrads glanced at Adrenache as if anticipating her to defend her own abilities.

Feletra wondered if this was all some sort of test and looked gradually more confused. *If this is a test I'm probably going to fail and end up back in the cage again,* she thought.

Nil, however, could tell she was answering truthfully and knew nothing of what they were implying.

'They think you're kymic,' he interjected to encourage her.

'Kymic?' Feletra repeated, raising her head and straightening her spine. 'Not this again. No, not me. My family abhor Blackcraft, and so do I. Now I do know you have the wrong person.'

'It doesn't have to be Blackcraft, Feletra,' said Nil.

'And as I said, Adrenache has never been proven wrong,' Mathenhis quickly added.

But Feletra felt adamant.

'But if anyone were to know of its existence, it would be me,' she said. 'I have lived my whole life as a normal girl, with a normal childhood. None of my family are unusual or kymic. So why would I be?'

'Your family is irrelevant to this,' Adrenache spoke in a low and meaningful tone. All eyes turned to her. 'A power such as yours need not be inherited.'

Feletra suddenly realised that she was the sole focus of the discussion, and no longer desired to be.

'But what about Nil?' she said, looking at him. 'There was something you felt from him as well, wasn't there?'

Adrenache looked down, 'I thought I did, but now...I may have been mistaken. Your sheer presence has created an overbearing aura, Feletra. I believe it may have clouded what I felt from Nil.'

'So why have you brought us here?' Nil asked.

Adrenache looked on but did not answer, and so Mathenhis spoke instead.

'The Efordrads believe you are both genuine people, and were not associated with the crew who tried to kill my men. But we also know, through Adrenache, that Feletra possesses a gift which is beyond her control at present. Because of that, we want to help.'

'Help what?'

'Help her to recognise it. But more importantly, to control it.'

'You make me sound like a weapon. Like you plan on using me...' Feletra chipped in, feeling somewhat distressed at their claims about her. It all felt so foreign and unheard of: dangerous, powerful, gifted. It wasn't her.

But Nil had looked at her directly then.

'No one is going to use you again,' he reassured, and for all that he'd done, there was nothing but the absolute truth there in his eyes this time, Feletra could see it plainly. He wanted to protect her.

'Of course we won't use you,' said Mathenhis, 'we do not mean to scare you, Feletra, but you must realise that...there *could* be a danger to yourself and others, if you ignore what you have and do not learn to control it.'

Feletra looked up at him, 'How can I do that?'

'By recognising what it is and what it can do,' said Adrenache. 'We can help you with that. Stenahn and myself have been discussing the possibilities; you know what Blackcraft is. Well, there are other kyms, stronger ones, even – four altogether: Blackcraft, Artrenium, Konexa and Helum. Blackcraft is the most commonly known and used. The others are scarce, most of them were possessed only by a select few. Many of the commonfolk of Esilence have long since forgotten they ever existed. But the Efordrads remember; we never let go of history.'

Feletra found she could not hold her tongue at this.

'If that were true then how could you forget the Artrenium?'

There was a silence that fell hard amidst the group. The Efordrads looked uneasy, Feletra anxious for an answer and Nil sighed quietly. But Adrenache was unshaken.

'Tell us, Feletra,' she continued, 'have there been any strange incidents you have experienced? Things that cannot be explained?'

'No,' Feletra replied, shaking her head. She kept trying to convince them all that 'strange' was not her, when she now realised she was trying to convince herself more.

'Then let me help you. The felled trees in the forest were caused by you.'

'No –' Feletra felt preyed upon now; she looked to Nil for support, who also appeared somewhat surprised at the claim.

'Then it *is* Blackcraft you think she has?' he questioned.

'No,' said Adrenache, 'we suspect something else. Think, Feletra. Cast your mind back.'

All focused on Feletra again. She disliked the attention immensely, and tried to recall any odd events. Her first thought was the attack under the Valley House, but she buried this for now. Then she remembered Whiteblind Wood.

'I...there was a burst of fire. I was underwater, in Whiteblind. It looked like it had happened beneath the surface, but I just thought someone else had created it. I had this idea that someone did that to try and help me.'

'And did you ever find that person?' said Adrenache.

‘You were in Whiteblind Wood?!’ came Raneao’s voice without warning. He suddenly looked upon Feletra with a new admiration, and the belief that there was indeed something special about her to have survived the foreboding death trap.

‘Yes, I was...and no, I did not see anyone when I came out of the water. But I was being chased, I couldn’t think straight at that time. Actually, maybe you could help me understand something else that happened to me in there. When I first entered, something came over me and my horla; my head was pounding, everything felt hot even when it wasn’t, sounds of things became so loud and clear, then everything began to fade to black – I couldn’t see or hear, then I think I fainted.’

Stenahn had been nodding throughout.

‘Yes, that is not unusual,’ he said, ‘do you recall seeing things that looked like tall, white lifeless trees poking out the top of the forest from afar?’

‘Yes.’

‘They are the forest plutes, and they keep the entire place alive. They have such a great lifeforce that excess energy spills out of them, it is a gas which is inhaled by any living thing present. But nothing can withstand that energy for long –’

‘That’s why it appeared so dead inside, nothing could survive in there?’ said Feletra.

‘Yes. If I may ask, who was chasing you?’ Stenahn enquired gently.

‘Oh...I don’t really know what they were. Wolf-like animals. In a pack. On their backs they had those plutes, just like the forest; I didn’t think I would escape them, they were strong. But I managed to kill one and get out. That’s when I saw the fire, showing me the way.'

Raneao had stumbled into a gaup in Feletra's direction, he was genuinely impressed. Even Nil looked upon her differently.

'Those were the Dirim,' said Mathenhis, 'a vicious and ancient race, older than men.'

'And very intelligent,' Stenahn added, 'they understand all languages passed around these lands. By killing one of their pack, particularly if it was a superior member, you will have earnt their respect. The victor, they believe, must be one of strength and courage, and they honour that greatly.'

'I suppose that explains why the others stopped chasing me,' said Feletra. 'And they started drinking from the pool where it had died.'

'Yes, they mean to inherit the strength of the member that was lost to them, drink the blood or eat the flesh and continue their legacy,' Stenahn said, 'they will ritualise every death of their own kind.'

And then Feletra began to piece things together.

'And on their backs – like the forest, those –' the word escaped her.

'Plutes?' Adrenache encouraged, raising her eyebrows. 'As Stenahn said, the energy of the forest plutes is too great for any other living thing; they must leave or soon perish, with the exception of the Dirim. I am sure you know already of the extinct race Belarahn?'

'The bringers of Blackcraft,' Nil said from the shadows.

'Nevermind Blackcraft,' Feletra interjected somewhat heatedly, 'they brought life to Enphiah.' She had heard the tales of these beasts many a time; they were one of the earliest races to inhabit Enphiah and lived during the

Valistehn Period, large horla-like creatures who would stamp and shake the earth, said to have released Blackcraft from deep beneath.

'Feletra is right,' said Adrenache, 'Blackcraft was merely a consequence, a snake waiting to be coaxed from the earth. Nevertheless, the Belarahn were hunted by the Dirim, until the last few were cornered in the south of Droha. The Belarahn released excess life here as a result before they were killed, and the great forest plutes of Whiteblind were born. It became the home of the Dirim, they adapted over time and were the only creatures strong enough to withstand the energy. The lifeforce took hold of their bodies, and now they share Whiteblind's legacy just to survive.'

For some reason, the story sent a shiver down Feletra's spine.

'But come, Feletra,' said Mathenhis, his blue eyes flashing in the dim firelight, 'what else has there been?'

She thought again. Her mind stretched back to Elenia Forest now.

'I was sat by a fire with my brother in Elenia, and...' she glanced at each of them, and no longer felt foolish for what she was about to say. The faces of these new people were serious but tender, watchful. Their approach fair and cordial, 'and a layer of ice grew over it. The whole fire stopped moving in that moment. It was frozen, and then the ice disappeared again.'

The stares continued curiously, struck with the wonder of the impossible: frozen fire. All but Adrenache, who looked to the floor again, followed by Nil, whose eyes were lost in the soft flames.

'It seems fire must be easily manipulated under your

abilities. Is there anything else?' Adrenache said so quietly.

Feletra could see she was thinking. This was a process of elimination to her; she would soon be able to reveal what Feletra was afflicted with. She suddenly wondered if it was the curse of the Sorpha that Adrenache could feel so poignantly. Was she mistaking this for a kym? *But then, hadn't I forgotten I was ill with the curse anyway?* Feletra thought. *Where are my symptoms? Why don't I feel ill? But mother did say it varies from person to person...one day it will all hit me at once. And then I will fall to the ground in a pool of my own blood and vomit, and my life will be over.*

'Feletra?'

Nil's voice sounded far away, but it was closer than the others. It brought her back.

'I can't do this,' she said, her tone subject to defeatism, 'and you can't help me.'

She suddenly left the circle and walked out into the cool air. Nil was immediately on his feet and Mathenhis went to follow, but Adrenache placed a hand on her brother's arm.

'Let them be.'

Feletra felt dizzy, even in the outside air. She paced aimlessly between the trees, one to the next. For everything else that had happened so far, the curse had no longer existed. For so long, the Sorpha was something unheard of, its waters had dried up and all there was left was a great dry chasm. But Ataleka, and what affliction he had to suffer from that same dreadful, pure fluid, was never far behind in the crevices of her mind. That is what spurred her on from the start. But the reality of a curse upon her own soul shook it about like a delicate flowerbud lost in a hurricane.

For the first time, she was afraid of what her own life would come to, and not just that of another.

‘Feletra –’ Nil called, ‘talk to me. What’s really bothering you?’

‘Nothing, I just want to leave so I can – I can carry on.’

‘Stop holding back. The Efordrads are trying to help you –’

‘They don’t know what they’re helping. They can’t. There is nothing they can do for me!’ her voice was shaking. She stopped giving Nil eye contact and looked to the stars in despair.

But Nil very calmly took hold of her arms and looked her squarely in the face. She felt soothed all at once.

‘If they can’t help you, maybe I can,’ he said. His voice ran like a clear mountain creek. It all spilled out too perfect, every word said in the right place at the right time.

‘I am cursed, Nil,’ Feletra blurted without thinking. But it had been eating away at her, the burden must be shared now or it would drag her down with it. ‘Me, and my brother – we are cursed. And I cannot save him unless I go to Chriah and find a cure.’

Nil’s expression had not changed.

‘What curse is it?’ he enquired sternly.

‘The Sorpha’s.’

And then it changed. A dark shadow passed over Nil’s brow and he felt compelled to pull Feletra in closer just to protect her.

‘I don’t think it’s some kymic aura that Adrenache is feeling from me,’ Feletra said, ‘I think it’s this – the curse.’

‘But what you’ve said in there is not explained by that – the things you have described are purely kymic, the curse would be making you suffer, not –’

‘See things? Nil, that’s exactly what it can do.’

Nil fell quiet and looked into her eyes unwaveringly.

They were so dark yet now overcast, glassy and sorrowful. There was an obscurity to them; there, right in the centre, was a moon, a caliginosity of scattering clouds passing over it one by one, and nestled between them a thunder of dormant impassion and vividity.

'So this is the real reason you were on the ship. You *do* need to get to Chriah?'

'Yes, to Leohreten – my brother and I worked out that the caves holding the cure must be near that village.'

'Caves? What makes you think it will be there?' Nil said quickly, though at the mention of Leohreten became dark once more.

'I had some sort of vision when I was back home; it's what started everything. It showed me what to do. Do you...?'

'I believe you, Feletra. And the Efordrads can help you get there, they can. But first, you need to tell them everything.'

Feletra began to develop some unfounded trust for Nil. Suddenly she realised that all words he spoke were of wisdom, and he had done nothing but help her since they had met. Then this made her think.

'I will tell them...' she said feebly, 'but why are you helping me so much?'

Nil's head tilted back slightly. He didn't seem to have expected this question.

'In honesty, I don't really know,' he let his hands fall from her arms. 'I haven't been able to shake this feeling that you will need me though. I know, I know, you're independent and don't need a minder and all...'

Feletra looked distant for a moment.

'Actually, you've saved my life twice already,' and then

she smiled, ‘you might have more use than you think.’

Nil grinned with appreciation. Then he beckoned her back to the house. They could see Mathenhis outside, waiting for them by the door.

Before he was within earshot, Feletra stopped.

‘Wait,’ she said, ‘before we go in, I want you to agree to tell your side as well. I still don’t know anything about you.’

‘It might surprise you to hear that you know me better than my own family,’ Nil replied.

But Feletra looked confused. Strangely, Nil looked around briefly as if he had heard something untoward.

‘Nevermind,’ he said, ‘yes, I agree.’

Feletra felt satisfied enough, and strode back into the stuffy warm house, Nil in front and Mathenhis behind.

She took her seat, and began.

x

‘We could have followed him into the city –’

‘No. We can’t afford to have our faces seen at this stage.’

An exasperated sigh.

‘He’s in there – telling them everything about us –’

‘Dox is right. We could have killed him by now.’

‘It doesn’t matter. They won’t believe a thing he tells them.’

‘How can you be so sure? I think we are wasting our time like this!’

Amanyl shot an ill-tempered look about the men.

‘I am sure because the Luminors have lost their way. They barely remember their duties to Enphiah,’ he said, ‘and even if they could see the truth before their eyes, they would rather be in denial.'

There was some thinking passed around in silence. Some nervous glances that this was merely a fool's hope.

'Then what do we do now?' said Dox, a slender young man, black and untidy hair. His eyes were small, they glinted and flitted about like a serpent's.

'We wait,' Amanyl replied with ease. 'Emmet can't stay in there forever. Very soon he will declare his claims, they will be dismissed and he will be thrown out of the city. More likely for wasting their time than insanity.'

'If he can't raise the alarm to the Luminors of Enphiah why are we even chasing him?' said another of the men, unconvinced. 'Why not just let him walk around as the madman he'll be labelled as?'

Amanyl rolled his eyes in vexation.

'It's not the Luminors I'm concerned about,' he said, 'it's the common folk. All it takes is one rumour to spook them and suddenly it spreads like wildfire. As soon as it reaches Setra, it'll be our necks on the line for letting information escape too soon from Betharanei.'

His comrade looked confused and agitated.

'And what?' he said.

'You ignorant fool,' Dox snarled. 'Not only will you be a dead man walking, it means we'd have been responsible for ruining the entire plan. Chriah is still waiting for the right moment, it's crucial. And Setra cannot make its move until then.'

'If anything happens before the time is nigh, if word gets out –' Amanyl added, '– Enphiah will have had its armies assembled by then. We are not ready. The preathins are not ready.'

The ignorant fool gave one succinct nod in solemn

agreement.

'So, we wait...' he said dully.

'So we wait,' Amanyl affirmed.

They looked to the great gates of Rukur before each of them were allocated a station outside different exits of the city. Each and every conceivable escape was covered. But Emmet might have had the advantage of the inconceivable.

Inside the grand city, there were more turns and twists than a snake could coil around a small mouse. The place was littered with staircases and sharp corners. After all the confusion to navigate the streets and asking for directions ten times, Emmet had finally found the place he sought – a huge building constructed almost entirely of lucrin, though the house now was tired and weather-beaten; it was the Chandre, and had stood as far back as the Nyvean War, built in the victory of the Lorahk army led by the Western Enphiahn leader, Rukurehn.

Within the Chandre the descendants of Rukurehn convened every so often, though today was not one of those days. After arguing incessantly with two unhappy guards, Emmet waited an hour before he was granted entry. Closing the doors behind him, they cursed and jeered that he would only be thrown out again in a few moments.

Inside the house was no exception however; it was well cared for over the years; pillars polished and impressive stone statues were still white in colour. There was but one window which was narrow and stretched all the way from the rafters to the floor, permitting one great shaft of bright sunlight – everywhere else was torch-lit.

The light fell upon two high-backed chairs, both of which appeared so regal and monumental, though these were not for a king or queen. They were built for the

Luminor of West Enphiah, and the Luminor of Mid Enphiah. Upon approaching them, Emmet could see that one was adorned with the emblem of Lor:

And the other of Penthor:

Emmet heard a heavy door close somewhere behind the chairs, followed by flat, echoing footsteps. A stout, slow man and his tall son appeared from the shadows.

But the great chairs of grandeur were abandoned and Emmet was beckoned to sit at a long table further in. The stout man coughed a little.

‘Who are you?’ he said laboriously.

‘My name is Emmet. And I come with urgent news.’

‘Oh, well, then you had better hurry and tell us,’ there was an element of sarcasm detected. Emmet knew already this would be a difficult task.

‘Wait,’ came the young man at his side, ‘do you know who we are?’ he sounded pompous for his age, too sure of himself.

‘Yes. Though your names, I confess, escape me.’

‘Jekron. And my father, Menkhrist, Luminor of Lor.’

Emmet nodded politely.

‘Now that the formalities are over,’ said Menkhrist, ‘come. Tell us your news of urgency.’

He spoke as if expecting some sort of show. Emmet shuffled further forward on his seat.

‘It’s Chriah. They’re forming some sort of plan against us. A conspiracy. Betharanei has become a secret breeding ground for preathins. I think they mean to overthrow us once their forces are assembled –’

‘Wait, slow down, slow down –’ Jekron interrupted, smirking, ‘you mean to say that Chriah will declare war on us?’

Emmet looked between them and hated how fiercely he was about to be judged.

‘Yes.’

Menkhrist laughed openly.

‘Using preathins, no less?’ he jested. ‘You realise we killed them all in the Nyvean?’

‘They’re not extinct!’ Emmet retorted. ‘No, see I thought they were gone too but, but they’re not – they come from the earth –’

‘Yes, we know where they came from.’

‘Then why the resistance? You must realise that this is happening as we speak –’

‘And where is your proof?’ said Jekron.

‘My proof? My own eyes, I-I have seen the foul things myself, been in their lair – killed one even just to escape!’

There was a noise behind one of the pillars. A torch bracket moved slightly.

‘And this was what, in the middle of your village then, for all to see?’

‘Where is he from again?’ Menkhrist muttered to his son.

‘Betharanei.’

Menkhrist grunted. ‘One of those common places.’

Emmet now felt penalised for no good reason.

‘Please,’ he implored, ‘do not disregard what I am telling you. There is a movement which threatens all of us. I have no doubt that there are countless of those breeding grounds in secret locations across Enphiah, right under our noses. And they are just waiting for the right time to strike and catch us off-guard. But we can have a chance if we are prepared –’

‘And what would you have us do?’

There was a new addition to the discussion, a female voice.

Emmet saw a hand in the shadows of a pillar, it placed a torch into an empty bracket. And then she stepped forward.

‘If this were all true and our old enemies were just waiting to pounce, what would you have us do?’

She looked young and dynamic, a fresh mid-twenty or so. But her features were not soft; her eyes and nose were sharp, symmetrical, yet her lips blossomed from her face, round and tender. And upon her head, a torrent of bright blood-red hair that collapsed in thick, untidy strings to her elbows.

Emmet required an extra moment just to take her all in.

'Consult the Ranis. Assemble what we have, then strike these breeding grounds before it's too late. Shut them down.'

'How are we to know you speak the truth?' said the woman.

Emmet looked between the three of them.

'You won't know...' he said, 'not right now, at least. But you're my last hope. You are the only ones who can form some kind of defence. My evidence lies outside the walls of Rukur, hunting me – the men who are in league with Chriah. Oh –'

He fumbled around, and then carefully extracted the poor remains of the knife he had stabbed the preathin with.

'And this,' he said.

The young woman stepped down to join them and took a closer look at the weapon, turning it over gently in her fingers.

'What is that?' said Menkhrist, craning his neck.

'This is the weapon I used on one of the preathins, to defend myself.'

'Preathin blood is renowned for its properties,' said the woman, 'like disintegrating common metals such as pnapsor. The dried liquid on this is also black, like the blood.'

Emmet felt some relief, it sounded as if she actually believed him.

But then Menkhrist changed his tone suddenly.

'So it's true!' he exclaimed. 'We must waste no time – bring forth the Ranis! Gather only our very best! Alert the authorities of Penthor and do it with haste!'

Emmet breathed a heavy sigh and his blood rushed at his success, but it was momentarily lived –

'You'll do it then?' he said. 'Thank you – thank you for believing me; and if you'll let me, I can help –'

Menkhrist was laughing again.

'Young man, the only one of us that needs help is you.'

'W-what?'

'You will leave the Chandre with haste, and then you will leave Rukur with greater haste. If you so much as breathe a word of this insanity to the people of the city, I will have you personally escorted to Chriah where you can deal with it yourself.'

'I am telling the truth! If I leave Rukur now those men will kill me on sight!'

'You will send them our regards, won't you?' said Jekron derisively, a taunting smirk across his face.

Emmet was furious. He rose to his feet and stood tall.

'I am not a madman!' he yelled, but the two guards from outside were moving in on him. 'Now you will listen to me –'

'No, *you* will listen!' Menkhrist interjected. 'We will not tolerate any such madness in this city. You are banished from this house and may you pray that I never set eyes on you again.'

The guards took hold of Emmet, which only enraged him further, but they were too strong to shake off and dragged him to the door. The young woman watched him go.

'You are lost in your ignorance!' said Emmet, his voice echoing about the place. 'It will be too late when they come for us! You bring death upon us all – women, children, families – all of us!'

But his last words were in vain just as much as his first,

for before he knew it he had been tossed outside like a piece of meat to a stray dog. The real dogs were out there though, outside the walls of Rukur, waiting for him hungrily.

The guards chuckled at the state of him, and he glared back darkly. Picking himself up, he strode away into the city streets, and was about to enter the stable where he'd left Syndrex temporarily, when someone collared him.

Clueless, he was pulled into a narrow side street, prepared to explode into curses, when he saw her face.

It was her, from the Chandre. The unnaturally radiant red hair escaped her hood like wisps of fire, and she was dressed in a rather manly fashion: clumpy leather, two thick metal belts at her waist and hips, and large, hard-wearing boots.

'How did you find me so quick?!' said Emmet, 'I'd left before you –'

'I know all the ins and outs of my city,' she replied, 'a little better than you, I think. Which is partly why I'm going to help you get out of here.'

Emmet paused.

'And what's the other part?' he said, at first feeling unsure if she had been sent just to mock him further.

'That I believe you.'

Her eyes looked truthful. Emmet wanted there to be some seed of doubt left in him, but she had not treated him like Menkhrist and Jekron. His flicker of hope crept back.

'You...believe me? After all the humiliation I was put through by those two numb-sighted fools who can't even –'

'Those two numb-sighted fools are my father and brother. And don't worry, I'm not offended. You're right, they are fools. And cowards; the threat of Chriah would terrify them. The luminors of both Lor and Penthor have been this way for a thousand years. They listen to no one, thinking the peace will hold forever.'

Emmet was able to quickly bury his embarrassment at slating her relatives.

'Then why are you so different?' he said, finding it sorely difficult to draw himself away from her eyes.

'Because I am not afraid,' she said shortly.

'And have sense,' Emmet added, to which she raised a friendly eyebrow. She was intelligent, straight forward and a little wily. He liked her already.

'My whole family are well learned,' she continued, 'but my mother encouraged me to read past the facts written in books, see the colour between the black and white. And I discovered so much more about the past, present, and even the people we lived around. Suddenly I could read who was lying, genuine, loyal or a traitor, And I see only the truth in you.'

Emmet could barely suppress a grin. Finally, someone was on his side.

'Then what can we do now?' he said. 'Your father will not listen.'

'There is one thing, but it will involve some...unorthodox methods, and the men out there who are waiting for you.'

Emmet caught on quickly enough.

'You mean to force it out of one of them,' he said. 'But there are too many. How are we even going to capture one?'

'Well, one is all we need. I'll take care of the rest.'

'You?' Emmet said dubiously.

'Yes. You can help if you want.'

‘Oh – I see. You mean you can have some of the guards that work for your father help us.’

‘No. I mean, *I* can take care of them.’

Suddenly Emmet caught the flash of fierceness in her eye and no longer felt so dubious.

‘Now, come with me –’ she said, taking his arm roughly, ‘I will lead us out of the main city where they won’t expect us. Then we take them down one by one.’

‘Wait –’ said Emmet, ‘if we’re going to work together I need to know your name.’

She did not stop or turn around.

‘It’s Dynetii.’

Chapter 14
A Quell on Death

'Are you sure that's what you saw?'

Ataleka was facing his mother. She was holding him to stop him shaking; the sickness had banished the weight off his bones and affected a deathly pallor to his skin, it was like holding a small boy again. Banu lay dead in the stable, he had told her. Something was feeding off him, off his belly. Something foul which he had never seen before. And then it had looked at him, he said (though it had no eyes that he could see) and sprang for him.

'I locked the doors in time. I didn't know what else to do,' he said.

Estra looked at him sternly.

'You can't tell me what the thing was?' she said.

'No. I didn't know what it was. But it was white and made strange noises. Mother, you don't think I'm seeing things, do you? You don't think it's just part of the curse?'

Ataleka could not stem the tears that welled in his sore eyes.

'Don't say such things,' said Estra quickly and dismissively. 'I'll not hear you speaking of the curse.'

'Is Ataleka unwell again?' Leao interrupted.

'Hush,' Estra ordered. 'Now I will go out to the stable and see what is going on myself.'

'I'll come with you.'

'Ataleka, if this is something dangerous you must stay in the house –'

'I'm coming too,' said Flior.

'And me,' came Skepreo.

Estra flapped her arms in defeat, sighed, and proceeded to the stable with her three sons in tow.

There, Flior stepped up to the doors and peered through the gap between them. Ataleka had not been seeing things; inside, Banu's hind quarters could be seen spread across the floor, his blood coated everything. But the more macabre sight was a small, pale and skinny body, hunched over him. It was no larger than a child. There were unusual devouring noises that were sickeningly clear. Long fingers digging fervently into the flesh, a sloshing sound when an unfavourable chunk was dumped into the hay on the floor, a deep gulping swallow that was all too quick. The last of Flior's three horlas had met the same fate in the neighbouring stall. But almost as soon as Flior had a good view, the thing raised its bloody head and stared straight at the door. Although it had no eyes, he could feel that it had detected his presence.

And it was fast. Suddenly it was at the door, screeching and clawing at the other side.

Flior staggered back in alarm.

'I think I know what it is,' he said, though the realisation turned his skin paler than usual. 'But there needs to be less of us here – Skepreo and I will deal with it together.'

Estra said nothing and ushered Ataleka towards the house, who kept looking over his shoulder at his brothers fearfully.

Skepreo dashed round the back of the stable and returned with two spears and a shovel.

'It's all we have – everything else is in the stable,' he said.

'It's fine,' said Flior calmly. 'I'll take the shovel. And

Skep – this thing will be aiming for the house. We can't let that happen.'

Skepreo nodded apprehensively.

'Just do it.'

Flior then heaved one of the doors open. The creature's scrabbling had since stopped, and there was nothing there, though the heat of Pytheria had already hit Banu's flesh, and the smell was bordering on rancid.

Skepreo gave the closed door a timid poke with the spear, and suddenly the feeble creature awoke once more. It scrambled out quickly and advanced on Flior, who swung too high and missed. Then Skepreo jabbed at it, but it was too quick and nimble. It screamed and screamed at them, then changed course.

As Flior predicted, it was heading for the house, and was already ahead of them.

The brothers sprinted after it.

'Lock the doors!' Flior called to his mother inside – 'Barricade yourselves in!'

They saw doors and shutters slamming shut from a distance, but the bedroom window was left open for too long –

Inside, Ataleka was straining to pull it to – but his muscle strength had waned so much from what it once was that even pulling the shutter in was a challenge now.

Estra saw it, and ran to help him – a second too late – for the creature thrust its entire body through and the wood shattered. Some sort of black fluid burst out of pores in its skin and it spat the same stuff at them as it launched at Ataleka.

He kicked it away, and then it sprang for his head, about to sink its teeth into the back of his neck.

Bri screamed. Estra was on it immediately, pulling the vile thing from her son, but for such a skinny, fragile-looking creature its strength was immense.

She looked around the room desperately as Ataleka could only squirm beneath the putrid face and breath that was thrust into his.

There was a long feather quill on a bedside table, taken from the hardy wings of the Kestinoch Eagle, the feather shafts were as strong and unyielding as a broadsword.

She reached for it, took the nib end and without a moment more to think she drove the implement steadily into the back of the creature's rubbery-looking neck. It shuddered ungracefully, screeched helplessly and by the time the quill was poking out the other side, fell limp upon Ataleka.

Estra ripped the little body off him and embraced her pale and shaken son, her expression still as hard as nails.

Bri went to answer the calls of Flior and Skepreo from outside and unbolted the door for them.

They beheld the scene in the bedroom with awe – Flior nudged the vicious creature onto its back with his boot.

'Are you alright?' he said.

His mother nodded slowly and solemnly.

'It was a preathin,' Flior confirmed.

'No,' said Estra instantly. She was in denial, perhaps for the children's sake.

'Yes. An infant one. I learnt more about them in when I was in Penthor.'

'But they're extinct, Flior,' Skepreo added.

'I thought so too. But I am certain this is a preathin larva. I also knew it would go for Ataleka the most.'

'Why?'

'Because he desires the most out of any of us, and they hunt their prey on desire. I would imagine that Banu was just the appetiser of its meal.'

Ataleka listened, silent and upset. He wished Flior hadn't added that last part about being a meal, it made everything more real. But falling prey to a preathin was the least of his worries. *I am cursed,* he thought. *They all know that now. And I desire so much it should be selfish. I want my strength back. I want my health. And when my hearing, my sight, taste and touch finally go, I'll want them back so much there'll be an entire fleet of preathins after me then.*

'I want a cure,' he said aloud.

They each looked uncomfortable, and he knew what they were thinking. That there wasn't one. But Flior looked slightly different to the others, he was the only one who held eye contact.

Estra changed the subject.

'If this is a preathin, where did it come from?'

'I don't know,' said Flior worriedly, 'I didn't even think they could come back.'

Estra was shaking her head whilst staring down at the wretched thing.

'This is impossible...' she whispered, then saw that Bri and Leao were coming closer to inspect. She led them away into the kitchen.

'Come now, come. Skepreo, dispose of that thing and burn it.'

Skepreo left to retrieve the shovel, leaving Flior with Ataleka, who was slumped onto the edge of his bed sadly.

'Listen to me,' said Flior, crouching down before him. 'Feletra is going to come back. And she's bringing a cure, she's going to cure you, Ataleka.'

X

Afax had a small scar across his left cheek. The fur had never grown back there since. He'd gotten into a scrap with a scerou once (an animal like a large cat with jet black fur that breathed through its belly, native only to Pyra) and it had lashed out at him.

It was the only feature Nil could distinguish him by when he was frolicking in the treetops with a dozen other gipterns.

Afax leapt back down to the ground where Feletra and Nil sat on a bench in Adrenache's own personal garden. She stood tending to a vine gently. Everything here bloomed and grew more than anywhere else around the settlement. Feletra watched Adrenache's tender care with the vine and knew exactly why that was, but she had other things to consider now.

Like the kym she had to remember to control.

After Feletra's story, Adrenache made it clear to her that it was indeed a kym she could feel from her and not the curse of the Sorpha.

'You need to keep trying,' Nil encouraged.

'I don't know how to try,' Feletra sighed. 'When it happened before, I wasn't thinking about it.'

She held a flowerbud in her palm, and was attempting to grow a layer of ice over it like she had done with the fire in Elenia Forest. This was apparently but a taste of what she could do with the Konexa, Adrenache had said.

It was the second rarest kym of the four, she had explained to them, and is a thought-based power. The thoughts of the wielder, even metaphorical thoughts, can be interpreted into physical matter, although how this matter will take form is never clear. The Konexa usually begins to establish itself with the becoming of age, as it did with Feletra, although it can be spontaneous with others.

'It is a good thing the Konexa is showing itself in you now, Feletra,' said Adrenache, approaching them. She was carrying a small basket filled with fleshy green tubes that were covered in grey spores; they were growths that took hold of the vines and would sap their energy if left. 'Some develop it later in life and they don't have as much time as you to control it. Eventually they destroy themselves because of that. And being young means you are reaching the peak of your development and understanding, you are still letting knowledge flow in – this is the perfect time for the Konexa to rear its head.'

'To rear its ugly head...' Feletra muttered. 'I don't want to have something like this in me. It's a time waster. I need to get to Chriah for –'

'For Ataleka, we know,' said Nil. Afax chirped. 'But the more you let the kym fester within you and are not dealing with it the more dangerous you are to everyone and everything around you. Even if you do go home with a cure, it will mean nothing if you're a constant threat to your brother and family anyway.'

'Nil is right,' said Adrenache, 'I understand the curse is something you and Ataleka are facing, but the Konexa will demand far more of your energy. I think it may even be the reason you haven't felt any symptoms of the illness yet; this is the most crucial time for the kym to inaugurate itself, it has preoccupied your body and mind.'

As Feletra stared at the limp, ice-less flowerbud in her hand, a memory suddenly struck her. In the crop field at home, when Ataleka's skin cracked open and bled for no reason...

'Feletra, what is it?' asked Nil.

She looked at him hesitantly.

'I-I think I hurt Ataleka with this, with the Konexa. And I didn't even know it was me. I just thought it was his first symptoms of the curse.'

'What happened?'

'I remember what I was thinking about – I wanted to talk to him about what happened at the Sorpha, but he kept avoiding me, I think he was scared. Then I finally got a moment when he was alone, and I felt like I'd caught him and he couldn't escape me this time. I remember thinking about chains because they would hold him there. Then I turned around and saw he couldn't move, could barely breathe, and his arms and chest began to bleed as if those chains were cutting into him. I wasn't trying to be malicious though, it was all an accident, I'd never hurt my brother. But it makes sense now.'

'The chains were the metaphor in your mind,' said Adrenache, 'and your desire to speak with your brother became so great that the Konexa took over. I think your emotions might be playing a part in this as well, Feletra.'

'But wasn't that situation all head, no heart?'

'No, your emotions must be steering it,' Nil cut in, 'when you walked off at the beach you were so angry with me, and that's when all the trees came down.'

'You still think that was me?' Feletra still hated being blamed for this, though the evidence was mounting against her and she knew it.

'It *was* you,' said Adrenache, 'that is when I sensed the kym the most. The power was enormous and yet the

Konexa is still capable of so much more.'

'Then what, I need to be emotional in some way for it to work?'

'No, I think your emotions are your downfall. The Konexa responds easily to both head and heart, but in this case your heart is greater, Feletra. You need to bury it and open your mind more. Then you can control it to your will.'

'That's another thing,' Nil chipped in, 'from what I remember learning about it back in Pyra the kym is based on will power. Once fully grasped, the possessor need only imagine an object or situation, and it will invisibly occur.'

Feletra sighed heavily, dropped the flowerbud and placed her head in her hands. It was confusing and exhausting, learning about this 'gift' she was infected with. Don't be emotional, do use your head, control and focus, open one thing, close another, don't give up, it's now or it's never, learn or die...she'd have happily ignored the whole thing were it not such a danger to everyone around her.

She decided to take a walk over the bridge and into the forest to clear her mind, although the desired effect lay far from her. Mathenhis soon found her; his bird appeared first and swooped past with its blood-red tail feathers.

'That bird of yours nearly caught me on the head it was flying so low,' Feletra criticised jovially.

Mathenhis laughed.

'So how are you finding it? The Konexa?' he said.

'I haven't found it. That's the problem,' she replied sedately. 'I don't know what I'm meant to be focusing on.'

'Then don't. Or rather, don't ignore it, but wait for it to happen naturally like before and then take control half way through. It might give you an insight into what it actually feels like in you, and then you can recreate the feeling next time.'

'Adrenache and Nil think I should learn how to control it as fast as possible, before something serious happens again.'

'They're not wrong, but this isn't like learning how to sew. It's like taming a wild animal that bites whenever you try and tie a leash about its neck. It will take plenty of time and patience, and only you will know when you're ready to unleash it.'

Feletra deliberated.

'You know, it's all very well everyone talking to me about the Konexa,' she said boldly, 'but every time I mention the Artrenium you all avoid the subject.'

Mathenhis wore an expression between a nervous smile and an awkward pursing of the lips.

'It's because it is the only divide between the Efordrads and Adrenache. They don't believe in it anymore, but she never stopped. For years she's tried openly to convince us, then eventually gave up.'

'Why didn't she just use the Artrenium itself to show them?'

'She can't. The Artrenium is said to exist in a hierarchy, therefore whoever is leading the Efordrads is usually the most powerful –'

'You and Adrenache?'

'Yes. But – treetops cannot reach great heights without their roots. And that's where the rest of the tribe comes in. Without them believing in it or using it, the abilities of the leaders wane in turn, and the Artrenium will disappear.'

'And what do you believe?'

There was the awkward mouth again, but the eyes pondered.

'I'm uncertain,' said Mathenhis, smiling now, 'I want to believe in the Artrenium so much, I want to share the hope that my sister has for it, but I struggle to see that when there is no proof with my own eyes.'

'You don't need proof, Mathenhis, you need faith. You said yourself it needs belief to exist. I think you believe in it more than you don't, and you're afraid of feeling foolish in front of the tribe if you speak out.'

'We all need faith, Feletra. Unfortunately it evades us more skilfully than we can hunt it.'

Feletra looked down.

'Agreed,' she replied ruefully.

Mathenhis picked some small nuts and handed them to Feletra to feed his bird as they walked on. It was called a fareon; most of them lived in the mountains, and when Mathenhis ventured there one day, he found the bird as a chick alone and stumbling in the deep snow, his leg had been crushed from a fall from the nest above. Too young to yet fly, Mathenhis had taken the chick with him to find the mother and nest, but upon his discovery on the next shelf up, he saw that the nest had been savaged by some fierce predator. There was only blood and downy feathers left blowing in the freezing wind. That same predator was the matirii, the huge grey mountain beast of unsurpassable temper and a love for only the sweetest flesh between its teeth; Mathenhis had faced the matirii and escaped with just a scar across his head. Unable to fend for himself, the chick was brought back to the settlement where Mathenhis raised him and helped him to fly, though his leg had never recovered. Since the fareon's daring leap to escape his attacker, he had never been able to stand on his own two feet, instead relying on the claws that tipped his wings for grip upon landing and the good leg to steady himself. For this reason, he rarely ever touched the ground, instead landing in the trees and rooftops. And he would do anything Mathenhis asked of him, never going far from his side. He had been named Ren, which meant 'loyalty' in Old Beltrorn.

'So, when can I leave Ira?' Feletra asked affably. 'That's not to offend – I appreciate everything you've all done for me, but as you know, it's important I find the cure quickly.'

'I understand,' said Mathenhis. 'We are in the process of gathering the Markhim, they're a group of mirikites, creatures of the sea. They've always come to the aid of the Efordrads, the trouble is finding them. They are flighty animals, and don't like to stay in one place for long. But they will be the quickest way for you to cross the sea.'

'And how exactly are you gathering them?'

'I'll show you. Take a walk with me.'

Mathenhis led Feletra to the foot of the mountains on the northern reach of the island. As they approached an outcrop that jutted over the forest, there stood at the very end four white stone pillars surrounding a beacon. But for the intensity of the light that was emanating from it, Feletra felt amazed she had not noticed it in the sky before. A great blue beam lit the way from there to far out in the sea, nowhere did it falter.

As Feletra looked closer, she saw a beautiful pale stone in the beacon sat before a small glass enclosure, and within this was an unusual insect, trying in vain to escape. It appeared to be glowing with the same blue light; the more it struggled, the brighter the light shone.

'See the stone, Feletra?' said Mathenhis. 'It was carved by the Artons, made from a primitive rock of Enphiah known as selteb. They called this stone Emptera, and there is a second stone, its sister, which the light meets, called Liminep. But – to produce the light that channels through the stones, we need a reefly, like this one. As soon as you trap one, they emit that blue light as a signal for help to their own kind.'

'But why not just use a flame?' said Feletra.

'That is where things get specific. When the beam hits the other end, Liminep splits the light into a fan-like projection, which penetrates the water's surface down to the depths of the sea. But within the water, the light becomes a brighter blue and the fan disperses into shafts, and the shafts then flash the light. However, this is a particular shade of blue that can only be seen by the Markhim beneath the water, and they know that it is our signal to them to gather here at the island. The reefly is the only thing that can produce the right shade of blue, so we take one, and let Emptera magnify the light. Don't worry about the fly, we replace it every day. Adrenache insists. She seems to attract them for some reason, so at least they're easy to find.'

'Interesting,' Feletra mused. 'How long has the beacon been lit?'

'Since you told us your story,' said Mathenhis. 'You needn't look so surprised, we aren't the oppressive captors you once thought we were.' He gave her a wry smile. 'Unfortunately, mirikites scatter themselves across the Sea of Dalpha, so it may take a while before one of them sees the signal.'

Feletra looked uncertain about this. How long would she have to wait?

'How many days does this normally take?' she asked.

'I know of your urgency, Feletra. But I cannot say, I'm sorry. The last time we requested the help of the Markhim was before my time. But it's the only way to leave Ira. And safely.'

'What about a boat?'

'Wrong season. The storms out at sea are too severe, and mirikites are faster. They may be able to miss them. You and Nil were lucky to come off your ship alive. I am surprised the ships are even engaged in faring at this time of year, but then, I suppose there will always be a penchant for money in the main land.'

They left the mountains and were on their way back through the forest, when Feletra's sharp ears heeded something untoward.

'What is it?' said Mathenhis.'

She felt the ground rumble beneath her, claps of thunder, but the skies were bright and clear and nature had not to answer for this. Faint cries and screams.

'Something's happening.'

Back at the settlement, Nil had been spending his time with Adrenache in the garden, where they discussed Nil's part in the matters at hand.

'Have you told her everything, Nil?' said the matriarch.

'Yes. Everything was said the past night. It's what she asked of me.'

'I am glad. Because you know already how she will react if she were to discover you had been lying.'

'I know. She would feel betrayed.'

Adrenache stretched up to unhook a creeper from a thorn that had it growing astray. She was so slight of frame, sometimes even appearing brittle, not tall and imposing like the stories would have painted past matriarchs of the tribe. There were curves in her gown where womanhood allowed, but these were somewhat under-generous, distended at the waist rather than drawn into tight half-moons. The hips and breasts, too, gave cause for forgiveness, though for the subtle roundness and skin as white as milk, there was somehow still much to be left to the imagination, shy invitations gone unspoken. Still, she would seem to sweep the ground, not walk it, glide where others trod like mortals. Ever did she hold her head high.

'You must work together now for the same thing. It is strange that fate has brought you to the same path. Keep her close, Nil, for I would not desire to be her enemy when she reaches full strength, and she will.'

On the night that Feletra had told them all of her plight, Nil had been obliged to follow on then with his own account. By the end, the two stories were not too dissimilar, and Feletra discovered that Nil's heart also rested with his family.

He was a lone child, with only his mother to care for, and she for him. Together they had lived in Stura, in a quiet village with few inhabitants. Nil undertook all the manual labour about the house, with a few favours for neighbours here and there, whilst his mother earnt a little money doing what she loved, as a teacher for young children. But there was something different about her: she was a woman of Blackcraft. Whilst she meant no harm, she and her son were forced to keep this a secret, for Blackcraft was as frowned upon in Pyra as it was in Enphiah, to the point of imprisonment. Or if caught by extremists, death.

Nil hated how often she came so close to revealing herself, for she helped others with the craft: the thatcher would land in a bed of straw when his ladder broke under him, a child's picture book was straight and pristine again after a classmate had stamped on it, an open wound could be stitched in seconds. But she could be clumsy and did not exercise caution. Many a time Nil urged that they move to one of the secluded houses, where no one else would find them, so that she would be safe from suspicious eyes. But her love of teaching kept her there.

Not long ago, however, a man had arrived at the house in the middle of the night. Neither Nil nor his mother knew him, or how he had managed to enter without breaking the doors down, though he looked eerily upon them as if he knew them well. *'I have been watching you for some time,'* he had said to Nil's mother, *'and I believe that you are worthy of my circle.'*

After enquiring what this circle was, the man explained that it was known as the Sabrine, for the best craftsmen in the land, and that with twelve fully fledged members, they would do great things, and that the common folk would soon be at their mercy. They needn't hide from prying eyes anymore, but instead walk forth as proud craftsmen.

But Nil's mother sensed the evil in him, and refused immediately. The man left quietly that night, but three starbands later he returned and attempted to change her mind again. She refused once more and Nil threatened him protectively. He left quietly. Another three starbands later, four unknown men visited in the night while they slept. Somehow they had entered the bedroom of Nil's mother without a sound, and the doors were still locked.

Nil awoke in the next room to screams, and ran to her aid. She was writhing in pain on the bed, her body fed by a stream of something dark and terrible from between the four men stood huddled at the foot. He tried to stop them, but they overpowered him, completed their dark ritual, and vanished. Nil's mother was left screaming in pain for days after; insomnia took her and she cast her food away. She knew what it was they had done. It was the Craft of Wraiths.

After five days, she fell into a complete state of trance. Barely responsive, the most she would utter were dark or fanciful things that were planted in her mind, things that made no sense. Others were strings of words that had no meaning in this world, but of another, Nil was sure. Sentences came in whispers and rasps of the throat that sent a chill through him.

On the sixth day, the strange man that had visited twice before had returned to them. He told Nil that he could remove the curse at once if she were to join them. Nil refused again on his mother's behalf; curse or no curse, she would never have forgiven him if he had given her to this stranger. The man made him one last offer, and said there was another powerful craftsman who lived in the Hills of Durun, and if he could bring him instead to take her place, he would lift the curse and leave them in peace.

Nil travelled to Durun in Enphiah as the man said, but quickly discovered that the craftsman he spoke of died seven years ago.

He was furious, and then furious with himself, for in the wasted time he left Stura the man could have returned for his mother. He saw only red, and vowed to return to Pyra, find the man, and kill him.

But before he could cross the sea again, he met Feletra, a girl he was so drawn into protecting he could not begin to fathom what she had over him. And then he met the Efordrads who, after hearing his drastic intentions for the mysterious man of Pyra, tried to convince him otherwise, not to go seeking vengeance and death, for this would put him just as low as the craftsman. Instead he should find the cure with Feletra, and use it between his mother and Ataleka.

Nil listened to them, and agreed, though Feletra had observed no change in his expression, no crack in his determination and honestly believed he was saying this just to please them. But she had said nothing.

'This man you thought to seek, is he in Chriah?' said Adrenache.

'Yes. I am sure,' Nil replied assuredly, 'before the captain of the Weeping Dove died, I discovered that he supported the Sabrine, and he knew where to find that man. I would have followed him after the voyage, but then he tried to harm Feletra. By then, I didn't care how he could have helped me; I wanted him gone.'

'Feletra was not pleased about being your payment for the information you needed,' said Adrenache softly, but then Nil saw she was smiling. She understood him. There was no judgement in this garden.

'That won't happen again,' he said firmly.

But then Adrenache's smile faltered slowly.

'Our members are in trouble –' she said, '– there is blood in the forest.'

'What?'

Nil stood to attention immediately, he knew Feletra was in the forest also. Then he heard cries from afar, beyond the garden walls.

Adrenache's head was tilted back and her eyes a bright white – it was something kymic.

'They are helpless,' she said in that low tone of hers. 'He

has trapped them.'

'He? Who is he?' said Nil, but Adrenache had become paralysed with the kym that sought her body from the forest yonder. Nil turned on his heel and ran for the garden passage that led straight into the heart of the forest. Afax had caught up and bounded on beside him – the clever creature had remembered the dagger his master had left on the bench, and flung it to him. Nil caught it without having to turn his head. All he could think now was that Feletra must be there – she must be one of the trapped. First he had thought that she had lost control of the Konexa again, until Adrenache said 'he.' Who was he?

As Nil approached the grassy knoll that overlooked the vale, he caught an open sight of the offender and quickly crouched to avoid being seen. Stealthily he crept down the bank to the vale's level, and then he recognised who this man was.

Stood in the lazy stream that fed a cove beneath the knoll was the marked man, the crew member who left them stranded in the sea. He had trapped four of the Efordrads into the cove; their weapons were nowhere to be seen and two of them appeared to be gravely injured. Feletra was not there.

The marked man raised his hand, then he stopped and caught sight of Nil to his side.

'You,' he said.

'Who are you really?' said Nil boldly. He looked fearless.

The attacker mocked him with a curtsey and a broad smile.

'Korsthr,' he said, 'at your service.'

'What do you want here?'

Korsthr paused, and then looked back at the Efordrads as if peering through a keyhole.

'Them,' he said simply, and before any of them could react he raised a hand to the great knoll above them, pulled down on nothing and the huge mound followed suit, crushing each of the four Efordrads to nothing.

Nil did not hesitate – he sprang for Korsthr. Afax came up from behind and aimed for his head, but he was expecting all of it, and slung the giptern into the hard ground.

Nil prepared to drive the dagger into his marked, greasy flesh, but Korsthr halted him without touch and then the Blackcraft held him there, still and powerless.

And then he came closer, until his outstretched hand came into contact and wrapped firmly around Nil's neck.

'Don't stand in our way,' he said maliciously, and in that moment Nil saw over his shoulder Feletra and Mathenhis had arrived – his eyes widened and he wanted to tell them to run, but he was rendered helpless in the grip of the craft.

Korsthr caught that small reaction he expressed in his eyes, and turned to face his newcomers – but Mathenhis had already drawn a bow – as the arrow flew for his heart Korsthr quickly tried to deflect it entirely, but not quickly enough, for the arrow then struck Nil, plunging between his ribs.

'Nil!' Feletra exclaimed, and she ran to him, heedless of the craftsman.

Korsthr wore a momentary look of fear as Feletra approached, though his adversaries had not the time to notice his subtleties at that point – he darted off into the forest towards the settlement. The hold on Nil was broken and he collapsed to the ground.

Feletra knew how Nil could so easily look in the face of adversity and stand his ground unshaken, but even she thought that lying on his deathbed would break him.

She was wrong. He lay there, half in her arms, half out, and was in full control. His breathing quickened a little, but his eyes were focused and as his gaze glided up to hers, she thought she could hear some unearthly, mellifluous melody. It was an uncanny and eerie sound, lasting but a second, fragmented and without substance. It reminded her of a lullaby her father used to sing to her as a child, but where there would have been words there was just music, murmurs and sighs on the ebb of breath.

'Mathenhis!' she called desperately, 'Mathenhis! Help him!'

The Efordrad approached with the bow hanging sadly at his side. Five more members of the clan appeared behind them, led by Raneao.

'Mathenhis, what happened?' said Raneao.

'It was a craftsman,' came the low reply, 'he's heading for the bridge, and he's powerful. Go, stop him now!'

The Efordrads wasted no time and ran for the settlement. Feletra looked at them go in despair.

'Why won't you do anything?' she said. 'Please!'

Mathenhis hesitated, then looked her in the eye.

'It's a poison barb. I'm sorry, Feletra, he only has a few minutes.'

Feletra looked horrified, she felt as if someone had taken a hammer to her chest.

Afax had been left unscathed after his rough handling, and came now to paw at Nil's skin where he was turning pale. And then Feletra lost control of something inside her. *I won't bury him*, she thought – the earth beneath them began to lift – *he's not going to die. I won't bury him. He's not going to die.*

The ground shook and lifted higher – higher – a great pointed hill was forming with each of them still atop –

'Feletra –' said Mathenhis, 'the craftsman –'

'It's not him –' said Nil, his breath slipping from him, and he looked up at Feletra proudly as she held him tighter to stop him from falling.

'You're not going to die,' she said to him with tenacity, and she suddenly felt stronger than ever before. It was as if she could feel the raised earth surging through her, in her blood.

Then Nil's breath caught somewhere in his chest, he inhaled sharply and looked about in surprise and confusion.

'What is it?' said Feletra.

'I don't know –' he spluttered, 'but something's changed. I could feel the poison moving before – I think you stopped it.'

'I-I what?' she said with a gasp, then she looked up at Mathenhis. 'Does that mean it is over? He's going to be alright?'

'No,' said Mathenhis gravely, 'you've stopped the poison from circulating, but as soon as you lose hold of the Konexa it will begin again, reach his head and that's when it will kill him.'

Feletra felt sick. The hill rose higher again. Nil's fate was in her hands, his very life swung helplessly from a pendulum of strings rooted in her struggling mind. This kym of hers now truly was both a curse and a blessing; she could not hope to hold on forever, already it was slipping.

Then something bold struck her, an idea that might have been fruitless in the moments that fled from Nil like grains of sand upon a merciless gale.

'Heal him, Mathenhis!' she said suddenly.

'What? Feletra, I ca –'

'You have to heal him now, while he still has a chance! Use the Artrenium!'

'There is no Artrenium! You know this –'

'No – you just don't believe it! Even your sister believes in it. I know she does – please, you're all he has left –'

The hill rose higher still. Nil's eyes widened.

'The poison is trying to move again –' he said, 'it's like something cold –'

Feletra looked at Mathenhis despairingly. She could feel the Konexa slipping from her grasp.

'I can't do what you're asking, Feletra. I'm sorry,' said Mathenhis, his eyes beginning to reflect the melancholy abyss of hers.

'Yes, you can!' she cried. 'I believe in the Artrenium, please just try – I can't let him die –'

Nil made another strange noise – Feletra knew that was when she had lost the Konexa, and her heart sank.

'Mathenhis, please!' she implored, but then Nil was tugging at her sleeve.

'Don't –' he said, though it pained him now to speak, 'just look at – look at me.'

She did so. Though she hated it. She'd never had someone die in her arms before. She kept trying the Konexa over and over again, but to no avail.

His hand was loose, she took hold of it and he gripped it in return. He began to shake a little and his face was pale now.

The poison had entered his head.

Feletra stared into his green eyes; they were still

dancing, like when she first noticed them on the Weeping Dove, they were still alive somehow.

And when she thought it was all over, when Nil's last moment was but a heartbeat away, the world stopped.

Suddenly she thought he had gone, for his eyes had stopped moving. But the dance in them was still there, even now. And then they moved.

A blue light entered them, and it grew stronger and stronger. Nil blinked several times, then he inhaled sharply and looked down at his body. Feletra followed his gaze.

There, at the site of his wound, the blue light emanated powerfully, almost blinding them. Amidst the light, they could just make out the two hands of Mathenhis, laid one atop the other, above the wound.

Feletra couldn't believe it – it was the Artrenium, and it was working. In a matter of seconds it was all over; towards the end of the healing the blue light increased in intensity and then disappeared suddenly.

There was a moment of silence between them as Nil sat up, one hand feeling at the smooth skin where the arrow had pierced, the other still clutching Feletra's unknowingly.

'Is he...?' Feletra said delicately.

'He'll be fine,' Mathenhis replied.

Feletra and Nil exhaled deeply.

'Thank you,' said Nil.

Mathenhis shook his head with an almost coy smile. 'Please,' he said, 'it was Feletra who saved you.'

They looked at each other. Feletra flung her arms around Nil without thinking, she wanted to say things, she felt astounded, but was interrupted.

'We have to get to the others,' said Mathenhis.

Feletra and Nil snapped into the moment, in the midst of

everything that just happened they had forgotten that Korsthr was still at large and was heading to kill the rest of the Efordrads.

Hastily they slid down the steep hill that had raised from beneath them and Mathenhis jumped. It was too soon in her ability for Feletra to return the ground to how it was, and now was not the time for practice. Afax was so overjoyed his master was well again he glued himself to Nil's arm lovingly, until they began to tear through the forest, and he swung from tree to tree to keep up with them.

They ran on with all speed to the settlement – the closer they came, the louder the despair rang out in the air. Feletra's heart was quickening, she didn't know what to expect. But as they were approaching the bridge they were faced with stray patches of fire in the trees and undergrowth – the trail of destruction worsened, and then they saw everything from the other side of the bridge, awash with catastrophe.

With not a moment to lose or look back, the three of them sprinted across the bridge to help, Mathenhis poised with his deadly bow, Nil with only his short dagger and Afax ahead of them with sharp claws. Feletra had nothing and missed her bow even more now, but she was planning on using a different weapon. It may have been too soon for her to use so brashly, and she risked harming the others in the process, but there was no time to wait for perfection now. Maybe this was the only way she'd ever be able to wield the Konexa, when there was something worth using it for.

Even from a distance, the damage to the settlement was already so vast that they could spot its source easily – Korsthr walked amongst them audaciously, manipulating fire, crushing homes and seizing those who tried to run.

Raneao could be seen ordering a group of Efordrads, but many of the warriors emerged only to their deaths – Korsthr used Blackcraft to break bones, impale, suffocate, and he laughed mercilessly every time they tried to come near.

‘Every one of you will be destroyed!’ he said, and he raised his hands in a gesture to come forward.

Feletra and the others crouched behind a crumbling stone wall as Mathenhis shot one deflected arrow after another.

‘He’s too fast,’ said Nil. ‘He’ll see everything coming.’

‘Why is he even doing this?’ said Feletra.

‘I don’t know –’

‘No, no –’ came Mathenhis, for suddenly they heard a familiar voice across the way, clear and strong. It was Adrenache.

‘Why do you slay us so?’ she said. ‘For revenge? Your men threatened *us* –’

‘I don’t care about the crew,’ Korsthr laughed. ‘But orders are orders, and before I leave this wasted island, I will see that every Efordrad is no more than dust beneath my boot.’

‘Adrenache!’ Mathenhis called to his sister. She was so close to Korsthr, too close. And she stood tall with her chin held high, her eyes gleaming white like her hair and her pale green dress floating about her ankles. Against all the destruction she appeared so ethereal and innocent, a beacon of light and hope.

‘Orders?’ she said. ‘Then you do have a purpose to kill us. You are working for someone else?’

‘Quiet!’ Korsthr bellowed. ‘You are nothing more than an obstruction.’

He raised his hand to her.

Mathenhis could hold back no more – he leapt out from behind the wall and fired at the craftsman, striking him squarely through the hand that was raised.

Korsthr bent at the knees in pain, ripped the arrow from his flesh and turned to face Mathenhis.

'Nil – he'll kill them both!' said Feletra, 'I have an idea.'

'You're not that strong yet, Feletra!'

'I have to try!'

Feletra ran onto the scene, Nil following suit with Afax, and as they watched Mathenhis ready to release an arrow for the head and something dark begin to manifest from Korsthr's good hand – he stopped.

As soon as he saw Feletra, he lowered his arm, and the dark craft that was building within his palm began to dissipate. Mathenhis stopped too, he was confused but held fast with his bow.

They formed a triangle with Adrenache and Nil looking in. Feletra mirrored Adrenache's noble stance but she didn't know what to do with herself. Upon being closer to Korsthr she felt her anger rising for what he had done and it was causing the Konexa to stir within her, but nothing was expelled.

'You,' said Korsthr, pulling a cruel smile at her. It was as if he had forgotten the Efordrads were ever there, and as he acknowledged her as if she were significant she felt a pang of fear in her stomach and the ground before her began to shake – she knew it was wanting to raise between the two of them and protect her.

No, stop it, she told herself. *I don't need a wall.*

The Konexa had listened, for suddenly the earth gave way instead, and created a shallow dip between the three of them. But then Mathenhis lowered his bow, for Korsthr turned pale and fell to his knees.

'It's the poison,' said Mathenhis.

The craftsman reached for something in his pocket, it was a vial that looked empty from a distance, yet when he opened it and raised it to his lips, he inhaled heavily.

His head dropped, as did the vial. There were a few seconds in which nothing happened, but Mathenhis raised his bow again in suspicion. Then Korsthr lifted his head and rose to his feet once more, his empty-looking pallor completely gone. Feletra noticed something with her keen eye – the arrow wound on his hand had also disappeared. Her heart suddenly brimmed with hope and dread that mixed in a sickly concoction: *he had a cure.*

Mathenhis' mouth fell open and Adrenache looked grave from afar.

Suddenly they heard an eagle's cry – it was the same one that Feletra had recognised over and over, she knew it – but there was a greater creature that stole her attention and left all but Korsthr aghast.

'It cannot be...' said Adrenache.

From the direction of the mountains, a great and beautiful swenph swept down and landed beside the craftsman, screaming and beating its wings at the others, almost blowing them down. Feletra saw its eyes, they were small but the blue was incredibly bright, unnaturally so. They were wild, ice cold, rolling about without any real focus.

Korsthr mounted the erratic bird easily, then he looked directly at Feletra, held out his hand and without warning she felt her body pulling towards him, unable to fight it.

'No!' shouted Nil, and ran to pull her back. 'Leave her!'

Feletra fell to the ground in the drag to the swenph – she dug her fingernails into the earth but he was too strong – Nil grabbed her arms.

'Don't let me go!' Feletra cried.

Korsthr made a simple flicking gesture, and Nil was thrown off.

Mathenhis shot more arrows – all deflected – then he and Adrenache were thrown away just the same. It was too easy for Korsthr.

Feletra was reeled in upon the swenph like a fish trapped on a hook – he had her. Before she could do anything, he touched her throat, there was a strange sensation that ran through her flesh in an instant, she was paralysed. They took off into the skies as Korsthr held onto to her to stop her falling.

'It won't be for long, my little konexic,' he said in his grating voice. *This is it, then,* she thought. *He will take me back to whoever he is working for, then they will kill me.*

She wished she could move her mouth, she wanted to spit in his face. *Why is the Konexa so unpredictable? I need it. I need it now. I must harness it.*

Out of nowhere the eagle joined alongside them, and when it called Korsthr could understand its language.

'I know what I'm doing,' he replied. 'Trust me, it's easier my way.'

But it seemed there was an argument here, for the eagle would not heed, and cried ever more frantically at him.

That sickly feeling in Feletra's chest returned to her. Suddenly she remembered the faces of her family, and the feeling increased. She could feel something inside of her – it was breaking free –

She flexed her fingers – and then the entire hold on her

was broken. The eagle saw it first and screeched loudly – Feletra struck Korsthr round the head as hard as she could before he could express his disbelief.

He took hold of her arms, but the commotion had sent the swenph off-balance and they were heading down to one of the beaches of Ira. The swenph softened the blow into the sand but Feletra had rolled off, spitting out the grains that had found their way into her mouth. She quickly got to her feet and was ready to attack any way she could, but Korsthr was already drawing the swenph back up, with the eagle at his side.

'Fine, you were right,' he said in an undertone to the bird, followed by something in Fadic, then he looked to Feletra.

'I'll see you again,' he said with a wink, 'but don't be too long.' Then he flew off with the two birds.

Feletra didn't know what to think. For a moment she felt that this must be some game of his and that he would quickly return for her, but he did not turn around. As she watched the swenph fly over the beam of light to Liminep, she saw something else stir within the water. Was it a trick of the twilight?

Something was arching its back above the waterline as it prepared to surface not a quarter of a league from where she stood transfixed – the closer this thing came the more she could see it was simply enormous.

The first mirikite had arrived.

Chapter 15
Thick Blood

Elegantly, majestically, the swenph landed safely upon a wide balcony of a Setran tower. Set in a grey, desolate land, the tower was undeniably stunning; overly cautious precision and better-spent effort had gone into the architecture; the walls were etched deep with sweeping lines that pointed, curled, swirled, soared, plunged and pressed into the black stone.

The room was dark and full of gloom. Before a blazing fireplace stood a tall man, enriched with a heavy blood-red cloak that dusted the ground and grey attire beneath, made of enna. A thick belt was bound about his waist.

Korsthr dismounted the swenph carelessly.

'Akeon,' he called loudly, addressing the man, who had the eagle swoop in and land upon his shoulder as he turned. 'Why the change of heart? I had the girl. We could have sped things up if I'd brought her here –'

'Your only order was to eliminate the Efordrads,' Akeon said with a deep voice that carried well. He had not shouted, yet it had the same effect somehow and Korsthr did not interrupt. 'If you had kept her on that swenph a second longer than receiving my warning you'd be a dead man.'

'She's just a girl –' Korsthr smirked.

'She is a konexic, and can outweigh your craft with ease. She can destroy you from the inside out, if she wanted. Don't think for a second you had it under control.'

'But she's new to the kym. She didn't know how to use

it.’

‘That is when it is most dangerous. She could have done something unexpected to both of you. You’re a fool. If you wish to maintain your new place within the Sabrine I will need to start seeing some intelligence.’

Korsthr held his tongue for retaliation. It would only end badly for him if he didn’t.

‘What now then?’ he said.

Akeon turned away.

‘Well, this is progress,’ he replied. ‘The Efordrads are out of our way. Or rather, out of Feletra’s way. The rebuilding of their community and grieving for their dead will take precedence. Now when she arrives in Chriah, I can be the one to show her how to use the Konexa, and the rest.’

‘I don’t understand. The Efordrads were teaching her how to control it; why not let them do the dirty work and put their lives at risk rather than ours?’

‘The wrong teacher produces the wrong student,’ said Akeon, ‘they will only restrict her capabilities. I can unleash her full potential, and then utilise it.’

‘Against...?’

‘Yes, you know the rest.’

‘And you are sure it was a good idea to let her go?’ said Korsthr. ‘If you want to use her you could have had her by now –’

‘You are thinking in the wrong order. First, she must do something else, it is the key to all of this. Only after that can I have my way, but she must do it herself, and find her own way to Chriah.’

‘How is she even going to do that? I, for one can tell you that no ship is going to make an easy journey across

Dalpha.'

'The Efordrads have their ways,' said Akeon placidly. 'The remaining few will have helped her with that. She will find her way here. Besides, she has motive.'

'Don't forget the boy.'

Akeon paused.

'He will find his way here as well,' he said finally, then gestured something to the eagle, and the bird took flight to the north once more, where Pytheria still shone.

x

Feletra wandered down the quiet beach aimlessly. She tried to figure out which direction the Efordrads lay in, but it never seemed right. One thing she was sure of, the smallest mountain range now lay between herself and the settlement, dividing them.

The night soon set in and engulfed the island, the cold followed. The beach was endless, it curled and spread as a spit that pointed out to the eastern sea.

Feletra sat down upon the sand, and looked out at the spit tirelessly. She wanted to walk the length of it, right to the end, for no other reason than wanting to. And then she didn't know what she'd do at the end. It must have been a league long, maybe two.

Then she wondered why she was thinking about this, of all things. Something so simple. For this was the first time in so long she wasn't worried about anything, nor did she have the creeping curiosity nibbling away at her insides, hungry for answers. There was some sort of inner calm here, a foreign and unusual feeling in Feletra's library of expressions.

Shouldn't she have been thinking about the craftsman, all the lives he took and why he had wanted to take her away? And after that, think out a logical plan of how to return to the others, identify where she stood currently, analyse the quickest and safest route across the island. Gather any necessary supplies and head out. The night came and went, morning broke and Pytheria rose; Feletra hadn't moved or slept all night.

A thin-legged spider crawled over her hand. She brushed it off. The waves crashing upon the shingled shore were hypnotising. The sea was whispering into the sky, calling. But then she heard it becoming louder, until it was so clear that she recognised the call.

'Feletra!'

Nil's voice.

She turned around, and sure enough there he was, scrabbling his way through the entangled forest towards her. Afax was slashing at the undergrowth for him, and Mathenhis was close behind.

Feletra ran up the beach to them.

'Nil?' she said, unable to believe her luck.

'So it's true,' said Nil, 'you are still on the island.'

He was smiling at her, and she was overjoyed to see them.

'But how did you find me?'

'Adrenache knew,' said Mathenhis, 'she said the craftsman had left you on the far eastern beaches of Ira. We followed her directions and Ren helped from there.'

Feletra looked overhead as the shadow of Ren circled them above. She felt elated that they were here, and that her luck was turning. Then she remembered all the Efordrads that had been killed in the Blackcraft attack, and her own happiness was dampened again.

'What's it like back there?' she said cautiously.

'Not good,' Mathenhis replied, but not hopelessly. 'There are many of us to bury, and many homes to rebuild. But there is some hope among us – I have shown the Efordrads the Artrenium.'

'That's wonderful news,' Feletra jumped in, 'now they have seen it with their own eyes they'll have no choice but to believe it.'

'Yes, that is true. But at the same time, a lot of us are still mourning. It's difficult for anyone to think about the Artrenium after what they are suffering. The kym has saved a few lives, however. Those that were wounded badly will live to see tomorrow.'

Feletra felt guilty somehow. Nil seemed to notice the change in her eyes, the glint of relief that died and was then consumed by bitter remorse, but said nothing.

'I have some other news,' said Feletra.

Nil and Mathenhis looked at her, half with anxiety and half with expectation.

'One of the Markhim has come. It's been swimming around the spit –' she said, pointing to the lone finger of land. 'I think it's waiting for the others.'

But Mathenhis lowered his eyebrows.

'Are you sure it was a mirikitc?'

'I think so...' said Feletra, now beginning to doubt herself.

'It's just that they will usually come onto the beach and speak to us.'

'Oh, but it did beach,' Feletra insisted, 'then after a while returned to the water. But I have seen it around the spit, it hasn't left.'

‘I see,’ said Mathenhis. ‘Let’s take a look down there before we head back.’

To the very end of the spit they walked; it felt desolate yet so tranquil, an island all of its own that seemed entirely broken off from the mainland and floating about in the turquoise waters like a great lillipad that could never quite tether its stem. The east side of the island was indeed closer to some far-off paradise.

They looked into the shallow shores. Pytheria was flashing blindly off the stuttering face of the ocean.

‘I don’t see anything,’ said Nil.

‘That’s because they don’t like to be seen without knowing an Efordrad is nearby,’ Mathenhis replied, then he picked up a stone, threw it as far out to sea as he could, and waited.

He knelt down, looking intently across the surface.

There was movement. A large ripple appeared where the stone had disappeared, then another.

Feletra and Nil stepped back warily.

Something smooth and oval-shaped surfaced shyly. Mathenhis smiled and said something in ancient Fadic to it.

There was a pause after as it submerged again, and then the water turned chaotic. As the mirikite heaved itself into full view, the waves became feral and subservient to this great beast; it was as if it had been summoned from a spell – one moment everything was so calm and the next the sea was ablaze with anarchic ambiguity.

As the creature unfurled a beautifully long neck Pytheria was blotted out and they stood in the shade – deep rumbles emanated from its belly as the sounds from the ocean’s depths now graced the skies above Ira.

‘It didn’t look this big before,’ said a gaping Feletra to Nil as their heads were tilted back uncomfortably to meet the soaring heights of the mirikite.

‘Edego, I might have known you’d be first,’ Mathenhis called upwards.

The mirikite bent its neck to gaze down upon the ant-like Efordrad. It truly was a king of the sea; its body was streamlined and plump in the middle, then flattened out into a bluntly pointed fleshy tail. It was a dull, stony grey all over except for the head where the colour faded into orange around the eyes and crown.

They were there for a while longer as Mathenhis spoke to Edego in Fadic, explaining the favour they needed.

Feletra and Nil sat upon the sand in the meantime, bathed in the shadows of the mirikite.

‘You looked as surprised as I did when it came out,’ said Nil, ‘I thought you said it beached in front of you already?’

‘Yes...’ said Feletra, her eyes darting, ‘I hid.’

Nil looked at her and had to contain himself. She glanced at him with a blush.

‘What? It was huge!’ she exclaimed.

Nil sniggered.

Finally Mathenhis approached them.

‘Edego thinks his master will most likely agree to take you both overseas.’

‘His master?’ said Feletra. ‘I thought he was the...?’

‘No, Edego is actually a lesser. He is one of the smaller mirikites.’

Nil looked past him at the towering beast, ‘If you say so.’

‘Anyway, be glad. Your plans are in motion. Edego will return to the sea around Liminep and emit his own call to draw the others in faster, and we will return to the settlement for now.'

'Mathenhis,' said Nil, 'why don't we just take Edego now? Why do we have to wait for the others? You could carry an army on him.'

'The Markhim don't do favours for others without council first, and after the final say of their master, Rodim.'

Feletra was suddenly distracted. From the north, a bird was flying straight for them. It glided between skittish flaps as if it stopped mid-air every so often. Nil and Mathenhis followed her gaze and appeared equally bewildered, until the bird finally landed upon the sand and pecked off a sealed and battered letter affixed to its leg before throwing it towards Feletra.

Feletra dropped to her knees and edged forward. Plunged into the sand, she saw the first half of her name poking out upon the front of the envelope, the letters written in the common hand, leaving much to elaboration. She plucked it out just as the bird sat upon her lap and proceeded to stare directly into her eyes. It was deathly still all of a sudden and Feletra felt that something was not right – it was gazing into her soul, taking something from it –

Mathenhis shot the small creature dead with an arrow. Feletra was left nonplussed, but the previous sensation had thankfully passed.

'What was that?' she said.

'A harmena bird,' Mathenhis explained, 'they can learn all there is to know about a person just by looking deep into their eyes. We know there are spies out there now, I could not let it escape.'

A pause followed as Feletra gazed at the tiny pierced body coated in sand, then down at the letter. A part of her did not wish to open it for fear that it was from her ever-watchful enemy.

'Tell us what it says,' said Nil placidly.

Feletra picked at the red wax seal until it popped open. She unfolded the letter and was somewhat startled to see it was from Emmet; she read it aloud for them to listen, her expression falling with greater alarm the longer she went on.

'This is the man you met in Betharanei?' said Mathenhis.

'Yes, Emmet. He was a good person, but I had no idea he would he would do this. Going back under that Valley House is madness, especially if what he says is true about the preathin. I almost died in there, what if he is walking straight to his death?'

'There is nothing you can do to stop that,' Nil commented bluntly, 'in fact, it is likely he has already been there by now. What intrigues me are the dark affairs of Chriah he mentions. If that was indeed a preathin you faced and Chriah is behind it, then we should all prepare for terror.'

'He tells me to steer clear of Chriah, but I *need* to be there. We both do.'

'And the Markhim will see that you make it there,' said Mathenhis firmly, 'I promise you that. But keep your head at all times in that country, it seems your friend has taken a great deal of risk sending you such content this far. I would heed his words and move forward with caution. I will inform Adrenache later of this information.'

Upon their return to the settlement, Feletra almost wanted to leave again; she could feel her eyes begin to shudder in their sockets as her fingers still loosely clasped at Emmet's precognitive letter, and it were not for the dead smoke in the air. Some small fires still burned weakly in corners, the wildlife had scarpered, leaving a macabre silence behind. The only sounds that could be heard were the faint sobs of women and cries of pain. A baby was crying somewhere – with dread, it struck Feletra that its mother might be gone forever. She added Emmet's face in her mind to those who were lost in the drift to the afterlife, did he make it out alive?

'Feletra?'

Without realising, she had stopped within the flow of Efordrads who were running and darting about her to help, just staring.

Mathenhis approached.

'Adrenache wants to speak with you. Come.'

Left together inside a royal blue shelter of leaves from the forest, Adrenache turned to Feletra unexpectedly jovially. She wore a soft smile; her eyes had returned to blue but her hair still shone silver. All her dark roots had disappeared.

'So much has happened and continues to happen, Feletra,' she said. 'You have awakened the Artrenium, for which I cannot thank you enough.'

Feletra had never seen her so alive. With all the detriment just outside, it confused her.

'It was really Mathenhis who did that –' said Feletra.

'Not without your belief in him. And there is more – the mirikites have joined us. Soon you and Nil will be able to cross Dalpha.'

Feletra failed to respond. She stared, she felt blank. Everything was working out for her, whilst everything had just collapsed for the Efordrads.

She sighed rapidly.

‘Feletra,’ said Adrenache, again in that low, eloquent tone of hers, ‘let go of the loss you have seen here. It is not yours to bear.’

‘But I am to blame. Korsthr came for me, he treated everyone else here like they were just in the way of that.’

‘But did he come for you?’ said Adrenache. ‘He changed his mind, Feletra, and left you here on the island.’

‘There was an eagle that spoke to him. It said something to make him let me go. And then, I broke free of his hold.’

Adrenache nodded.

‘I know. I saw that part happen. But the craftsman’s decision to take you could have been closer to opportunity than a thought-out plan. Wouldn’t you agree? Do not mistake me, as insightful as I am, there is still much hidden even to me. I cannot tell you what his intentions were; perhaps his ancestors were enemies of the Efordrads. We have known a few in our time, particularly craftsmen. Or perhaps you were connected, do you know him?’

‘No...but I did meet him before, just the once when he left us out there in the sea. He was one of the crew.’

‘He would have known the captain then, and did you not say the captain knew things about you that he couldn’t have? The link is clear, I think. Korsthr may have been attempting to finish his master’s job.’

Feletra’s eyes mulled into a deliberative gaze.

‘There was something else,’ she added, ‘Mathenhis shot Korsthr with poison; he should have been killed, but he wasn’t. He had an antidote.’

‘Yes, the gas within the vial...I do not know what it was, but I am almost certain it is the same cure that you are seeking.’

‘But it gets complicated now. Korsthr was on his way to

Pyra, most likely Chriah. This means there are Chriahks that know about the cure, Chriahk craftsmen, in fact. How are we ever going to get past them?'

Feletra looked wide-eyed, and then Nil walked in with Afax at his feet.

'You're stronger than them,' he said succinctly. 'You're a konexic.'

Feletra scoffed a little.

'That doesn't fill me with hope. I still can't control it, and there's only one of me. Something tells me there will be a whole host of them to protect the cure.'

'Well, when that fails, you'll have me.'

'And what will you do?' said Adrenache with interest.

'I'm the brains of all this. We can't lose.'

Feletra and Adrenache laughed together, then Feletra felt solemn once more. It seemed wrong to laugh, but she didn't want to cry and appear weak.

Adrenache took her hand.

'There will be time for you to weep and remember us. But to weep now will hinder you, blind you, give false judgement. I urge you to think forward only, and keep your head. You didn't cause any of this.'

Feletra stopped for a moment as her eyes drifted between the shining silver strands of Adrenache's hair where she became lost in their ethereal light, but safe and sound and warm...where no one could reach her. And then came back slowly.

'I just don't understand how these people know anything about me.'

Adrenache glanced at Nil.

'I have a feeling that will come clear when you get to Chriah,' she said, 'but until then, focus on the cure. This is for both you and Nil now. You must support each other.'

Following the discussion, Feletra and Nil helped the Efordrads where they could. The Artrenium was now in use by a select few who had been strong enough to abstain from the grief, namely those amongst Raneao's men. They had formed a team of healers, who were benefiting from the aid of those like Feletra and Nil to run around to fetch supplies for them. At one point, a patient was in urgent need of fresh water, and Feletra, already sweating from running to and fro in the roast of Pytheria, obliged. But as she returned, Nil saw that the water was bubbling and issuing steam heavily. They had only looked at each other, eyebrows raised in the knowledge that the Konexa was seeping through Feletra's mind again.

Mathenhis led the whole affair, he was an adept leader, prioritising the injured, instructing the healers, reassuring those who had lost someone. And every hour or so there seemed to be one or two more Efordrads who had awoken from the anguish and asked Mathenhis to show them how to use the Artrenium so they too could join.

Each time this happened it became easier to teach them, for that was how the Artrenium worked; the greater its use, the more pronounced the hierarchy became, allowing the kym to flow naturally through them again. And its capabilities stretched beyond healing the wounded; many of the homes that had been burnt down had been made from entirely natural resources of the forest, meaning that with the Artrenium, the Efordrads were able to encourage new green life to grow on a far quicker scale than nature intended.

Two more starbands passed. New homes were rapidly coming into shape, spirits were lifting following two mass burials for the unfortunates who were killed, the Artrenium was almost entirely accepted by all (those grieving were still slow to conform), and by late evening of the third approaching starband Mathenhis returned to the settlement with hopeful news.

‘Rodim has arrived,’ he said, ‘the mirikites were reunited last night for council and have agreed to take you to Pyra.’

Nil nodded with anticipation, Feletra smiled weakly.

‘Thank you,’ she said, though not with the enthusiasm Mathenhis had expected.

‘Aren’t you happy? No more waiting, you can leave whenever you want now.’

‘I know. I am happy. It’s just been a draining time, I think.’

There was a frankness in Feletra that even she could not place, for it certainly never used to exist within her. Some might have said it was a spark that had died, but that didn’t quite seem to explain it. A sincere sobriety had commandeered, or if daring towards one extreme, a well-accepted moroseness. And the change could also have been observed in both Flior and Lampaea; once they had tasted the world outside of that secluded Elpuran house, the wild abandon and the inventive voices of story characters began to dissipate quickly.

Perhaps death did that to a person. Nil was no less surprised; he seemed to have passed this phase long ago.

Two days later, when the effects of the Artrenium were beginning to show and the green shoots of new life were tall and prosperous, Feletra visited a shrine in the forest built in memory of the lost Efordrads. It was a stumpy looking thing made of stone, and sat in between the twisted trees like a plump, ugly cousin at a family reunion. Two stonemasons of the tribe had been in the midst of carving all the names of the deceased into the stones. Half were there, they had then retired for the day, either because darkness was falling or, Feletra observed, the name of a close one came next, for the latest entry was not complete. Even the dust still lined the edges. She thought one of them had found it too upsetting for one day; the three letters thus far were: *'MAR.'*

Without a thought put to it, Feletra leant in, parted her lips in a soft, delicate 'O', and blew all the dust away. It scattered into rolls in the air, glittering sublimely in the shafts of sunlight.

For a moment, she wished that spirits looked like that, if they must look like anything. Just a wisp of dust teased by light, playing catch me on the wind, or descending onto a still lake's surface like ashes laid to final rest and swept off on the ebb.

She was captive in the thoughts of dust and decay and lights and eyes that had burnt through the afterlife to watch her and accuse her of their passing.

Nil approached her so soundlessly it startled her.

'How are you going to get over the next ones?' he said.

Feletra turned and looked at him with hooded eyes.

'What do you mean?' she said quietly.

'You're going to kill in Pyra. Will you have time to grieve for them too?'

'I don't have to kill anyone. I won't.'

'Then you won't get the cure.'

Feletra took a step back from the shrine.

'No one has to die from this. Not everyone is a killer like you –'

'The Chriahks won't see it that way. They will do

anything to protect what they have. They're a savage people, and you might change your mind when you see what they're capable of.'

She felt her anger rising, a hot bloom of pink was ascending to her face from her belly.

'There are other ways – there are other ways than just death.'

'Yes, it means you lying in the ground instead of them –'

'Then I will have gone down honourably.'

Nil glanced sceptically.

'It's not like in the stories, Feletra. All the war heroes you've heard of have killed a thousand men each.'

And then she drew in one quick breath and stopped bothering, her composure a waned entity.

'Fine! Then I will kill them all!' she exclaimed, her voice resounding about the forest. 'Is that better? Now I'm like you.'

Nil paused.

'Did you know you blush when you get angry?' he said delicately.

Feletra made a stomp at him, to which Nil's flinch surprised even him. He had his hands in his pockets and made that crescent smile at her again. She couldn't stay angry at him when he did that. It was infectious.

She let his words flow over her as they walked back to the settlement together, mainly because Nil had never been wrong, and she wanted to avoid the truth. Her hands were still pure and unsullied from the taking of life – she knew that could change in Chriah. It would have to. And yet there was no fear within her that this would come to pass; it was a fear that it *could.* That *she* could. She was able now, equipped with something in her very bones and spirit that once lay sleeping.

She could tear a man's heart right out of his chest. Have it beating in her hands.

Could I? she thought, and she glanced down at her hands and grew afraid of them. Nil walked on ahead of her, and saw not the fear, the dark foreboding, the terrified shadow that crossed meticulously into the black of her eyes.

Was life so easy to take? she asked herself. *When I am the taker, is it that simple?* As simple as Nil had shown her on the Weeping Dove? A quick cut, and it was all over. No more light. No laughter, no love, no family, only blood – the blood was endless. Rich and thick. The Konexa would hunger for it, she was sure. There was blood on her hands.

'Feletra, there's blood on your hands.'

She knew it was Nil's voice, out there somewhere. But she couldn't see him. Nor could she reply. Out of the slumbering crevices of her mind a deep darkness had exuded, and had overcome the forest. The sunlight had been ushered away, and lurid shadows took hold of the place as if to the click of a finger.

Feletra was stood rooted within the thicket; her eyes were unclear, only blurred shapes she could make out. But whatever had taken control of her body prevented her from moving an inch.

Then she felt something faintly brushing her arms, it was warm and wet. It tickled her skin and rose upwards from her hands –

Nil had taken hold of her shoulders now, she had seen him coming towards her. He was saying something urgently, though it was laboured and slow to her ears.

Then she understood what it was.

There was blood pouring out of her fingertips; it was pushing its way upwards, up her arms in tiny streams. Streams that quickly became rivers, faster and faster – the blood was forcing its way out now, spluttering and bursting –

'Come back to me, Feletra! Come back!'

The blood quickly drained into her own gaping mouth.

Feletra gasped, she choked and fell to her knees.

Instantly, the light returned to the forest again. The blood wrenched itself out of her mouth, travelled back down her arms and sealed within her fingertips. Not a mark was left on her skin.

'Don't let it – don't let it take me!' she coughed, 'I will put it all back, I promise, just don't let –'

Nil grabbed her firmly.

'Put what back?'

Then she swayed a little to a stop, and looked into his eyes in a melancholy daze.

She whispered, 'All the life I took.'

Nil shook his head in confusion.

'You haven't taken any,' he said softly.

'But I will,' Feletra said through tears, 'I felt their blood. So many will fall at my feet and never get back up.'

Nil did something then that she would never have anticipated; she felt as if she was still in that dark, foreboding world she had created, but no more when he leant in and opened his arms to embrace her, whilst she sat kneeling upon the earth before him.

When he had pulled her forward, a blink of Pytheria's light caught her in the eye through the canopy above. There was no more darkness at that moment, either in the forest or inside her. His arms were larger than they had appeared, or perhaps she hadn't noticed before. She felt the muscles flex in them, signifying she was safe.

'Whatever loss comes your way,' he said, 'I will be there to help you bury it.'

Nil lifted Feletra off the ground, and escorted her through the thicket, over the bridge and back to the settlement.

x

Lampaea laid a hand gently upon the horla's neck. He could not think how he would explain to Halemedra that Fitaeba was dead, he had been there for her entire childhood. Bren had also passed his horla on the way to Olonath, slain by the fadres.

'You have served her well, Fitaeba. I will see that she is brought home,' Lampaea was left with no choice but to leave him lying there, he wished there was a better way to pay his respects to such a loyal creature, but there was no time to bury or burn. Neither was there time for the innocents of the party who were just as unfortunate, they came across four on their path and the guilt mounted with every new body.

'Come, Lampaea,' said Bren when Lampaea paused next to another.

'We were charged with their safety. We should have saved them.'

'We were overrun, this is why we need my men. The sooner we reach Olonath the better, let's be gone.'

There was no forest nor any land that could dissuade Lampaea from a challenge, but Olonath was a place to be reckoned with. The Great Forest of Beltro was studded with great soldiers of trees, grown deservedly fat from an age of unquestioned conquer and dominion of the solid earth. Never was such variety seen in any one region of land; there were trees and plants of all species here, all blooming richly and greedily leaving no space unaccommodated.

There were many shades of colour to be seen, some blindingly bright; where the great fanning petals of blossoms failed to gain notice there were tremendous blades of leaves to fill any void. Electric blues, vain scarlets and ostentatious oranges were spread everywhere generously – the ground beneath could scarcely be seen save for the path that the Beltrorns had marked out.

The forest fauna was no less abundant, many of the animals here Lampaea had never seen before, or their images confined to the pages of old textbooks. The diurnal creatures were very tame, venturing daringly close to the two men, especially Bren, who they all seemed to recognise and revere respectfully.

Bren pointed out each creature as they made their way through the forest, though there were so many that he had to name them at a speed which was unfit for Lampaea to remember them all. Nonetheless, each was as unique as the next; there were lattels, keepers of the earth, burrowing and resurfacing continuously. Trelespies, the most graceful and nimble. Regratims, the playful, trinket-loving thieves. Reeflies, congesting the air with their fat bodies and the weerasuhn, a herd of huge black-skinned beasts, slow in nature and conservative with a tough hide. Lampaea had been startled when four of these crossed their path so unexpectedly, one of them an infant as large as a horla. For beasts so large and commandeering in presence, their emergence from the foliage was subtle and quiet; the bottoms of their feet fell soft on the undergrowth, and they moved so slowly that one could hardly feel the vibration of their steps.

Some of the night creatures were less friendly, Bren warned, and it was best not to venture out alone at dusk unless you knew the forest well.

It took an entire day to work their way to the heart of Olonath, where Bren's men were based. They might have taken half the time were the terrain of the forest more forgiving and set out levelly. But there was rarely a flat piece of ground to make footing, and nowhere comfortable to rest. Lucky for Lampaea and Bren then, that they were men of energy. Bren tackled the walk with ease from the aid of his knowledge of the path, and Lampaea trekked on similarly for the youthful excitement that stole him whenever he found somewhere new.

One could have struggled to call Olonath a forest at all, for the slopes became hillsides, and the hillsides almost mountainous. The rocks doubled in size and number, but the boulders were scaled effortlessly, the clear streams that wound in between leapt over tirelessly. As they traversed the freshwater springs, the reeflies became more abundant, as this was their breeding ground. Lampaea was not used to these insects, they sang a lull of buzzing that would have soothed the soul on a quiet night of rest and reflection, but the high-pitched ringing and clumsy flight only irritated when trying to reach somewhere quickly. He went to swat one out of his face, but Bren cautioned him not to, for they were the harbingers of the Artrysiptic. This was a realm any mortal knew little of, Lampaea was even unsure of its existence, but it seemed best not to mention this. For all his bold and dignified presence, Bren was more learned than he appeared, and with it came a knowledge of the ancients and all that was ethereal and slept dormant within Esilence.

The moon was high and waning when they reached the camp of Bren's men, or Kenduhn, as they called it. The camp was small, for there were only fifty or so men, and was situated on one of the more forgiving slopes that embanked onto a great ridge at the top. To the bottom, a lip of jagged rocks curled around and a good lookout could be placed here, level so that a far reach of the forest ahead could be discerned.

The men all stopped what they were doing when Bren and Lampaea approached, and surveyed Lampaea with suspicion, despite that he walked as an equal in the midst of their leader. Slowly they gathered closer.

'Bren,' one man said, 'you look like death.'

'And we weren't expecting you to bring a stray back.'

'Alright, come on, move it.'

From between them, another man strode confidently to greet them, his black hair dishevelled, though he maintained a neat beard, and his great brown eyes were huge and searching.

'Bren, you are returned to us some starbands early. And you are without your cousin and her aaron, I fear the news you have for us.'

'This is Lampaea, a good man who helped me,' said Bren.

'Taiso,' said the dark-haired man, regarding Lampaea levelly. He extended his hand courteously and gripped in a friendly but authoritative manner. 'Lampaea, that's a western name. You have come far?'

'Elpura,' Lampaea replied. 'But I have not seen home for

over four years, I have long since been travelling around Mid Enphiah.'

Taiso made no reply. He seemed uninterested in learning any more of Lampaea's travels, and Lampaea in turn was thankful, for he was not in the mood to be social and share stories, only to set out for Setra as soon as possible.

'Taiso,' Bren addressed, 'I must speak with you, with Lampaea present. Time is pressing and what we thought about Eastern Enphiah was true.' This last part he said in an undertone, and the expressions of the men gave away why. They were all eager to hear the news, but for some, their faces were pained more than they wanted to show. It was clear Bren was not the only one with loved ones missing amongst them. But the time had been too soon to break the truth to them, that their lovers, mothers, sons, daughters and brothers were being held in the deep chambers of Setra against their will. Bren wanted his men to keep a level head, to keep irrationality at bay for as long as he could for them.

'Come,' said Taiso, his voice under control. He led them up the slope and into a large wicker den. Upon the sides were tapestries displaying the emblem of Beltro, the same symbol sewn into Bren's mask; many called it, 'The Feral Eyes of Beltro.':

Inside, it was littered with weapons; there were beautiful bows with Fadic letters carved into the wood, throwing knives laid abundantly in a pile and broadswords galore. They were gleaming new and all looked lethally sharp.

'You'll have to excuse the mess,' said Taiso, leaning against an enna-covered table, 'we made a large collection yesterday from the smith in Isbre.'

Bren looked over the weapons, then back at Taiso with a small frown creasing his features.

'You sought to prepare before I gave the order to move out,' he said.

'The men know, Bren. You don't need to break any news to them, we have all suspected the Setrans' schemes for some time. The time for seeking evidence is gone, we need to prepare a strike now.'

'That is why I wanted to speak to you,' said Bren sombrely. 'I need an immediate discharge. We will ride north to Setra, and set this straight before anyone else is taken over the border.'

Taiso looked taken aback.

'I know I said prepare now but there is too much haste to this –'

'Haste is needed,' Lampaea interjected, 'but numbers are not. To ride with a party this size to Setra is folly, there would be no way to conceal us all. Three, maybe four should go, I insist on being one of them. Our focus must be on infiltration, releasing our prisoners and then later returning with enough of a stronghold to take them down.'

'My men are the best, Lampaea,' said Bren.

'Granted. But you need a strategy. Return there with your party later, when the captives are safe, and let them have their revenge. But the Setrans will be expecting some resistance, they're no fools. At least if we get to Maliste with stealth, we will also know where the strengths and weaknesses lie in their fortifications, and use it against them next time.'

'Unless we are caught,' Bren said heavily, 'in which case they will be reinforcing all those weak areas. And worse, bring death on all of us, prisoners included.'

'Maybe not,' Taiso added thoughtfully. 'They clearly need these people alive for something. We'd all be captured and held there, not killed. Either way, I wouldn't like to find out what goes on behind those walls.'

The reality of this hit Lampaea again. He felt his heartbeat quicken, his blood run hot with anguish and wrath. It worsened with every day; he must find Halemedra, he must take her away from that accursed place. He hid the searing emotion well for now.

'But I agree with the Elpuran,' Taiso continued, 'we must first pass by unseen, get them out of there, and we learn their layout at the same time. Two birds killed with one stone.'

Bren folded his arms and touched two fingers to his temple. It seemed he might have been warming to the plan, albeit reluctantly. Lampaea was already familiar with his stubbornness, but now even Bren could not deny it was a far more logical approach, lest he march in with all force and lose his fifty or so men to a preventable slaughter.

'Beltrorns do not know stealth, Lampaea,' Bren said, his voice flowing in a sigh. 'We are built for brute force. You are slight of frame, your abilities I would not doubt, but you cannot do it alone either. You have a well-thought plan, but I think you may have the wrong contenders for the job.'

‘It’s either this or we lose all. Surely you must know what will befall your men if you all ride out together? It’s not an option.’

Bren had not moved a muscle, he beheld Lampaea grimly, whilst Taiso was shaking his head gently, not looking at either of them. They all recognised the risks that would be waiting for them behind the enemy’s border, all coming to terms that this was the best way they could hope to make any difference.

At length, Bren unfolded his arms.

‘Tell the men of our plans, and have five stationed at the forest front when we leave. I am off to find Miksandh, I want at least four of us in company.’

Bren did not wait for a reply, and made out swiftly. Taiso was regarding Lampaea once more, though his look had changed now. There was respect creeping through, but still he appeared to be weighing him up.

‘You have quite the analytical and decisive mind,’ he said finally, ‘and you can fight as well? Where did you learn these skills? I would not have expected this from an Elpuran.’

Lampaea glanced at him somewhat dismissively. Why was it so unheard of that an Elpuran would be skilled in combat? For they too fought in the Nyvean War, they too had the skills passed down from their forefathers, and they too had their family names inscribed upon the Ranis of Lor. As he thought of this, Lampaea considered the Ranis again. Was his name on there? His father’s, and his brothers’? It was unknown if his ancestors had even partaken their duty in the Nyvean, but if the men of that day had indeed served, their names and all male descendants were recorded automatically upon this paper, regardless of whether the soldier lived or died.

A coldness then came over him. When the rest of Enphiah discovered what the Setrans had been doing, a great wrath and a terrible thirst for vengeance would sweep across the lands, burying itself in every simple villager and townsfolk like a parasite that dug its way to the heart. Such an offence the Easterns had not committed for over two thousand years, they could not have expected this to go unnoticed for long, surely. Although there was no apparent motive for land seizure like in the past, Lampaea wondered, his conscience heavy, if the crime might draw out swords of justice, arrows of retribution and the blood of the innocent. All in a war that could tear Enphiah apart again. Whether or not war would be declared, or thrust upon them, or kept hushed for the prevention of an outbreak, it could not be said. Lampaea shook the foreboding thought off.

'My father taught me,' he said. 'And my brothers, as soon as we each turned ten years old, we began. He hates the idea of leaving his sons without skills that could save their lives. There was also more than combat that we learnt. Basic survival skills, domestics, hunting...the Western Enphiahns are no less educated in brawn and brains, I assure you.'

'Clearly not,' remarked Taiso, raising his brows. He did not appear enlightened, but the impression had been left, nonetheless.

When they left the den to find Bren, they found him engaged in quiet discussion with another well-built man who was known as Miksandh. Lampaea noticed then a small boy not far from them, huddled against a tree with his arms wrapped tightly around his legs. He looked apprehensive as some of the men tried to offer him a slice of cold meat or bread, and could not meet their eyes or speak when he dismissed them.

Bren turned to Lampaea gravely.

'The boy is from our party,' he said, 'the only captive that made it here alone. The men think he may have lost his mother on the way, I've sent two scouts to look for any survivors. He will stay here for now.'

Lampaea looked at the boy again, whose darting eyes met his gaze but the once. It was as if he feared what they might do if he gave any sign of interaction. He must have been ten or eleven, but his fidgeting movements and the flitting wide eyes made him appear younger and more fragile. There were grass and soil stains all over him, the once credible and humble jacket was ripped at the collar and elbow, bracken lay tangled in his hair.

'Something terrible has happened to him,' said Lampaea. 'He looks feral. Does he have a name?'

'You can try asking him. But he says little, the pain is still too near.'

Bren left to arrange the provision of supplies for the road, giving clear orders and taking swift charge. Lampaea walked over to the boy and crouched before him. He had to crane his neck to see his face for the youth chose to duck his head to avoid him.

'Are you hurt?' asked Lampaea. He saw the boy's eyes dart up to him, then down again, and he gave a quick shake of the head.

'You should look at a man, when he is speaking to you.'

The boy seemed to have been brought up with respect, for when Lampaea said this his head rose to meet his face, though his eyes were still unsteady. It was only fear that restrained him.

'You were with your mother, weren't you?' Lampaea continued, 'I remember seeing you with her, when we rescued you all. Can you tell me where she is?'

These words struck the boy hard. He held his head in his hands, then shakily raised a finger to point above them. Lampaea looked up, but struggled to understand.

'The sky?' he said uncertainly.

The boy pointed more fervently. No, not the sky. The trees. But not just any trees. He pointed to a lesser hardwood tree, known as a teril. But it was between the branches of these trees that a malignant parasitic plant tended to foster itself.

'Tym...' the boy whispered. It pained him deeply. 'Tym –'

'The tympana?' said Lampaea, and the boy's finger fell, his hands clasping his head again, his breathing quickened. He could no longer hold his gaze, but Lampaea needed no more than this; a grisly image began to take form in his mind, one in which he hoped was only born of a mistake, or imagination.

The tympana hung from the teril tree thickly in light, feathery cones of pale pink flowers. An enchanting sight only to those who knew not the nature of this plant. For the price of its charming, picturesque looks there was an impending peril to any who came by curiously. No man could hold the stuff, lest his skin and bones rot away before his very eyes; what one would have experienced after death for the earth to take a few seasons, experiences the process of decay in a matter of seconds, alive. There was but one race that were able to handle the tympana: fadres. Their tough skin did not reject the plant, there were many toxins and natural offenders of Esilence that they could touch unharmed, as well as many theories why they bore such an immunity, all of them dark and impure.

Lampaea looked up at the teril, and feared the worst of what the scouts would find.

Chapter 16
The Edge

There was no side-stepping with Dynetii. If a job needed doing, it was done. From one point to another, in a single straight line, there was no room for deviation, nor any time to consider the 'what ifs'. And if someone didn't like the way she did things, that was their issue, not hers.

Emmet found her difficult to keep up with, she was so ordered and forthright. But it was just another thing he appreciated about her, though it could be a little overbearing at times, for she applied this to her skills, skills which he could not match. She possessed judgment far beyond her years; if there was one liar amongst a hundred truth-tellers, she could point him out. She was adept at building and handicraft, having made items from the rough weaving of hunting traps to fine embroidery. She could read, write and speak Fadic, a broad branch of language secluded usually only to a few select Beltrorns outside of fadres themselves. And Emmet was quickly to discover he should leave no doubt as to her abilities in combat.

Enquiring as to whether all the descendants of the Luminors were this skilled, she informed him that it was purely choice. Whilst there had been other descendants who had excelled as a fine warrior or astute scholar, some had not the enthusiasm and allowed whatever degree of power they had left to consume them with arrogance and conceit, all born of a desperation to relive the homage and respect the people once paid them. Jekron and Menkhrist were just such, and their laziness had led them into squander and neglect. It was Dynetii who the people of Rukur knew, her face whom they trusted. She oversaw stock and supplies, goods export, instructed builders, settled disputes between neighbours, visited the sick and managed the harvest each year. They knew her father and brother were there, up at the Chandre, knew their names, but had never laid eyes on them.

The first thing Dynetii did was buy new, robust clothes for Emmet, for his soft villager's attire and travelling cloak would only hinder him.

'You're a wanted man, now. You need protecting,' she said, paying the tailor. He gave her the boots for free, out of friendship.

Emmet controlled his look of disdain. He did not want her to think of him as some helpless baby, but it was too late for any resentment now, for it was indeed help he had rode to Rukur for.

There was one last stop to be made at the armoury. There seemed to be plenty of these down the main street, but Dynetii quickly led them away from here, down a narrow alley that opened into a small courtyard, darkened and sheltered by a bridge overhead. The armoury lay before them, with a house attached to the side. There were no other customers around, the place was so quiet that the owner had heard them approach. He stepped outside boldly, almost threateningly, as if he received trouble regularly, then saw who he was facing and his features relaxed into a wide, welcoming grin.

'Dynetii!' he said amicably. 'You are well?'

The man was massively tall, towering over the two of them, and thickly set. There were a few scars across his huge, exposed arms and one at the base of his neck, though his eyes were bright and full of life, like a child's, for he must have been no younger than thirty-five. Emmet could see instantly the loyalty Dynetii placed in this man.

'Indeed so, Mov,' she replied. 'Though I come in haste. I'm afraid this cannot be a social visit today.'

'You'd better come inside,' Mov glanced at Emmet, then back at Dynetii. 'Is he...?'

'Yes, he's alright,' she said, 'his name is Emmet. I must tell you the rest inside.'

'Very well,' Mov nodded once, and they followed him into the armoury.

Emmet almost banged his head on the low doorframe as they stepped inside. Everything was cramped and the air was heavy for it. The weapons were by no means laid out as if for customers to browse; they were strewn carelessly across a network of work benches, though the variety was vast, and the level of craftsmanship and detail that had gone into them was emphasized in the dim lighting. Clearly Dynetii sought out only the best in the city, although the secluded nature of the armoury and the lack of customers suggested the business was less than thriving.

There were several wooden chests beneath the benches, all under lock and key, and Mov moved to one in particular, bending down and producing a ring of keys.

'Off to the south hunting again, are you?' he said, turning the key, 'I can give you something new along with the usual gear, if you like.'

'Actually, Mov, I will need my mother's blade,' said Dynetii, straight to the point.

At this, Mov paused, then turned and stood to face her gravely, a slight stoop in his shoulders before the low ceiling. Emmet wondered how a man so huge could stand to work here.

'I should hope just to show it off to your new friend,' he said, 'but I have a strong feeling it's not for that. Am I right?'

'There are men stationed around the city walls,' she replied, 'men waiting to kill Emmet.'

'Dynetii,' said Emmet, 'are you sure you want to tell this man everything?'

Mov gave Emmet a dangerous look and folded his arms, such was the emphasis on his muscles then, but Emmet was not perturbed.

'Mov is a good man,' Dynetii assured him, 'I trust him with my life.'

Emmet raised his eyebrows and said nothing. That was a deep trust to claim to. His own trust he once thought he had for friends had been shattered, and his mind seemed to be re-evaluating the depth of any other loyalties held to him now, if they could even be called that. But then, he had decided to trust Dynetii almost instantly, had he not? He could have explained that to himself though, he could have said that he had had no choice. Trust in Dynetii and either come out with answers, be betrayed, or walk away from Rukur and face a hunt with probable death. There was only a one in three chance that he would come out of this well. And even if Dynetii did prove to be loyal, there was still the chance that he might die by the hand of Amanyl, or any of the other hunters as soon as he stepped outside of Rukur with her.

For Emmet was no warrior. He understood how to shoe a horla, how to keep a stable maintained, how to make friends, how to crack a joke that would leave a table of full grown men in stitches. Of killing, he knew nothing. It struck him, then, that he was not sure what Dynetii expected him to do out there; did she want him to kill, maim, or just stand by whist she did it all? In any case, there were at least eight men and but two of them. Surely Dynetii was not so arrogant as to think they could take down all of them? Emmet wondered if she would ask Mov to help, the brute strength in him was an advantage if nothing else.

'You are free to insult me, but not under my own roof,' said Mov patiently, but with an unmistakable growl in his tone.

'I'm sorry, but events of mistrust have led me here. The line between friend and foe has since become blurred to me,' said Emmet.

'Well, there are no blurred lines with Dynetii. You have chosen well in her.'

'Actually, she seemed to choose me.'

'Which is why we are here,' said Dynetii, stepping forward, her eyes becoming fervent with impatience. 'Emmet has fled from his home village after uncovering information that may relate to Chriah's movements within Enphiah. For that, his conspirators want him dead, they followed him here from Otra.'

'Did you say Chriah?' said Mov, his eyes widening. 'What's their part in this?'

'We cannot say for sure,' said Emmet, 'but they are breeding preathins underground, this is what I discovered, and there can surely be only one reason for this.'

'War...' Mov said darkly. His shoulders drew outwards at the thought, as if to make himself larger-looking for a fight.

'But nevermind that,' said Dynetii briskly, 'it might not

come to war, not when fate has brought Emmet to us. His warning could save thousands of lives, but only if we act now.'

Emmet felt his chin lift without realising. At Dynetii's words he felt a sense of self-worth, and hadn't even thought of how significant his decision had been to ride out to Rukur until now. He had acted on instinct at the time. Death is upon you – leave immediately – seek those who could put a stop to the darkness that was gathering across the land. There hadn't been time to stop and think of the impact his information could provide. And what was he going to do if Dynetii hadn't have found him? Ride out of the city to face them, and give up after one try? Perhaps he wouldn't have done such a cowardly thing, perhaps he had been on his way to the stable to calm himself next to Syndrex, and then return again to the Chandre to make them listen. He didn't even know. That was a path of possibilities that fate had taken from him, and for the better, he thought.

'I am a little concerned as to what your plan is,' said Mov, looking at Dynetii soberly, 'you were always one to cut the rope, rather than untie the knot.'

'Emmet thinks there are eight of those knots out there. Seven of them, I will cut.'

Mov sighed shortly, 'And the other?'

'The eighth returns with us. We need one for information,' Dynetii's tone was becoming fierce again. 'I know I need not ask you to keep your silence for us.'

Mov nodded, his expression kept simple and sincere. He reacted as if she told him such plans every day, and then disappeared briefly into a small back room. There was the sound of a key turning in a lock, and when he returned he held a great sword across his two huge hands.

A faint smile graced Dynetii's blossoming lips as she took it from him and fleeting memories of her mother holding the same weapon beset her. She withdrew the blade and admired it from hilt to tip.

'That is a fire blade,' Emmet said in some wonder, for the edges of the sword curved in and out to create waves, the length of the blade reminiscent of an ascending lick of flame.

'Indeed. It was made especially for my mother by Mov's father, for she saved Mov from a craftsman.'

Emmet would not ask how this story unfolded. It was not the time for it, and the fact that Dynetii's mother was nowhere to be seen in the city suggested it did not end well. Dynetii's eyes had not lingered on Emmet as if to encourage the questions from him either, for which he was thankful.

'A strong woman,' said Mov, looking the blade up and down as if it held the memory of her within it. 'Now go. And have that sword returned to me how it left when you're done, no one will look after it like I do.'

Dynetii had Emmet keep a short sword with him, of which Mov said is his to own, for even after this, he should still consider himself in danger. Emmet was ordered to stay the night with Mov in his armoury as eventide greeted them, and to keep out of sight of all. Dynetii returned punctually at dawn the following day, thrusted a bowl of natsa before him for breakfast and dragged him out of the armoury without hesitation. As they passed through the city again, they drew curious looks from all, but none ventured to question Dynetii. She led Emmet up higher and higher into the outer fortifications, where sentries paced to and fro, a couple of them acknowledging Dynetii with a nod. The wind swept fast up here, it was cooler and a vast scope of the plains surrounding them could be gained.

'I am engaging my friend in stealth and combat training up here. You and your men take the day off,' Dynetii called to one of the sentries.

'My lady, I am sure your father would prefer we stayed, if at least for your own safety.'

'This is my father's command. He wishes me to test his newest recruit without any distractions.'

The sentry gave a nod and called his men to depart. Dynetii then led Emmet across the first traverse, where she peered down to the plains. There was no one to be seen for a long time, and then she caught movement.

'There,' she said to Emmet, pulling him over roughly to one of the narrow look-out points. Below them, a man, no more than a spec on the ground, made his way slowly trotting around the south city wall on a horla. He seemed to look over his shoulder, and then cantered further in hurriedly, where they could no longer see him.

'That was a signal he just received,' said Dynetii, 'because he was within range. They know not to be seen. No matter, this makes our job easier.'

'How?' said Emmet.

'They will be closer to the underground chambers on the perimeter, and a network of passageways that no one uses save for a few merchants for storage space before crossing the plains. I know those passageways better than anyone, and I can keep us hidden.'

Emmet looked into Dynetii's eyes, which were calculating everything. It dawned on him that this would be a far stealthier mission than he thought, rather than charging at them with swords flailing and mad intent. Less impulse and more organisation. The men outside had practically fallen into Dynetii's trap, played to her advantage, for she knew the city like the back of her hand. Emmet thought this played to his advantage too, for direct combat was not his strength. Surely it was easier for him to catch his opponent unawares, in the darkness, on silent steps...it was easier to attack from behind, wasn't it?

Would that be better for you? a dark voice crept into his mind. *You won't have to see their faces that way. That's the only way you could even think about killing them, isn't it? Stab to the back, like a coward.*

Emmet felt the plunge of the knife at that point, the power of the sword that was all his yet that which he did not want.

'Dynetii,' he said, 'I don't think I can...' he wasn't looking at her. But he knew she was looking at him forcefully as soon as he opened his mouth.

'It's this or you die,' she said finally. 'You don't have much of a choice, Emmet.' There was no sympathy in her tone, but he didn't want there to be. What good would it do if someone simply told him not to worry and that he could back out now if he wanted to? He should be worried. He should be nervous. He should be terrified even. His life was on the line; he would never be able to go back to his life in Betharanei, for even if he did 'cleanse' the village, it would never be the same for him. The memories of deception would always be there.

Together they made their way swiftly down to the passageways; it was dark everywhere, no torch light was spared down here. They had only the scarce daylight to cast shadows round corners, to separate the veils of black and grey. They passed many foreboding stone staircases leading down from the passageways to these chambers that Dynetii spoke of; no doubt she planned on using one to interrogate their captive. Emmet hoped, much to the sickening of his gut, that any sound from those chambers did not reach the surface.

Narrow archways opened out onto the plains from where they crept precariously. Dynetii was leading them around the perimeter until there was some form of life. But then Emmet halted at one of the archways and peered out from the shadows, for there were three of the men not ten paces away. Their backs were to them, and they spoke in undertones between their horlas. Amanyl sat in the middle.

Dynetii sensed Emmet had stopped following; she turned back in a half crouch and made a hand gesture to forget them. Emmet tried unsuccessfully to signal back to her across the open archway: *It's perfect, three of them there now – let's go.*

But after much refusal from his companion and moments wasted in the peril of being caught, finally Emmet gave up and scurried over to Dynetii without the men seeing him.

'Not them,' said Dynetii in a hushed voice, her expression almost scornful. 'We leave any groups till last. The individuals will have all their senses keen, they will be listening and need taking care of first. But if we attack a group first they have more chance of raising an alarm.'

It made sense, although a part of Emmet wished he hadn't sought any approval and just charged at them, for that might have been the only way he could quell this fear. If he could kill without purpose or accident, or even without logic, the pain would have eased, the burden lighter to bear. But this was premeditated, and there was logic in it, for there was no sense in waiting to be killed if you could prevent it, or if you could prevent a war threatening the lives of all. Emmet knew that that logic was a dark one, nevermind that he had no choice. There was simply something terrible in waiting to be labelled a murderer.

They moved stealthily from archway to archway, passing by like ghosts, checking them all the time for their first target. They had nearly passed the entire eastern wall with nothing, when suddenly Dynetii stopped.

'There's one,' she said, pointing to the plains, where a lone member of the men stood staring into nothing, his fingers twisting idly around the reins of his horla. A sword the length of Dynetii's own hung at his side, making Emmet feel evermore insignificant with his short sword. Dynetii would have no doubt told him it was about the skill one could exert, not the size of the weapon, but the former was somewhat laughable when applied to Emmet; unless he carried a great spear, his enemy would run him through first. Then it dawned on him he'd be better off with a shield, if not for protection then at the least to shelter him from blood spatter...

'Stop doubting everything,' said Dynetii, interrupting his thoughts; she was indeed adept at reading people. Without warning she strode out of their hiding place, a head of deep crimson trailing down her back. The rider turned to the sound of her footsteps. Emmet remained unseen with his back against the wall, and his heart began to beat fast. It was happening and he wasn't prepared. Not yet.

'Who are you?' said the rider, hand on hilt.

'I run this city,' Dynetii was smiling.

The rider was due to open his mouth in reply, but Dynetii

had already moved. At the sound of her sword being unsheathed, Emmet couldn't help it, he had to look, and emerged to stand watching from the archway. But by the time he came out there were only two seconds more to witness. In that time, the rider lost an arm and then his throat was slit, his horla was unharmed, but he fell next to the bewildered beast in a limp heap. Not a scratch was left on Dynetii.

Emmet stood gaping at the body, the detached left arm strewn carelessly not too far away, and the pools of blood that were drying up so fast in the heat of Pytheria. The first kill was over. He tried to control his breathing in front of Dynetii as she walked back casually into the shadows of the archway and looked at him plainly.

'Yes,' she said, as if answering some question of his that he had asked without words, 'you will feel that shock to begin with. Are you ready to find the next one?'

Emmet attempted to compose himself. 'Y-you speak of them as if they are just a chore on a list, as if they are bred to be killed –'

'They bred themselves to be killed when they chose an allegiance to Chriah and they decide to breed preathins to eliminate us. Don't let your kindness excuse them, Emmet. They want you dead more than anyone else at this point. Now are you ready to find the next one?'

Emmet nodded reluctantly. There was no hope of winning an argument with Dynetii, she was used to getting what she wanted. Moreover, he knew she was right. He just had to learn to block that human side of him, treat blood like water, screams like simple speech.

'What about his body?' said Emmet.

'We get rid of that first. Bring it into the central chamber;

only my father, brother and myself carry a key for that, so he won't be found. We'll put the others in there with him. You've gone white, Emmet...don't worry, we will organise a ritual burning later on, they won't be left here.'

This was a lesser worry of Emmet's for now, when placed next to the task at hand.

Together they dragged the body of the rider down the widest passageway, the only one left in darkness with torches extinguished long ago. Unlike the others, this one was not a maze, and led directly to a large descending stone staircase. At the bottom was a door crafted entirely of lucrin, and when Dynetii produced a key it required the both of them to pull it open, a layer of stone was shown sandwiched between the precious substance. Whether this was designed to keep things (or persons) in or out, Emmet thought, there was surely no better place for either.

Inside the chamber was darkness save for a glass jar from which a flickering blue light was teased onto the flagstones. The narrow room would have appeared ethereal were it not for the carcass they had just dumped onto the floor. Looking closer, Emmet could see the curled up remains of three reeflies inside the jar. From his research on preathins, he had stumbled across articles on many animals and learnt more of their ways, knowing now the reefly was native in the south and Pyra, and that their light shone dimly for years after their death.

As they circulated the perimeter and brought back two more riders into the chamber Emmet was no less uncomfortable. There was blood on his shirt and hands now, though his sword was still clean. Dynetii uttered not a word of complaint that he had done little to help; she seemed to appreciate that he must cope with the ordeal that was so new and brutal to him, despite her harsh tone. Three more individually carried back; Emmet had forced himself to watch Dynetii end their lives, and nearly all of them from Betharanei. Each of the riders would catch Emmet in their sight just before the last stroke, and their eyes would widen in a last realisation that the prey was there, right in front of them, but he had outwitted them somehow. He wished they hadn't seen him, hadn't bound him to memory as their last point of recognition as their spirits departed. He felt as if he had betrayed them in some way, in spite of the fact that they had betrayed him first.

What was this soft side that knew no evil? Were there even sides?

Emmet gripped the hilt of his sword harder, trying to impart with it that aggression, that feeling of being unstoppable. They had found the last two riders, and one of them was Amanyl, the ringleader and Emmet's long-standing friend. Their backs were still turned, and they were laughing quietly at some underhanded joke.

Emmet drew in one breath and wanted to say something – he was prone to hesitation now. But Dynetii knew not the meaning of the word, and ran out from under the arches this time, her arm raised high with a throwing dagger at the ready.

'Wait!' Emmet called, and the two riders turned.

Dynetii released the dagger for Amanyl, but he deflected the shot with his own blade, and it plunged straight into the head of his comrade, who could not scream, cry or speak, only fall. Amanyl didn't give him a side glance. He dismounted his horla and charged at Dynetii, she at him, but he was sprightly for his age and his training was not lacking. He dodged her strike and kicked her hard in the shin. When she was down, he gave another to her stomach.

Dynetii did well to suppress a cry of sheer pain, but Emmet was alerted and approached gingerly with his short sword. When Amanyl saw him, he burst into laughter that rang out across the plains and echoed in the arches, but Dynetii was signalling; with blood exuding past her full lips, she pointed subtly to the fallen man next to Emmet and then to her head, tapping it.

Emmet bent down and reluctantly pulled out the throwing dagger that had just about cleaved the man's head in two. There was a sickening resistance to it as the weapon sucked free. But as he did so, Amanyl had lifted Dynetii up by the ends of her hair, stamped a foot onto her lower back and held his sword edge to her throat.

'Now, there is a good question,' he said mockingly, 'how many weapons can Emmet wield before doing harm to himself first?'

'Let her go, Amanyl,' Emmet's voice raised louder and bolder than he expected it to. 'Aren't I the one you want anyway?'

'Yes, you are. And you've made this ten times easier for me. I didn't even have to come looking for you. You know how to make friends though; the girl is valuable I see, and I don't just mean her fighting skills. For that, I can't let her go.'

Something snapped within Emmet then, when Amanyl spoke those words about Dynetii's 'value', when a thin, disjointed smile crept across his face. That was all he could see, a disturbing grimace full of power and lust, the same suggestive expression that he would have once known as friendly, approachable, genial. In the moment that followed, Emmet launched the dagger with the stance and aim of a warrior, and it settled cleanly between the shoulder and neck. Amanyl had no time to react, the fact that the quiet stableboy of Betharanei had attacked at all had thrown him, and now he stared at Emmet more wide-eyed than any of the other riders had.

Dynetii felt the grip on her hair slacken and rolled away from Amanyl's blade safely as he collapsed to the ground.

'I'm sorry,' said Emmet, 'that was reckless, I should have put your safety first –'

'Emmet!'

Dynetii was struggling to her feet in a frenzy, looking to the archway, but Emmet was not quick enough – as he turned, an arrow struck him in his upper arm without warning, and the pain left him standing there in shock, unable to respond. Unbeknown to them, there was a ninth rider, and he came forward from the shadows now, his bow ready – but Dynetii had recovered.

She charged at him with the fire blade, deflected his second arrow with it, and then met his flesh. The hand that clasped the bow was gone in an instant, and the rider curled up in a ball of agony on the ground, clutching his severed wrist in chilling screams. Dynetii took a strip from her tunic and quickly gagged him before anyone from the city was alerted, then took advantage of a loose belt of leather from his quiver, and bound his feet.

The man kicked at her like a child refusing a bath. 'Get your hands off me!' he wailed behind the muffles.

'Oh, stop whining,' Dynetii muttered. Emmet had markedly maintained composure and was still standing, much to her astonishment. 'Emmet, I know this isn't the best time but I could use your help over here.'

Emmet made his way over slowly, and then he

recognised the small, feverish eyes and untidy black hair of the rider. A young man his own age who he had grown up with.

'Dox!' said Emmet with disgust, and gave him a hefty kick that winded him. 'You tried to kill me!'

'Enough!' Dynetii sounded like a firm mother to two sons. 'We need to get him off the plains. Take his top half.'

With a grunt, Emmet was forced to ignore the pain that was spreading from his wound to his hand and shoulder. The arrow still protruded from his muscle like a branch on a tree that couldn't conform. Together, they carried Dox all the way into the central chamber, Emmet now grateful for how much easier it had been to carry dead bodies rather than live ones. Dox was flailing his stump of a hand everywhere, and Emmet grew irritated at all the blood that smattered across his face and torso. They dumped him onto the chamber floor with even less care than his dead comrades.

'What is this –' said Dox, reeling back into a corner as Dynetii took the gag from his mouth roughly, 'you killed all of them?! You ought to burn for this!' he spat at their feet.

'Interesting set of morals,' said Dynetii dryly, then she tended to his wrist and wrapped it tight to stem the bleeding.

'Why bother...' Emmet uttered, staring darkly at Dox.

'If he loses too much blood, he's no good to us. Come, we need to collect the last two bodies before they're found. I'll see to your wound after, for now it's better if the arrow just stays there.'

As they left the chamber, they heard Dox break into a pathetic peal of laughter, slumped in the corner. Amanyl and the other rider were quickly brought into the chamber, which had now become a tomb. Emmet had not complained once about his wound, despite the pain.

‘Finish me off, then,’ said Dox weakly, glancing around the eight dead. ‘What’s eight out of nine? That’s a job half done.’

Dynetii took a cloak from one of the riders and placed it round Emmet’s shoulders to cover the arrow, to which there was a slight wince of protest as it pressed into the wound. Then they each turned from their prisoner without a word and locked the door behind them.

They started off down the passageway, when Emmet stopped.

‘We could just do this now,’ he said, something reckless stirring within him that was not present before, ‘make him talk.’

Dynetii narrowed her eyes at him. ‘First, we clean you up. He’s not going anywhere. And we stop, take a moment. We just killed eight men in a row, remember? Earlier today that scared you. But then you have your first taste of a kill and now something has changed you.’

Emmet walked on past her, a wide stride on him.

‘Maybe you’ve rubbed off on me.’

x

Adrenache’s hair was shining brighter than ever. Her eyes, too, spoke brilliantly of kymic energy. The Isle of Ira was brimming with it now, the Artrenium had returned home, and was enveloping all that lived. The island was alive. But it was the konexic, also, that affected her. She knew about Feletra’s episode out in the forest, knew how the kym was trying to drag her down.

'My hair was once as dark as yours,' she had said to Feletra. 'Then I had begun to feel the Artrenium around me as a girl. If I held my palms to the earth, I would feel a beat, like a pulse. The kym had chosen me to help free it again. Its presence began to change me, I saw strands of silver appear in my hair; I thought I had become cursed with old age, but my skin became softer, my eyes brighter. It was not the change into a crone, but one into enlightenment. But then you arrived, Feletra, and it seemed the change was complete. That energy you carry around is unstoppable, greater than anything else I have ever felt. I hope you learn to use it, before it learns to use you.'

Adrenache's words had stayed with Feletra, and she began to wonder if the Konexa would eventually change her too. Or perhaps it was just an Artrenium thing, she didn't know.

There was some goodness in between all the heartache and mourning on the day of the stalok; a stalok was a well-known ceremony across the lands for marrying two persons together, but this was not a ceremony to be taken lightly. Each estehss, the term given to an individual who has undertaken the rite, must take the love of the other to their grave and into the next realm for eternity; one who breaks a stalok and leaves their stelon (male) or estehn (female) is forever out-casted, for this was a love considered to be profound and unbreakable. Many lovers existed simply as ayres, as Estra and Padryl did, which Feletra was reminded of as she intently watched these two Efordrads gaze into each other's eyes adoringly and take each other's hands, Stenahn wrapping chrysana web about them thrice over. Mathenhis leant over quietly to explain when he noticed

Feletra’s frown.

‘This is a very old tradition, if one of them struggles against the chrysana, their love must be questioned. The idea is that if they must suffer, they will suffer together from here on.’

The celebrations that followed into the night were wonderful, the misery of the recent event could be washed away for one starband as if it had never happened. There were cheers, songs and laughter for hours until the couple finally retired. It was a welcome distraction for Feletra, but not enough to kill the burning anxiety about Chriah; by will power alone had she avoided reading Emmet’s letter over and over.

The Markhim had gathered on the same shore the next day where Feletra and Nil had washed up. They formed an arrowhead, with the monumental Rodim at the head, closest to the beach. Edego was lying low in the deeper waters. They were ready.

Mathenhis had provided them both with a change of clothes fit for travel, with a sword from the Fadic times for Nil. He had nothing more for Feletra, but gave her a wink and told her to be patient.

Gone were the trousers of innumerable pockets for Nil, Feletra thought he looked strange without them. Instead he donned thicker hose, tall black leather boots, a sleeveless jerkin and a hooded coat. The hood he had insisted on, and had been added especially. Mathenhis even saw to it that the Efordrad stealth mask was included. Feletra had been dressed in the same style, though with blacks, woody browns and greens. Her jerkin was short and sleeved, and she had a cloak ready for the cold in Pyra. Together they had been given some of the best hunting gear on the island, even their shirts were lighter, pliable and any strings were dipped in wet mud to better conceal them.

Feletra, Nil and Afax stood upon the shores before the Markhim, where there were four Efordrads to bid them farewell: Adrenache, Mathenhis, Stenahn and Raneao.

'Rodim will lead the way,' said Mathenhis, 'you and Nil should ride separately, the journey is not comfortable on a mirikite with more than one person.'

Feletra looked around at the Markhim waiting patiently. There were ten of the great beasts.

'Do we really need this many?' she asked. 'Ten mirikites seems a little excessive, even with the current storms at sea.'

'I wouldn't worry about that. They haven't had a reunion in many years, some are just enjoying each other's company again. And they all know that you are a new konexic, a group of them travelling with you makes them feel more at ease.'

Feletra felt startled. Nil was no more surprised.

'They're afraid of *me?'* she said.

Mathenhis smiled warmly at how much she underestimated herself. 'We all are a little bit, Feletra. You have improved, but still not fully grasped it. There's nothing stopping you destroying each and every one of the Markhim.'

Feletra felt a tingling somewhere in the back of her brain when he said this. It could have been the Koncxa or it could have been her nerves, although she knew that the former liked to take the hand of the latter and not skip with it merrily, but drag it through the mud just to be heard. Nevertheless, she had indeed improved her control on the kym during her time on the island. She could create that layer of ice when she thought of the freezing water on the Weeping Dove, fire when she remembered that burst of flame beneath the pool in Whiteblind Wood. By recalling the impossible she could channel it through her mind and bring it to the fore, though there was still much to learn, Adrenache had said. With time she would become stronger, she still had only minimal control. And yet with so many questions answered there were still other mysteries to dispel; even Adrenache had been unable to provide the answers to the conundrums of Leao's behaviour and in particular the woman and man at the Sorpha. What she did believe confidently however, was that Feletra did indeed face a preathin in Betharanei, and the ill prospect of their return to Enphiah would bring ruin to all.

'May your voyage be calm,' said Stenahn, stepping forward with Raneao. 'You have returned our legacy to us, I only hope we have done enough for you.'

'More than enough,' said Feletra earnestly, 'without the Efordrads, I would have brought myself and all I know to destruction.'

Stenahn smiled.

'Farewell, young ones. And thank you,' said Raneao.

Adrenache turned to Feletra and Nil. There was a tenacious sea breeze, and it whipped playfully at her silken white dress.

'I have something to give you,' she said, directly at Feletra, and as if from nowhere produced a great longbow. Feletra felt astounded at such a gift, for she had never seen such a beauty among bows; the carvings from end to end were minute, there was a picture of a fareon in the middle, and around it were Fadic words which were foreign to her.

'It was made from one of the new trees, grown from the

Artrenium. And it is lightweight, it will not slow you down.'

Feletra accepted the gift carefully into her hands; it was indeed so light, lighter than even the training bow of Lampaea's, and yet this was twice the size and thicker.

'It's beautiful, thank you Adrenache...' she said. 'But I do feel undeserving. I shouldn't be thanked, or rewarded for what I brought to Ira.'

Feletra's eyes, as dark as they were, looked cast with grey and Adrenache saw the sadness within her.

'Life does not come back from anything stronger than death,' Adrenache said to her, 'and you brought a life even stronger than that. I cannot describe to you the enlightenment we all feel. Take no heed of the bow, for I assure you, the Efordrads are forever in your debt.'

A waning smile graced Feletra's lips, and when Adrenache embraced her she didn't want to leave, the Isle of Ira had become a home to her, and she had found a second family here.

As Feletra moved on towards the shoreline, Mathenhis went to help her mount one of the mirikites. Edego had waded forward and laid down his neck for her. But as Nil made to follow, Adrenache stopped him firmly for a moment, and discreetly pushed something into his hand. He looked down and there was a smooth stone. It was dark grey, the colour of a vast storm over mountains. Shaped like a symmetrical leaf, it bore a hole in the middle, through which two small rings were hooped and linked to the bitten edges on either side. Within the hole, the rings were bound by a network of threads spanning the circle, like a spiderweb.

Nil looked at Adrenache, expressionless, but she looked

back knowingly.

'For when you feel the need,' she said.

Nil simply nodded once, and stowed the pendant away in a pocket. It had been too quick for Feletra to notice anything.

The two companions soon discovered that the journey would indeed have been uncomfortable with two to one mirikite; the only place to sit was in a steep curve between the long neck and abdomen. Nil's mirikite was named Rydha, and she swam alongside Edego, with the rest of the Markhim behind and Rodim to the head. They were soon being carried swiftly away across the glistening waters; the ride was smooth and fluent, though the waterline rested only an arm's stretch away from Feletra's feet, and she watched the waves warily, then looked back at the shrinking shore. The Isle of Ira was fading away into just another horizon, she could no longer see the Efordrads, but the brightness of Adrenache's hair was the last thing she could make out.

For half of the time Feletra and Nil only shared glances, and there was something ominous in each look, for they both knew what land they were approaching, and only had each other now. Around sunset, the Markhim slowed down and Edego and Rydha swam closer.

'Can you see the shore yet?' said Nil, no longer drowned out by the distance or the sound of the crashing water. The sea would be calm tonight.

'No. I don't know know how I feel about Chriah now. It's becoming a real place when before it was all imagination,' Feletra reflected, looking ahead.

'Just keep your wits about you,' Nil warned, 'and keep your Konexa under control. There are more craftsmen in

Chriah than any other land. They will not hesitate to take you down if you show that you're kymic.'

Feletra paused.

'I may have to, Nil,' she said with clarity, 'you know that.'

Nil gave his solemn nod in reply. Another day and a night passed by, the starband shone brighter than ever at sea. Feletra loved to watch Ilysehr, blinking back at her from the highest point in the sky, she loved this star more than the moon, and always felt its presence closer than it truly was. There was an old fairytale about the starline; there were four lights in the beginning, bright and blinding globes of light that were the Wardens of Esilence. When Esilence was nothing but darkness, the lights were all that wondered the desolate world, but the darkness was greater, and would absorb their great energy, bit by bit. Eventually, the tiny parcels of light that were stripped from them began to take form. Parts of Drenaas became the air, the wind and storms, unforeseeable and ferocious. Ilysehr scattered into water and vapour, forming the world's great seas, oceans too deep to comprehend and breathtaking waves that crashed into flecks of passion. The light of Astalien exploded to form Pytheria, a ball of fire so intense it trailed excess energy to create Desporsa and the rest was lost, hidden somewhere in the darkness. It was said in folklore that when one strikes a flint to create a flame, that another piece of Astalien has been found. These three lights took to the sky when there was little left of them, as great stars, to watch over their creations. There was a fourth light known as Phaos, and Phaos raised phenomenal mountains, moulded valleys and ripened magnificent forests. But Phaos was late joining the skies, and when the first daylight broke across the new world, it was too late, and Phaos could not see the other three stars to join them. Lost, Phaos drifted across Esilence tirelessly until nearly all its light was spent and eventually, there was just one thing left to do, and another realm was formed. Phaos created the Artrysiptic and the afterlife with all there was left to muster and there, would wait for Drenaas, Ilysehr and Astalien to join its side. Many who had faced near-death had claimed that they had seen Phaos, the last light waiting for them at the end.

The Markhim would only slow down during the night, but they never stopped. Feletra slept uneasily; every time she stirred awake she saw Nil still wide awake, sat upright, looking ahead into the darkness. At one point she saw him twisting something over and over between his fingers, then he seemed to sense she was watching, and stowed the item away carefully.

Feletra knew there was far more to Nil than met the eye. Her curiosity was burning about him sometimes, but she had to let him open doors at his own pace. She trusted him, but she still hadn't figured out why.

On the following starband, when Ilysehr was brightest in the sky, Feletra had somehow managed to fall asleep, for the winds had gathered a biting chill and the sea was beginning to show its temper again. She had managed to forget the drenched feeling to her feet, as the waves stretched quick, ghostly arms out to her, and slipped into an impossible slumber of salt spray, shivering exposure, and channels of air that whistled past her ears bitter and brisk...

When something flew past.

Her eyes were open in an instant and she saw it. A great

eagle had swept past, its talons inches from her head. She now would have recognised the creature anywhere, it was the very same one that she had first met back on the Elpuran plains. The beat of its grand wings was heavy against the sea air and it continued ahead of them to Pyra.

With much delay, Feletra rapidly fumbled for the longbow and an arrow and took aim, anger suddenly rising in her.

'It's out of range now,' came Nil's voice across the way.

Feletra held her aim a second longer, then lowered the bow and looked at Nil.

'That bird has been following me since I left home,' she said tenaciously, 'I know it's a spy.'

'It's flying towards Chriah,' Nil replied, 'if it is a spy for someone there, I am afraid this won't bode well for us.'

'Both that eagle and Korsthr are working for the same person. If I see that bird again I won't hesitate to shoot it down: I'm not letting anyone get in the way of me and that cure.'

Nil's eyes had lingered on Feletra, and then they shifted away passively, but Feletra observed his lack of reply.

'Nil,' she said, 'why do you seem to have so little passion, unlike me? Your mother suffers as much as my brother. Are you not wanting this cure as much as I am?'

'I am wanting it, Feletra,' Nil replied, 'but I fear I am too late to save her. I fear what I may go home to.'

'You left her alone?'

'No, I left her in the care of a friend of hers. But neither of them will be able to stop that craftsman if he returns. Even if my mother still lives, and I cure her, what is to stop him making things worse?'

Nil looked at Feletra, yet still he retained all emotion

within him. His mouth was straight, his eyes were dry, his composure was faultless.

'I am sorry, Nil,' said Feletra, feeling that she had let her own needs for Ataleka overshadow his, when it seemed now that his were greater and more critical. 'I could come with you, you know. To face this craftsman. My Konexa could be perfected by then, I could stop him.'

'I'm not bringing you anywhere near him, Feletra,' Nil said firmly, 'I want you safe.'

'Then what will you do?'

'I will find a way.'

Feletra disliked his incomplete answers immensely. But to spare his feelings on the matter she kept quiet and tried to sleep again. She knew they were in there somewhere, deep inside him, damaging him because he would not share them. To her, it seemed there was indeed no hope for his mother, not unless Nil accepted her help, but he seemed more intent on keeping Feletra safe than his own family. Why? She couldn't comprehend it. Unless Nil had truly lost that much hope in saving his mother, that he was compensating for failing her by protecting Feletra, someone who showed promise and hope. Yet also vulnerability. Perhaps it was a way he could secretly save his own soul. Nil was too complex a creature.

Feletra leant awkwardly into Edego's neck, and watched Afax nestle under Nil's arm before closing her eyes to try and forget it all until sunrise.

They awoke at dawn. Or at least, Feletra did, she could never tell if Nil slept or not, for he always seemed wide awake at any time of day.

'Feletra,' he called clearly to her, 'look ahead.'

She did. There was land, closer than she thought they

would have reached by this point, the Markhim must have sped up again at some point. Pyra, at last.

Feletra hugged her body tight. The air was brisk and the temperature in the south was far colder than the scorching Plains of Nemenon that she was accustomed to.

'Stura or Chriah?' she called back.

'Stura. We will have to make our own way into Chriah, but at least we have nothing to fear from Sturans. They are quiet, helpful people.'

'Just like you,' said Feletra, throwing him a cheeky smirk.

He returned it with his crooked grin. 'Yes, just like me.'

Feletra could see the great snow-capped mountains in the distance, and the sweeping green forests that smothered every inch of land. The sky was a stone grey-purple and Pytheria was trapped behind oppressive thick clouds. Desporsa was painted out entirely.

Edego and Rydha beached onto a shingled shore, all as grey as the sky. Feletra stepped down onto the land and she immediately experienced a foreboding sensation creep under her skin. A sadness hung in the air here. When the wind stopped whistling she thought she could hear a droning sound, punctuated with something frantic and terrified.

Mortal despair. It was everywhere.

She stooped and picked up some of the dark shingle, turning it over as the edges crumbled like ashes and were whipped away by the wind. Behind her, Rodim had come forward, he bowed his head to them and gave a drawn-out cry before retreating back out to sea.

'Thank you,' said Nil, and in only a few moments the Markhim had disappeared beneath the surface, returning to their deep and mysterious kingdom. Edego left last, he gave them one last look of farewell before vanishing with the other mirikites.

Nil turned to Feletra, watching her look downcast at the shingle in her hand.

'We should move on,' he said decisively, and began to walk inland. Afax bounded over to Feletra, chirped twice and dashed the shingle she was holding.

'What happened here, Nil?' said Feletra, following him, 'I have a terrible feeling from this place. There was suffering here. Do you feel it?'

Nil stopped slowly before they entered the woodland.

'Yes, I do feel it. For ten leagues or more along this shore, this is where Sturan families tried to flee to Enphiah in the Stalespic Period. The Chriahks found them. The Sturans begged for mercy, but all of them were butchered, children as well. The ships from Beltro and Ferin were on the horizon when it happened, come too late to save them.'

Feletra stood aghast. She knew the story well, but not this feeling that came with it, this feeling of such reality that stung her skin whenever the salty air pinched it, or the texture of blood that had dried into the shingle and never washed away. She looked back once, and could almost hear the departed voices pleading with her as they might have done the Chriahks.

Chapter 17
Unleash

The moon was waxing when Feletra and Nil had stopped for the night in Sevtern Wood, the huge forest that rubbed shoulders with the length of the northern shoreline. They had supped on some of the food from the Efordrads, wild boar meat with a few fresh vegetables heated over a small fire.

Feletra had been poring over Emmet's letter half the night.

'Staring at it will not change what it reads,' said Nil to break the silence. He sat with his back against a tree, arms folded and knees cocked outwards.

'Do you think he's right?' said Feletra, sharing her thoughts. 'That it was a preathin?'

'Chriah is capable of dark things, I would keep an open mind and say yes, it is very possible.'

Feletra looked onwards between the ominous blackness of the trees. With the firelight before her, nothing could be discerned within the forest.

'But it shouldn't be possible...not when we eliminated them all in the war. If Blackcraft can be used to bring an extinct species back to life then maybe it is more twisted than I thought.'

'What if they never went extinct?' Nil suggested.

'We haven't seen any since the end of the Nyvean War. And Penthor and Acro checked all of the eastern holdings to be sure the enemy wasn't keeping any, they decimated all the breeding grounds.'

Nil's face was in darkness with his hood drooping over his head, but Feletra knew he was watching her.

'You know your history, but do you know your nature? Preathins are not bred like sheep or cattle. They begin life in the very core of Esilence, old Fadic scripts read that it takes two thousand and six hundred years to fully mature and emerge from the surface.'

'Then how does that add up? It's been just over two thousand years now that they were first seen emerging. It's not enough time for them to be maturing already.'

'That part I cannot answer. But I am sure the craftsmen behind it all have found a way around it.'

'Craftsmen for certain? Couldn't they be something else, or even the morotehm?' proposed Feletra.

'No. A stunt like that would need every ounce of Blackcraft. They could be konexic, like you, I suppose, but we both know there are not many of those out there.'

Feletra digested what he had said for a few minutes, then put the letter away and withdrew Flior's map instead, realising she had no plan of how to cross into Chriah without being seen. Next to her, Nil tilted his head a little.

'You won't be needing that,' he said, sure of himself, and Feletra looked up questioningly, 'I know of a way into Chriah, no one else knows of it.'

Feletra looked down at the lovingly-made map, and her eyes lingered on home and Elpura, then drifted up to Betharanei, where she tapped gently.

'Emmet...I hope he's alright. I feel as if I've led him to his death.'

'You led him nowhere,' said Nil from the shadows again, he seemed quick to answer everything tonight, 'you fell down a hole and nearly lost your life. He willingly goes down the same hole, knowing he has put his own life at risk. There's no good to be had fretting over something that is neither your fault nor in your hands to control.'

Feletra couldn't help it, but she broke into a broad smile at him. The pause that followed must have been Nil trying to understand this reaction, but she continued to grin nonetheless, biting her bottom lip a little and shaking her head.

'Feletra...' said Nil slowly after a time, 'why are you smiling like that?' he sounded like someone who had just figured out they were the subject of a very elaborate practical joke, but this only caused Feletra to release a peal of laughter at him, a sound she had not heard in a long time.

'Come into the light, will you?' she said, flinging a stone at him. 'I can't see your face with you looking like the mysterious bringer of death over there.'

'How charming,' replied Nil dryly, edging closer to the fire and throwing his hood back. His eyes flashed in the light of the fire.

'Sometimes I think you were reborn from a wiseman,' said Feletra boldly.

'I'm not wise,' said Nil simply. 'I could be more proud of myself if I was. Wisdom is one great virtue, my virtue is just several small pieces of sense.'

'Something a wiseman would say.'

'Or a modest man.'

'If you are modest, then you hide that you are wise and prove me correct,' Feletra argued back jovially.

'Great starbands above, you've seen through me,' Nil jested with his straight expression and steady gaze. 'Takes a wiseman to figure out another.'

'Not wise, but witty. And quick.'

‘And stubborn.’

‘To the bitter end.’

‘Good. That’s when you’ll need it most.’

Feletra smiled again, coyly. Then she replaced the map back in her pack, but as she pushed it to the bottom, the little wooden horla toppled out. Both Feletra and Nil tried to catch it, but in the fumble of fingers in the air the ornament bounced away and fell straight into the fire.

‘Oh, no!’ Feletra exclaimed.

Nil reached behind him for a long stick to fish it out and all the excitement had awoken Afax into a frenzy, who began bounding around the tree roots.

‘Wait, Nil, look!’

As Nil turned around with his weapon of choice, he saw to his amazement that the fire had stopped burning. The fire could still be seen, but now there was a solid block of ice encasing it entirely. In the middle and lying untouched in the ashes was the horla figure, waiting to be rescued.

Feletra’s eyes were ablaze with wonder. She came close and touched the sparkling ice, it was sticky cold, so cold there was a chilled smoke unmistakably burning at the edges.

Nil looked on with mild interest.

‘So that’s...?’

‘Yes!’ Feletra blurted. ‘It’s all me, and I’m holding it, I can control it. It feels easy.’

‘But do you know how to create it?’

‘Not exactly. But I’ll get it. This is...this is something I’ve never achieved until now. Not for this long, anyway. Watch this.’

She focused on her unnatural sculpture for but a moment’s breath, then suddenly the ice and fire together transformed into dust about them. Black scatterings like chimney soot formed a quick murky haze around the clearing, and then nothing was left except the horla.

Feletra and Nil coughed a little from the black dust and swiped at it in the air. It was like some magician's trick.

'Well, at least you saved the little horla,' said Nil with difficulty.

Feletra was too elated with her abilities to care for it, but she plucked the figure out of the base stones and put it away. It was scorching hot.

Then something else strange followed; the cry of a true horla could be heard in the distance and rang out through the silence.

Feletra and Nil looked at each other warily, it seemed that company was nearer than they thought.

'Keep the fire out for tonight,' Nil instructed, rising to his feet.

'Where are you going?' Feletra said with concern.

'Just to scout for any signs that we've been followed. I will be quick. Try and sleep.'

It was with a heavy heart that Feletra watched Nil disappear with Afax into the darkness, she noticed him pick up his dagger before he left. But she managed to lay down and sleep while he was gone, knowing she needn't worry about Nil. He could recognise a danger greater than himself, and could take care of any others.

But as Feletra wrapped her arms around her shoulders and pulled her hood up against the southerly cold, there was a greater comfort now knowing she could protect herself.

x

On the following morning, Lampaea was selecting a new and better sword out of the collection from Isbre. Every choice was a fine one, the smith of Isbre must take much care in his work.

At length, he chose a short sword, something light enough to keep him quick on his feet.

'Is that all?' Bren came up beside him, 'I'm sure you can wield something larger.'

'I can,' Lampaea admitted, 'but I am taking my bow as well, and will be relying on that more. I hope we can avoid a bloodbath, anyway.'

'As do I. But, as you wish.'

Lampaea followed Bren out of the tent, then stopped to gaze ahead at the hill above the Borderknot Meander opposite. At the top, he could see the young boy there, on his knees, looking up into the boughs of a great, twisted tree whose roots spread to the bottom of the hill and upturned everything. Wrapped up the trunk and hanging from nearly every branch were the electric blue petals of the forest, strung from one to the next in the most florid fashion that Bren's men were capable of.

They had found the boy's mother, along with six others from their party. They had all been lifted into the trees on the eastern front of Olonath, with tympana draped over every limb. There was more tympana left to see than there were bodies, the flesh barely there when the scouts had finally found them. It was difficult to say how long they had been there, but the smell and number of flies it had attracted suggested it had not been long acted out after Lampaea and Bren had escaped the Well of Oxena.

One thing everyone at Kenduhn was certain about: it was

laid as a warning. Fadres did not like to be cheated out of their own plans. The victims were originally being taken to Setra, but once Lampaea and Bren interfered, the fadres had been alerted and angered. That was enough of a reason to respond, respond with a malicious message...to stay away. They had no way of knowing how many of the others had escaped or been recaptured.

Bren had his men create a shrine as best they could, more for the boy's sake than anyone's. The boy visited it every day since they had made it, just staring into the boughs above him. But not once had he wept.

He will be a strong man, one day, Lampaea thought as he watched him, then went to join Bren with Taiso and Miksandh.

'Are we ready to set out?' said Lampaea, looking eager to make tracks.

Bren looked at him with amusement and then back at his comrades. 'One thing I appreciated most about Lampaea when I met him, was his enthusiasm...'

Miksandh laughed as he fastened the bridle on his horla, and Taiso slapped Lampaea on the back. Taiso, it seemed, had completed weighing up Lampaea's character quickly enough and deemed him trustworthy to walk amongst them.

'I think we are ready, Lampaea,' Taiso replied.

They had four horlas dressed in riding gear and waiting at the base of the camp. Lampaea took the pale grey female, her name was Alefthera. She was placid and amiable with him, with huge hooded eyes that were primed and ready to indulge in fresh adventure.

Taiso set off with Miksandh, and Bren turned to Lampaea with a sombre look.

‘Are you certain you wish to join us, Lampaea?’ he said, ‘I do not want to see your emotions cloud your judgement out there.’

Lampaea appeared indifferent. ‘You have close ones there, too,’ he pointed out.

‘I have a cousin. You have a lover. I think I know who will be able to maintain a clearer head.’

‘I’ll be fine.’

Bren said no more, and cantered off. Lampaea could see he didn’t believe him. He barely believed it himself, he had no idea how he would react if he found Halemedra, dead or alive. It did not bode well for his heart to think of her at that point, let alone how it might affect his head.

He rode out after the other three, and noticed the faces of the men in the camp as he galloped past. They feared for him the most.

x

Nil had found no trace of any followers, either on foot or riding. Feletra remained wary. As they made their way through Sevtern Wood, she looked around and over her shoulder constantly, believing that more than just eagles could have been sent to watch her. After all, an eagle would have felt suffocated in a forest; she fully believed that whoever had sent the eagle also had a chemnon with the creature, that way they would see through each other’s eyes. A chemnon was a deep and sacred kymic bond between man and beast based purely on love and trust; the bond itself however, could be formed naturally or by a craftsman. The strongest chemnons were those naturally formed, as an emotional connection would be preestablised. In the event of the man's death, the creature would die with him, but in the event of the creature's death, the man would endure terrible illness and death later. Some rare individuals however, had been known to survive the trauma, but were never the same again.

Pyra, known typically as The Woodlands, was not too different from the Isle of Ira, save that the woodlands did indeed appear to be everywhere. Feletra spied many different forest birds that startled her whenever flocks of them catapulted into the skies at their approach; the place was otherwise quiet and peaceful. The sound of a creek babbling wispy murmurs nearby was soothing, and Feletra locked eyes with a huge wader that raised its head curiously and fanned out pale yellow feathers.

They stayed another starband in the wood, though Nil said they were close to the edge now. It was safer to sleep under the cover of the trees.

When Drenaas was reaching out to Ilysehr, Feletra looked up and saw the same great bats she had seen a long time ago in Droha.

'They'll tear your throat out,' Nil observed.

Feletra shivered, watching the last silhouette disappear in a hush on the breeze, 'I can believe it.'

She offered to provide fresh food that night and hunt, and half expected Nil to doubt her skill but he had responded fairly, knowing she was adept with the bow.

And Feletra had not disappointed, returning with a temeron as her prize. Nil raised his eyebrows in some surprise as this was indeed quite a prize; a temeron was a timid creature, related to the horla and near impossible to catch, for its hearing was impeccable. Feletra's solitary trek across the Plains of Nemenon had accentuated all her senses perfectly for such a challenge. The rustic flavour of the meat was within reward, and there was plenty to save and take with them.

'What is this way into Chriah then?' Feletra said over a mouthful.

'There is a long tunnel passage that crosses the border.'

'And no one else knows of this? That seems a little too fortunate for us.'

'As far as I know, no one else knows of it. I found it when I was young, I liked to keep it my own secret, not that I had anyone to share it with anyway.'

'No friends?' said Feletra, careful to avoid pity. Nil wouldn't have liked that.

'Do I really seem the type to have friends?' said Nil cynically.

'You have me,' Feletra reasoned.

'I don't have you. You have me. You have something that keeps me walking by your side, because it feels that peril will befall you if I am not with you.'

Feletra looked away in discomfort. She never understood it when Nil said this. It seemed rather speculative of him at first, filling gaps with reasons for the sake of filling them. But the longer she knew him, the more she thought this was a feeling that came to him as naturally as breathing. And there was discomfort for him also, when he admitted this feeling; it was unusual to witness Nil outside of that stony, hard and placid exterior, but Feletra could sense the slight change as it happened. It solidified what she knew to be genuine of him, for it was the guessing she found most vexing.

'Do you think you will ever find out why?' said Feletra somewhat timidly.

Afax clambered up Nil's chest and held onto his neck.

'I hope so. Though unfounded feelings like that are normally the work of Blackcraft.'

Feletra then looked taken aback. 'Must you always assume there is Blackcraft behind it?' she said glaringly. 'Sometimes we simply cannot put a reason or a value to what we feel. Sometimes there is no more to unearth than what the mortal mind gives us, and the world would rather keep us asking questions than finding the answers.'

The smoke of the fire drifted curiously between the trees to be lost to the night sky. Nil smiled lightheartedly.

'The optimistic Feletra,' he said gently.

Feletra rolled her eyes. 'That's a rare thing by itself.'

'I like it,' Nil mused, 'and I will take on board what you said.' He laid back to rest and Afax scurried back down to his chest to avoid being crushed. Feletra sighed lightly, and then concentrated on the fire.

Too much concentration? The Konexa was not wishing to be roused tonight. There was still a learning curve to conquer.

Feletra gave up wearily and unloaded their pile of earth onto the flames.

Nil woke Feletra before Pytheria had even surfaced. Desporsa could not be seen to have risen yet either, but Feletra knew it would be a fiery red today, for the winds were high and a light frost embellished the leaf litter.

Feletra stopped short when she noticed small clouds form before her eyes.

'Nil, what is that?' she said suspiciously. 'Every time I breathe and speak…?'

'I forget you're not used to this weather,' Nil replied, 'that's your breath. You can see it when it gets cold enough, that's all.'

Feletra breathed deeper to create thicker clouds and watched them rolling away; it was fascinating, and yet menial to anyone else. When they came to the end of Sevtern Wood on the eastern side, they were faced with an overgrown, sorry-looking meadow. There was a small lifeless lake over to the south with furry black and grey moss holding the stones and reeds captive, and the tall grasses directly ahead some distance away would twitch and quiver spontaneously.

Finally Pytheria joined them, though it was a pale and dull sun, suppressed behind lazy and intrusive grey clouds.

Nil had paused for quite some time at the forest front, assessing the scene intently before setting out. Feletra could see why, the meadow was so open and quiet, it was all too easy to be seen or heard. They were incredibly close to the border now, if Chriahks caught them crossing over without permission she was sure they would be attacked. And with the eagle relaying messages to whoever was watching her, it paid to be prudent now. The eagle knew Korsthr, and he was evil enough.

'The tunnel mouth is over there, on the other side of the lake,' Nil nodded in the direction of the south and spoke sparingly. 'And Feletra, keep –'

'Keep quiet, don't worry, I know,' Feletra reassured.

'I was going to say keep calm. There are two things you need to know, the first is that the Sturans call this the Singing Meadow.'

'Why?' Feletra's eyes narrowed into a frown.

'You may hear a sound as we are walking through, don't run if you hear it. Just keep walking and ignore it.'

'And the second?' Feletra felt some anxiety was

deserving of this place, she kept it at bay for now.

'The second is if you don't ignore it. This meadow may look dead but it is teeming with life, it makes the forest look tame. There are no friendly creatures here, if you run or shout, you will stir them, and then we're in trouble.'

Feletra looked generally unperturbed, surely there were few beasts left in Esilence that she had not faced and come out alive.

'What is the worst that we could find?' she asked.

Nil did not even hesitate. 'An eraiik,' he said.

Then Feletra became a little more perturbed. Though they were not found in Western Enphiah, she knew what an eraiik was. It was a vicious beast, quick on its feet and leapt upon prey from impressive heights. Their skin was armoured all over in a striking black and gold; they would either travel in pairs as mates, or in groups of four or five until a mate was selected for life.

Nil ordered Afax to sit on his shoulder, for he could grow excited and become a liability on his own, and then led them on through the meadow.

Feletra remained calm and as alert as she had been through Sevtern. She stepped on some hard frost and it crunched too loudly for her liking. Nil turned briefly with a finger to his lips. They each kept a level head and proceeded with the utmost caution from there, and before long they were half-way to the lake. And then she heard it.

That eerie, high-pitched sound that seemed to be gliding and sweeping between the grasses and reeds, or even from them, it was hard to tell. It would become louder, then quicker…and louder again. It was like pipe music, with notes enveloping the senses like vapour on a wisp of breath, as clean as the hiss of water upon a single flame.

Ignore it, said Nil. Oh, how she tried. That sound was more than just music, it invaded her body and shook the bones about inside. Feletra found herself swatting at the air when there was nothing there. It was more than just distracting, it was commandeering. She glanced ahead at Nil, he was completely unaffected, she wondered if he could even hear it. He must be able to, he must simply be used to it from his childhood.

Feletra stumbled a little. It sparked Nil's attention and he turned with a gesture to enquire if she was alright. She returned it adequately and Nil carried on. The cold sound was there again, it felt as if spirits of unrest were rising from the ground to taunt the visitors of the meadow.

Feletra swiped the air again, but the sound only seemed to become louder. She covered her ears, it was unbearable. She wanted to run, run until it was behind her and gone forever. But running was not an option. *Remain calm, Feletra,* she told herself.

She made an involuntary sound of exasperation and swiped at the grass with both arms in wide sweeps.

Nil heard her and stopped abruptly.

'You have to overcome it,' he whispered urgently.

'I'm fine, Nil, keep going,' Feletra urged. She could barely tell how loud she was speaking.

'Feletra, you need to keep quiet.'

Feletra placed her hands over her ears again and screwed her eyes shut. There it was again, that insufferable sound that would give her no peace. It felt like an age she had kept her eyes closed, so long she thought Nil must have gone on without her. But then she opened them again, and he was still stood there. The first thing she did was follow his gaze, for he was fixated on something behind her, his look piercing.

Over her shoulder, Feletra set eyes upon an incongruous sight. Something stood there on two legs, at least ten feet tall, looking straight at them. Feletra was paralysed; this thing stood hunched and poised with scything claws hanging limply at its sides, a long snout tasting their scent on the meadow as a thin, worm-like tongue whipped out slowly to reveal three rows of perfectly parallel, lethally tapered teeth. And plastered over its entire body, black and dull gold…

The serenity with which it fixed its gaze upon them was uncanny, the singing reeds of the meadow had ceased.

Feletra felt rooted to the ground, she dared not move. Then she remembered, these beasts do not travel alone…

True to form, next to the entity already looming before them there then rose another, as if in slow motion. The mate.

'Eraiik,' said Nil.

The word then snapped inside Feletra like an elastic band and she reached for an arrow, but Nil grabbed her hand and the two eraiiks leapt for them.

'Run!' Nil shouted.

Feletra left her arrows in their quiver and moved as quick as the fear would carry her. Nil was sprinting ahead, and Atax ahead of him; they were heading for the tunnel mouth, but the eraiiks were so close already – Feletra knew it without having to turn around.

No man-made weapon would be able to stop these wild animals, that armour was simply too thick. But could the Konexa be strong enough?

Feletra then stopped abruptly and turned to face them, she was petrified. She didn't know what to do with them, but she raised her hands and thought of a wall.

'Feletra! What are you doing?' Nil called urgently.

The eraiiks were hurtling towards her through the reeds, their jaws opening wide – Nil was running back to her from the opposite direction –

What was he doing? *Stay back, Nil.*

She began to feel something. Not in her palms, but in her mind. The Konexa was awakening, begging for release.

Something then flashed bright white before the leading eraiik and the beast was momentarily stopped by some unseen force – but the second took over, breathing rapidly and heavily – within close enough range of Feletra, it leapt to a soaring height, aiming straight for her – the landing would be all too perfect, she had no time.

'No, Nil!' she cried at the very moment that Nil had reached her, dagger blazing in his hand.

He swiped at it with the blade, and then recoiled when the metal bent and broke – the eraiik had landed on something, but it was neither of the two companions.

A konexic barrier had formed between them – a wall of sheer white light that shimmered and overlapped itself like vexed ripples. Both eraiiks were there now, beating at the wall viciously in vain.

'Run to the lake, Nil!' Feletra ordered, but she expected no less of his stubbornness.

'I'm not leaving you to hold them off – can you keep the barrier at a distance?'

Feletra looked around the kymic wall desperately; it had curled around their heads protectively and formed half a sphere, thin layers of liquified crystal that were impenetrable and – incredibly – growing in diameter.

'I don't know –' said Feletra, she lowered her hands and

found that she didn't need them. The eraiiks were becoming worse, one continued to slam the barrier whilst the other was attempting to bite its way through with futility.

Then she felt something new, something pressured forcing its way from the earth into her feet, her legs and moving up her body. In her mind there was a storm, a great gust had formed and was bursting within its vessel, she had to release it from her head.

The pressure surging through Feletra had reached the top of her body and without warning it escaped – the two eraiiks were thrown to the sky from where they stood, the konexic wind had spirited them away and they landed at the edge of the meadow.

There was a moment of awe like a lost breath or a skipped heartbeat. The next thing Feletra knew, Nil was grabbing her hand again and pulling her towards the lake. Despite the great defense there was still no time to waste, the eraiiks' thick armour left them unharmed by the blast and they ran on again at full speed, anger now blended with their bloodthirst like wildfire rising to the temptation of a tower of autumnal leaf litter, dry and ripe for feasting.

Afax led the way; Feletra's heart was pounding in her ears not just from the chase, but from the kym pulsing through her blood, it had unfinished business to attend to.

If only she could stop and turn around again, the beasts would wish they had never been born…

But Nil pulled her on, relentless – they had reached the lake and now it was a race against time to skirt the edges to the other side, for the eraiiks were closing in again.

One leapt into the air once more – Feletra felt its presence, she was prepared. Nil felt a sudden yank as his hand was ripped away from hers – he and Afax were propelled into the lake by Feletra's Konexa, but Nil had not the time to see that the water had dispersed below him, as if he repelled it, and his fall – somehow slower and softer than nature intended, was into the gritty lakebed that had lay slumbering.

In the half-moment that followed, Feletra stared directly at the eraiiks with eyes now blacker than burnt ebony. Without warning, a narrow ridge fell away in the ground between them and a great wall of fire erupted as if pushed toward the surface from an underground hurricane.

The eraiiks fell back in surprise and the heat was too much to bear; Feletra stood directly before the fire, unaffected as Nil watched from afar in amazement. She turned her head to him swiftly and pointed to the other side of the lake.

Nil nodded. He would meet her there. The slightest movement – and the lake's waters would shift and open the way for him; Nil took advantage and ran straight towards the liquid wall before him, creating his own dry path across as the water sprang away from him forcefully and instantaneously.

He could see Feletra running at the same pace on the land, a thick trail of fire in her wake with every impact her feet left, it was absorbing to behold. Still the eraiiks would not cease however; whilst kept well at bay, they dodged the fire where they could and kept on her tail. The mate trailing last kept a careful watch on Nil and Afax in the distance, timing the wait anxiously for when they would step back on land.

Nil sprinted on with Afax – as Feletra's fire began to falter she was forced to run faster – the far end of the lake was now within reach. She could not see the tunnel that Nil spoke of and could only run in his general direction. Finally Nil left the lake and the heavy waters collapsed and clashed inwardly behind him – he remained dry as a bone. Then Feletra saw him signalling her over and he disappeared into some dense undergrowth. Not once did her eyes leave that area where she saw him vanish – she *must* find the tunnel.

The eraiiks were insatiable, on and on they raced, their determination limitless and fuelled by the wrath of humiliation. But Feletra had no intention of returning that dignity to them – she saw Nil ahead, waiting in between the thick bushes and thorns. Without hesitation she plunged forward into the vegetation, caring nought for the deep scratches and cuts from the thorns that graced her skin.

Nil led them on, further and further with what seemed to be no end in the haze of panic. And then there it was – a tunnel mouth so small Feletra feared they would even fit.

'Nil! How –?'

'Trust me!' Nil called back firmly. He pushed Feletra through first – they could hear the eraiiks snarling behind them, 'Go!'

Feletra crawled faster than she had ever crawled before – in the scramble, Afax climbed over her head to the front to lead the way, she could see no more than the fading light on his twitching fur.

Then they all heard the echoes of the eraiiks; she and Nil looked back at the seething mates as they snapped their jaws and spat maliciously. And then much to Feletra's astonishment, one of them pointed straight at her with open scythes and spoke.

'Konexic!' it growled, and with one great swipe of its fist thrusted all its weight down onto the tunnel roof above them. Catching on that they had no hope of fitting through the mouth, the mate followed suit in a bid to break through the top – a notable indent was forming in the earth and pieces of soil and stones rained down upon them.

'Move! Go!' shouted Nil, and Feletra wasted no time. But although the tunnel was widening, it felt as if their attempts to move any further were futile. The eraiiks were bringing them an earthquake – finally the earth was giving way and light streamed through a gap as big as a head between two boulders –

The claws reached down and hooked perfectly into Feletra's side.

And as she screamed in agony – a great force burst forth from the wound – the Konexa took some of her blood with it, a crimson tint mixed into that otherwise invisible kym rose through the gap faster than a beam of sunlight and blasted the eraiiks like nothing she had ever felt before.

The power was shortlived, for the pain was searing.

'Feletra –' said Nil, able to see now with the light from the tunnel hole, 'throw me your pack!'

Feletra was the one carrying any medical supplies; with much effort and by momentarily releasing one hand from her gushing wound she threw it to him.

'Are you still with me?' Nil enquired, his voice a regular pace whilst his hands moved swiftly with the bandage and string.

'I'm – s-still writhing, aren't I?' Feletra replied breathlessly. As she looked at him Nil could see her eyes were still blacker than night. 'Did I kill them?'

'I don't know, but I'm not going up to check.'

Impressively quick, Nil had dressed the wound and was urging her on already.

‘I don’t think I can move with this, Nil,’ said Feletra.

‘Yes, you can,’ Nil concluded, ‘we can’t stay here, knowing the eraiiks could still be alive. Make it a little further down and I’ll be able to help you the rest of the way, I can’t do anything until the tunnel widens out.’

Unable to protest about anything greater than the pain itself, Feletra reluctantly moved on, though she made a point of crawling on her right-hand side to prevent any ground contact with the wound. Her breathing became more labored and with every movement it felt as if her side might burst wide open.

Finally, the tunnel widened enough to crouch, but Feletra was slowing dangerously. Afax was watching her eyelids sink and called frantically to Nil.

‘Feletra!’

She could hear the music of the reeds ringing in her ears again, even now when her eyelids failed her and her body crumbled into a chasm of shadow.

x

A moment was indeed what was needed with Emmet. The bloodlust and thirst for revenge died down for the better after a hot drink and a period of brief reflection over dinner. Meanwhile, Dox awaited them in the main city chamber. Emmet hadn’t thought about what he would ask him, the obvious questions about Chriah were clouded by personal betrayal.

At sundown, Dynetii beckoned him to the chamber. He nodded and touched where the arrow had pierced his arm; Dynetii had treated the wound well, though it was his lingering energy that dulled the throbbing pain. Mov had decided to join them as a lookout in the chamber passage, even Menkhrist's sentries would have trouble fighting their way past him.

'Dox…' said Emmet casually, 'how's the hand? Or there be lack of?'

Dox was dripping with sweat, he let his severed hand fall limply to the ground, and glanced up at Emmet with amusement at his remark. His good hand was shackled to the wall behind him.

'Always knew you had a sense of humour, Emmet. You've changed in other ways though. Fully-fledged killer now.'

Emmet lunged down at Dox and struck him hard in the face.

'I'd have expected pride from you then,' Emmet snarled, he seethed with anger.

'Calm, Emmet,' said Dynetii, and he retreated silently. 'What is the purpose of Chriah's breeding grounds?'

Dox held his gaze with the flagstones to his side. The skin on his cheek tumbled and rolled from the back of his jaw to the front like a Nova Snake beneath desert sand. He gave something a flick with his tongue, and spat out a bloody tooth.

'Chriah will be unstoppable,' he said thickly, peering at Dynetii now through lank threads of his black hair, sodden with grease and sweat.

'That's not what I asked,' Dynetii sighed. She looked at Emmet imploringly, who seized the opportunity and struck Dox again with his full weight behind it. Dox was driven further towards the flagstones again, he spat blood pitifully.

'I hope you are willing to lose more than just teeth for your silence,' said Emmet.

Dox raised an eyebrow wearily and began to snigger, he seemed delirious. 'Take me to death and back, Emmet. You'll not have me betray my country.'

'Your country?' Emmet laughed disbelievingly, 'I grew up with you in Betharanei. Now you mean to tell me that all these years you were a Chriahk?'

'No. The Otrans preach a dull life and they practice a dull life. But I confess, that is all I have ever been. I did not want to be that mundane Otran that has no name in history. Amanyl was a Chriahk and he began to see potential in me as a boy, the affairs of Chriah became known to me and the thrill of just being someone was incredible. I was lost in the feelings of importance, schemes, excitement, so much so I began to love Chriah and called it home.'

'This story of yours is wonderful,' said Dynetii, 'but I'm not hearing the answers to my question,'

'Find a real traitor then.'

'We've already found him,' Emmet laughed, 'I'm glad you were the last, you're the most treacherous of the lot. Squeezing the truth out of you should be easy.'

Dox remained tight-lipped. Emmet and Dynetii glanced at each other and they moved into position. Dynetii took a step back; Emmet's force was brutal as he laid a heavy kick into Dox's exposed elbow, all the bone cracking at once and changing shape entirely.

Dox cried out but let the pain course through him without saying a word. With one arm missing its end and the other mangled beyond repair, even charity would have saved its breath.

'Tell us and you will live,' said Dynetii.

Dox struggled to inhale breath to form words. 'You expect me to believe you? After – after you butchered all the others.'

'I swear it,' Emmet said irrevocably.

Dynetii looked at him curiously for a moment but she knew that decision was now final, there was no lie to Emmet's eyes. The beatings continued; when Dox seemed ready to pass out and uttered 'stop,' they listened, but nothing would follow. Dynetii sighed in exasperation and drove another fist into the side of his skull.

Emmet stood back to survey the scene and think. Dox was not a strong man, neither was he honourable. Something would break him.

'Emmet, this isn't working,' said Dynetii, 'we're doing too much damage for him to talk anyway.'

Emmet saw the short knife at Dynetii's hip. 'Or not enough. Give me that,' he pointed.

Dynetii was somewhat taken aback but then he took it from its sheath and quickly knealt down before Dox, lifting his head forcefully and pressing the tip to his lower eyelid. Suddenly, Dox's eyes were wide open and his breathing doubled in speed.

'Do you feel this?' Emmet asked. 'It's pnapsor. That means it blunts easily, and popping your eye out will not be that quick. In fact, it could take a while –'

'Emmet, please –'

'You've lost the use of most of your limbs, but we all fret the greatest when our senses are on the line. Will you value your sight?'

'Yes! If only you would put down the knife –'

'You will speak then?' Emmet's voice was strangely smooth and hair-raising, even Dynetii felt uncomfortable. This plan was wholly unbeknown to her, she was not able to gauge how genuine his threats were.

‘Come now, Emmet,’ said Dox desperately, ‘this isn’t you –’

But then Emmet began to edge the blade beneath the delicate skin.

‘Stop! Alright – alright!’ Dox flailed his stump of a hand pitifully, tears of blood streaming down his face, and Emmet withdrew the tip of the knife.

‘War is upon all of you. Chriah and Eastern Enphiah are allied once more, they will take back the land and the seas, and purge all with an army none can defeat.’

‘The preathins?’ said Emmet, the blade still poised.

‘Preathins…led by craftsmen. There can be no darker force.’

‘We defeated the preathins before,’ Dynetii said confidently, ‘we can do it again.’

‘You will have no time to react. The breeding grounds have been under your very nose for centuries, we have already infiltrated. There are two beneath Rukur, you might like to know. Why, you are standing above one now.’

There was a deathly silence, almost as if they were trying to listen for signs of activity from below. The agitation was beginning to show.

‘And the waiting game?’ said Emmet in suspense. ‘Back in Betharanei, I heard the discussions in the back streets. What are they waiting for? Why haven’t they struck sooner?’

‘The preathins –’ Dynetii interjected, ‘a new generation is born every two thousand and six hundred years. It’s a long but dedicated wait…’

‘In the know your lady is,’ Dox said, and there was that twinkle in his eye, a twinkle under hooded lids that was all Emmet needed to know.

‘Why do I feel you’re leaving something out?’ said Emmet.

‘Because my guard is down and you have deduced well, Emmet. There was more to wait for than just the preathins, though the timing of the two was undeniably impeccable. They have been awaiting an Enphiahn girl, whose future was seen. She is the key in all of this, she will start this war, and end it.’

‘Who is she?’

‘The most powerful konexic Esilence has ever seen. Feletra of Elpura.’

What silence followed then was even more deathly than the last. At her name, Emmet’s heart thumped so hard he thought the chamber might echo with it. It couldn’t be. The same Feletra he met? It just couldn’t. Without knowing it, the knife began to slowly fall away and his grip became slack.

Dox’s laughter interrupted his scattered thoughts. ‘She’s walking straight into Chriah’s trap,’ he said gleefully, and then he must have noticed the steel fade from Emmet’s eyes, for he added, ‘oh, no. The travelling girl in Betharanei? Not that one?’ and he laughed louder than ever, but his breath to reach for a second round was stolen from him brutally, for the captor made his move.

‘Emmet!’ exclaimed Dynetii in shock.

Emmet plunged the knife deep into the socket where it was warm and calamity ensued. He scraped around, not wishing for a clean cut, the blade juddered inside his head. Finally it gave way, and the eye came free. A tangled mess, it popped and bounced to the floor like quivering live bait before meeting an abrupt end.

Chapter 18
A Vision of Beyond

‘Death is not with you. Death is not with you. Death is not with you.’

The five words that lulled into Feletra’s heart over and over, as if they were a melody from a harp.

Then she awoke, her vision blurred, and she could make out Nil’s lips shaping the words carefully, one after the other. As her eyes came into focus she found she was looking deep into his two pools of green, the ripples within them at slumber. He had been watching over her until she awoke, stitching her wound, washing her face of the dirt, and chanting unknown words to her.

‘Nil…eraiiks?’

‘The eraiiks are gone, we made it,’ said Nil, helping her to sit up. She touched the wound in her side.

‘I thought that beast cut me deeper,’ she observed, ‘it does not hurt that much.’

‘Oh, it did. Deep enough for anyone else to die, you lost a lot of blood. But it seems the Konexa provided a temporary seal after you passed out, there was a shield hovering around your wound for some time. Thankfully, it didn’t resist my touch so that I was able to stitch it.’

Feletra looked around and shuffled into a better position, they were at the mouth of the opposite end of the tunnel now, the moonlight streamed in and a thick Chriahk forest lay before them.

‘Why were you saying those words to me, Nil?’

Nil looked uneasy for a moment. ‘I had to be certain the

Konexa wasn't just feeding off the last of your energy, I had to do everything to keep you alive.'

Feletra studied him for a moment. 'Thank you, though I did not think you believed in blind hope so much.'

'I know when it is blind and when it is not.'

Pain scorched Feletra's flesh in waves. She tried to keep the wincing to a minimum.

'Is it safe out there?' she nodded to the forest.

'Nowhere is that safe in Chriah. But there are no eraiiks here, if that's what you mean. Are you strong enough to move on?'

'Yes,' she replied firmly, her body resenting her somewhat. Nil did not argue, disagree or lecture her otherwise. He helped her out of the tunnel, from there Feletra needed no aid. No complaint would pass her lips, though the wound was like no pain she had ever experienced before. It felt like surges of electricity being forced through her, embers burning at her nerve ends.

They ventured out into the forest quickly in spite of the setback; Feletra was taken aback, the trees rose as tall as mountains here, the slender trunks black as ash and as straight as a lucrin longsword. At their tops they fanned out into branches and skinny boughs that looked like deformed claws or tangled veins, blindly reaching out to anything in one big confused mess. Each tree was barely two persons apart, much to Feletra's consternation as it notably slowed down their journey.

Even with just the wound I'd have moved faster than this, she thought.

The day was grim, the clouds folded over themselves with heavy descent and flecks of snow began to drift down. It perplexed Feletra to begin with, the flakes tingling her cold senses as they settled on her eyelashes or nose and then melted instantaneously. Afax seemed to dislike the cold immensely and disappeared under Nil's cloak for warmth. The snow fell heavier, quicker but soft, there was a calm yet enervated feel to this place…and then amidst all the pure white, the looming lines of trees, the traipsing grey silhouette of Nil's figure ahead and the blurred edges that made him real, something walked with them.

Feletra came to a stop. The sense of that particular something was pressing and imminent, finding seed within her mind. She looked around twice and could make out nothing, the reception for some essence of evil growing, deepening, leeching…

She turned a third time, and it was there, a tall dark figure not twenty paces from where she stood, the face blurred out by the snow. She strained her eyes and took a couple of steps closer, when without warning, the silhouette cascaded instantly and the shape had melted into the ground.

Feletra gasped and stopped again. Blackcraft?

She swallowed hard and her eyes darted about the blind scene, awaiting an ambush. Then as she turned to face forward again, she beheld to her horror a man hanging by one arm from the tree before her, a single rusted hook through his wrist, blood staining the snow below him.

Feletra let out a cry and stumbled backwards – she fell onto her haunches and pulled herself away hectically. She couldn't tear her eyes from the body, the taught limb that suspended the whole gruesome thing, but in particular the head – the head was thrown back, the pale jawline sharply protruding and all facial features hidden.

All manner of defence had fallen away, she could not even feel the Konexa at this moment. Nil had been alerted and ran over without hesitation.

He dropped to his knees next to her. ‘Is it your wound?’

Feletra pointed frantically, Nil had run straight past the body, apparently oblivious. ‘It’s that!’

Nil looked over his shoulder and poised one hand over his sword hilt, but he failed to spot any danger.

‘There!’ Feletra cried. ‘Can’t you see it?’

‘I don’t see anything,’ replied Nil honestly, but Feletra could not ignore the gentle swinging between the snowflakes.

‘He is there, plain as day! A man hanging from the tree – not ten steps away.’

Nil looked again at the tree but still his eyes failed where Feletra’s revealed the morbid picture. He pulled her up from the ground and led her away, back towards the east. Still, she could not tear her eyes away, and looked back all the time, fearful of that lolling head returning to life to look her dead in the eye. Only until they descended a hill was he truly out of sight.

‘Nil, what do you know? You did not tell me I was wrong, or losing my mind. Was that a spirit I saw?’

Nil continued walking.

Feletra grabbed his sleeve in agitation, ‘Nil!’ and he stopped. She noticed he was rubbing the stone pendant again.

‘I think so, yes,’ he said quietly, he drew his hood in closer about his face and stowed the pendant away calmly. ‘Some Chriahks once took pleasure in hanging their enemies from trees until they bled to death. I am sure their mark is all over this country, the trails of death they left everywhere.’

‘You have seen things before as well?’

‘No. I have felt the evil here many times, but to see it materialise…no one can see that, Feletra. No one can see the dead, that is something coveted, something that people would kill for.’

‘Why would people want to see? It’s terrible,’ Feletra was reminded again of the paralysing fear.

‘Seeing is next to communicating. For years, craftsmen have undergone trials, sacrifices and every dark craft they could find to achieve it. Once you speak with the dead, you have a gateway to the Artrysiptic.’

Feletra felt colder now than just from the snow.

‘The Artrysiptic? Where all kymic beings go after death…did they even succeed?’ she said through chattering teeth.

‘Most died trying. But I believe a few did, as far as I know they took their secrets to the grave. But you are something to be feared, Feletra. Promise me you will keep this gift to yourself while we are in Chriah.’

Feletra nodded awkwardly. ‘I’ll try,’ she quickly wondered what she might do then should she have another encounter in front of a Chriahk. Worse still, if said encounter attempted to communicate with her. And then it struck her that this was not the first time after all. ‘This has happened to me before, Nil. I even forgot about it; I saw a woman in that house by the Sorpha, she was an ill thing, deranged. I think it was Zenika.’

‘The mother of Nephele?’ Nil’s eyes widened some.

‘Yes. This is the Konexa, isn’t it? It’s the only reason.’

‘It could be. This gift is rarer than the kyms, it could simply be who you are.’

Feletra had no answer for that. What words could have sounded complimentary and unique of her were soiled for their true meaning; there was no good to be taken from looking upon death, only fear and nothing to control it.

'Or the curse. It is true that I should be receiving dark visions.'

'Somehow, it just doesn't seem that way. You have not suffered anything else, I'm beginning to wonder if you are cursed at all. Let's walk another couple of leagues and then make camp,' said Nil, 'the snow should ease by the other side of the forest.'

Feletra walked closer to Nil, although she accepted the fact that neither of them could fight away the dead. She almost wished it were indeed a symptom of the curse, for if it were not then she would never be rid of it. And Nil was right, somehow it simply didn't feel like the curse; it felt like a gift, despite the macabre characters and their stories. There was almost an enlightenment to it, seconds in which she would experience this divine skeleton beneath the morbid flesh. The essence of evil was still thickly with her however, and it was not of the spirit itself but of Chriah and all the wrongs that could no longer be righted. This was the Konexa enhancing everything, all the terrible reality of the world that the morotehm could not feel.

And all the while her mind only repeated that one line she felt she had heard a thousand times…

You are something to be feared.

x

On the eve of the second day, the sky above Acro had become an angry scarlet red. Lampaea felt how close Setra was, he was eager to cross the border and find Halemedra. He was sure Bren was of the same mind, but he did not showcase the excitement or anticipation.

The four were making excellent time, stops to eat and rest were kept as short as possible and sleep was constantly monitored with one of the party as a look-out at all times.

Lampaea appreciated the company of these men; they shared many of his own qualities. They were quick, ambitious and driven as he was and made no time for quarrels. Miksandh was bright-eyed and quick-footed; he had many plans to fulfil and many places to see when this was finished, he would say. His youthful output was infectious and he would often drive Taiso to tears of laughter. Taiso, on the other hand, was somewhat older and the wear of time was expressed in his eyes, the creeping lines about the mouth and the growing shadow on his brow. He was slower to trust others, took pride in his judgement and had a softness about him that he was ready to share with a woman and children.

Then there was Bren, a serious man built for leadership. Without knowing him better, Lampaea would have thought him fierce and brutal in his decisions. But this Beltrorn had proven himself diplomatic, fair and understanding even in the face of adversity. The wild side of Beltro was well mixed into his blood however; there was no better evidence to this than when he had followed his gut more than his head and rode the raging rembrorhg out of the Well of Oxena. Bren never cared to mention any mortal fancies such as home, family, good food or jokes. Even his cousin and her aaron, whom he deeply cared for, were not mentioned openly with fondness. He often reminded Lampaea of Flior and his mother, whose heads were always in the moment, and had memories aplenty but locked every last one away.

The sun had been scorching the northern plains today and even as Pytheria began to set, still he challenged how much sweat could leave their brows. As Lampaea wiped his face, he stopped the others, for he felt something was afoot.

'Do you hear?' he said.

The men peered about the wilderness, perplexed.

'Hear what, Lampaea?' asked Bren.

'Complete and utter silence. The birds were with us the whole way, now there is nothing.'

'We are close to the eastern border now,' said Taiso, 'perhaps even the animals will not stray too near for the darkness the land bears.'

'The border is still eight leagues off. Something has shaken them.' Immediately Lampaea withdrew an arrow and reached for his bow.

'Come now, Lampaea,' Miksandh implored, 'your senses are too keen. There is nothing here.'

But Bren had automatically followed Lampaea's surmise and placed a hand firmly on the hilt of his sword. 'I trust in Lampaea's instinct. Be on your guard,' he ordered, and the three of them withdrew longswords.

Lampaea then caught sight of something above them; a great bird in flight, the clouds gave way and parted before it, no more than smoke about a deceased candle.

'There!' Lampaea cried, and the men followed his gaze.

'What is that?' said Taiso.

Lampaea strained his eyes, he glanced at Bren and together they knew. It could only have been one thing.

'That's a swenph,' said Bren.

'Surely it can't be!' Taiso said, though his tone questioned them little.

‘It is,’ Lampaea replied, confident, ‘the swenikga follow eastern rule now, do not expect that to be a friend.’

The swenph was clearly not passing by; with a great cry it flew down and swooped once around them before landing squarely in their path. The men were ready with their weapons.

Lampaea had never before seen a swenph in the flesh, for after they were all taken from Acro the east had kept them confined for years, slowly breaking their spirit. It truly was a great and magnificent creature; a long slender neck snaking out from its body and wings that beat harder than a warrior’s heart. Even the tail was a thing of splendour, as long as it was formidable, a man could die quickly beneath its mass. Indeed, the swenikga were once some of the midlands’ best allies; when Acro suffered the greatest during the Old War due to sharing the largest border with Setra, they were granted immediate permission from Penthor to breed vast numbers of swenikga, the largest and strongest fliers known. The Acrounians defended their land well on the backs of the birds and pushed the Setrans back, until Setra saw what huge benefit they were in battle and ordered the Delicans to steal them away, thus they had stolen the ‘Acrounian Wings.’

Lampaea was proven correct in his estimations, for the swenph had nevertheless been changed dramatically from its former glory. The eyes were most notable, red raw and absorbing, the whites were gone. They darted about the men madly, bulging and full of contempt. The bird’s feathers looked beyond ruffled along its body, battered almost. Where once this elegant creature boasted a rich and brilliant sky-blue, now was reduced to a flaky ash-grey, such vibrancy that had been decimated by cruelty and manipulation. The tail end too, had been pierced with stakes and left there to fester.

The swenph was not alone, there was a single rider perched upon its back. Hooded though the face was, Lampaea recognised the stony-blue colour of the hand that lay across the flea-bitten feathers.

And then he lifted his hood back. Lampaea had seen that face before, at the mouth of a well.

'The fadre,' he said aloud. Bren remembered him too, and his eyes narrowed fearsomely.

'What is it you want?' Bren called.

At that moment, the swenph was still, it cocked its head and stared, fixated on them. The insanity in that eye was immense, inside it the trepidation of sorrow's last tear, the quickest of them to roll down the skin and fall from the glazed cheek. A single drop of rain to its fragile hold the only villain to bring it crashing down forever.

The bird snapped. With a deranged cry it charged at them – the men held their ground – then there was dust as it reached them and the swenph lifted into the air, the force of its launch was enough to knock each of their horlas to the ground.

Bren, Taiso and Miksandh were all thrown off their guard, but Lampaea had been ready and managed to roll off his horla and back into a crouch. His bow was still intact and he immediately shot three arrows before the swenph had ducked behind the clouds again. All a miss, the bird was too fast.

'Miksandh, ready your bow!' commanded Bren, while he and Taiso bore their longswords in a tenacious grip.

'Where is it?' said Taiso.

Lampaea caught the shadow on the clouds of red dusk.

‘There! Spread apart!’

The swenph revealed itself once more and came at them with all speed.

Lampaea and Miksandh shot arrow after arrow, the fadre controlled his pattern of flight well, until Lampaea’s finally shot straight into the bird’s side. There was a short cry of anguish and a waver in balance, but no sign of detainment. The swenph was in line for Taiso, who ducked with his sword above him – he caught the wing. It was enough to bring it down, its hope of flight now impaired. The beast limped about but was too weak to fight them.

The fadre was not fazed, calmly stepping down from the swenph’s back and leaving it to its fate. He carried a crossbow, and aimed first at Lampaea.

‘Lampaea, move!’ yelled Bren, but Lampaea was quick-handed with his bow and struck the fadre in the chest. He fell backwards and hit the ground.

It seemed too simple and Bren was indeed of this opinion. ‘Wait!’ he said as the men were just lowering their weapons. ‘Stay on your guard. Fadres don’t die that easily.’

They maintained all manner of defence on Bren’s advice, and edged in closer to the fadre, who still had not moved. The swenph snapped and snarled at them nearby, but had no strength to advance. Lampaea approached gingerly, his sword in hand now, and leant over the body.

The fadre moved just as fast as Lampaea. As soon as his eyes flicked open, Lampaea had launched forward for the throat but his opponent had shared the same idea, and now – to the indrawn breath of suspense from the men around them, they each had a blade laid bare against the other’s flesh.

Miksandh quickly prepared his bow. ‘I can hit him.’

'No –' said Bren firmly, 'it's too much of a risk to Lampaea. Hold fire, Miksandh.'

The fadre looked deep into Lampaea's eyes, and Lampaea into his. They were bright green, unnaturally so, exploding out from a cruel, malicious face of stone-grey skin. Even set so dangerously against it Lampaea could feel the resistance against his own sword – it was the first time he had been properly able to look at a fadre. He not only looked but felt impenetrable, it was incredible but no wonder either that his arrow had left but a scratch.

'Who are you?' said Lampaea.

'Alaxas,' the fadre replied, his voice deep and raspy.

'And who are you working for, Alaxas?'

The fadre frowned with huge-set eyebrows, everything seemed slightly more pronounced than the face of a regular person. 'You fight for the people you cannot free.'

Lampaea was becoming agitated. 'I will free them. If it is my last move, they will breathe good air again.'

Bren moved in close enough to listen as the fadre began to smile, revealing two sharp fangs to the front and another two behind these.

'Esohgenedin mera menke, Halemedra.'

He startled Lampaea then. With just her name his heart sank, but that was not all. With an evil smile still painted across his stormy face his body began to shudder, and suddenly the earth he lay upon seemed to be turning into a great mound atop of him – his body was becoming the earth itself, and he was gone.

Lampaea knelt there, shellshocked.

'Lampaea, let's go,' said Bren. The swenph lay bleeding out, death not far on the horizon.

'No, no, Bren –' Lampaea protested. 'What did he say?

You know the language, you know Fadic, what did he say about her?'

'It matters not. Taiso, Miksandh, get the horlas ready.'

Lampaea couldn't let it go. 'It matters, Bren. I need to know.'

'He was a craftsman, Lampaea. You can't trust anything he said to be true.'

Lampaea grabbed his arm, 'Tell me.'

Bren looked him carefully in the eye. 'He said Halemedra was the best,' he placed a hand on Lampaea's shoulder and then tended to the horlas.

Lampaea knew exactly what to make of the words, and then also not. It was as vague a statement as he could have heard, and that was just what Alaxas wanted. But no matter if Halemedra was dead or alive, Lampaea wanted his head on a pike. And then something else struck him, but Bren mentioned it first.

'It appears the enemy know who we are, or at least some of us,' he said, glancing at Lampaea. 'They know our links to the captives. More importantly, with that fadre escaping us they will know we're coming, and I have no doubt that there will be more to intercept us. From now on, we must all have our senses on high alert.'

As Taiso and Miksandh re-mounted, Lampaea quickly drew Bren to one side again.

'Bren, how is it they know who we are to the captives? I have only ever been alone with Halemedra, it's not possible.'

'Blackcraft,' said Bren bluntly.

'That's still not possible.'

Bren then paused and wore an expression as if he truly wished he did not have to speak his next words.

‘The craftsmen have become more cunning and more versatile than they were in the past. In Chriah, I believe, they have found a way to…*bend time.* And fate, possibly. The two things we cannot exist without. I only know this from a Sturan who joined us in Kenduhn, he left Pyra after witnessing this strange craft. They can shape our lives, Lampaea, they can control us.’

x

Gathering over Rukur, dark clouds had drawn every man, woman and child out into the streets, craning their necks to the skies. Rain began to fall, soft at first, and then it came in droves, pounding the city so hard a few even thought their rooves would collapse atop of them. Some withdrew inside, but many stayed to witness the anomaly, even rejoiced. Lor had not seen rain like this for decades.

Emmet was running, running through the downpour, Dynetii was ahead. But all the people became obstacles in the streets, there they stood with their hands raised to the sky, feeling as blessed as Emmet and Dynetii were feeling despair. They were racing back to the Chandre for help, Dynetii had sent Mov back to the armoury and instructed him to wait for their return after she had spoken to Menkhrist.

Emmet caught up and stopped her briefly. ‘Are you sure we should be doing this?’ he said. ‘Your father didn’t believe me the first time.’

‘We had no proof back then,’ Dynetii reasoned, ‘and you have me now.’

‘Wait – I have a bad feeling about all this, Dynetii. It might be better if we go straight to the Lor Nimh Ring.’

Dynetii rolled her eyes. ‘He is the head of the Ring! It will make no difference.’

‘Alright, alright, fine. And I need to send a message to Feletra, I must warn her immediately.’

‘It will be done, Emmet, I will send scouts to the south to find her, but first this. Come on!’

She ran on before Emmet had another chance to protest, reluctantly he chased after her. It seemed wrong, he knew it. He knew Menkhrist would not respond well, even with his daughter to contest. From that single meeting he had been able to surmise everything about the man; selfish, absorbed, close-minded. Everything that Dynetii was not, she knew this herself. Yet Emmet knew not the relationship between the two, it appeared clear to him that Menkhrist’s favourite child was Jekron, he only hoped Dynetii could prove him wrong and convince her father thus.

Outside the Chandre, there were guards that reacted when they saw Emmet again, Dynetii silenced them with a gesture of her hand and they entered.

Emmet saw Menkhrist in deep conversation with Jekron, they found them in the library, poring over old scrolls and tablets. They looked up expectantly and Menkhrist squinted initially, when he then recognised Emmet he was roused instantly with wide eyes.

‘You dare show your face back here?’ he yelled, ‘I banished you!’

‘Father, wait –’ Dynetii interjected predictably, ‘I brought Emmet back here, we have evidence –’

‘Evidence of what? That our old enemies have been busy breeding preathins and mean to destroy us?’ Menkhrist scoffed.

‘I know it sounds insane Father, but you must believe us.

We shouldn't be wasting time arguing about it, we need to inform the Nimh Ring and our allies!'

'Pray tell,' said Jekron callously, 'what is this evidence?'

Emmet stepped forward and stood by Dynetii.

'One of my chasers,' he spoke clearly, 'we held him captive, and terrorised him until he talked. He confessed all, the preathins, the plans for war, everything. And there is a breeding ground beneath Rukur, you need to evacuate the city.'

Menkhrist looked between them with what could have been confusion, then at his son, who shook his head without deliberation.

'What of the others?' said Jekron. 'Those that hunted you?'

Dynetii felt far from pensive. 'Dead,' she replied bluntly, 'we killed all of them.'

Jekron had already known the answer to this, but he had to poke the dormancy out of his father, he had to fish and tempt the raging reaction forth. Menkhrist, in his old age, was less receptive of conspicuity, and Jekron, fully aware, was only ever too happy to be his aid.

'I had thought there was more strength in you…' Menkhrist said to Dynetii, and then his eyes darkened for Emmet. 'You have caused all of this madness, you have corrupted my daughter, bent her mind to carry out your depraved will –'

'No, that's not true!' Emmet objected.

'You will hang! By my hand, you will hang for your sins!'

'Father, no!' cried Dynetii. 'Do you not see? Do you not see it is all true?!' she instantly ran to him and filled his view with her face in anguish, but her attempts were in vain, for guards were already arresting Emmet and taking him away. He did not try to fight them, he knew he was powerless now.

My judgement has come then, he thought, to die for the truth.

They dragged Emmet away to be imprisoned.

'You can't do this!' said Dynetii. 'He is innocent!' she was grasping desperately at Menkhrist's arms, shaking him, but he was set in his decision, and looked uncomfortable as if he had to swat a busy fly away.

Jekron was becoming frustrated at the scene. 'Will someone restrain her?' he said. 'Her senses are warped.'

Immediately two more guards were there to hold Dynetii off her father. She looked at them like a cat glares at one who has stood on its tail.

'Get your hands off me! What are you doing, Father? I have not lost my mind!'

Menkhrist peered at his daughter for a few moments, the expression of sheer disappointment, with Jekron faithfully at his back.

'You must listen to me,' Dynetii implored. 'Chriah will be on our doorstep – they are already here! The city will fall if you do nothing!'

Then Menkhrist continued the look a little while longer, his face newly tinted with melancholy eyes, until he reached out and dragged a rough index finger down her cheek, and Dynetii was momentarily silenced.

'You are so like your mother,' he said, 'passionate, radical, untameable…always pretending to be something she was not,' his gaze flicked up to the guards, 'take her away.'

Dynetii was furious, she fought and kicked against the

guards pulling her away. 'You are the insane one! You are an ignorant old man who will single-handedly bring us *all* to ruin!'

'My Lord, the tower?' said one of the guards.

Menkhrist shook his head. 'The storc.'

At mention of this, Dynetii fought even harder, and she caught a glimpse of Jekron's smile. Storc was the Fadic term for dungeon, but they were like no man-made dungeon. The storcs were first built by the fadres themselves, and drove inmates insane. They were built with many layers surrounding them, bringing the heat within to an unbearable degree and a lack of any light rendered the prisoner blind. Traditionally, the fadres would play cruel games with the prisoners in the heat and the dark until the will to live was gone forever. Even the guards had shown some subtle surprise in Menkhrist's decision, and Dynetii swore she would never forget what he did.

All the way down, until she was cast into the chamber, her resistance and her screaming had not ceased. They had been too strong to fight off, but she would make her wrath known nonetheless. No matter how long they kept her there, she would have her voice heard.

Menkhrist would not kill her, she knew that, instead he would try and change her. Mould her. Manipulate her.

All in the darkness.

x

Feletra felt numb all through her body, and that was before her death. There was a stream running through the caves, and she was edging her way around the sides, stepping cautiously from rock to rock, it would lead her to the cure.

There was no feeling left in her feet, or her cold hands as she steadied her balance against the smooth walls. It felt like light rain in here, but it was damp and felt stale, she craved the crisp frozen air outside.

She slipped – it was inevitable, her ankle caught between two boulders, wedged deep. The panic ensued, but she couldn't express pain the same way anymore.

'Nil!' she called, and she could hear him behind her, at her aid immediately. He wasted no time and managed to winch her free.

No sooner had she picked herself up…searing pain shot up her spine and down again. A heavy knife was ripped from her back, and she collapsed, rolling off the boulder and into the stream, where the trickling water carried her blood to the cure. She would never reach it. The Konexa had no power left in her, she tried to summon it and nothing happened. She felt normal again, vulnerable.

Laying helplessly on her front, her laborious breath pushing at the water, she saw Nil's boots as he jumped down next to her. He stepped back, and she noticed he was holding the stone pendant, fumbling with it as it slid between his thumb and forefinger repetitively. Until it dropped into the stream as if he too had fallen numb.

From the other hand, the knife fell.

'Feletra. Feletra?'

She broke free of that world. It was morning, the cold was biting, but she was alive. There was Nil, standing above her, waiting for her to move on. During a stop for a quick breakfast, Feletra had fallen into a trance, and her eyes had shown her a fearsome turn of events. She looked back at Nil, trepid, anxious, disquieted. It did not go unnoticed.

‘Did you see them again?’ he said plainly. ‘Death?’

Feletra hesitated, ‘My death,’ she said. ‘I had a vision of it. Someone drove a knife into my back.’

‘You don’t know who?’

‘No…I could not see them,’ she had been locked in eye contact with him the whole time she spoke, but nothing in Nil quavered.

What is he thinking right now? she thought, her mind now turning wild with possibilities and great doubt. *Should I tell him?*

Nil adopted one of his rarer but unique expressions then, one that settled perfectly between determination and understanding.

‘I had better walk behind you more often then,’ he said.

Feletra privately raised an ironic eyebrow at the comment, and then rose to her feet. Nil had already covered any trace that they had been there, and they moved on through the snow. The east coast was still many leagues off by foot.

Feletra felt conflicted again. She had grown to trust Nil, he had proven himself a loyal companion. But this vision reminded her of the first back in Elpura that led her here to begin with. It had been of the same ilk, the same aura, only she was awake this time. The message delivered in it had been real before, there had to be something real in this one now. Should she fear Nil? Should she run from him? Would he wait till her back is turned and betray her?

Suddenly she thought back to the vision in Elpura again, at the time she had only paid attention to the curse and the caves, but there was a boy…a boy whose face had not been clear. Could it have been Nil, and not Ataleka all along? A warning inside a message, an answer at the expense of threat.

The snow began to fall again, and the forest felt like it would never end. Chriah was a dire place to be, the sky was always grey, the great trees bore down on them as if they were watching their every move, and there were uncertain noises both at night and in the day. Feletra found the caution but not the fear, not since the Nova Snake, the Dirim, the eraiiks, everything.

There had mostly been silence for the past three leagues, until they heard something not far off. Nil extended his hand to Feletra as usual to signal her for quiet, but she too was scanning the scene. It was like a trudging noise, a sound of arduous footsteps through thick snow, much like their own had been, except this was enough to account for five or six people.

Nil had withdrawn his sword slowly and the two of them assumed a crouching position, and then the sound stopped.

Feletra held her breath and her eyes were darting everywhere for signs of life. Eventually they relaxed.

'Must have been some animals,' said Nil in defeat.

'Heavy boots for animals,' Feletra mused, and then she spied something in Nil's other hand, it was the stone pendant.

'Nil, what is that?'

Nil followed her gaze carefully, and momentarily appeared as if he had been caught off-guard.

'It's just a charm,' he answered. 'Adrenache gave it to me, for luck on our journey.'

Feletra nodded, inside she felt dubious. He was too difficult to read.

'I saw you holding it when we rode over on the mirikites. You play with it a lot, don't you?'

Nil looked somewhat agitated. 'I just want to reach Leohreten safely, Feletra, that is all.'

Feletra was suddenly occupied with more pressing matters, for in the blink of an eye, an arrow struck the tree dangerously close to her head. Nil turned and saw five men approaching them from the hill to the east.

'Behind the tree!' he shouted.

Feletra spun backwards on her heel and took cover from one of the tree trunks. They were thin and looked like poor shields, but there was nowhere else to run or hide. Abruptly she felt three more arrows pierce the same trunk. Nil sent Afax scurrying up to the top of the tree for his own safety, no arrow would reach these heights.

'They're craftsmen!' said Nil from behind his own tree across the way. 'Their bows are shooting themselves!'

Feletra ventured a peek from where she hid, and Nil was right. Three bows were just hanging there in mid-air, arrows alongside, positioning themselves one after the other. She was ready with her own, but the enemy's bows were fast and kept her trapped.

'I don't have time to aim with those arrows firing at us!' she yelled.

'You don't need time, Feletra,' said Nil, and she looked at him curiously, 'I've seen you shoot.'

Feletra lingered, she had not applied her skill in a situation like this before, against actual craftsmen. Even against Korsthr she did little…but she couldn't stay there all day, that was not how they won in battle.

With a leap of faith and something brazen in her gut, Feletra threw herself out from her hiding spot and shot at the craftsmen with lightning speed. She hit one of them instantly, hearing a cry, though she would have called her aim poor from the falling snow and the rush to stay alive. She was quickly forced to shield herself again. The bows of the offenders were far closer than the craftsmen themselves, and continued to move in on them.

‘Staying here is suicide, we have to run!’ said Feletra.

‘We won’t get far,’ said Nil, ‘not with those arrows trained on us either way. I will run out and take down the bows, that leaves you free to shoot the craftsmen –’

‘Nil, you can’t, you’ll be killed –!’ she was interrupted by an arrow whooshing straight under Nil’s nose, there was no time to talk. ‘I have an idea.’

‘Feletra, if you’re using your abilities, it has to be right now, the bows are nearly on us –’

‘Shh!’ Feletra fell into focus, it may have wasted all the time they had left if she failed now, but she had to forget the bows. She blurred them out of the picture entirely…in their place, she positioned a seed, and as the seed just floated there, it began to crack. The sound of it was loud in her head, as loud as the bow of a ship dividing as it crashes into an iceberg. The seed she saw was bursting open, and from within came thick vine leaves and a single delicate yellow flower that lifted its head…

Nil had been watching the whole time – he witnessed the wood of the bows split apart just as Feletra’s seed had done, and incredibly, the same leaves and flowers that sprouted forth from them. The cleaved bows fell to the ground in splinters and the vines continued to grow, curling themselves around the arrows and snapping them in two.

Feletra opened her eyes, feeling certain she had achieved what she set out to do. Still, even at the silence of firing arrows, she looked around the tree, and smiled seeing the weapons in pieces. Nil was subtly overjoyed next to her.

Then they were met with a response that echoed impressively around the forest. 'So, it is games you want to play?' it crowed with amusement.

Feletra held her breath as kept as still as a statue. She glanced at Nil, who shook his head, though she could not say what he was shaking it at. To be quiet? That he knew their next move? Or some remote arrogance of their abilities after Feletra's example?

It didn't matter which it was, for his expression quickly changed again – suddenly they felt their trees, their only protection, vibrate from the roots and judder through their spines. They each took a step back and watched the trunks as they creaked and groaned and the bark shifted of its own accord.

Nil shot Feletra a knowing look, the craftsmen really were playing with them. The trunks began to split outwards from the middle, wrenching open a gaping hole in the wood that would tear both the trees apart to leave them exposed.

Feletra looked on in indignation; these men could have walked right up to them and killed them in cold blood in a heartbeat, but no, they preferred point-scoring and playing the game, using Feletra's own idea against her. They needed to make a decision; only Nil's mind seemed made up.

'Ok, now we should run,' he finalised, 'keep close and –'

'No, no, wait, Nil. Just wait.'

As soon as she said the words, she wondered why she had. What plan did she have? No plan. But she felt she should make one. Why did it seem Nil never had any faith in her? He should give her more chances, she was improving her control with every passing day. Every day she got stronger, she just needed to prove it.

Time was running short in her split-second thoughts – the tree before her was dividing wider, the gap was large enough to shoot arrows through and she ducked down for cover. *Think, Feletra, think.* Doubtless, her father at a time like this was have told her not to be hero unless she had it all figured out. Father. Where was he now? She almost forgot he was out there, hunting her. No. Stop. Mind in the game.

The game…the game of copy-cat. You couldn't copy what you couldn't *see*.

Out of nowhere, Nil had made a leap for where Feletra knelt and missed another arrow.

'We need to act now,' he roughly grabbed her bow.

'No, Nil, stay down. I have it!' Feletra protested. She went to snatch her bow back as Nil tried to pinch an arrow from her quiver in desperation.

Too late – the tree shattered to pieces around them and they covered their heads.

They didn't move, fearing it was over. There was a brief laugh from one of the craftsmen, more of surprise, and then he said. 'Clever ones, you two. Come out, come out to play. We can up the stakes a little.'

Feletra slowly lifted her head, he was spinning a dagger in mid-air above his palm. He was but ten paces away, standing between the other four craftsmen, and she noticed her own arrow protruding from one of them in the shoulder. *Just the shoulder? I need more practice in these conditions…*she thought.

Their lead stood fearlessly among them, his were the darkest features; intense oil-black eyes like a horla, a tidy beard framing his heavy jawline, shaded Chriahk skin, thick wintry wear with military detail and a woollen hat to tuck away a mass of charred curls. And yet he looked right at her. Once. Maybe twice. He was scanning the forest for them.

Nil noticed it too, but neither of them dared speak. Could they really not see them?

Feletra slowly rose to her feet, soundless, and Nil followed suit. They waved their arms in front of them, and felt confident enough to smile at each other. There was an invisible sheen between them, or a sphere surrounding them, she couldn't quite tell yet. But she had done it, this she did know, for the Konexa was bubbling in her blood at that very moment. Afax could be seen poking his head out from between the evergreen needles above them anxiously, took one look at the men before them and delved back up high again.

Nil gave Feleta a congratulatory nod, which she basked in for a few moments. But how well were they hidden? The craftsmen, whilst blind, did not appear fazed, they were accustomed to the abnormal, and began to disperse themselves from the group.

The lead craftsman came forward towards them, they could not wait there idly. Together, with all stealth, Feletra and Nil slinked away from their destroyed tree refuge. They stepped onto the pieces of shattered bark and branches that lay strewn everywhere, conscious of avoiding leaving footprints in the snow. They watched where each of the craftsmen were going cautiously.

'How far do you really think you can get?' said the craftsman, and he held up his bow, ready to strike in the wrong direction. Then he slowly swung the bow round in a circle, when it reached them was exactly when Feletra looked back at him; suddenly she thought they were visible again and that her power had worn off. In a panic, she slipped and fell face-down into the snow.

The craftsmen were alerted to the noise. ‘Over there!’

‘Get up, Feletra – move!’ Nil yanked Feletra back onto her feet and they ran.

Arrows were firing past them at all speed, but the aim still remained poor unlike before, and Feletra guessed, gratefully, that they must still be invisible.

The snow seemed to deepen the further inland they ran, Feletra thought they must be making barely any progress to escape, for they had to wade through the knee-high snow like water. Every step felt sluggish and they were acutely reminded that had they been visible, they’d have both been long dead by now.

Feletra knew not how to run in such challenging conditions, she gave no thought into perfecting her escape as effectively as Nil’s vaults and bounds, and was driven to stumbling more than once, driven by the craftsmen’s hunting calls behind them.

Noticing her struggle, Nil grabbed Feletra’s hand firmly and pulled her onwards, he led them successfully to the east until they reached a river. Feletra felt her heart sink, there was no way across, but to her amazement Nil did not hesitate.

He grasped her hand even tighter. ‘Jump!’ he yelled.

Feletra had no time to protest, and she thought in that heart-stopping moment as she leapt, that she did not want to protest. She was through with making a fuss, delaying the inevitable, and resisting those things she feared. The water ran rapid and turbulent below her. It was deep – her feet would not touch the bottom, she could see that. And it was guaranteed to be freezing, she would be lucky to come out with a chill, let alone alive. And yet she leapt forward – with all her might she leapt, and the water was every part as she imagined and more.

She was fortunate to have Nil still holding onto to her, or she might not have made it to the surface, but he miraculously raised her to safety. She gasped hoarsely at the raw, stony air. The current dragged them downstream a little, but the river was littered with stray rocks and logs and Nil found it easy to attach themselves to one of these.

Feletra made an attempt towards the bank but Nil warned her off.

'Stay in the water,' he instructed quietly.

Feletra then realised his incentive, they would never get away so long as they kept leaving tracks in the snow to follow. Afax had followed them racing through the treetops above, until he had made that leap with them with instant regret – now he scrambled to the very summit of Nil's head where he was furthest from the water and shivered violently.

The craftsmen all appeared at the top of the river bank and came to a halt, searching the scene with their eyes hungrily. Still they were blind to the two companions. Feletra found it searingly difficult to control and regulate her breathing from the biting cold, but she couldn't afford to let them hear her. Yet the heavy current must have been loud enough to drown that out, and what of their breath? Could they see those thick, translucent clouds billowing out of them? Feletra carefully placed a hand over her mouth.

Nil's plan appeared to be working.

'Very good,' said the lead craftsman, and he began to

laugh to himself as they all walked away towards the south.

Chapter 19
Dark Territory

It had been too long, Flior knew it had. Padryl should have returned with Feletra by now. He knew the land better than her, how had he not found her yet? Where was he? Where was she? No, he knew where Feletra was, in a hateful land, where deceit flowed in the very water they drank, animosity bleeding out of the air they breathed and ashes that contaminated it without the need for fires.

Flior realised, sitting by the fire in silence with Estra, that the next time he saw his sister, he may only be greeting her lifeless body, if that benevolent bounty was even granted. There could be nothing, nothing but a message from an ebrat, nothing but an educated guess that she was gone. Nothing but a memory. Yet he had let her go…she had been young and inexperienced but he had let it all happen, even helped her.

Flior trusted Feletra, he trusted there was always a reason for everything she said or did, he had watched her grow up this way. Feletra had always had good foresight, though it had been overlooked by her other brothers and sister, and even she overlooked herself for it sometimes. Flior fondly remembered one day, in the blistering heat, when they all took turns to refill Banu's water, and each of them would trudge back home from the River Kestors with a single canister, but Banu drank so fast that Feletra took it upon herself to take Banu, her father's trailer and three barrels. Banu was rewarded with a drink from the river itself, and the family were rewarded with no more trips to and fro. Lampaea, Skepreo and Ataleka had argued of course that they would have done the same if they had known how hot the day would become. But Feletra had known, she had anticipated how much it would affect Banu on a working day, but she had been the only one to do anything different. Padryl was very attached to his tools and equipment, including his trailer, but when Feletra felt certain of something, nothing could stop her. She was not one to ask for permission or advice when she saw that a solution was absolute, and she took that trailer that day, without a trace of conjecture. Flior admired this about his sister above all else.

'I know what you did, Flior,' said Estra monotonously, the firelight casting wild shadows in the hollow between her hair and her cheekbone. Flior did not feel the obligatory flutter of the heart that one experiences when they have been caught at something. His mother was sharp, sharp as a razor even, he needn't have guessed how far the wool had been pulled over her eyes. But he no longer cared, his agitation had been growing at the same rate as Ataleka's curse, day after day ever since he had watched Feletra take his horla away over the plains. And a fear, a fear that merged with everything in his head and was becoming unbearable. No doubt Estra would mention some guilt he must be feeling, he waited for it patiently. And he had made up his mind, he had made it five starbands ago, but hadn't found the heart to act upon it yet. Feletra would have acted upon such a mind.

Finally, he made eye contact with Estra.

'She trusted me to keep it quiet,' he said, 'and I trusted her to do the right thing. She knew her own mind better than anyone the night she left.'

‘That, I do not doubt. Feletra has always been headstrong, stubborn like her father. She has always tried to solve every problem, even those that were beyond her. But this, my son, is beyond her; what I fear is that her heart leads her, for Ataleka, and stamps over her head. She seeks the cure…but at what cost?’

‘Do you believe in it?’ asked Flior all too suddenly, he could barely draw a reason why he had indeed asked, for he secretly believed, and he had forced himself, for Feletra’s sake, to come to terms with that. Steady, down to earth Flior believed in a myth. ‘The cure? Do you believe it is out there?’

Estra studied her son with a slow-forming frown.

‘I believe my eyes,’ she replied succinctly.

Flior knew her response was just as viable and logical as the one he would have once given had he been asked the same question long ago, but her disbelieving tone irritated him now, and he fought not to release the sigh that would have inevitably signalled controversy.

And then Estra, right on cue, ‘How long have you fought with the guilt for letting her go?’

Flior’s eyes darted away again, in the blinking firelight it might have seemed there was no movement in them at all.

‘I have no guilt, only fear,’ he told her, careful that his tone was not too attacking, ‘I fear for her life, that much is obvious. But I have made my decision, I will find her.’

And then Flior was about to disappoint Estra.

‘Go to your father first,’ she said, ‘he must be lost, else they would have returned by now together. Then find Feletra and bring her back.’

‘No,’ Flior replied without hesitation, and Estra snapped

to attention. He knew that was what she assumed he would do, but bringing everyone home and continuing to do nothing would solve…nothing. Ataleka would only worsen, but Feletra was giving him a chance to live again. She was risking life and limb for him, and Flior was not prepared to let her waste that.

'I want you to listen to what I'm about to tell you, Mother. Feletra did not leave without guidance, she had a vision, and in that vision she saw Ataleka's curse and her own, and then she saw a way out, she saw the place she could find this cure and end it all, and I have wished her well ever since. But I can't keep standing by and waiting, not when she could be in trouble. And something is changing in Esilence, I can feel it. That preathin was enough of a warning that something isn't right. I think if anything else happens, you should take everyone and go to Orpegh. Promise me.'

'Flior, this is –'

'Promise me,' Flior reiterated sternly. He had learnt it from her, and now he used it against her.

Estra paused, it was all Flior needed to see to know she complied, though she showed no sign of wavering.

'I promise,' she said earnestly, 'but Flior, what of this vision? You know how Feletra is, she sees or hears one thing and that is all it takes for her to go gallivanting off. She needs to come home, she is stricken with grief for Ataleka and has clouded her mind with her own emotions.'

'Feletra has a clearer mind than you think. I will not bring her home, I'm going to help her.'

x

Lampaea was out for blood. The face of Alaxas had burned into his skull almost more than Halemedra's, he would have his head. There were times on the last leg of the journey, into the early hours when he took watch and his comrades slept, that he feared what these new thoughts would do to him. The need for revenge was consuming him, it was buried deep into his flesh, as if from those moments of being so physically close to Alaxas he had passed it on like a contagion.

Lampaea let none of these thoughts slip to Bren or the others, they had already thought him a liability at one point, and this was simply not the time for confiding. Perhaps it never was the time; Lampaea had never been a sharer, it wasn't his way. Skepreo would have heard the most, but even he had never been told about the first meeting with Halemedra, the way he adored her, or the fact that he almost ran away at the age of fourteen after the most intense argument with his father and that, if Estra hadn't talked him into staying because Skepreo looked up to him, he likely would never have returned.

On the last day of their journey to Eastern Enphiah, just as Pytheria was setting once more for the night, they had reached the border. The easterns, proud of their statement that this was their land, had erected a magnificent wall dividing their region from the midlands; it was as brilliant a grey as they could have hoped for and certainly as high as they had set out to achieve, for it reached into the sky as high as the Markhim and sported deterring spikes along the top.

The emblem of Setra had been carved into the wall from top to bottom and blared animosity at them:

There was no welcome to this place, and Lampaea thought with audacity that the Setrans would have built all their walls out of lucrin had they and Chriah won the Nyvean War. Nevertheless, westerners were still permitted to cross the border, although they were often subject to questioning. The party braced themselves for this eventuality, and Bren stepped forward as their speaker, Lampaea noticed him tucking his Beltrorn-adorned black bandeau away out of sight.

'Setra!' he bellowed. It was a good, strong voice on Bren, a leader's voice. Bren was right about one thing, Beltrorns did not know stealth…here was a man who vocally and physically dominated all those around him. Men of his country strode wide, shook the earth with their boots and left large footprints in the minds of all those whom they met. 'Memorable' did not seem to justify.

There was a long wait, but Bren did not call again or look back at the others. Lampaea was about to say something, when the two great doors that halved the Setran emblem cracked open slowly. The noise was like thunder, roaring and cavernous across the Acrounian plains.

Once the doors were fully open, the scene was followed by more silence; Lampaea could see leagues of Setra laid out before them in rolling hills but there was no one to greet them. He supposed a greeting was too close to a welcome, and approached Bren's side, Taiso and Miksandh followed.

'Should there be someone here?' said Lampaea curiously, during his short trip to Mereta there were guards immediately on hand to interrogate. 'It feels like a trap.'

'I don't know,' Bren answered, 'but someone is clearly watching us. Don't go for your weapons or they may quickly change their minds about letting us in.'

'Bren!' Taiso piped up, a frown of deepest concern creasing his forehead. 'If this *is* an ambush –'

'My gut tells me otherwise. Be on your every alert but just keep away from those swords for now.'

Taiso looked horrified at the idea; it was clear that if his trust for Bren did not run deep, he would have been riding back to Olonath by now. Miksandh's anxiety, too, was showing greatly and he appeared more boyish than ever. Lampaea was past anxiety, fear, reluctance. He wanted in, and he wanted Halemedra back. He pictured her weeping, weeping at the terrible way they'd treated her, weeping with joy when she looked upon his face again. He could feel her arms around his neck already, desperate for him to take her away from the darkness. He was determined to show her the light still existed, burning bright and waiting. He would coax her into the warmth again.

They rode on forward and past the gate warily; Lampaea could sense how much Taiso was just itching to lay a hand on his hilt. Straight ahead of them, the Setran Valley opened wide its hands to the River Hadrican that banqueted from them with voracious appetite. And from the river all the veins of those hands spread down the valley in cracks of streams all feeding or being fed from their mother, the heart that was the Hadrican. All around the great valley there were steep hills and dales that might have once been thriving with life, but where there had been teeming forests years ago, all that remained was a dead, almost barren land. The surviving veterans of the day were scattered leftovers of fat, swollen trees that no longer bore fruit and lay strain to the earth to even beget some meagre greenery. For the aching and neglected thirst that infected the earth here it was fractured; careless long grasses and reeds that leeched onto what they could amidst the shade of boulders and dusty crevices. There was no denying Setra was once beautiful, captivating even, an envy of neighbours, until she was taken by those who cared not for her beauty, those who were driven by greed and lusted after Mid and West Enphiah to take as their real trophy.

Lampaea noticed the land was burnt black in many places, and Miksandh also marvelled at the Setrans' recklessness. 'What happened here?' he pondered.

'You need to ask?' Lampaea replied.

Taiso added his own disgust to the observations with a shake of his head, and then he turned to his lead, 'Bren, how do we even find Maliste? Should we just keep going towards the valley?'

As soon as he had finished the question, three men on horlas were galloping their way over from the northern hills. Bren halted the others until they arrived.

'What is your business in Setra?' said the lead of the three. He was a tall man, even on horla-back, though from his shock of unkempt blond hair he appeared weatherbeaten, as if he had been on watch at this gate for too many days. One of his lackeys behind him carried the Setran flag proudly.

Obnoxious, thought Lampaea, not even at war and still shoving it in our faces like we are inferior. There indeed was the traditional Setran welcome.

The men had perhaps assumed they would venture through Setra honestly, fuelled by their own patriotism for the West and the Midlands. That was the Beltrorn way, wild, unabashed and only action. It came with some surprise then, when Bren answered instantly with a rather different story of his own.

'We are summoned from Tethip,' he announced clearly, 'here to aid the trafficking from the north into the east. We are all highly trained in combat, and for our skills Setra has requested our help.'

Lampaea was impressed with Bren's quick thinking. Not only had he provided a viable excuse but he had also explained the presence of their weapons. And to claim they were from Tethip (despite the fact that Taiso was forced to hide his expression of disgust) was the most believable part he could have added. The Tethirians had been branded for their treachery for two thousand years, it was not unheard of for them to be seen with the enemy.

'We are unaware of any Tethirians due to be visiting. Summoned by whom?' said the weatherbeaten lead, he did not yet seem convinced, but then perhaps it was his job to appear as sceptical as possible. Scepticism induced pressure, and pressure broke weak links such as what Bren's story should have been, but Bren remained staunchly credible in his delivery.

'A commander under the lead of Alaxas. He has requested we do not share his own name until we have arrived at Maliste, there are fears of information leaks, I am sure you understand.'

The lead gave no acknowledgment to this, he looked between the four of them inquisitively.

‘Alaxas?’ he said.

‘That’s right.’

‘It is unusual for him to deal with men –’

‘He never talks to us,’ one of his lackeys interrupted regrettably, ‘just flies straight past on that big old swenph –’

‘Quiet. Alaxas avoids sharing his business with anyone other than fadres unless it concerns the master. He conducts most of his dealings outside of Setra, I suppose this is what he has been doing, recruiting…’

‘And killing innocents,’ added Lampaea suddenly, he couldn’t help himself.

‘What’s that?’

Bren stepped in quickly. ‘My comrade was recalling the great feats of his, he truly is a credit to the master.’

‘Yes, I was admiring his…*methods* with the common folk,’ said Lampaea, seething beneath his sycophantic tone.

The lead studied Lampaea in silence, until his subordinate with the flag spoke up. ‘Typical Tethirians,’ he sniggered, ‘always ready to lick someone’s boot.’

‘If you would but show us the way to Maliste,’ Bren stressed, ‘we have never set foot inside Setra before and are pressed for time, a guide would be greatly appreciated.’

They could not tell how much this man suspected them as frauds and intruders, he maintained the face of utter dubiety. Lampaea felt not even half the concern of the other men that he might not believe their terrible story. In fact, he felt it was slowing them down, an attack would have been far more efficient. After all, they were Setrans, an attack was imminent at some point.

‘Very well, I will show you.’

Much to their surprise, the lead was preparing to take them inland. As he instructed his two men to stay on guard at the gate, Bren glanced at Lampaea for his intrusion with a hint of glare. Lampaea couldn’t blame him, he knew it had been reckless.

They began to make their descent into the valley, it appeared the easiest way was to follow the river directly, although their guide explained that the winds in the east were the worst, and for that it was best to avoid the high ground and the mountains. Once he was far enough ahead and out of earshot, the four men sidled their horlas in together.

‘Tethirian!’ Taiso kept his outburst as stiflingly quiet as possible. ‘You could have picked anywhere, Bren, but Tethip? That is an insult that will follow me to the grave…’

‘You cannot fault the logic for saying Tethip,’ Miksandh grinned, ‘at least Bren thought of a way to get us to Maliste.’

‘Though I might have lost it for Lampaea’s addition,’ Bren reckoned.

Lampaea said nothing. He was already steeped in a state of dampened rage to keep them happy, if he had ridden out alone to Setra it could have been all swords blazing by now, no one standing in his way, the stealth saved for when he would arrive at Maliste. A part of him did think it was a blessing he had anyone for company to keep his heart on the ground and his blade in its sheath; ever since Alaxas had said those horrific words the anchor chained to his brain had snapped just like string and any sense he had left was begging for all six eyes of the men to be trained on his every move in case he ruined everything.

They were led down to the riverbank, where the land was flattest and the horlas were able to canter at a reasonable pace; the party were able to spot parts of the land that still flourished and preserved Setra for all its former glory, great canyons that collapsed in layers around the winding river, the folds of moss-smothered rock were smooth and rolling, until the greenery turned to grey and brown again and they rode deeper into this intriguing notch of Enphiah.

Even the wildlife was different here in the east; mostly they saw cattle up on the hilltops, but their cattle appeared stranger, larger but skinny with spiral horns on every one and a crazed look in their eyes. Western cattle would have moved on but these froze like cats sensing prey was near as the men came close, eyes bulging blue and fixated on them.

'Don't let the camah bother you,' said the Setran, 'they have greater problems with the foxes.'

Lampaea followed where he pointed to the tops of the valley. Looking down upon the scene were nine or ten imbruvia foxes, or the Imbruvium as they were sometimes known. No ordinary foxes, these beasts were huge and their heads reached a grown man's crown; clad in thick, auburn-sunset fur, they were fierce and answered to no one but the fadres. The most curious thing about the Imbruvium however, was their night-casting abilities. At their will, they could blanket a place in pitch blackness, darker than any corner of the wildest night. In Blackcraft practice this was known as the Craft of Shades, but no craftsman had ever matched the dark arts of the foxes. Lampaea could not explain why but he felt a cruelness from them, a sense that they detested the world and took joy in sucking the light out of it. He could not tell if he might have felt different had they been travelling though some other land, or if he hadn't a new found hatred for fadres and knew very well from his mother's books the affinity these beasts had for them.

'Will they attack?' asked Taiso.

'Only if we stop,' came his answer.

Once they left the valley the Setran took them south across a vast plain of marshlands. The winds whipped high here and battered them in all directions. The terrain too, upset the horlas as the sludge restricted their every move and progress felt slow and laborious.

Miksandh's horla stumbled into Alefthera after another sudden assault of the wind.

'Do you think he is leading us astray?' said Miksandh with his new doubt.

'If he is, he's an even greater fool,' Lampaea replied, cocksure that the man stood no chance against the four of them, but then even he thought it bold of himself to underestimate the situation. They were in Setra, and if Alaxas had any sense he would have alerted this apparent master of his that four men were at large and on their way into the country…if there was indeed an ambush waiting, they would need to think one step ahead.

The marshlands thickened out into a meadow that stretched for at least ten leagues; far ahead were the snow-capped mountains of Eristenon, and to either side were sparse woods. And then Lampaea was on high alert. They were too exposed here, he looked to the trees in the east, and he looked to the trees in the west. Something was not right.

'What is that?' said Bren, nodding straight ahead. Lampaea had been so busy inspecting everywhere else that he missed what sat right in front of him. Specks of rain began to fall.

'That is Maliste,' said the Setran, slowing down. *Why was he slowing down?* 'I am sure your services will be well received here in Setra.'

Nestled in the heart of the meadow between them and the mountains stood an enormous black tower, topped with what appeared to be the Setran emblem. There was a wall encircling the whole structure, at least a league wide. The rain grew heavy.

'Thank you. Why do we stop?'

The Setran failed to respond. Bren rode in closer to his horla and looked him dead in the eyes, 'Why have we stopped?' he repeated with intimidation. The man blinked and glanced momentarily to the eastern woods.

Lampaea saw it. That was all he needed. Silently, he withdrew a knife.

'This is where I leave you –'

'Take us to the gate at Maliste, I insist,' said Bren firmly, 'you must tell them who we are.'

The suddenly anxious Setran hesitated, and then said, 'Very well, follow me.'

Lampaea stole his opportunity.

'Forgive me, Alefthera,' stealthily, he drove the knife into the horla's shoulder muscle, not far enough to do terrible damage, just enough for her to bleed profusely. When she reared up on her hind quarters in utter shock, Lampaea managed to rapidly hide the weapon under his coat as the company set their eyes on him after the horla's cry.

'My horla is wounded!' Lampaea called above the pounding rain, he pressed his palm to the wound delicately to stem the flow.

'Lampaea!' Bren approached from the front to inspect the commotion. 'What happened?'

'Something in the meadow grass attacked us – it caught Alefthera in the side. She cannot go on, I must stop the bleeding.'

The Setran lead appeared next to them.

'Your horla has served. Ride pillion with one of your friends and let us be gone.'

Bren wore an expression of irritation as his patience grew thin with this man; this was no way to treat any horla, least of all a Beltrorn-bred one.

'I need the cover of the trees,' said Lampaea, confident of Bren's acquiescence, 'I can do nought in this rain. Come, I won't keep us long.'

Bren nodded without delay and signalled to the others. The Setran's irresoluteness was sensed by all but they moved on to the woods contrary to his advice.

Taiso turned back to him, his aggravation also beginning to show. 'Why do you linger? Is there something in those woods we should know about?'

The Setran dawdled a little longer, then all at once rode off to join them. 'No, nothing.'

Lampaea was dressing Alefthera's wound as carefully as he could with Miksandh by his side but his hands were notably feverish and his distraction was escalating. He had led them to where the assailants lay, he knew the situation was not too much of an improvement but at least they were even now; it was harder to shoot through trees than out of them. The rain was also held off impressively by the canopy, now it was simply a case of warning the men, he was certain they had no idea. But the Setran, he knew everything.

'What is your name, Setran?' asked Bren.

'And why is that necessary?' the man replied defensively.

'I merely mean to mention your name to the commander in light of your good service leading us here.'

The Setran's mouth stammered opening and closing. 'Ebenaea,' he said finally.

'Thank you, Ebenaea,' Bren shook his hand, though his eyes were cold. Lampaea wondered how long he could keep up this amicable, receptive act, it was some achievement but far out of character. It was about to disappear.

'Alefthera is stronger than she looks,' Miksandh observed, 'we stemmed the bleeding in good time. She is well enough to continue.'

But Lampaea had other things to observe. There, he saw it – a fadre crouching in the undergrowth, aiming a crossbow straight at Bren's head.

'Ambush! Bren – get down!' he cried.

Bren was quick to act – he dodged the arrow narrowly as he dived to the ground but found himself at Ebenaea's feet who swiftly drew a sword to slash his throat. Taiso reacted just in time and threw a small axe in Ebenaea's direction, where it struck him neatly in the abdomen. He fell to his knees, clutching at the wound and malice shining in his eyes for them.

Lampaea had slammed himself to the ground and whipped out an arrow for his bow immediately as flurries of the fadre arrows hissed and flew past them from every direction. They seemed relentless, there must have been several attackers waiting for them to arrive.

Lampaea carefully turned to lie on his back; he could not see any of the men for the undergrowth lay thick around them.

'Bren!' he called, and there came a reply instantaneously.

'Lampaea – do you see how many there are?'

'The forest is too dense, I can't tell. Ten, maybe twelve at a guess. Are Taiso and Miksandh there?'

'They're with me –' said Bren, he sounded as though he had just avoided another arrow.

'We must make a stand!' came Taiso's voice.

Just as Lampaea began to think this was not the wisest of ideas at that moment, he was forced to change his mind. The shooting stopped almost immediately, they were moving in on them. For a second, all he could hear was his own heartbeat. And then he heard it, and he could not understand it. Someone spoke words in Fadic, the voice was calm, wispy yet powerful.

'Get up, Lampaea. Slowly,' Bren spoke to him now, he was responding to someone else's request.

Lampaea rose gradually from the undergrowth, poised as if ready to pounce, his bow strung tight in his hands. Thirteen fadres encircled them, long bows and crossbows at the ready. Three of them each held a short sword to the throats of Bren, Taiso and Miksandh. *They had moved so silently, how was it even possible?* Lampaea thought. All the fadres had their faces covered with hoods and red bandeaus, all but one.

Alaxas stepped boldly through the middle of the entrapment towards Lampaea, who held fast on his defence, his eyes ablaze with fury.

'You are…outnumbered,' Alaxas smiled, referring to his

comrades surrounding him.

'But I could still kill *you,'* Lampaea spat, his fingers trembling on the strings.

Alaxas took a step closer, his face inches from the arrow tip. 'And if you do, you and your friends will lose your lives in the blink of an eye. Tell me, Lampaea of Elpura, is my life, and your insatiable thirst for revenge worth that much to you?'

Lampaea hated his voice. Had it emanated from fadre or man, he still would have hated it; it was like a wound that not only bled but gushed with repugnance.

He looked over at the men, their faces were as brave and steadfast as ever, and he found himself lowering his bow.

Alaxas looked at Bren patronisingly. 'Tell him.'

'Drop it, Lampaea,' said Bren thickly, 'and your sword.' Lampaea was forced to oblige, and let the weapons fall into the undergrowth. 'Now run.'

'What?' Lampaea thought he heard wrong.

'Run!' Bren yelled.

In a flash, Lampaea saw his training days with his father again: *what do you do when they're encircling you? What any sane man would do, dive and roll.* And he dived straight down. With not a second wasted, Lampaea missed all nine arrows that had been trained on him, some of them striking the fadres themselves – he rolled out of the circle until he was behind one of them, slit his throat with his own knife and backed away with the fadre as a shield as more arrows were fired.

'Kill him,' Alaxas looked murderous. He was down to five archers on Lampaea's tail, the other four had been struck with Fadic arrows, strong enough to pierce their skin. In men, they would split skin, flesh and bone.

Lampaea had dragged the fadre as far as he could, then dropped his lifeless body and tore through the woods. He ran faster than them, and could hear their cries shrinking away. But still he ran, on and on, driven by energy, fear, anger – he had no idea where he was going. Half the time he had been running there had been silence and no pursuers left; finally, he stopped. His breathing was hoarse and his chest was heaving – he looked around him everywhere, spinning in circles.

He was alone.

x

As Emmet lifted free his ankle from one of the heavy chains that snaked across him, he peered up at his open cell window which felt leagues away. The dawn was breaking, but Pytheria still shied away from Rukur, the rain from yesterday had continued its relentless slog all night, and Emmet began to wonder if it was here to wash away the terrible things he had done, or just wash him straight out of Esilence when he hung today. They had kept him there for sixteen days.

He heard faint voices outside that came to him like murmurs, they were congregating, it must nearly be time.

Why must they always gather a crowd for executions? Can a man not die in peace? They do not even know why I am sentenced to death.

Now that his cause had been stripped from him, and all that he had done been rendered worthless by the people he had relied on, Emmet suddenly felt that his whole life had come to nothing. Since the day he was born, he had accomplished nothing. He let his brother die, likely sent

Feletra to her death for not stopping her and now all of Enphiah would perish, ripped apart by preathins because he foolishly thought Menkhrist would help. And Dynetii. Fiery, untamed Dynetii…what had they done to her? She had been Emmet's beacon of hope, and now even that light had been quenched in a stone cage somewhere. How he wished he could see her one last time…he knew they had imprisoned her. Dynetii had cunning, intelligence and impatience, she would have found him and released him by now if that were not the case.

Emmet watched as a rat scurried up to him and sniffed around his shoes curiously.

'You had a choice, and you chose to live in the dark,' Emmet said, just as curious.

A sound of sliding bolts came sudden, and the rat dashed away. A burly prison guard appeared at the bars to Emmet's cell, he unlocked it and then stepped aside, revealing Menkhrist.

Emmet rose to his feet hastily, his blood beginning to boil at the sight of the man.

'How did you find our quarters?' Menkhrist said airily. 'Did you sleep well?' he stepped inside.

'Dynetii. Where is she?' Emmet had felt certain his words would spill with venom, but they only poured into the cell with despair.

'She is learning the error of her ways, she is no longer any concern of yours.'

'You wouldn't harm her,' Emmet's tone came out half question, half statement, but deep down he wanted reassurance. It never came, for Menkhrist felt no shame in allowing him to believe the possibility.

'The man you maimed half to death –'

'Dox?'

'Yes, we let him go. It took him a while to recuperate, of course. You are quite more mad than we first thought, gouging out an innocent man's eye and that –'

'Innocent!' Emmet's anger echoed around the stone cell and his chains shook dangerously. 'That man wanted both me and Dynetii dead!'

Menkhrist sighed, 'I had come here with the sympathy that you might have come to some remorse. I see now that perhaps I was wrong to think that.'

Were Emmet not physically and emotionally drained he might have laughed. The man's sympathy fell as brutally short as his intelligence. He said no more.

Menkhrist hovered on the moments that he naively expected Emmet to squeeze all his begging and pleas for mercy into. When he saw that his prisoner would not be wavering today, he wore a look of expectancy and surprise and ambled out of the cell.

'He is ready,' he said to the guard, who wasted no time in unlocking Emmet's shackles and gruffly leading him out and up a stone staircase. He was led outside into the rain, where two more guards marched behind; the city folk stopped and stared, many of them hanging out of doorways and windows, craning their necks to get a better look at the criminal. Emmet had been wrong about one thing, no crowd had been formed at all, they had no idea what was happening, their faces all of confusion yet steeped in intrigue. Menkhrist had not kept the silence for Emmet's sake though, he had done it to keep them all there, in his beloved, rotting Rukur. Any whisper of preathins and they would flee, as they should have done days ago. Emmet pitied them, they were blinded by a man already blinded with fear.

'I want to see Dynetii,' Emmet said suddenly, or uttered, his words began to fall down his throat with every swallow as he took each step closer to his end. The guard dragging him seemed not to hear.

'I need to see Dynetii!'

Suddenly the guard answered with a blow to the stomach. 'You don't make demands!'

Emmet buckled as the wind was knocked right out of him. There were a few gasps from the onlookers; Emmet wished this was normal practice in Rukur, and that they would all go back to carrying out their mundane lives, bored of seeing yet another criminal walking to his execution.

They reached a set of heavy gates leading to a courtyard, and in the centre of the courtyard there stood a stage, a wide table to one side, and three dangling nooses to the other. Emmet bet Menkhrist wanted him on the middle one. They pushed and poked him in the back until he was indeed in line with the middle noose. Emmet tried to ignore the frayed cords, hanging in the air like the tongue from a beast looming over him, a hot breath was the breeze and hungry spit dampened his skin in the soft rain.

There were louder cries of excitement and morbid curiosity now, the city folk pressed themselves into the closed gates, pushing and pulling each other away for a better view. Others were climbing the surrounding stone walls of the courtyard in an attempt to peek over the top. Four guards went to stand before the gate and block their view, but they only became louder and began to call out, 'What's going on? What did he do? Who is he?'

Below Emmet, standing smugly off-stage, was Jekron

with his hands clasped behind his back zealously. Next to him stooped a portly old man holding an open book out before him. Emmet was not surprised Menkhrist had gone back into hiding, although he imagined him watching the scene from afar somewhere.

'Emmet of Otra!' Jekron announced heartily, he was enjoying himself already. 'You stand before us, in Lor's Court of Justice, guilty of crimes for which you have been sentenced to death. Have you –' he checked the book quickly, '– any last words?'

The crowd at the gate fell silent. Emmet took the hush as a blessing, if the last sound he heard was the falling rain he would die with a clear mind. For all his failed endeavours, there would be nothing and no one to compete with that sense of black and white clarity, not even Dynetii.

'What is my crime? Name it.'

Jekron was taken aback. 'Your sentence has already been delivered by my father, you know your crimes –'

'Name it! Your people would hear the answer, not I,' Emmet stared Jekron down staunchly. He felt at that moment that he were the one with the power, the same evolved feeling he'd had when he had dragged Dox back to the chamber, despite the fact a noose had just been looped around his neck.

Jekron glanced to the gate at all the eager faces, even witnessing him outside of the Chandre was an exciting notion, it could only mean that Emmet was indeed the worst criminal that they had ever set eyes on.

'Very well, where to begin?' said Jekron at leisure. 'You disobeyed the Lord Menkhrist's orders when he banished you from the city, accused our fellow Enphiahn and Pyraihn leaders of conspiracy –' there was a hurried murmur at the gates – ‘killed eight innocent men out of your madness and paranoia, maim a ninth and have corrupted the mind of the Daughter of the Chandre, my sister, Dynetii.’

The murmur fell into cries of disarray and gasps of disgust. Dynetii, the favourite of the whole city, had been targeted and warped by some madman from Otra. How they looked upon him with loathing now.

Jekron appeared mildly uncomfortable for a moment, thinking of how Menkhrist had not wanted a riled crowd, and particularly no mention of conspiracy. He gave the final nod to the executioner on the stage.

Emmet did not fight it. He heard the executioner shuffling into position behind him, and then, as he tried to focus on just the rain again and its song of soft forgiveness, he saw a figure huddled low within the throngs of people cursing through the bars. There was too much shadow across the face to see properly, but a pair of hands rose up to the neck, and a gesture was being formed. What is that? A signal – the hands squeezed, opening and closing on thin air – the rain made it too difficult to see –

Emmet gingerly touched the noose about his neck, watching this entity ahead of him all the while. His fingers curled and tucked under the rope, was that right? The executioner was ready, his hand grasping the lever.

The figure continued opening and closing, it became frantic, and then the whole body began to move forward.

The executioner pulled in one go and the crowd hushed once more – Emmet desperately tried to shove his hands beneath the noose – but too late.

He hanged.

Chapter 20
Lightless and Legend

Feletra had never witnessed before such a lack of reaction to the cold. The river had been freezing, deathly so, but as soon as they had lifted themselves back onto the riverbank Nil was ready to press on. His body language had perfectly conveyed the phrase 'no time to lose!' whilst Feletra had been physically unable to stop herself shaking so violently.

The urgency to be as far away from the craftsmen as possible spurred her on, but whenever they stopped she thought the shivering was so uncontrollable that all her organs might fall out onto the snow.

Nil had whipped his cloak off and placed it around her shoulders, his body still impervious to the cold.

'How – how do you not feel it?' Feletra stammered. She sounded weak and was becoming deathly pale, Nil noticed. Even Afax had left the confines of his master to burrow under her cloak and share his body warmth.

'It's just one more league to the next village, Feneryth, do you think you can make it?' said Nil.

Feletra showed whatever surprise she could. 'A village? We can't stop at any settlement, we must keep to the wilderness.'

'You cannot go on, Feletra, not like this. You need shelter, warmth and food or you won't make it to Leohreten.'

'And the craftsmen? They're still out there, l-looking for us,' said Feletra through the shivering, though with only half the vehemence she usually had. She could not deny her strength was waning fast.

'I will take care of them if I have to, but not even your Konexa will protect us next time unless you recover,' Nil had no need to encourage her, Feletra was overcome with the urge to lie down, sleep, forget the world. She trusted in Nil's judgement for now and let him lead her to Feneryth.

When they reached the village, Feletra's body finally buckled and she fell unwillingly to her knees. Nil supported her, only thankful she had made it this far, and there were others – village folk that had seen a girl collapse. A man and a woman from a house nearby came forward and aided Nil; together they carried Feletra inside and laid her on a bed.

The woman tended to her immediately. 'What's her name?' she demanded in a rough voice.

Nil was cautious. 'Atrika,' he said.

'Alright then, Atrika,' she said a little more soothingly, though the tone was only just discernible in her grating Chriahk accent. 'My name is Cercha, we need to get those damp clothes off you and into dry ones.'

Feletra was reluctant to comply initially and held tight onto all her layers; Afax leapt out from beneath them with a ringing chirp and startled Cercha and her aaron.

'Great Ilysehr, I was not expecting a giptern to fly out at me!' Cercha exclaimed. 'Keep that thing away, will you? And gentlemen, if you wouldn't mind, this girl needs to undress. Find the boy some of the potato soup from earlier, Rhachok.'

Nil turned back before being ushered out of the room by Cercha, 'I will just be next door, Atrika,' he said with a lingering look.

'Thank you, Themson,' Feletra replied. Perfect, their

identities were set and matched.

Feletra regretted watching Nil walk away and the door close behind him, and he seemed to have something of the same look about him. They had relied on only each other for so long, it no longer made sense to be separated. But swiftly now Cercha began to remove Feletra's clothes, she did not wait for permission.

'I can do it myself –' Feletra replied weakly, she suddenly remembered her wound from the eraiik.

'Quiet now,' said Cercha firmly, 'I'll have you sorted in no t –' and she saw it then, the scar upon her side, an unnatural shade of blue not from bruising, but from the Konexa's touch. It almost glowed.

'Oh, my…' Cercha observed, then she looked Feletra square in the eyes. 'Did he do this? That boy? You can tell me –'

'No!' Feletra reacted strongly, she did not like the idea of someone accusing Nil. 'I had an accident when we were travelling, some thorns – it's nothing to worry about.'

'Some thorns as I've never seen before,' Cercha sounded clearly sceptical, but she asked no more. Her eyes however, were brimming with disbelief and Feletra could tell she was beginning to create stories in her head, most of them involving Blackcraft. It was no normal wound, anyone kymic or not could see that.

Cercha had proceeded to draw Feletra a hot bath; initially the heat and steam were a shock after bracing the biting cold in the woodland, but soon it transported her away from everything, the luxury she could indulge in and she could feel the Konexa passing though her bones at peace. She never thought she would feel its presence this way, soft, remedying and alleviating, and had only witnessed before its intensity and power, its wrath…

As she submerged her whole body under the water and closed her eyes, she listened to a steady beating that was not her heart, but her kym. It pulsed through her spirit like a dormant volcano, stronger that the Sorpha's current, waiting for only the slightest signal to come forth and erupt in all its unstoppable might. And yet here it breathed in the quiet darkness within her, mending her body with all haste.

Feletra opened her eyes. She felt strength in her again.

'Atrika!'

A pair of rippling hands thrust their way under the water and tore Feletra away from her trance by the shoulders. Startled at the disturbance, she spluttered and coughed a little as she looked into Cercha's frightened face.

'I knew I shouldn't have left you alone! To think, you could have drowned but a moment later –'

'I was not drowning,' Feletra reassured her, 'I was healing,' she spoke the words before thinking.

'You were what?'

'Nothing. I think I am ready to get out.'

Cercha passed Feletra a robe and retained her suspicion, even with a little added caution now. 'Go into the room next door, I have laid out clean clothes for you and dried your old ones. I'll bring some soup in and then you should get some rest for the night.'

'Thank you,' Feletra quickly retreated into the bedroom and changed rapidly. Cercha was there serving the soup instantly, and Feletra felt uneasy when she sat and watched her eat the entire bowl until she was finished. She whisked the empty bowl away and blew out the candle; Feletra suddenly became wary of the change in her, she seemed to be fearful almost, not wishing to linger long in the same room.

'I must thank you for your kindness,' Feletra said before Cercha could close the door, 'but…you ask nothing of us, my companion and I, who we are, where we came from?'

Her hostess hesitated before she could reply. 'My aaron, Rhachok and myself, we have been told everything there is to know from Themson. Now sleep. We can talk more tomorrow,' Cercha closed the door promptly, and Feletra felt on edge. She wanted to see Nil, what had he told them? And why had he not come to see her yet?

Feletra was then reminded of her vision again, or whatever it was…Nil betraying her in the caves at Leohreten, bringing her to death…could this have been a trap…

She tried to sleep, but it was a fruitless venture. She tossed and turned and could find no peace in her mind, and when the night was at its deepest, the doorknob turned. Instantaneously she sat bolt upright, preparing for anything.

When Nil delicately sneaked in and closed the door behind him, Feletra sighed with relief. All thoughts of betrayal had been temporarily forgotten, she looked to him with hope.

'What's been happening?' she eagerly enquired.

'We need to leave,' said Nil in a hushed voice.

'What? Why?'

'I was wrong to have brought us here. That Rhachok, he suspects something, and I do not trust him.'

Feletra looked sheepish, 'I think Cercha is the same.'

Nil frowned at her tone. 'Did she see something?'

'I tried to stop her, but she saw my scar from the eraiik –'

‘Feletra!’ Nil whispered urgently. ‘You know that scar is not normal!’

‘I know, but it was too late before I could do anything. I made something up to keep her quiet, but what of Rhachok? Tell me about him.’

Nil had been pacing softly to and fro, mulling everything over. He approached the window discreetly and stopped to peer outside. The village was calm and silent, the snow had ceased. There was opportunity to leave.

‘I saw him outside, speaking to a man on horlaback, and they looked often at the house. The rider gave Rhachok something, it looked like payment. Then he left quickly. I fear we have been betrayed.’

Suddenly, they heard a creaking floorboard from down the hallway. Together, they froze. There was another footstep, slow and deliberate.

Nil flew into action. ‘Out the window, quick.’

‘Nil, I am half-dressed!’ said Feletra desperately. ‘My shoes, my pack –’

‘Throw it all outside and get dressed out there, get far away first though. They could be craftsmen. I will follow.’

Feletra carried out the deed as quietly as she could, she was thankful her room was at ground level. Hastily, she stepped barefoot onto the snow outside as she clambered out, and gasped at the terrible sensation. Her skin mourned the warm ground of Elpura in that moment.

Feletra crept through the freezing cold as fast as her numb feet would carry her, but only reached the third house along before she was forced to fumble for her shoes. As she slumped down against a barrel, she hurriedly pulled some thicker clothes on and her coat.

Without warning, there was a loud explosion from where

she had escaped that must have woken the whole of Feneryth. Feletra crouched her way to the front of the house and peered down the main road. Debris of rock and stone had flown everywhere and littered the snow, there was a gaping hole in the wall where Feletra had slept – but where was Nil? The villagers began streaming out of their homes to witness the destruction, children wailed in fright, the women kept them close by and their hands shook with feeble candles, the men approached the scene with caution.

'Rhachok? Cercha?' they called. There was no reply.

Feletra grew anxious and craned her neck for a glimpse of Nil, still she saw nothing. Had he been out of his depth this time? She could stand it no longer, and prepared to break cover and return to the house. Instinctively, she reached over her shoulder for an arrow, but her back was bare of ammunition. She had forgotten her quiver, and now held only a bow like a half-wit.

'Feletra.'

The voice from nowhere startled her, she fell into a cart and quick as lightning there was a hand over her mouth, she was looking closely into Nil's eyes.

'Quiet,' he said, 'don't alert them.'

She shook his hand off in irritation. 'What happened in there?'

'I was right about Rhachok, he used Blackcraft on me. And missed, as you can see. I got out, found a horla and then came to find you. You didn't get that far, I see.'

'My feet were about to fall off, I had to stop. And did you say you have a horla?'

'Yes. Come round the back, before we are seen. We must leave Feneryth immediately.'

Feletra followed Nil carefully into a back alley where a

great white horla was waiting patiently, though some of the riding gear was missing. She was wary of the fact that this was one of the Chriahk horlas, it had the look through and through.

'Nil, can we trust this horla?' Feletra asked dubiously, the horla had not once stopped solid eye contact with her.

'Yes,' said Nil confidently, 'get on. Oh, and –' as Feletra mounted first Nil handed her an unspoilt quiver full of arrows, 'you might need these.'

Feletra strapped her quiver on guiltily. 'You cannot say I wasn't pushed for time.'

'All's well that ends well,' said Nil, ignoring her excuse. He mounted the horla behind her and prepared to ride, when Cercha appeared without warning at the main road end of the alley. She hobbled towards them, fully dressed, looking battered and bruised. Slowly she began to raise an accusing finger at them.

'You!' she wailed. Feletra could hear tears in her voice, and she became confused – were they not the victims here? Nil set the horla off at a powerful gallop down the street before there was any time to exchange words. Feletra looked back, but no one was following; they rapidly hit open ground once more, and Feneryth fell behind them. The snow was no hurdle for this horla, he was native and his roots ran deep here. Feletra was amazed at how well and obediently he responded to Nil's direction.

'Nil, where are we going? Leohreten?' said Feletra.

'Straight there,' he reaffirmed, 'but we will go around it. I have a feeling the caves are by the shore, under Leohrebor Mountain.'

And soon did the mountain come into view, it was magnificent. Two tall, snow-capped peaks crowned with breaking tides of cloud stood in grandeur and were united above a sweeping mass of trees that formed the Serensis Brake like a king and queen on a chessboard with their pawns.

'Where is Leohreten?' Feletra asked as she looked ahead, unable to find any give in the trees.

'Inside,' Nil answered, 'we enter the Brake.'

They were fast approaching the eastern shoreline that was garnished with the greenery of the Serensis Brake, Feletra had no idea what to expect in there. Were there more craftsmen waiting? Or Chriahk beasts fiercer than anything else she had encountered? Or was the brake a self-sufficient trap, like Whiteblind Wood?

Once inside, the horla reduced its speed to a canter. No snow fell here, the forest was dense with peculiarly-shaped trees and huge boulders, and all of it bathed in knee-high murky water.

'This is more of a swamp than a forest,' Feletra muttered as the water became deep enough to only accommodate a trot at best.

'Yes,' said Nil, slicing away at some vines that blocked their path, 'there is a darkness that lurks here, they say there are shadows that walk beneath the water. Better that we keep moving and do not stop for anything.'

Nil urged the horla on as much as possible, but there was only so fast a beast could wade. The water was not just that but also sludge, it mixed and swirled like a cauldron of poison every time they took a step. Feletra could barely take her eyes off it, anxious that she should watch for any sign of something otherworldly rising to the surface.

'There it is, Leohreten,' Nil nodded straight ahead. Feletra looked on with narrowed eyes. There, beyond the trees, rose a great white stone ridge, jagged layers took it higher and higher. And between all these layers nestled wooden houses in every nook and cranny. At the top of the ridge, a long hall reigned in white, its edges adorned with what was surely lucrin. But one thing was off, Feletra noticed.

'Where are the people?' she said.

'I don't know,' Nil replied uncertainly, 'I've never seen a town so dead.'

'It's like a graveyard…'

'I don't like it. We need to leave this place behind us quickly.'

They rode on around the town and further into the brake. Feletra did not like the look of Leohreten at all, there was a ghostly foreboding aura to all of it, not least because there were no signs of life to be seen, but a cursed feeling to the place as potent as that which seeped from the forest surrounding it.

'Wait, Nil! What's that?' Feletra had been watching the town fall into the distance behind them with scrutiny. At one of the highest houses, not too far from the white hall, something black issued from between the cracks and the foundations – it was formless, neither solid, liquid nor gas but a constant transition of all three. Gracefully and fluidly it seemed to be tasting the air almost, and then disappeared within the house once more.

'Those are the shadows I spoke of,' Nil explained, a dark tone passing into his eyes, 'but they should not be in Leohreten. Someone is working an evil here.'

Feletra felt the hairs on the back of her neck stand on end. 'What will happen if they find us?'

'I cannot say, but I do not know how to fight them.'

‘Ride on to the eastern shore. Now.’

Feletra and Nil did not see any more of the black entities known as shadows, and they had not ceased riding to witness any more, or even take the chance. The swampy terrain of Serensis tapered off as the forest came to its end; they came onto the shoreline as Pytheria began to die away beyond the clouds. To the north-east, the sea tossed and turned viciously, a beast in chains awakening from some traumatic nightmare.

The horla, still as obedient as ever, cantered across the shore beneath the watchful eyes of Leohrebor, with not one of them knowing where they should be going. There were few signs of life, and Feletra grew suspicious.

‘We are out in the open here, the guard of the forest is gone, but there is no one around? No craftsmen waiting for us?’

‘I do not think we should count our blessings yet,’ Nil warned, ‘they may be waiting at the caves. There is every chance we could be walking into a trap.’

‘Do you think these people know we want the cure?’

‘It’s possible. It’s more possible they know you are a konexic, and that is why they hunt you.’

Feletra looked on tenaciously. ‘Whatever they know, they will not come between me and that cure, I must go on for Ataleka. That is if we ever find these caves, it seems impossible to find.’

Nil halted the horla all of a sudden.

‘What is it?’ said Feletra warily.

‘Something I should have thought of a while ago,’ Nil delved into his coat and pulled out a cold and reluctant

Afax by the scruff of his neck, 'don't argue with me, get out.'

The giptern scrambled out of Nil's grasp onto the ground and glared up at him moodily.

'What are you up to?' Feletra observed curiously.

'Gipterns are notoriously good at finding rare things, within reasonable distance, of course. You have no idea how many gems and unusual plants or rocks I've been brought since having Afax.'

'That's perfect, Nil!' Feletra beamed, and then her smile faltered a little. 'But, what if I am wrong and the cure was all a lie? He won't find anything.'

'We've been through this before, you don't just believe it's out there, you know it, and I do too. And if it helps, Chriah undertook a mass culling of gipterns across the land in Men. 56, and they're not even native to Pyra.'

'That's true? They were desperate to hide something then.'

'What else could that be but a cure to everything? The very one that the Chriahks were said to have stolen from Penthor. It's more valuable than the Sorpha.'

Feletra nodded resolutely, she would find this cure with every means she had. And somehow, against all the odds, she had reached the east of Chriah and was still alive, that surely had to count for something.

'Afax, find that which we seek,' Nil commanded, 'lead the way.'

Afax turned inland, he bobbed up and down a few times slowly, grasped at the air twice, and then shot off. Nil gave the signal to the horla immediately, for Afax was a rapid creature to keep up with. They followed the shoreline at full gallop travelling south, back the way they came.

Afax had brought them further inland, closer to the mountain, he slowed down at this point and grasped at the air again whilst facing a sheer cliff face.

'Is he lost?' Feletra asked uncertainly.

'No, he knows where he needs to be, but he cannot find a way in. It is within the mountain, are you certain you saw waves in your vision?'

'Yes, without a doubt. Waves or at least some large body of water.'

Afax had had enough of staring at a dead end and sprinted off once more. He chirped at them to follow, and after another half-league stopped so abruptly the horla very nearly trampled him. The giptern sat proudly before a small opening in the rock face, just wide enough for Feletra and Nil to crawl through.

'This is not what I expected…' said Feletra with dread. Nil dismounted and went to inspect the hole, there was nought to see inside but blackness. He dipped some rags from his pocket in a little oil, lit it with flint and steel and then flung it down the tunnel like a pebble skipping across the sea. Feletra joined him to examine the result, but the passage barely widened at all as far as the illumination would indicate.

Afax leapt into the opening lightly, and continued into the tunnel without waiting for their approval.

'That's it?' said Feletra, watching him go. 'We're not going to find an easier way?'

'Afax knows the best way, we shall have to trust him,' Nil scrambled inside but sensed that Feletra was not following, 'what is it?'

Feletra backed away involuntarily, her gaze fixated on the darkness ahead. Her mind began running fast, she saw flashes of the Valley House, of Emmet, and then she heard her own struggle, her screams as a thin, bony hand grasped her ankle…it was feeding off of her…

'Feletra.'

Suddenly, Nil was stood before her; she registered his close presence instantly.

'Is there another way?' she said, her voice low, laboured, and somehow intense.

Nil shook his head. 'No. Is there something you have seen?'

'No, just memories. If there is no other way, then lead on.'

Nil followed Afax into the tunnel, Feletra took one last look at the daylight and the white horla standing by loyally, then reluctantly followed Nil. The tunnel was pitch black save for the meagre torch that Nil had thrown in; the walls were cool and damp and there was a rich smell like rotting fruit mixed with mildew consuming paper and old books. The whole thing made Feletra feel sick, and the air became as cramped and suffocating as the tunnel itself, she prayed it would open out soon.

Led by Nil's torchlight that he had collected further down, Feletra got her wish finally as the tunnel expanded into a cave that reached high into the mountain. From another tunnel above them, a beggarly waterfall issued pitifully, but it formed a stream along the bottom that led into what appeared to be an endless collection of chambers.

'Is any of this looking familiar?' asked Nil.

'I'm afraid not,' said Feletra dismally, 'I don't know what to expect anymore, I thought we'd find the cure on the coast, not inside a mountain.'

'Leohrebor is well connected to the sea, full of hidden

passageways and caves, all we have to do is find the right ones. Besides –' Afax bounded on down the stream, indicating eagerly, '– we have Afax as our guide.'

They followed the giptern downstream precariously, for the light of Nil's torch grew scarce and the ground was not only wet but rough terrain; the rocks in here were strange and like no other caves, many of them glistening blue in the firelight but also jagged or pointed, one needed only to slip in the wrong place…

'Wait,' Nil said suddenly, their path had created a fork at the edge of a steep ledge, and each new path snaked up high against the cave walls, between them both the stream widened out below. They waited for Afax to decide, he pawed at the air again, then quickly sprinted away to the path on the left.

Nil let Feletra walk in front, and then it became all too real to her; she was painfully aware that this scenario she had seen before – she died from a ledge like this, with a stream running below her, because Nil had killed her.

She tried in vain to keep an eye on him, glancing over her shoulder whenever possible.

'If you keep looking at me you'll fall,' Nil warned, 'look ahead.'

Feletra attempted to follow Nil's advice, but it was difficult to silence the voice from her gut at the same time; she tried moving faster instead, but this only made the path more slippery.

'Slow down!' Nil called, but before Feletra could stop she lost her footing and her leg was instantly trapped between two boulders, just as she had foreseen. She cried out in pain, scrambling about desperately before Nil could reach her – was this happening? Had she predicted her death?

'I'm coming!' said Nil, and he approached her too quickly for her to react. Without warning, driven by panic, Feletra rapidly grabbed her bow and arrow and aimed directly at Nil, inches from his face.

'Step back,' Feletra said viciously. Nil obeyed but had not the look of fear nor even perplexity upon his face. He kept his arms by his sides, and softly gestured with one hand to Afax, who leapt for it and climbed to his shoulder faithfully.

'Are you going to shoot me, Feletra?' he said calmly.

Feletra could barely tell if she was holding her breath or not. Her arm stood fast with her eyeline but inside her heart trembled.

'Is my life in your hands?' she said darkly.

'It has always been in yours.'

'And you would not betray me? Would you not leave me here to die?'

'Betray you? Is that what you have seen? That it was I who drove a knife into your back? Your mind plays with you but it is your heart that knows me, tell me which one you truly believe.'

'You do not seem to be a man of the heart, Nil. It's all about the mind, isn't it?'

'But yours cannot be trusted. Who knows if it is the Konexa, the curse or just your paranoia that plagues you? You need to trust me or you will die. Do you trust me, Feletra?'

Feletra tried hard not to become detached from the notion as she bored into those dancing green eyes, but she knew she was detached from the start. Slowly, she lowered her bow, she couldn't do it.

‘You’re right,’ she said in resignation, ‘I am plagued. I can no longer see who is friend and who is foe. I’m sorry, Nil. This is not me, I wish only to find the cure but now I find myself hunted by men who would see me killed, and for what reason I cannot even say.’

Feletra had almost forgotten her ankle was still trapped, until Nil bent down and helped winch her out.

‘None of this is going to be black and white, we know that,’ said Nil heavily as he faced her, ‘but if I can inject just a little grim colour to help you there, I will.’

Feletra sighed, ‘If I let you.’

‘I do not ask for permission,’ Nil took a stride around and took the lead. Feletra drew in a long breath. She was amazed at her self-control and her ability to prevent the Konexa from being coaxed out of its shell, but evermore amazed at Nil’s…loyalty? Stubbornness? Determination? She had no idea what to call it, but after everything, he was still here with her, and for that her fondness of him had only grown. That same fondness had stilled her hand, the arrow choked of its swift flight to his heart.

They approached a steep and narrow incline, peering down to the bottom they could see a shallow but active pool – Feletra was alerted to the sound of rapid running water.

‘Do you hear that?’ she said with wide eyes. ‘The water that I saw, it must be down there.’

Nil gave Afax a questioning look, to which the giptern returned confidently.

‘Well, he seems to agree with you. The bad news is, I see no steps down, the good news is that this *is* an incline, we could slide down.’

Feletra craned her neck dubiously, ‘I don’t know, it’s still a long way down –’

‘It’s just a little bump at the bottom.’

Feletra and Nil spun on their heels like lightning, they knew the sound of that ugly voice.

‘Korsthr,’ Nil said with loathing. Afax bared his teeth and revealed his long claws menacingly.

‘It has been a while, hasn’t it? It’s good to see you are exactly where we want you,’ Korsthr began to raise one hand, and Nil was quick to take the signal.

‘Move, Feletra!’

Feletra did not wait for Korsthr’s Blackcraft to brew within his hand – together with Nil and Afax she jumped down the incline and fell into the shallow pool beneath. The bare rock gave a hard impact but there was no time to linger on the pain.

‘Go, run!’ Nil urged, but Feletra scanned the great open chamber they had landed in, it seemed to be closed off entirely.

‘We can’t,’ she realised frantically, ‘there is nowhere left to run!’

Suddenly there came a great cracking noise from where they had come – a huge fissure formed in the wall followed by an explosion.

‘Get down!’ Nil shouted as the rock sprayed everywhere before them.

Out of the rubble and dust in the air strode Korsthr casually, and Feletra and Nil stood aghast at the man’s power. Behind him he left a gaping hole directly from the pool to the passage they had taken.

Feletra knew it was now or never, she had to take action or admit their death; with all the strength she could muster to the tips of her fingertips and the very edges of her skin she called to her Konexa and thrust it towards Korsthr.

'You'll need to be quicker than that,' Korsthr tutted, untouched. Feletra couldn't understand it, she had released the kym – but nothing had happened. She narrowed her eyes, noticing her vision was blurred.

'What's happening? What have you done?'

'We're divided by a shield or barrier,' said Nil, 'it's their protection craft, your power cannot reach him whilst he holds us here.'

'Not me. Him,' Korsthr replied amusedly and nodded forward.

Feletra and Nil followed the line of his gaze to where a beautiful waterfall graced the dim and abysmal cavern. Below it stood a tall man, drenched in a long grey coat that reached his ankles. His look was young but somehow wizened, his presence ominous with a tremendous cause for caution, roughened skin like chopped timber and if granite could wink – those hard, grey eyes glinted like the entrapment of a thousand silver pieces.

Feletra would have stood in some exhaustive awe had she been viewing him through another's eyes. 'Who are you?' she said, curtailing the curiosity.

The man raised one straight arm out ahead of him silently, and the waters below him began to stir; a moment passed before something swelled at the surface, and what emerged had Feletra step back despite the craft that encircled her. A beast rose like no living thing she had ever seen before, a great serpent snaked out of the depths and onto the cold rocks, its enormity sprawled out in coils sitting cramped beneath the cavern roof, twice as large as a Nova Snake. It loomed over them perilously with eyes like a cat's, Feletra was momentarily reminded of Byte at home, but Byte had no fangs like this, no jaw like this, no terrible, treacherous air like this. It took one look at Feletra and Nil and instantly charged forwards at them, but the moment it touched the sphere the beast recoiled in pain, unable to penetrate it.

Feletra knew then what this was.

'Is this what you seek?' said the man lightly. Ever so lightly. His tone was that of a polite and humble shopkeeper finding a particular item for his customer, yet the timing was just so that Feletra could detect an abundance of derision beneath it all.

It can't be, she thought with dread, *but it is.*

'I know not the name of this thing,' she said strongly, 'who are you? Tell me.'

'This is the nyrox, the creature that would turn your fortunes around. "*Cure to the wound, cure to the age'd –*"'

'"Yet lightless and legend, kept still and cage'd" ...the cure was never an object or some potion, but this beast you have kept imprisoned.'

The man circled the pool in which the nyrox lay patiently and approached them closer. 'There is much for you to learn, though I cannot deny your courage, or even your stupidity for leaving home with so few answers, Feletra.'

'Tell me who you are!' Feletra yelled, riled at the very use of her name. 'Are you the one who has been following me?'

Korsthr snickered from behind her, and out of nowhere an eagle descended before her to land squarely next to the nameless man, the same eagle she had first met on the Plains of Nemenon.

'Akeon, and yes,' he replied with ease.

'Why?' Feletra could feel her blood boiling.

Akeon paused with a distinct look of interest about him.

‘You know what you are, don’t you?’

‘Does it frighten you?’ said Feletra with tenacity, her curiosity began to overlap her fear of what this craftsman would do to her.

‘No, it rivets me. Though I should be frightened.’

‘Why would you torment me? Dangle the cure in front of me like this when you are to kill me?’

‘You will not be killed, Feletra, you misunderstand. I have much use for you yet. Chriah – has much use for you. Do you see that beast behind me? It belongs to Chriah after a pact was made with the House of Demata. Any Enphiahn spies or in your case, thieves attempting the steal the nyrox, are ultimately considered an act of betrayal of that agreement, and a legitimate cause for war.’

‘What? Demata? That’s-that’s the House of the Penthoran Luminor?’

‘Very good,’ said Akeon softly.

Feletra’s eyes widened with disbelief. ‘No! I came to Chriah seeking only to cure my brother, not to steal it for Enphiah!’

‘It matters not,’ Akeon cocked his knee and rested one foot against a thick coil of the nyrox, then he peculiarly plucked a cherry from his pocket and ripped the fruit from its stalk with his teeth, ‘you are an Enphiahn seeking the cure, the agreement is violated. Korsthr, take the declaration to Penthor, we have wasted enough time.’

Korsthr gave a succinct nod and took his leave.

‘No, wait! You can’t go to war over this – I am not involved with the House of Demata! This is a mistake!’

Akeon turned to Feletra directly, there was the silver flash in his eyes. ‘There is no mistake, you have been an asset to us, Feletra.’

‘This was planned all along…I was just a pawn in your grand scheme. You would have gone to war with or without me, and tricked some other poor Enphiahn.’

‘You do think so little of yourself,’ said Akeon simply, ‘it had to be you and no one else. Who but Feletra of Elpura would have travelled to the Sorpha and cursed her brother?’

‘How do you know that?’

Akeon glanced past Feletra curiously. ‘Your friend is a little quiet.’

Feletra had found herself so lost in the ebb and flow of outrage and bewilderment that she had forgotten that Nil shared the sphere with her, and his lack of input had suddenly become disturbing, it was decidedly unusual of him. She looked over her shoulder, and thought her eyes had tricked her, Nil stood outside of the sphere with Afax at his heel.

‘Because he has the Souls,’ said Nil darkly, his eyes trained on Akeon, ‘he commands the Time Soul and the Fate Soul, that is how.’

‘Nil? How did you escape the barrier? And what Souls? What are they?’ seeing and hearing Nil the way she did now caused the fear to swell in the pit of Feletra’s stomach, she began to wonder if she should consider herself alone again.

‘The Souls show all that was, all that is, will be and all that could be or could have been. Few craftsmen have ever been able to control them, but he can. He can create realities within realities…I think I know now, he is the reason you are cursed, Feletra.’

Feletra had never felt so overwhelmed before, and her sheer confusion unsettled the Konexa terribly. The craft sphere shuddered and it caught Akeon’s eye. ‘I don’t understand,' she said, 'how is he responsible?'

'The man and woman you saw at the Sorpha, he created them,' Nil explained, 'I don't know who they are but they are known to him in some other reality that he accessed using the Souls. He had them appear at the exact moment you would be there, so of course, it had to be you who came for the cure. It was all too perfect, you were the Enphiahn konexic he wanted, and I am right, aren't I?' Nil directed his question at Akeon, he was fixated on him. Feletra knew not what to make of it all, she began to feel a coldness from Nil – *how did he know all this?*

'I had never doubted your cleverness,' Akeon mused, 'although leaving Chriah was certainly an exception. What throws me is your decision to let her come here, knowing she cannot take the nyrox so long as you are bound in a chemnon.'

Nil looked down. Feletra's mind was swirling with everything new Akeon said – *Nil shared a chemnon with this thing?*

'I had to protect her from you,' said Nil after the droning pause.

'Based on your whims and fancies, was it?' Akeon spat the cherry stone out into the pool forcefully, 'Still, I will take no merit from he who has guided the konexic straight into my hands. You have served well, Nerehr.'

Nerehr? Nil's full name. It hit Feletra like an arrow into her already trembling gut.

'I would never have guided her to you,' Nil said unquestionably. Feletra saw that his fists were shaking, the craftsman saw it too.

'You should not bring Arton stones into Chriah,' Akeon flexed his fingers gently, across the air he took the stone pendant that Adrenache had bequeathed Nil, 'do you know what this is, Feletra? It's a Blackcraft suppressor, but the Efordrads cannot suppress what you truly are, can they?' he was addressing Nil.

And Nil shook even more. There was something dark within him that Feletra could not relate to in that moment, a rage to end all rages, one that had festered into some toxin of immeasurable potency over every year of his life. The nyrox shifted position, seeming to also sense the change in him. Afax must have known it too, for he scurried away up onto a high stone ridge and hid there. Feletra could not have prepared herself for that which she was about to see.

'I left that behind.'

'That will never change what you did, what you are capable of,' Akeon spoke fiercely now, relentlessly, 'she knows not what you are, does she?'

'What is he saying, Nil?' said Feletra apprehensively, she was desperate to reach out to him, a part of her wishing to stand strong by his side but another part confused, afraid and despairing that would have the barrier kept between them.

'Nor of the torture,' Akeon continued, 'the sheer power you drove into their bodies until they finally stopped screaming, the Craft of Wraiths –'

'Stop!'

'The Craft of Wraiths!' Feletra exclaimed, 'the Blackcraft your mother suffers – is this the craftsman, Nil?'

There followed a deathly pause, still Nil could not bring himself to look at Feletra, and then he answered, 'My mother is dead.'

'What? You don't know for sure –'

'She is dead,' Akeon said bluntly, 'by Nil's own hands,

no less. She tried to interfere with forces she could never have even dreamed to control. The consequences were…sublime.'

'Enough!' Nil closed his eyes as if some unbearable agony had accosted him from within.

'You killed her? Is that true, Nil?' Feletra began to shake.

'She suffered, didn't she, Nerehr? Never before had she felt pain such as you had inflicted upon her, no wraiths as dark as the ones you had choked the very joy out of her with, no end to her screams –'

'No!'

Something happened then that Feletra could not have anticipated, she had to ask herself in that split second, *was that me?* But no, it was not her, it was not the Konexa losing restraint, it was Nil. What burst forth from him was some unseen power, driven forcibly by his wrath – Akeon had been prepared, the attack was parried as he held out one arm to it, fighting craft with craft – but there was some struggle in him, as his knee began to bend a little he looked directly at Feletra, held out his other hand and lifted her straight into the sphere.

Feletra cried out – the pain was unbearable, her eyes glazed over and she could barely see through the kymic mist – the sphere came alive around her body and ensnared all that she was, long tentacles of Blackcraft curled about her arms and legs and another began to feed its way in through her mouth –

'Let her down!' Nil yelled, but Akeon would not yield.

Nil ceased his attack and Akeon followed suit, Feletra fell to the floor in a heap, she felt breathless but stood up nonetheless. She knew what he was.

'You…you are a craftsman,' she said hoarsely and with

disgust.

'And a powerful one,' Akeon added with a distinct pride about him, 'he should be, after all that I have taught him. No father could have asked for a better student.'

After what came to a moment but seemed an age, Nil finally turned to look at Feletra with an indrawn breath that she could only have assumed was the sound of misplaced courage.

'I couldn't tell you,' he said, his voice the quietest she had ever heard it.

'You're…his *son*?' Feletra was horrified. *Lies. Lies. Lies. The whole time.*

'I am. I cannot hide who I am from you anymore, I'm sorry,' just like every other time, there was no waver in him, no expression, no nervous twitch, nothing.

'You planned this, there was betrayal in you from the beginning…how…?' the sphere juddered dangerously.

'You don't yet understand, Feletra.'

Feletra's eyes blackened instantly. 'Then *help* me to understand.'

She felt the kym breathing in her, with her, around her, alive and fully synced with her soul. Was there any way she could stop this power now…she had no answer, she cared not for the answer. Nil thought he knew wrath, he knew nothing, he could not begin to comprehend until he was consumed in her flames, eaten whole by a vengeful scarlet fire.

'I trusted you with all that I have,' said Feletra darkly, and then the sphere would not stop shaking all around her, 'you were one of his men, *his son,* leading me here under false pretence –'

'That's not true. I meant to lead you here but not to him.'

‘Enough of your lies. I will silence them.’

And the sphere burst wide open, like glass it shattered into pieces around the cavern. Nil had no time to react – at the first instant that Feletra was freed she cast a spectacular white fire, a great cylinder of an inferno imbued with every particle of her being – and every bit of her being in that everlasting moment was fury, a maddening storm of pure rage that she never could have felt before, unprecedented, untamed.

‘Feletra!’ came Nil’s voice, strangled above the intense roar, the fire grew and bloomed majestically. Nil did not even try to fight her power, he fell to his knees, overcome in the heat, and then his head fell to the floor. The nyrox began to writhe and thrash the water into great waves around it – it shared his pain.

It wasn’t enough, Feletra continued to burn a ring around him, for every flame was just another piece of her betrayal, of her desire to make him suffer, he would feel the pain that she felt. And then she heard Akeon’s voice to her side, shouting above the blaze.

‘If you kill him, the nyrox dies with him.’

Feletra turned to him swiftly with her ink-black eyes, a breath passed before the Konexa ceased; the column of fire vanished instantly with a hush of smoke, but Nil did not stir.

‘The chemnon?’

‘I am not really surprised he kept this one from you,’ said Akeon all too casually, he was wholly unfazed by Feletra’s display, ‘with Nil’s power invested in the chemnon with the nyrox, the cure has the best possible protection, but it seems you have now lost them both.’

The nyrox cried out with the suffering and slowly sank

deeper into the pool until it disappeared beneath the surface entirely. The cure was gone. That meant…

Feletra's eyes returned to their normal deep mahogany. She was lost as she walked over to where Nil's body lay, not shaking, not fearful nor vengeful, she felt numb, surrounded by death. A shift in fate, *his* fate.

Feletra knelt down and peered into Nil's everlasting green eyes. They danced no more.

'Seems a waste, doesn't it?' said Akeon, his voice cutting into the new silence with ease. His eyes were dry, Feletra couldn't help but notice that hers were too, but she could not tear them away from Nil's undisturbed body. 'Unfortunately, you have stripped me of my twelfth member as well. No matter, it's a minor delay. Still, there will be few craftsmen who will match Nerehr's power.'

'He's your son,' Feletra's words quivered, she continued to stare at the body, 'do you feel nothing?'

'I feel somewhat inconvenienced, if I'm honest. But then, it's rather like taking cake from a child and replacing it with a cake twice the size. I've lost nothing.'

'You've lost everything, you've lost your family, you didn't even fight for him. And you think I can replace him,' she turned to him suddenly, 'what is it you want with me?'

'Replace Nil? No one could do that. In truth, I was hoping to have both of you, but events have taken a turn. As I said, it is no matter, Nil would have taken his place as the twelfth craftsman in the Sabrine, but I will find another. To lose you however, there could be no greater devastation. I want you to unleash yourself upon Enphiah, you will stand for Chriah and Setra and purge the west and the midlands into squander.'

Feletra couldn't believe her ears. 'I will never fight for

the east.'

'Not even to save Ataleka?'

Feletra hesitated. *His name. He has no right to say his name.* 'The cure is dead. You said it yourself. I cannot save my brother any more than you can.'

Akeon suddenly whipped out his right hand and drew Feletra closer to him – she was moved through the air until she was rooted right before him. 'Do you know how the cure is obtained?'

Feletra had been blind before to the similarities between Nil and Akeon, but now that she stood inches from Akeon's face she could see it all. One could never have guessed they were family until they each spoke, or gazed upon a thing of wonder, or even smiled without a twitch of the lips. Akeon had it all, just like Nil. They even smelt the same, the hair of dwindling cinders and crackling embers, the skin of something dire but altogether seductive; if Feletra could have called it anything she would have called it the scent of peril at the hands of desire, the thrill that was both as stimulating as it was fearsome.

'One must capture the dying breath of the nyrox,' he went on, 'seal it within a vial, and combine it with the water of the Sorpha.'

'You're almost as good a liar as your son,' said Feletra. 'The nyrox is dead, yet the Penthorans and Lorahks had each of their soldiers carry a vial in the war. I even saw Korsthr use it in Ira; this cure has been used over and over for two thousand years. Unless you have an entire hoard of those beasts locked away to pick off one by one then I suggest you tell me the truth or face the same fate as Nil.'

She was sincere, and she stared hard into his soul, Akeon could see it, and he smiled a little. 'Fate. What if I told you

I could control it?'

'You can't. Nil thought he could tell me the same thing.'

'I can show you.'

The granite that winked – there it was in his eye again.

'I can show you how death means nothing with the Souls,' he went on, 'I can show you how you can save Ataleka, you can take the cure home to him once and for all.'

Feletra looked back at Nil again, she had killed him. She felt nothing for the deed, it felt as if she had killed her heart along with him. But Ataleka, he still had a chance, she would give up the world to save him. Anything.

And then she slowly looked back at Akeon, she was calm and collected. It was a foreign feeling to her, she knew she should have been screaming for the grief of Nil's murder, but everything within her was hushed. 'But only if I fight for Chriah. That's your deal, isn't it? How do I know my family will be kept safe in this war?'

'I will swear it. They will be placed under the protection of the Sabrine, my craftsmen, and no harm will ever come to them, if you uphold your end of the agreement. The pact will be bound with a Gorothra, that is a craft you do not want to break.'

Betray my country, betray my family just to save them. They will never forgive me.

'Show me,' she said finally. 'Show me the cure.'

Akeon lowered his head with a dark look about him. It was just like Nil whenever he wore a hood. Feletra hated the similarities, she was constantly reminded with this man of the life she took just by looking between his features. She dared not look back at the body again.

Akeon led Feletra out of the cavern, back the way she

had come and after clambering over the rubble left by Korsthr, they were faced with another solid wall of rock. Akeon barely moved but Feletra jumped when the rock face punched a door-shaped hole into itself and the force shot through the mountain until a rough passageway was left behind. The passage was a direct route into Leohreten, and opened out immediately beneath the shadow of the great white hall with the lucrin edges that Feletra had spied earlier when they passed the town.

It was no surprise then when Akeon led the way up an incredibly steep hill and into this hall. Inside, they stepped into an ancient and grand atrium, an arched ceiling of glass revealing innumerable stars tainted by typical Chriahk pale grey clouds. The place had been left to fester and decline from what was once clearly a monumental and imposing building, almost too impressive for the likes of the morbid Leohreten. They entered a side corridor off the main atrium and ascended a long and twisting stairwell; at the top, a long room stretched with an open balcony at the far end where veil curtains billowed inwards carelessly, cold flagstones paved the floor and the walls were adorned with strange and unknown artefacts, many of them appeared to be unusual weapons and dark contraptions of torture. And then Feletra saw something else between them all, an area saved for the mounting of skulls. Human skulls.

'To remember your victims, no less?' she observed.

'Sheep have no place amongst wolves in the Halls of Aberahn,' Akeon replied, 'those are the skulls of every craftsman who has controlled the Souls. There lies my own grandfather,' he pointed lazily to one of the fresher-looking skulls with its name plaque beneath it: *'Mahceo.'*

But to one side of each skull's cheekbone there glowed

a dim white-blue light where there should have been shadow. Feletra followed the source of the light with Akeon in front; he led her out onto the great balcony where it formed a trim around the entire north and east walls of the hall, and then curled up and over at the end as if the stones had once been a huge wave of the sea. Curiously, it dripped water from the top constantly like the cove behind a waterfall, and sheltered what appeared to be two globes of light, side by side upon a pedestal each, shrouded in a veil of enna.

Akeon softly removed the veils and the light echoed majestically about the wave.

'Behold, the Time Soul and the Fate Soul.'

Feletra felt her breath catch in her throat, she couldn't even explain why. 'What are these things?'

Akeon held his gaze with hers steadily and said nothing for a few moments, then he took her hand unexpectedly, she didn't resist, and brought it forward into one of the Souls. There was nothing solid there – she allowed her hand to become enveloped in its light, it dragged this way and that about her skin delicately in a constant fluid motion. Soft, ethereal, unreal and yet somehow conscious, it breathed in her presence.

Feletra had never experienced anything like it, she found herself lost for words. Akeon stepped closer to the Souls next to her, with his hands he formed a line of light between the two globes, inwards slowly, then suddenly forced his hands apart quickly and the light blinded them like a flash of lightning.

Feletra had no idea what had just happened, it was daylight and she discovered herself lying on the hard pebbles of a beach after what felt like a jolt of electricity to the stomach. Her ears were ringing and she remained disoriented for a few seconds as Akeon stood a short distance off, waiting for her patiently. He offered no hand to help her as she slowly rose to her feet.

'Where are we?' she called as she made her way over. A fierce gale blew all around them, the waves crashed down upon the rocks that fringed the shoreline. Everything looked real, even the sea spray felt real, but Feletra knew there was something amiss. Something not quite whole.

'The Dopror Islands, Yeracei, to be exact. In our world, this is where the nyrox was first discovered by man two thousand years ago. In this world, it's about to be us.'

Feletra had not the time to question what he meant by 'our world,' for Akeon raised a hand to the ocean, he focused for a moment – and then without warning the nyrox burst forth from the sea at least five leagues out as easily as one would pluck a shrimp from a rockpool. It writhed in the air furiously until Akeon pulled the great beast towards the beach where it came crashing down cruelly. As the nyrox roared at them Akeon flexed his hand once more and it fell still, breathing heavily with trepidation.

Feletra was not prepared for what came next, she wished she had looked away. Akeon poised a dagger in mid-air and followed it over to the nyrox, where it slashed across the serpent's throat and travelled deeper and deeper until the beast could no longer hold on, and faced its fated journey into the Artrysiptic with wide open eyes. Akeon whipped out an empty vial from his pocket and crouched down by the nyrox's gaping jaw at that moment.

Feletra saw it then – something flowing and sinuous, a rippling vapour that refused to simply disappear into the cold, coastal air but spiralled around each of the nyrox's teeth and appeared to drip from them into nothing. It was a ghostly and divine scene to behold. Akeon held the vial to one of the teeth, where he collected a few of the immaterial drops and replaced the cork.

'That's the cure?' said Feletra, transfixed. She had been watching the entire process.

'Almost, just a little Sorpha water –' Akeon withdrew a separate vial of unmistakable Sorpha water and added a few drops, the two were instantly attracted to one another and combined perfectly in a miniature burst of light, leaving a swirling grey gas that pushed itself off the glass sides as if vying for escape, '– and we have created the most coveted elixir in all of Esilence. Only with the Souls can this exist. Only with the Souls, Feletra, are we truly unstoppable.'

'And how you intend to win the war. Nil was right, wasn't he? These are not the Dopror Islands we know, they exist in some other reality, some world that you have created off the back of our own. How many worlds must you create just to go back and kill the nyrox over and over? When does it end before you are satisfied?'

'Man is never satisfied. Man lusts for power, for immortality. But he will protect it as fiercely as he hunts it. This cure could be yours, Feletra. I know of your own lust for it, I have watched it from the beginning. The curse can become a thing of the past.'

Feletra stared at the breath within the vial, it was so close…it was all she needed. She could have taken it off him, killed Akeon for it at that very moment, and she tried in vain to feel the Konexa, but there was nothing. It felt as unreal as the beach she stood upon, missing somewhere, like it never existed. Then she saw something appearing in the distance, not something – someone.

Akeon followed her gaze and it settled upon a woman, a woman who stood proud and bold where the beach met the trees inland, staring back at them as the wind buffeted her. She had a mission and a bow clasped in her hand. Behind her, a man, he carried much history and burden…but it was the woman who Feletra felt a reconnection with. She remembered her at the Sorpha. That magnetism could never be forgotten.

'Who is she?' she said.

Akeon hid the cure away in a pocket. 'She is one who also seeks the cure. She has not stopped for thirty years. She is you.'

Acknowledgments

My thanks go to all those who gave up their time to share their insightful thoughts on this story, and more importantly spared a great deal of passion for it as I do. These are the same people who will badger me tirelessly for the next book in the Esilence trilogy, which I am all too excited to finish and share.

Never have I felt more illuminated and motivated than since I have met Kris Turk, who has supported me every chapter of the way. I would also like to thank Debbie Leonardi, my best friend of twenty-four years and counting, who so generously aided me in the graphic editing of this book. And lastly my mother Shirley, who has since left this world, but not my side.

Maps of Enphiah, Pyra & Orpegh

ESILENCE
ORPEGH
THE BANDED LAND
TETHIP
ISLE OF AMFA
SETRAN SEA
ENPHIAH
FLUR
LIRA
LOR
PENTHOR
SETRA
ACRO
DEPRA
HALPRIGH
THENIGH
DELICA
OTRA
MERETA
DOPROR ISLANDS
BELTRO
FORPHON ISLES
PLAINS OF NEMENON
THE SORPHA
ERI
FERIN
ELPURA
DROHA
ISLE OF IRA
ASIRI
EMPHOR
SEA OF DALPHA
PYRA
MELII ISLANDS
N
CHRIAH
STURA

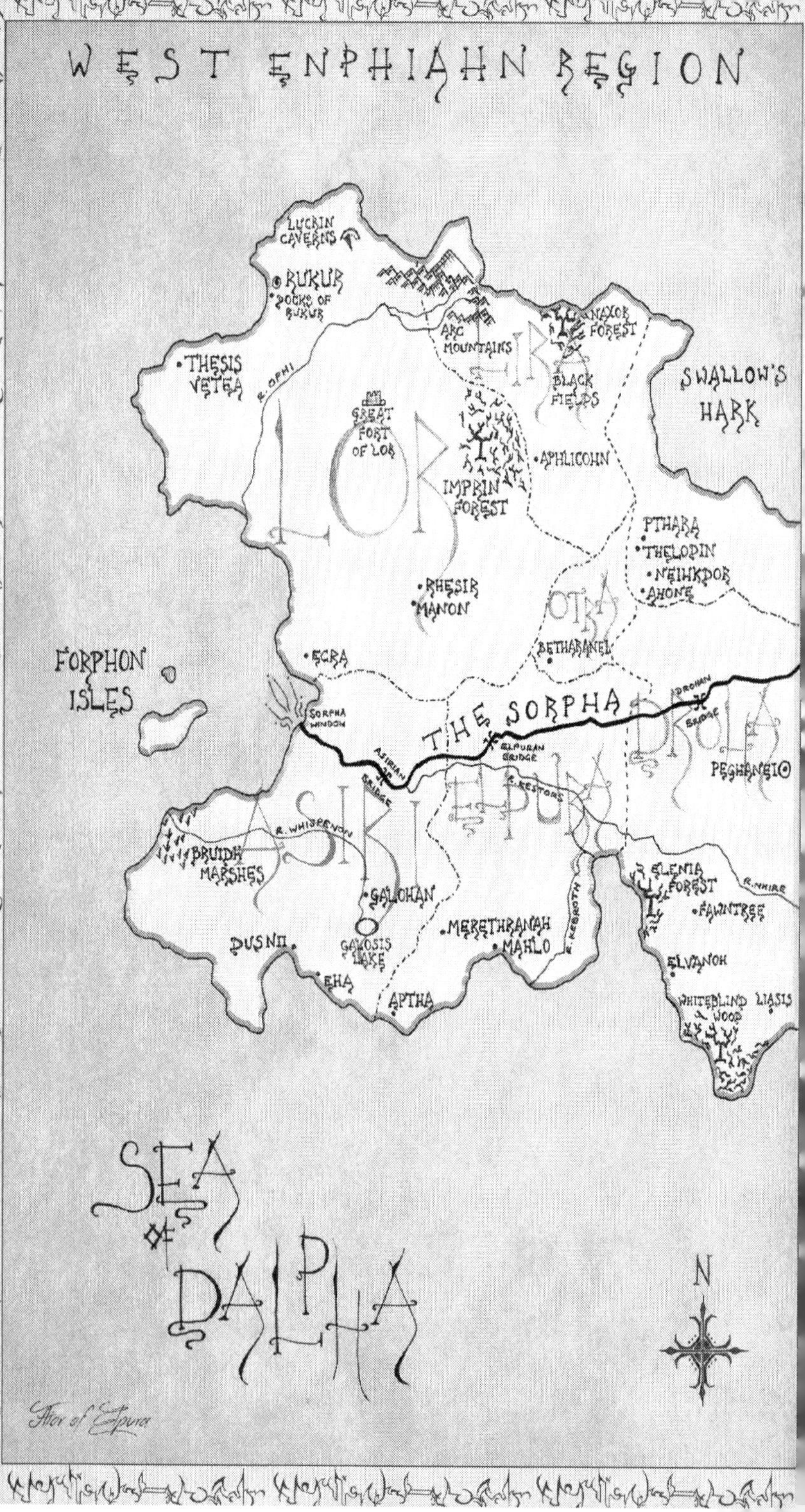

WEST ENPHIAHN REGION

LUCRIN CAVERNS
RUKUR
DOCKS OF RUKUR
THESIS VETEA
R. OPHI
ARC MOUNTAINS
HIRA
NAXOR FOREST
BLACK FIELDS
SWALLOW'S HARK
GREAT FORT OF LOR
LOR
IMPRIN FOREST
APHLICOHN
PTHARA
THELOPIN
NEIHKDOR
AHONE
RHESIR
MANON
OTRA
BETHARANEL
ECRA
FORPHON ISLES
SORPHA WINDOW
THE SORPHA
DRONAN BRIDGE
DROLA
ELPURAN BRIDGE
ASIRIAN BRIDGE
R. KESTORS
ELPURA
PEGHANEIO
ASIRI
R. WHISPENON
BRUIDH MARSHES
GALOHAN
GAVOSIS LAKE
DUSNII
EHA
APTHA
MERETHRANAH
MAHLO
R. KEBROTH
ELENIA FOREST
R. NHIRE
FAWNTREE
ELVANOH
WHITEBLIND WOOD
LIASIS
SEA OF DALPHA
N

SWALLOW'S HARK
MOUNT KYMA
ASBETHA
PYORIN
PENTHOR
PTHARA
THELODIN
NEIHKDOR
AHONE
THENIN BRIDGE
THE SORPHA
HILLS OF DURUN
FELISTEN
EBRETH
TEHMATAREI
BORODAO
PROVEHA
TREPTA
SHARN
SAPH NOIN
LUMBHN
MEDREA
SETRAN VALLEY
ERISTENON MOUNTAINS
R. HADRICAN
HURH CANYON
ISBRE
WELL OF OXENA
SLEN
BANSHOR
R. SPELONAS
GREAT FOREST OF OLONATH
RHOA
FERIN
LENAPHAN
THEOMARE
DROHAN BRIDGE
PESHANEIO
XENOR
CALABEN
ELENIA FOREST
FAWNTREE
ELVANOH
WHITEBLIND WOOD
LIASIS
DEAD MAN'S END
MID ENPHIAHN REGION
ISLE OF IRA
SETRAN SEA
TERACEI
BRATALACEI
DOPROR ISLANDS
GORON
SEA OF DALPHA
MELII ISLANDS
PYRA
STURA
CIRIAH
N

N
THE RISE
SETRAN SEA
TETHIP
ISLE OF AMFA
HEMONA
PHESA
BENUINN PEAKS
ZEH
TALATKE
VESKA
ANAROHR
PENTHOR
MOUNT KYMA
ASBETHA
NAGORAI
R. HADRICAN
SETRA
SETRAN VALLEY
ERISTENON MOUNTAINS
SUHNE
EXON
ELIR
EAST ENPHIAHN REGION

N
XENOR
SPELONAS
ISLE OF IRA
PYRA
MELII ISLANDS
MOKRA
SEVTERN WOOD
LEOHREBOR MOUNTAIN
FENERYTH
DEMELOR
SERENSIS BRAKE
LEOHRETEN
STURA
UKRHI MOUNTAINS
UKRHED
VARESHNA
VARCAN BRAKE
SIMIA
VYGOHR
CHRIAH
MADORMA

Made in the USA
Middletown, DE
04 May 2020

93636518R00326